THE

by Lindsey Mellon

COPYRIGHT

First Edition, published May 2025

ISBN 978-1-917393-15-7

Book designed by www.joi.agency

Paperback published by Northside House Limited.
www.northsidehouse.com

Dedication

For the peoples of the suffering lands of Sudan, and for my dear and gracious friends of old - Tigani, Mirghani, Mardi, Bella, Fatih and so many others from that place of boundless generosity and warmth.

Chapter 1

St James's Park, London, March 1989

"It was so degrading. As if he was taunting me. Posting me downhill to a nowhere shithole. Maybe it's his way of driving me out altogether." Haydon Talbot felt his face flushing. "I've lost my credo. For so many years the Service has defined my identity."

It could have been a scene from any decent spy movie. Two grey men in grey suits, shiny black brogues, one balding, the other with salt and pepper hair, sitting on a wooden-slatted bench and staring ahead at the ducks floating past on St James's Park lake. One MI6, the other an MI5 man. From that angle, looking up over the bridge, the skyline seemed Russian. Even the sky was suitably grey.

Haydon remembered coming here with his grandfather, holding hands, sitting on perhaps the same bench, looking at the same view over Downing Street. Duck Island it was called, he remembered. He'd been happy back then, his only worry was whether Grandpa would buy him an ice-lolly. Normally, he wouldn't.

He glanced over at Johnny Doyle, broad shouldered and brick solid. He envied his old friend his unshakable sureness. Of what was right and what was wrong. Of each sturdy step he took forward, never prevaricating or suffering regret about any decision he took. It had been that way since the day they'd first met.

That had been a terrible day – 27th August 1979. The day the IRA assassinated Lord Mountbatten with a bomb concealed in his motorboat in Sligo. But for the two of them it had been later that day and 100 miles to the east that was stamped black in their memories. Warrenpoint. That afternoon the IRA's South Armagh Brigade ambushed a convoy of Paras, setting off two giant roadside bombs just by Narrow Water Castle on the border with the Republic. The deadliest attack ever on the British Army in Ulster. 18 dead, 20 seriously injured. A bloody massacre.

Haydon and his Para company had been stunned and confused after the first colossal bomb had detonated. He'd been crouched on the road, unable to stand up, hands over his ears, and had watched as Captain Johnny Doyle arrived with the first reinforcements. Johnny had helped him to his feet, but then the second bomb had exploded, killing Johnny's commanding officer, rendering them deaf for hours. But they still worked away, loading the injured into choppers, trying not to look at the horrific wounds. He remembered seeing Johnny calmly giving orders, signalling with his arms and fingers, seemingly unperturbed by the scene of carnage, blood and body parts scattered and splashed everywhere.

They'd got ghastly drunk in the mess that night. From that day on, their friendship was rooted in the shared horror of those frightful scenes. So many of his colleagues had never been directly touched by the bitter gore of terrorism. To them, it was a remote thing, a topic for intellectual discussion. But for him and Johnny, it was about an officer's head hanging from a tree, an unknown soldier's leg lying in a ditch, and the brutal migraines that struck them both from time to time.

Their post-Army career paths had intersected over the years. When they met, they shared work confidences. Their bosses would have disapproved, had they known. Johnny himself had been the best man at Haydon's wedding and had stayed with him and Ros in all his overseas postings, while he'd remained a devout bachelor. Haydon realised he still didn't think of himself as a bachelor, but since returning to

London his marriage had drifted towards a stuttering end, even if some deep part of him believed he could win her back again.

"Sounds to me like you need to ride it out. Wait for the wind to change. It always does."

A small boy rushed past them and hurled a large hunk of bread into the water, then tripped over and fell. He looked up at the two men and began to yowl. Johnny reached out his hand. The boy took it, smiled, pulled himself up and ran off back to his mother. A flurry of ducks hurried towards the bread, splashing furiously and slashing with their beaks.

Haydon looked up. It was going to rain, the clouds were rushing past and darkening. He shivered. The two men sat side by side, watching the swans and ducks glide by, their heads moving and scanning the bystanders for potential sources of food. That's another factor. *What would be my source of bread?* Haydon noticed Johnny had lines in his face. We're aging fast, he thought.

"I can't make up my mind." Haydon broke the silence. "Perhaps he's doing me a favour and it's time for me to move on?"

"You need to relax. You'll have your chance again."

"But Sudan. It couldn't be any worse. There's been no real British interest there since Kitchener's day. Not even any serious trade opportunities to support. No. And Mark knows that. If he didn't want to give me the Director Ops job, he could have offered me Moscow, it needs new flesh. But Khartoum."

"Perhaps you're too nasty a reminder of how he sacrificed a friend in his rush to the top."

"After the Libyan fiasco, you'd expect him to make amends. Blowing the long-term penetration agent I had in play, just for his own short-term political gain." Haydon turned to face his friend. He felt the veins in his temples pulsing away. "Do you think he's expecting me to turn him down?"

"None of us likes to be around witnesses to our most shameful acts." Johnny rubbed his chin.

"He shovelled manure all over me. For what he did. And which I had opposed. Green-lighting the termination of an IRA crew, behind my back. Burning the top Libyan agent I'd turned, then shifting the blame onto me."

"Perhaps that's why Mark Glasson is the head of SIS and not Haydon Talbot?"

"He's a creep, you mean."

"He's a politician."

"And I've got no leverage."

"So leave then. Get yourself a board seat and earn some brass. You've earned it. What's stopping you?" He thumped Haydon's arm. "The Service has done for your marriage. Get out there into the wild world and learn how to enjoy life. Like me. You're single, you know. Get your leg over, in the ample pool of lovely divorcées. Come sailing with me."

"Maybe." He faced his friend, looking into his eyes. "Thanks, Johnny, for sage advice. It helps, talking it over with you. You're a solid mucker. I'm too angry to make sound decisions right now."

"Ask yourself if you believe you're going to make a difference to the world staying in the Service. If the answer is no, it's time to pack your bags."

"Sailing. Maybe that's the thing. And divorcées. Have you got spares?"

"London's flooded with 'em." Johnny looked at his watch at stood up. "I'd better get back to the office."

Haydon settled back on the bench, removed a sheaf of papers from his inner pocket and rifled through them. After his meeting with Glasson, he'd filleted the Sudan register but hadn't come up with any sign of any obvious threats, even of any warning signals. The country was run by what appeared to be a benign democratic government. The Prime Minister was Oxford educated, the scion of the Mahdi family, with moderate Islamic leanings and mildly autocratic tendencies. So why was it HMG policy to seek to unseat him?

There was a rumble of thunder. He felt raindrops on his head and returned the papers to his pocket. He didn't feel like going back to the Office. *Sod them.* He needed space to think.

He strode off in the direction of Trafalgar Square, head down, umbrella thrust forward against a suddenly gusty wind, chilly rain spattering his cheeks. His trouser legs were soon sodden, shoes squelching. He found himself crossing Piccadilly Circus. As he walked among the narrow streets of Soho, he felt a reassuring anonymity amongst the blank faces peering tentatively into hidden doorways. He paused outside a seedy shop, drawn by the red light flashing the word SEX. He peered in at the window display. *Who bought this tat?* Surely not to take home? In Frith Street, he stepped into a coffee bar and ordered an espresso. He sat on a bar stool and sipped it slowly, savoring the strong bouquet.

For years, ever since Rome, he'd been living in a cloud of negative energy. In that sad, final conversation he'd had with Ros, she'd told him, quietly, that he resembled a lost child, that he'd misplaced every ounce of the *joie de vivre* that had so captivated her when they'd first met. He hadn't replied, but he knew it was true. He felt like an aging bore with dodgy spark plugs.

Perhaps Khartoum was the right place for a burnt-out spy to hide and recharge his batteries. Hide from what? From himself, he supposed. It would be an act of masochism, but why give Glasson the satisfaction of letting him drive him out? He'd treat the posting as a sabbatical. All right, Khartoum wasn't Paris, but he'd make the best of it, brush up his

Arabic. He watched the rain splatter on the tarmac, torrents running down the gutter. At least the sun shone in Sudan; one less reason to be depressed.

Chapter 2

Khartoum, April 1989

Haydon shuffled along in a long queue of passengers stretching out onto the apron, waiting to enter the airport terminal at Khartoum airport. Most of them were Sudanese, just a smattering of foreigners. He felt the tarmac melting under his feet, and the midday sun scorching his newly discovered bald patch, an unwelcome harbinger of middle age. The terminal building was an old concrete structure, the same reddish colour as the dust that seemed to hang like a sheet in the air.

Broken and dirty windowpanes gave it a derelict appearance.

He'd expected to be met at the aircraft steps by Embassy staff, but this uncomfortable return to the ordeals of the third world reminded him of happier postings early in his career. He felt enervated by a sense of isolation and anonymity. It had been the right decision. Well, in the end he hadn't made a decision, he'd just let things move on, while he remained inert and indecisive.

Pathetic. Still, time spent far away from The Office and its envy-driven turf wars might reinvigorate his jaded psyche, give him back a sense of purpose.

None of the air conditioning units Haydon had spotted from the outside were working, and when he made it into the shade of the arrivals hall, the temperature didn't seem to lessen. Despite being the only flight to have landed, the arrivals hall was packed, and there was a long delay before bags started emerging in dribs and drabs on the squeaking conveyor belt. Haydon propped himself against a column and browsed an Arabic grammar primer, murmuring words to himself as he read.

A dark-faced man in an out of place blue blazer and Lord's tie tapped him on the shoulder. He looked like a Tamil, Haydon thought, and spoke with an old-fashioned public-school accent.

"Sorry for the delay." The man stammered and offered his hand. He resembled a recently appointed school prefect. "Ramesh Patel, Sir. Second Secretary. Poor start, I know, but the ambassador summoned me as I was leaving to pick you up."

Outside the terminal, a dark blue Embassy Land Rover with a driver awaited them. They set off towards the city centre, the traffic slow and unruly, the streets bustling with pedestrians.

Yellow taxis incessantly honked their horns, lorries belched out plumes of black smoke, highly coloured buses played musical tunes as they bullied their way forward. After a ten-minute drive, they turned down a sandy track and drew up in front of a three-storey red brick building. It had a fortress-like air, Haydon thought, designed to be defensible, at least from rioters armed with stones and bottles.

"The new Embassy building was completed four years ago, Sir. On the same plot as the Residency, that's over on the other side of the site there. Built in the sixties." He sounded apologetic as he pointed over a long, brown lawn to where a strange, boxlike building stood on stilts, out of place amongst the mature royal palm trees.

Ramesh took him on a tour of the Embassy, stopping frequently to introduce him to members of staff. He led him up a staircase running around an octagonal atrium and into a spacious office on the second floor, facing out over a large garden.

"This is you, Sir."

"Drop the Sir, Ramesh. Call me Haydon. Sit." He sat down behind the large desk, splayed his hands over the grainy wood and looked around him. This would do. He dabbed sweat off his forehead with his handkerchief.

"Give me a quick overview. Political sitrep, key ops, opposition activity."

"The ruling coalition has a parliamentary majority but is fractured and unstable. The Prime Minister is from the traditionalist Umma Party. He's piggy in the middle, squeezed between religious hardliners from the National Islamic Front and the secular Unionists. Who favour closer relations with the military regime in Egypt and fervently oppose *Sharia* law."

"Your prognosis?"

"The consensus view is this government will not survive more than a few months. Whether it ends by Parliamentary vote of no confidence or by military coup d'état is moot. There's a distinct *fin de siècle* atmosphere."

"London tells me we have a horse running in this race." Haydon looked over at the young diplomat. Reticent and inexperienced, he sensed a sharp intelligence bursting out from behind the schoolboy look. They'd get along fine. "Who he?"

"Ali Kabbani. Profile over there. Together with one pressing matter requiring your attention." He pointed to a stack of files on Haydon's desk.

"Thank you. I'll look through them later." He felt a blast of cold air from the air conditioning and felt goose bumps coming up on his arms. "The pressing matter?"

"Operation SEAMLESS. Awaiting a decision from London."

"Give me your take." Haydon smiled in encouragement.

"Money well spent?"

"We've been running this small hotel – The Forum – off books, for two years. Place was about to go bankrupt, your predecessor saw the potential. He convinced London and we snapped it up. For a song. Guests are aid workers and journos, the odd backpacker. Potentially useful sources who travel the length and breadth of the largest country in Africa. Great way to get real grass roots coverage."

"Who runs it for us?"

"Who ran it for us was Aphrodite Ratchett. Ex Balkans hand. She 'bought it' and managed it ever since. Half Italian. Splendid character. Built up the clientèle. The beardies all loved her."

"What kind of scale are we talking?"

"Fourteen rooms. Good occupancy. Manageable. We subsidise the prices for our target audience, so it makes small annual losses." Ramesh picked up a file off the pile on Haydon's desk and handed it to him. "The guests tend to stop in Khartoum on their way in and out."

"Product?"

"Invaluable. The guests tell Afra – everyone calls her Afra – their secrets over drinks in the bar. Alcohol is illegal, of course, but–" He shrugged. "The tape machines pick up the rest. We have the place well rigged. Famines. Mutinies. Militias. Drugs. Indiscretions. Details of agricultural production. Sexual peccadilloes. Islamic preachers arriving in town. An intel gold mine." He flushed and turned away. "Well, it is if you actually care about what happens outside of the capital. No other service has our depth of access. Not even our American cousins. And it's cheap."

"Why the urgency for a decision? It sounds like you've got everything running smoothly."

"Afra has cancer. She's gone home to die. We urgently need a replacement. Arabic speaking obviously. Which won't be easy." He rubbed his neck. Haydon realised Ramesh didn't know how far he could speak his mind.

"Spit out whatever is bothering you. I need to know."

"It's my opinion there's little appetite in London for intel out of this Station." He stammered. Haydon could hear bitterness in his voice. "I'm hearing that London wants to kill SEAMLESS. Cost savings. It will require your intervention if it's to be saved."

"What else?"

"I've recently filed reports about *takfiri* cells operating in the provinces. This is a new and worrying phenomenon, we haven't seen them around here before. Several SEAMLESS sources report their presence, moving amongst the *Baggara* and *Rizeigat* tribes in Darfur – especially within this new violent militia they're calling the *Janjaweed*. Also, across the border in Chad. Apparently financed by Qaddafi. Similar story in Eastern Sudan, among the *Beja* tribe, who are perennially restless."

"What does London say?"

"No interest. That's my point, you see. Maybe a new broom–" He broke off, looking at Haydon. "These *takfiri* represent a coming danger to Western interests. They operate in tight cell structures, they're difficult to penetrate."

Haydon tapped his fingers on the table. "H.E supportive?"

"The ambassador shows scant interest. I see little of him. Other than when he gets me to drive his boat on bird watching outings. He's keener on ornithology and lepidoptery. Not what you might call a 'hands on' diplomat."

"Wife?"

"Widower. No worries in that direction."

Just what he needed. No focus from London in the Station, and an eccentric ambassador who preferred peering at old rocks to playing a role in current affairs.

"Tell me some good news."

"Excellent cricket club, Sir."

Haydon lifted his head. He wondered if this wasn't impertinence, but Ramesh seemed naively enthusiastic.

"Plays every Friday. The unusual feature is donkeys on the outfield, normally they stand around mid-wicket. They get hit quite often. Then they make one hell of a racket."

"Thank you for your candour, Ramesh. Helpful. I'll nose through your files later."

Chapter 3

Haydon wandered across the garden from the Embassy, enjoying the pleasing tinkle of flowing water. Irrigation channels crisscrossed the lawn, fountains burbling a soft chant. A flock of guinea fowl surprised him as he passed through an ornate metal gate into the Residency garden.

Sir Robin Hutch, HM's ambassador to Sudan, welcomed Haydon at the door to the Residence and gestured him with an expansive wave of his arm to sit. He was wearing a crumpled white linen suit, a red rose in his buttonhole, and a stained Old Etonian tie. Frameless glasses lent him an academic look.

"Whisky? Water? Ice? Hmph." Without waiting for an answer, he walked over to the bar and poured out two glasses of scotch.

He turned back and handed Haydon a large tumbler, raising his own. "Welcome to the waiting room."

Haydon stared around the sparsely furnished room. It could be a waiting room, he thought. Not a personal item on show anywhere.

"Last posting, you know. Before we're pensioned off to munch grass, eh. I'm sure you worked that out, you look bright enough. Who did you upset then?" He chuckled. "Don't answer. But don't worry, there's plenty to do here."

"It doesn't seem to feature highly on Whitehall's radar."

"Mainly on the river. You'll need to get yourself a boat, eh. Extraordinary bird life. Particularly during the migration. Excellent duck shooting. And sand grouse, early mornings." He raised his glass and smiled. "Plus a plethora of fascinating archaeological sites. The Kushite and Meroitic are most interesting, and quite unexplored. You'll need to get about the country. For goodness' sake don't get stuck in this god-forsaken city, eh."

"I understand the political situation is tense?"

"Oh, there are always political crises. Governments come and go. But nothing changes. Hmph." He plumped himself down on a chintz sofa and leaned back.

The air conditioning made a clanking sound, the lights flickered, then went off. A uniformed servant came hurrying in with candles.

"Happens every evening, it's a sort of dusk ritual."

"Ali Kabbani. He's our candidate, I'm told? Should I cultivate him?"

"Well educated chap. Mind you these local politicos mainly are. Many of 'em have British passports. Half of them are Oxbridge. Other half Sandhurst, all berets and pistols. But they're all the same under their disparate headgear. Leave Kabbani to me, I lunch him frequently. Do you know that before Independence they used to refer to this country as the land of blacks ruled by Blues. Hasn't changed much, you see. Incidentally I hear you're a tennis Blue?"

Haydon nodded.

"I'd organise a doubles. Defence Attaché is a decent player."

"Do you have concerns about radical Islamic groups, ambassador?"

"Look, I don't get worked up about those things. The Sudanese political class are acutely intertwined, their disparate politics are significantly neutralised by intermarriage." He leaned forward and narrowed his eyes. "The main thing is not to go stirring up wasps' nests. You people from south of the river have a way of getting yourselves overexcited. Collect your gossip, yes, by all means. It's your job after all, eh. But in my Embassy, I like things quiet. That's the thing.

Understood?"

A *laissez-faire* ambassador, off studying ancient monuments, leaving him alone to get on with his work. That would give him unusual freedom to act. And with the fascinating reach of SEAMLESS. Clearly you needed to look outside of Khartoum to understand what was happening in the capital city. He'd understood that. Perhaps it was a dead-end post, of no interest to London. Or, as Ramesh hinted, was there something else bubbling under the hot, impenetrable clouds of dust.

Next morning Haydon got to his office early and started working his way through the pile of papers Ramesh had left on his desk. Nothing of importance. He paused for a cigarette, leaning out of the open window, blowing smoke and staring over the green of the ambassador's garden towards the Blue Nile. A peaceful scene. This was going to work out, he smiled to himself. He couldn't remember feeling so calm, ever. Spending time alone, focusing on himself, something he'd never done. Find himself. *Where would he find himself?* Reflect, set goals. Practical and moral.

The direct phone on his desk rang. He stubbed out the cigarette and walked to his desk. "Haydon Talbot."

"Welcome to the dust bowl!" A friendly American chuckle. "This is Pete Monkton, your Yankee cousin, looking forward to making your acquaintance and working closely with you. Mark Glasson gave you a good write up."

"I was going to call you once I'd got my feet under the desk. I'm not quite there yet. I only just got in yesterday."

"I know. But nothing is that important round here. Lookit. Get yourself over here to the American Club. I've reserved a great, big slab of prime rib and it's got your name written all over it."

Haydon looked at his watch. It was past two o'clock. He realised he was hungry. "Directions?"

"Any taxi driver will know it. Tell them it's next to the city cemetery entrance. Seriously. Half an hour?"

"OK. Thanks, I'll be there."

He leaned back and thought back to his last meeting with Glasson.

"Langley has posted a top man to Khartoum. Pete Monkton, their guy in Peshawar all the way through the Afghan war. Practically won it for them single-handed." He'd laughed. "Being in lock step with Langley demands I send an equivalent heavyweight as Station Chief to work alongside him. Shadow him as my personal rep. It's a senior role, operating in a hot zone. You like that sort of thing."

A prime rib of beef, he thought, and then I get to listen to a load of bullshit. Why not?

He might even learn a bit about what was really going on.

Chapter 4

Pete Monkton. 6'4" and brawny. Yale grad. Sidney Reilly with a buzz-cut and a Ten Gallon hat, although even Reilly didn't jump HALO out of airliners' belly holds from 34,000', at night, floating down behind enemy lines in the high Hindu Kush. All-American hero of the war against the Russkies in Afghanistan and scourge of desk-bound Langley analysts with their policies of prevarication and caution. '*Show me a hero and I'll show you a bum*'. Who had said that? Haydon was expecting to take an instant dislike to this supposed superman, although he'd still be obliged to laugh at his jokes.

Haydon had heard the stories. Within the spying fraternity, Monkton was a legend. Bill Casey's boy. At The Farm, raw recruits spoke his name with awe. How he'd helped thousands of 'black Jews' –*Falashas*– escape from revolutionary Ethiopia to make a new home in Israel. His last act as Station Chief in Khartoum, the night that President Nimeiri fell, was to crate up the two Mossad operatives who'd run the black op out of Port Sudan and dispatched them in a US 'diplomatic bag'.

You'd think he'd have needed a holiday after three years as Station Chief in Peshawar, helping the *mujahadeen* get their bulldozers and graders over the Khyber Pass and down the vertiginous tracks south from Jalalabad, siting the machine-gun nests that protected the approaches to the Tora Bora caves from Russian gunships. Taking covert, deniable, camel trips back and forth across the wild borderlands from Quetta, exhorting his *Muj* friends on night marches through narrow defiles, *Stinger* missiles - that he'd supplied - slung proudly from their shoulders.

He'd been there in the Zazi mountains when the first brutish Russian Mi-24 *Hind* attack helicopter had been shot down by a *Stinger*, racing directly towards them and loosing off salvos of screeching rockets before exploding in an immense ball of flame. From that moment, Pete Monkton had become a hero to the Afghan *mujahadeen*, who respected courage above all things. It didn't hurt that he doled out hefty wads of dollar bills. A billion in cash was the figure Haydon had heard.

Enough to buy yourself a major war.

Now here he was, back in Khartoum for a second tour as Station Chief, happy and smiling as if he'd got some major promotion. Perhaps Glasson was right, and this was a smoke signal from Langley that Sudan was no longer an intelligence backwater, "Good to meet you Haydon. Heard a bunch about you."

"I bet I've heard more about you." Haydon raised his arms in salute. "Your reputation precedes you."

"You shouldn't believe everything you hear. Just mainly."

Monkton handed Haydon an ice-cold beer. Children squealed as they leapt into the water. Mothers in dark glasses lay prone, their skin brown and oiled, on wooden sun beds that fringed the long pool. The other side of the high wall, a group of female mourners incongruously burst into a high-pitched wail. Monkton gestured.

"Figured I'd lay on the Embassy choir to welcome my new colleague in." He chuckled, then pointed at Haydon. "Mark warned me you're the depressive sort. Lunch next to the cemetery seemed appropriate."

"My chief is a piss-poor shrink, and I'd rather your choir sang The Star-Spangled Banner than carrying on with that awful screeching."

The two men sat under a large umbrella at a corner table set back from the tinder-brown lawn. They found they had a lot in common and chatted easily. About their military careers - they were both 'jump monkeys', and both dyed-in-the-wool Arabists.

Unlike many of his colleagues, Monkton was Anglophile, indulgent of his 'cousins' at SIS. He didn't bang on about the repeated security failures of the Brits – the Philbys, Burgesses and Blakes – he talked, with boyish enthusiasm, about the OSS in the times of 'Wild Bill' Donovan.

He'd met the legendary spy with his father when he'd been a kid, the two old men downing Old Fashioneds and exchanging stories of the 'glory days' when they'd sewed mayhem with SOE in Europe during World War II – 'setting Europe alight'– whilst donning white tuxedos and dancing 'til dawn at the 400 Club.

"Good to know I've one Agency colleague who doesn't think we're just a leaky and sinking ship."

"I wouldn't be so sure about that, although right here and now we have aligned interests." He poked his finger at Haydon, "It's why I asked Mark to make sure I had a counterpart that was right damn on the same page as me. He tells me that's you."

Monkton laughed, raised his glass then gestured to the barman with two fingers. He stood up and waved to a tall, dark-haired woman making her way along the far side of the pool.

"My wife Lena." He gestured. "We met in Beirut. We got married there too. Much easier the second time around."

She was wearing a white, flowing trouser suit. Haydon noticed piercing, green eyes, which warmed when she caught sight of Monkton. She kissed him, then looked over at Haydon. There seemed something familiar about the way she cocked her head. *Had he met her somewhere before?*

"Honey, this is Haydon Talbot. A new colleague. One of those tight-assed Brits." They shook hands. "He arrived yesterday. The poor man's depressed already."

He felt her eyes boring into him, he felt strangely vulnerable. "I'm ready to be convinced otherwise!"

"I felt the same when Pete brought me here." He noticed a slightly French accent, and a scent of gardenia. He had to make a conscious effort not to stare, there was something magnetic about her graceful movements. "Now I've grown to love this place. The stark discomfort disguises a world of beauty. At the centre of which is the River Nile, the bearer of life. Timeless and tranquil."

"We'll take you with us on the river." Monkton beckoned the waiter to bring menus. "As soon as you're settled in. Fridays we usually take a picnic and head upriver aways. Swim with the crocs, water-ski. Drink a lot of cold beer."

"I was raised around water." Lena ran her hands through her long, dark, hair. "Beirut was a wonderful city to grown up in, we lived right by the sea."

"Joining us for lunch, honey?" Monkton said, reaching over to stroke her cheek.

"I'm meeting Nadia." She touched his arm.

"She's over there, I'd better join her. And you two will want to talk boy's stuff." She waved and walked away. The two men ordered and drank their beers.

"I'm curious why you returned to this hellhole." Haydon leaned back in his chair and lit a cigarette. "It's not Berlin, or Moscow even. It's seems to be a junkyard for jaded spies, surely you'd have avoided it if you could have."

"Day two and you're impatient for answers." Monkton slapped the table. "Goddammit I like you already, Haydon.

"So, if you're not in disgrace, what keeps your drum beating here?"

"Coupla things." He screwed up his face. "Nostalgia isn't one of 'em, though I did have a blast here during Nimeiri's regime."

A waiter placed two ice cold beers on the table.

"My wife was born in Lebanon. During my postings in Beirut and Peshawar, it wasn't safe for her to join me. She had to stay home in Virginia. We don't have children, you see."

Monkton raised his mug and drank greedily. Haydon found himself warming to the man, the antithesis of what he'd expected.

"Five years pretty much apart. No good for any marriage. Here we can be together, maybe we re-stoke the flames, maybe we don't. But feeling safe feels pretty good for a change."

"A lot of nicer places you could have chosen to feel safe in." Haydon laughed. "It was the opposite for me, Pete. My wife Ros was with me in Rome, a great posting; but she told me it was as if I wasn't there at all."

"Our line of work is tough on relationships." Monkton frowned. "So much of what we do is concealment and dissembling. It becomes so much part of our being we don't realise we're doing it. We ingrain our invented stories into our memories until we're certain they're true, then we can recount them with confidence."

"A worrying thought. But in my case Ros has gone and I'm left alone with my untrue stories."

"Back to your question. Lookit, the Arab world is changing. Fast. I run the Middle East, as you know. Beirut used to be our wet dream, we ran regional ops out of our Station there. A perfect posting: sea, sophistication and an entrepôt of all the key players from all sides. We watched each other and back-channeled furiously. Then suddenly it turned sour and became our worst nightmare."

He frowned, his voice strained.

"Bill Buckley's kidnapping by Hezbollah. He was a close friend of mine, ex-special forces, our Beirut Station Chief. Great man, tough as nails. They took him and they kept him in a room just bigger than a coffin and they tortured him for months and months and finally they broke him. Then they rolled up every agent we had, every network. We had to start again from scratch. With Hezbollah a constant and dangerous threat. I got hustled off to Peshawar, to run the war against the Russkies. After that Beirut was over. Sudan is a perfect venue to manage the rebuilding. Out of everyone's eye-line, yet every important Islamic wire runs right through here."

He leaned back and swigged his beer.

"Here I'd got to know all the important military folk under Nimeiri, I made friends with the likely lads. I was on the same jump course at Fort Benning as Colonel Abbas el Daoud. An ambitious and clever officer, and a schemer. As you know, Jump School is another of those close bonding fraternities, like Yale. We became close. Very close. Now, Haydon, as I'm sure you've figured, regime change is right around the corner. You've got your horse running, in civvies, and I've got mine in a beret. Together we're going to ensure they have a benevolent regime, pliant to our interests, which provides me a safe base to manage area ops."

"It's that easy to ensure an outcome?" Haydon stubbed out his cigarette and exhaled. "There seem to be no shortage of different coloured hats tossed into the ring."

"O ye of little faith. Take a look at the last 100 years." He paused and took a cigar from a leather case, rolling it back and forth under his nose. "From Mossadegh to Allende, Philippines to Honduras and everywhere in between, we've shepherded in regime change whenever it's become necessary. Oiled by truckloads of dollars and intelligent cultivation of military pastures."

"Our guy gets along with your guy?" Haydon cut into his steak.

"Yes. And we need them both. The Army, obviously, but we also need 'civil society' onside - lawyers, technocrats, professionals. It reassures the fluffy European democracies and the UN. Daoud and Kabbani are cousins, which helps. Lookit, I'm going to fix for you to come on one of our duck shooting outings. Colonel Abbas and I."

"That would be great." Haydon rubbed his palms together. "Pete, this has been really helpful. Now I get the picture. If Glasson had explained it, I might not have been so disenchanted with the prospects of any meaningful operations here!"

"He told me you're a glum sumbitch. Don't worry, I'll work to make sure you don't stay bored for long."

The Sheikh

Chapter 5

Haydon shivered as he left the warmth of his Land Rover and strode along the narrow canal bank down towards the White Nile, 12 bore shotgun, broken, under his arm. The orange edge of sunrise was starting to peer through the palm trees that fringed the river, a biting easterly wind gusting over the water and blowing away any warming rays.

Two men stood warming their hands by a campfire close to the riverbank. A third man, a servant he presumed, was making tea from a pot hanging from a tripod. The tall figure of Monkton stepped forward and reached out his hand, gesturing to the other man.

"Haydon, this is my friend Colonel Abbas el Daoud. Haydon Talbot." He slapped him on the back. The Colonel smiled. A squat and powerfully built man, he had a round, expressionless, face. Not easy to read, Haydon thought, bluff and outwardly friendly. "Welcome to our exclusive shooting club."

"Where's the hide?" Haydon asked.

Monkton pointed upstream to three stubby shapes set 50 yards apart by the water's edge. "We each get our own wooden barrel to squat in for a coupla hours."

The servant handed Haydon a mug of sweet tea.

"Drink up quick. We need to be concealed before they start to flight in."

"Is this a regular activity?"

"We started popping quail together near Fort Benning in Georgia. Here it's more challenging – the Nile duck and geese are real savvy. You'll find Abbas here a difficult shot to better. His record is nine in one morning, which made for a great feast. You won't beat his record."

"I was lucky that day, you see." Colonel Abbas had a deep, hollow voice. "They came right over me and low, I could hardly miss, just had to load fast enough. Normally, you see, they climb high really quick and then we come back empty handed."

"What's the form?" Haydon asked.

"When they're flighting in, you have to remain motionless. If they spot you, they're off straight away." Monkton said. "And remember you gotta hit 'em as they're heading away from the river; so they fall in the field here."

They walked along wooden planks down to the riverbank. Belying its name, the White Nile was a deep muddy brown, uninviting and threatening. Haydon had difficulty climbing into his barrel, which was a tight and uncomfortable squeeze. By the time the birds splashed their way off the water an hour later, the sound of their wings audible as they burst into view, Haydon was so stiff and his muscles so cramped that he missed every shot. Abbas brought back three ducks and a goose and Monkton bagged two ducks.

The three of them sat on camp chairs around the fire eating breakfast. The temperature was rising fast and the early morning breeze had died. Haydon pulled his cap down over his eyes.

"Abbas, I have briefed Haydon on what we're expecting to happen." He chewed on a piece of kebab. "He's right on board with us and looking forward to meeting up with your cousin and providing assistance to him."

"You see, Mister Haydon." The Sudanese leaned forward and touched Haydon's arm. "What we will need is immediate recognition of the new regime. Within hours, not days. As soon as the US and UK governments recognise us, others will follow suit, and the coup will be solid. Can you give me assurance of your government's support?"

"So long as there is no excess bloodshed, then HMG will be on side. They will expect the usual statements regarding early elections, the involvement of technocrats, respect for human rights. You know the form."

"I do. Mister Peter bangs on about this often. We have all the right, reassuring, words prepared."

"Then I foresee no problems." Haydon wiped sweat off his brow. "Do you have a go date?"

"I'm sure you wouldn't want to know that. You will wish for full deniability."

There was something reassuringly sly about him, Haydon thought. A necessary quality in any successful coup plotter. His eyes were hooded, helpful for disguising feelings, but he was evidently bright and shared a deep level of trust with Monkton. *Would he have his soldiers on side?* That would be the thing that mattered on the day.

"Our main concern is about the increasing presence of radical Palestinian groups in this country." Monkton gestured with his fork. "This government is turning a blind eye to the growing threat. We've warned them many times, and we need this to stop before our beloved country ends up a madhouse like Iran or Lebanon."

"Our priority will be stability and economic growth." Abbas scratched his head. "We don't want international relations hindered by doctrinaire adventures. It's the PM's history, you see, that's the cause of his problem. He sees himself following in the footsteps of his illustrious ancestor - The Mahdi. That extreme egotism is putting our country at risk. Which is why we are obliged to act."

"Do you think you are under suspicion?" Monkton asked.

"No more than most senior officers. There are endless rumours of plots. Which is why we need to act fast, before some other group gets in ahead of us." He stood up. "I've got to go."

Haydon watched him pick up his birds and walk away, an athlete's spring in his step. A solid man, he thought, and he'll do what he says.

The Grand Hotel, a colonial edifice dominating the banks of the Blue Nile downstream from the Republican Palace, had seen better days. Haydon sat under a torn canvas awning on the long veranda, watching the river traffic floating by; a view that couldn't have changed much since General Gordon's time. The large *feluccas* with their billowing lateen sails seemed like giant swans sweeping past Tutti Island, with its rural scenes of mud brick-making, donkeys grazing and white-clad farmers hand-tilling the soil.

Haydon's circulation had returned after his confinement in the barrel, although he'd sworn to himself he wouldn't repeat the experience. He didn't like roast duck that much. But it had been a fascinating morning, Monkton and Abbas treating their plans for a *coup d'etat* and regime change like any routine work chore. Haydon wondered if the casual approach might not lead to catastrophe, the traditional punishment for failed coups being the firing squad. For Abbas at least.

Monkton had gone back to his house in Kafoury to collect Lena and drop off his birds. Haydon thought about Lena Monkton. She had that reserved strength he'd often noticed in Lebanese women; being married to a larger than life character like Monkton would require plenty of that quality. He lit a cigarette and leaned back, closing his eyes and letting the sun warm his face.

"Dreaming about your glory days, Haydon?" Haydon opened his eyes and donned his sunglasses. Monkton was holding a chair back for Lena. "That'd be some ways back now?"

"They are surely in my future, thanks to you!"

"My husband specialises in glory days." Lena pulled at her long hair. "Are you also an optimist?"

"I try to be." Haydon screwed up his face. "Often unsuccessfully. Today feels good, but my failed attempt at duck shooting, while tightly squeezed into a barrel, that was chastening."

"After watching my homeland destroy itself in a bloody civil war, I'm sceptical of heroic men. I've seen the damage they wreak in pursuit of their glory." She tapped the table. "Pete is the exception, of course, because he's always playing boy's games, and because he has God on his side."

"I lived in Lebanon for a year, studying Arabic at MECAS, until it had to close down when the civil war heated up. It was a wonderful time, my wife Ros was posted at the Embassy, in the early days of our marriage. It was a sudden and sad departure for us too."

"When is she joining you here?"

"We separated after my last posting. Rome. No children. She told me I'd changed and become unrecognisable." He sipped his drink. "I prefer to tell myself we'd both aged and lost our communal lustre. But she was probably right. I'll have plenty of time alone here to figure it all out."

"Avoid navel gazing, my friend; leave that to females, with their superior intuition." Monkton punched Haydon's shoulder. "Your priority needs to be getting close to Ali Kabbani and ensuring all the stars are aligned. My sense is things are going to happen in a hell of a hurry and will bite us in the butt if we're not right on top of them."

"Abbas wasn't giving much away."

"It's close by, you can smell it. This regime is going to fall soon."

"Why are you travelling then." Lena pulled a face. "If things are about to happen?"

"Quick trip to Beirut." Monkton reached over and touched her arm. "Need to keep the troops happy. Back by the weekend."

"Unlike Haydon, my superior intuition tells me that, unlike him, you haven't changed at all, darling. You just can't stop moving." Haydon thought he heard a tinge of bitterness in that husky voice. "Maybe it's you who should do some navel gazing."

"Not my style honey. I'm an extrovert. Haydon here's the depressive one."

"Are they mutually exclusive?"

"Shall we order." Monkton started reading his menu. "I'm famished."

Chapter 6

Khartoum, May 1989

He got to the party early, directly from the Embassy. It was still light. Diplomatic parties had become popular since the Islamists in government had forced the Prime Minister to ban alcohol. They were bread and butter opportunities for Haydon to scout for sources. As he stepped into the garden, his eyes scanned the crowd. The usual mix: Sudanese, Greeks, Armenians, Lebanese of different varieties, French, Italians, Kuwaitis. Business tycoons, government officials, diplomats, UN people. And spies.

The Italian Residence was a two-storey villa dominating a sharp bend in the fast-flowing Blue Nile, the terrace perched above a smooth, unnaturally green lawn running down to the water's edge. The evening was pleasantly cool, girls were wrapped in bright shawls, men wearing linen jackets or blazers. Coloured lights were strung from the palm trees that fringed the lawn. The Italian ambassador was an inveterate hunter, and a large wild boar, fruit of a weekend's expedition, was being hand-turned on an old-fashioned spit by a tall, very dark Sudanese in a long, white *jellabiya*. Haydon sniffed the intoxicating mix of roast meat scented with evening jasmine.

He saw his ambassador holding forth in a group near to the bar, boring his audience about butterflies, no doubt. Ramesh had let slip that the junior staff referred to him as 'Blather-too-much'. He turned away to avoid him and spotted the Embassy lawyer Yahya Abdelaziz sitting alone at a corner table, nattily dressed in a dark blue suit and striped tie, sipping a drink.

Taking a tumbler of Scotch off a tray he wandered over.

"I enjoyed my introduction to the Khartoum Cricket Club." Haydon plumped himself down opposite the young Sudanese. "I hadn't expected to see you there."

"Out first ball." Yahya smiled. "A good starting point for improvement."

"How come you play?"

"The British educational system." Yahya smiled. "Victoria College, Alexandria. Not much use to me though, deploying a straight bat in my business. For that you need a bat that goes around corners."

Haydon knew he'd gone on to study law at the Sorbonne. He was building himself a reputation as a proponent of human rights, taking on cases that put him at odds with the government. A risky choice, Haydon thought, the embassy picking him out at the start of a promising career; well, so long as he didn't get himself locked up. But he was wired into the political establishment and generally well liked.

"Waiting for someone? Or just feeling solitary?"

"Ali Kabbani. Have you met him yet?"

"No. Will you introduce me?"

"I'm your well-paid lawyer, I do your bidding!" Haydon sat down next to him and sipped his drink.

"I'm hearing a lot of talk of unrest."

"The dervishes are dancing, yes. They always do, but we Sudanese have this sixth sense, you see, we feel it under our skin when the pressure is nearing boiling point." He rolled his head around. "Endless rumours of planned coups. Who will succeed? Ah yes, that's the question."

"Who are the runners and riders?"

"Usual. Unionists, Communists, Muslim Brothers, Islamic Front. Every self-respecting army officer from Major to General, with or without a foreign backer." He twisted in his chair and poked his finger at Haydon. "Most of them trained at your Sandhurst place, that's where they learn how to do these things politely."

"What about you?"

"My work is a plot by itself. Even if I want change, I know another bloody regime will replace this bloody regime. It's our destiny, you see. *When God made the Sudan he laughed!*" He tilted back on his chair, which threatened to topple over, spilling his drink as he chuckled. "Human rights will be abused by the next guys just as well, they probably won't even bother to change the security bosses or the jailers, they're indispensable, you see. Look over there. The squat man in a white suit with the dishonest smile? Salah el-Fateh, do you know him?"

"Should I?"

"Classic example of what I'm saying. Big filing cabinet filled with secrets. Our version of J. Edgar Hoover. Bright and nasty. You don't want to meet him in a basement. He's head of the infamous *Mukhabarat* and will remain on top whichever group comes to power. Change his clothes perhaps, grow a beard if he needs one to fit in."

"You get on with him?"

"My services will always be in demand. I'll watch and smile and babble away in court and hope to get my clients a softer bed, or a mattress at least. Cheers!" They clinked their tumblers and sipped their drinks.

Haydon felt the whisky, almost neat, burning down his throat. The staple Khartoum drink – White Horse scotch – it came in half-gallon bottles and was served in large tumblers with a single enormous ice cube. The hubbub of conversation increased as the party filled up. A trio of local musicians started singing and playing percussion, and a few of the younger guests moved with the rhythm, hands in the air. A dark-skinned, elegant man with a walking stick limped towards their table. He had the slight stoop that tall men often affect. Deep scars on his cheeks gave him a sculpted look.

"*Yaaaa Salaaam!*" It came out as a low growl. The man raised his arms high and wide and smiled broadly at Yahya.

"They let you out, you rascal!" The younger man leapt up and the two men embraced.

The older man looked over at Haydon.

"Let me introduce Ali Kabbani?" Yahya gestured to the older man. "My cousin, well, of sorts, everyone's a cousin around here, you see."

"A pleasure to meet you, Ali."

"He's one of those politicos you should keep away from." Yahya held onto Kabbani's hand. "He's been under house arrest. For talking badly about the regime. I can't think why they let him out, probably because he's got a hot-shot lawyer."

"I'm still suffering extreme pain from the size of your bills." Kabbani rubbed his hands together.

"We were just talking about plotters, and here you are."

"Mister Talbot. You see, everyone here's a plotter." Kabbani sat down next to Yahya.

"And if you're not one, you're obviously a no one, but you'll be a suspect anyway."

Haydon was fascinated by Kabbani. He remembered he'd been a childhood friend of the Prime Minister, a liberal economist who'd graduated Stanford and spent some years at the World Bank. He'd been Minister of Finance until he'd spoken out against increasingly repressive security laws. Talked of as a future leader, he exuded a bright intelligence. Haydon saw hesitancy, or perhaps watchfulness, in those sharp features, a quality powerful men use, like charm, to disguise their thoughts.

"The ambassador told me you've been posted here as a

punishment?" A low chuckle emerged from the dark face. "What sin did you commit?"

"Plenty, I suspect. Mainly it's because my superior – he's an old friend – doesn't like me." He lit a cigarette. In the match's flare, Haydon made out a warm smile. "Of course I've read about your sins in the papers."

"Never trust the newspapers here. They're government propaganda! Even the football results are fake. If you want accurate news, sit in the camel market in Omdurman and drink coffee."

"What is the latest news from the camel market?" Haydon raised his eyebrows,

"Nothing you don't already know."

Kabbani turned to Yahya, and the two of them leaned in towards each other, heads close, whispering. Haydon took the cue and wandered off to get another drink. He was feeling light-headed. He lit a cigarette and looked around. Who should he pounce on? The ambassador was chatting with the Minister of Culture. Haydon threaded his way through the crowd towards a group of local businessmen.

He smelt her first, the scent of gardenia. Then, as he turned his head, a flash of colour. He moved towards her and their eyes locked and held.

"Lena isn't it. Hi. Where's Pete?"

"Away. Due back in a couple of days."

"Going for a walk?"

"I want to watch the sunset over the Nile." Bright green eyes, lit by a lantern on the bar. "May I join you?"

She nodded. The edge of a smile. They strolled side by side down the sloping lawn towards the river. The sun was sinking, reflecting and shimmering on the water, the dust in the air providing a bright orange tone. He felt a breeze on his face as they moved out of the shadow of the trees.

"It's magical."

"Sunset happens so fast here, accompanied by the noisy symphony of the birds."

"A poetic diplomat, are you?" She laughed. "Isn't that an oxymoron?"

"Never suspected I had it in me, but I'm willing to try."

The sounds of the party faded behind the whispers of the palms. She stood motionless, her right hand shading her eyes as if she were searching for something important on the horizon.

They stood close together, the sky filled with the evening flighting of huge flocks of ducks and geese. They could hear the loud swishing of their wings. A donkey started honking nearby. They both laughed. His hand involuntarily touched hers. He felt a shock as her little finger curled slowly around his. They stayed silent as they watched the sun dip behind the horizon.

"We met in Beirut once, you know." She squeezed his finger. "A long time ago. You don't remember that do you, just another embassy party."

He didn't answer, searching his memory.

"I suffer from nostalgia about my wonderful city. It's broken apart now."

"Sunset on the Nile, it's always melancholic." He inhaled deeply. The smell of gardenia was overpowering.

"I watched *Last Tango in Paris* last night. Alone." She said. "That left me feeling melancholic."

"It was about erotic anonymity, as I recall. They were called Paul and Jeanne?"

"Pleased not to meet you, Paul."

"Was it a tragedy."

"About obsessive intimacy between two strangers–"

"–nice to meet you too, Jeanne."

"Maybe what we need is another drink."

She laughed, turning her head and looking up at him. She

had an oddly angular smile, as if she was relishing a wistful joke. They wandered along the water's edge. Fingers linked.

"They say the crocs are friendly here."

"Never smile at a crocodile, my paw told me." Her voice was husky, assuming an American twang.

"Texas?"

"Pretty poor guess. North Shore Lebanese."

The stars were coming out, one by one; the sky grew brighter as the sun disappeared into the dusty horizon. She stumbled on a tree root and fell clumsily into his arms. He held her up and kissed her, her tongue flickering in response, demanding. He felt himself sinking. Then she pulled away. When he opened his eyes and looked up, she was walking quickly back towards the house.

Would he have been as direct if he hadn't been half-cut? He doubted it. Even though that first glance, which lasted a fraction too long, had been so unambiguous, so piercing. It had crashed through some chink in his reserve and stabbed into the core of his being. He felt a sharp pang of something. Maybe it was panic, he felt it run down his spine. His life had always been about keeping control. *This didn't feel like him.*

The Sheikh

Chapter 7

Khartoum, June 1989

When the ambassador was obliged to engage in diplomatic work, he transformed from his usual guise of dusty academic spending his days considering ancient monuments. Now he sat stiffly behind a large partner's desk, formally dressed in suit and tie, unsmiling. The neatness of the items laid out on the desk fascinated Haydon. Everything was so rigidly straight. Perhaps he should call a mechanic to rub him down with an oily rag.

"We need to be sure this is the coup we've been expecting. And quickly. Or has some other bugger hijacked it?" He reached down and adjusted a pen, placing it horizontally onto the blotting pad, then ran his hands through his leonine grey hair. "Can't you get hold of Kabbani?"

"The phone system's down." Haydon stood by the window, peering towards the roof of the Republican Palace, from where he could see dark smoke curling upwards. "And he won't be at his usual haunts."

"Get out there and find out how things stand." The ambassador directed the edge of a smile at Haydon, but his face was taut and distant. "It appears quiet enough."

"Quiet?" Haydon raised his eyebrows and gestured to the open window. "That's heavy machine gun fire, fifty cal, coming from the direction of the palace, a few hundred yards away."

"I need first-hand reports. How solid the rebels' hold is and so forth. Exactly who are they? Whitehall will want a cast-iron confirmation before issuing a statement. There's no room for error, bad for business. Get out there to the radio station. Whoever controls things there is on the winning side."

"Wiser to wait a couple–"

"–you're an intelligence officer, Haydon. Hmph. Go and collect intelligence." He reached down and pulled open a drawer, removing a coding machine, which he plugged into a strange-looking socket. "But don't take unnecessary risks."

"Like getting out of bed this morning." He said under his breath, turning and walking towards the door. The ambassador looked up and frowned.

"Don't be wet, Haydon. You're an Army man. Get to the officer in charge there. I want an on-the-spot report, and check out the bridges on your way back. Oh, and see if you can drive past the Palace and get a feel for the situation there."

He waved a limp hand at Haydon and started tapping onto the small keyboard.

As he was approaching the turning to the airport, Haydon saw a group of men running back from the crossroads and attempting to hurdle a high wall, which was when he'd shouted to his driver El-Haj to stop the car. They had just enough time to abandon the vehicle and rush to find hiding spots before the threatening gun barrel of a T72 tank inched out from a side street. It stopped. Haydon squeezed behind a wall.

There followed a worrying silence, which seemed horribly loud, broken by the bass growl of a large diesel engine. A cloud of acrid, black smoke floated by above him, then an ear-piercing series of screeches as the behemoth rumbled forward, emitting a sinister clanking sound as the tracks turned over. The ground beneath him seemed to move. He could feel the heavy vibration in his core. Thudding. Something pounding. His heart? He thought he could smell his own fear. It was odd. He had no clue whose side the tank was on. Was it there to defend the airport for the rebels? Or retake it for the government? It really didn't matter; he couldn't show himself anyway.

The screeching crept closer. He visualised the commander, erect head poking up through the turret, eyes scanning for a target. Fuck! He looked for the thickest part of the parapet to crouch behind and squeezed himself into the smallest ball. Eyes screwed shut. The wall wasn't thick enough. He felt exposed, as if the tank's eyes could see straight through the baked brown mud of the wall. Sweat was pouring from his forehead and down his cheeks. It ran into his eyes and stung. He wiped his face with a dusty handkerchief. He felt his shirt soaking wet.

He covered his ears with his hands. What am I doing here? He damned his weakness for accepting banishment to this godforsaken dump, for the admission of failure, giving in to his fear of leaving the cocoon of The Service for an uncertain future in civvy street. Punished for staying true to the principles he'd taken an oath to uphold. Seconds ticked past, slower than seconds. He should have stayed in bed this morning.

He closed his eyes and thought about Lena. She'd looked so lovely when he'd left her the day before. Snoring little snores. He'd bent down and kissed her forehead. She'd emitted a light sigh and reached her hand up to touch his face. He'd felt stirrings and kissed her again. She'd pulled away. He couldn't believe what he had done. It couldn't be worse. Against his interests as well as all his principles. It could blow his reputation out of the water, and he couldn't even blame it on drink. Some primal urge had pulled them together with an anarchic force of thoughtless and immediate desire. He wanted her more than he'd ever wanted any woman before. *Jesus!*

The tank engine roared again, pulling him back from his reverie. The metal clanking restarted. He sensed the noise was fading. It was moving off toward the airport. His stomach muscles unclenched. After some minutes, he peered over the wall and caught sight of a dark silhouette disappearing up the dusty road. He watched until all that remained of its threatening shape was a thick cloud of smoke.

A fuzzy head popped out of a concrete culvert by the side of the road. Followed by a skinny body that seemed to expand as it squeezed its way out. Dusting himself down, the man beamed, displaying several empty spaces where teeth had presumably once been.

"Mister Haydon." He wagged a thin finger. "You have to up my pay you want me to be hiding in the sewers of Khartoum."

"Me too El-Haj, same goes for me." They jogged together up the dusty road to the blue Embassy Land Rover, skewed across the front of someone's driveway. "Let's see if we make it to the radio station in condition to collect this month's wages, with our bits still attached."

"I drive you through fire, boss, you pay me enough."

Haydon reached into the glove compartment and took out a folded Union Jack pennant, screwing the mast onto the front of the car. "This is not strictly correct Haj. We have no Chief of Mission aboard, but I doubt anyone who's out and about with an RPG is going to argue about diplomatic niceties. It should make us a little safer. Should."

The roads were empty as they made their way slowly out of town, taking a wide detour to stay clear of the airport. A ragged group of soldiers manning a roadblock waved them through, after he'd wound down the window and pointed to the Union Jack. The soldiers' eyes all seemed bloodshot red. Maybe they'd been drinking *arak*. Which would make them extra jumpy. He noticed several figures seated on the ground, arms held behind their heads. One of them had blood streaming from an open head wound.

He turned on the car radio. Martial music, they'd been playing it since dawn. Did the radio station keep a tape ready on tap for the next coup? Then a crackly voice.

"This is the Revolutionary Command Council for National Salvation. We have overthrown the brutal and corrupt Mahdist regime. Martial law has been imposed. Citizens stay in your homes and await further instructions. Security forces are under orders to fire on looters. Stay off the streets! Stay in your homes!"

The music started up again.

They drove on, past the Russian-built oil refinery, tall rusty chimneys spewing out yellowish fumes, forming a cloud which obscured the wide River Nile behind. The steel monster gave way to flat brown desert, punctuated by a few bent and deformed trees, and a sea of waving plastic bags. A thoroughly modern landscape, he thought, a symbol of progress. As if little white happily waving flags had decorated the endless desert.

The antennae farm of the national radio station came into view. El-Haj swung the steering wheel and gingerly turned off the tarmac onto a sandy track, stopping the Land Rover in front of a barrier across the road. A group of nervous-looking soldiers in blue camouflage uniforms surrounded the Land Rover, rifles raised to their shoulders.

"Out! Get out of the car!" A tall soldier with puckered scars on his cheeks and sergeant's stripes on his shoulder banged hard on the door with his fist. "Now!"

"Diplomat. I am Engleezi Diplomat." He wound down the window and gestured to the pennant. "I need to talk to your

Commanding Officer."

"Get out!" The two men levered themselves out of the car, hands half raised in compliance. "Kneel. On ground. There. Quick!"

He felt his stomach churning again. El-Haj's face had gone from black to grey, beads of sweat were spraying from his forehead.

"Don't shoot! I am Engleezi diplomat–"

"–hands behind your head!" The sergeant barked instructions in Arabic over his shoulder as he loped off towards an office building. "Don't move!"

The two men remained kneeling on the dusty earth by the Land Rover, facing towards the two-storey concrete building that housed the national radio station. The sun was beating down, sweat was flowing liberally down their faces. Until recently, his life had been painfully dull, he'd craved excitement, something to jerk him out of a lonely malaise. What was it Wilde had said? *"When the Gods wish to punish us, they answer our prayers."* Now he was being punished in trumps. A group of soldiers were crouched by the building, smoking cigarettes and talking, eying the two men suspiciously, dangerous faced. Haydon's arms ached; he didn't dare lower his hands.

Bullet marks peppered the faded white facade of the radio station, with several smashed windows and a black scorch hole through the roof. Tank fire. He noticed the pointed ends of long gun barrels, 106mm recoilless rifles, he thought, sticking out from beneath camouflage nets at the side of the building.

The sergeant came striding out of the building alongside a tall, well turned-out army officer.

"Don't move, keep your hands where they are." The officer gestured with his swagger stick. "You say you're a British diplomat." Haydon nodded towards the Land Rover.

"Why on earth have you come here? In the middle of a coup. Are you mad?"

"My name is Haydon Talbot. Political Attaché at the British Embassy." He realised he was talking fast and took a long breath. "I'm under instructions from my ambassador to contact the Revolutionary Command Council. May I stand?"

"Remain as you are. With martial law in force, all movement is forbidden. And unwise."

"My government needs to understand the composition and aims of the Council, and to confirm the stability of the uprising."

"You colonials think you have some divine right to flout–"

"–I believe your leadership will wish–"

"Don't interrupt me–"

"–to open contacts with Western governments at the earliest opportunity." The officer glared down at him.

"You seem to be stupider and more arrogant than other diplomats I've met." After a pause, his face broke into a smile and he held out his hand, a tough, firm handshake. He yanked Haydon to his feet. "Braver too perhaps, Mister Haydon Talbot. Major Satti, Sapper."

He barked an order, and the sergeant motioned to El-Haj to get up off his knees. His driver's guileless smile reminded Haydon of a naughty schoolboy who'd been let off a beating. The Major led Haydon over to a wooden table in the shade and offered him a glass of water from a thermos. As they sat down, Haydon noticed the line of smudged shapes laid out under an awning in an outhouse. He shivered. So it hadn't been bloodless, as Kabbani had predicted. The pile of corpses a reminder that every outcome was still possible.

"It wasn't trouble-free driving here from town."

"Have a cigarette." Major Satti proffered a packet of Rothmans. "You look like you need several."

Haydon took one and lit it. He noticed his hand was shaking. "You're right! Tanks and nervy roadblocks. Hard on the nerves. Reminded me of Belfast, when I was a young lieutenant."

"I sensed a military air to you. I attended Sandhurst, you see, I have fond memories of Camberley, so I have a nose for stiff British officers. Infantry wallah I think?"

"Para. My army days are long ago. Now I'm a dull diplomat, lying for my country."

"You did well to get here. The streets aren't secure, elements of the regime are in hiding, resistance here and there. Bands of militia on the streets, dressed in civilian clothes." He slapped the swagger stick against his palm. "But we're mopping them up hour by hour."

"Holding the Radio Station will have been critical." Haydon said.

"We had to resist a determined attack, but as you see, we're still broadcasting." The Major stood up, dropping his butt end and stamping on it. He pointed towards the building. "I'll make a radio call to Army HQ and see what I can do. If they agree, I'll send you down with an armed escort."

Haydon drew deeply on his cigarette, feeling the burning relief travelling down his lungs.

Chapter 8

Major Satti was as good as his word and provided a battered 8-wheeled armoured car to escort them to Army Headquarters.

"Stay close behind."

"Thank you, Major. Good luck to you." Haydon waved. Satti saluted, then turned back towards the radio station.

El-Haj took the Major's instructions to heart and tailgated the ancient BTR-60, which, like all Russian machinery, emitted clouds of dense oily smoke. He coughed loudly and covered his face with a dirty handkerchief. Haj was a truly rotten driver, Haydon thought, but after their run in with the T-72 he had remained impressively calm.

They slowed to a crawl as they approached the Military area. Army HQ was a single-storey colonial building faced with peeling paint and flowering bougainvillea. The approaches were ringed with troops concealed behind steel and concrete palisades. He spotted the low shapes of tanks dug in hull-down, their guns aimed towards the arch around the guardhouse entry. Small blobs on the roof pointed spindly rifles downwards.

Their escort turned away as they approached the entrance. They waited whilst sentries talked to the NCO in charge of the APC. The tank gun barrels seemed to be trained directly on them. He hoped no nervy finger pressed a button by mistake. Nothing seemed to be happening. It was unnaturally quiet, yet they were at the epicentre of a military coup.

After an interminable wait, a sergeant waved them forward and raised the heavy metal barrier. They inched forward a few meters to face another steel gate. The barrier clanked shut behind them. While the car was being searched, a soldier ordered them out, and another soldier used a mirror on a pole to scan the underside of the Land Rover. They drove on, past concrete pillboxes and steel fortifications, then turned into a neat courtyard with geometrical flowerbeds leading up to the whitewashed Headquarters building. As he got down, Haydon flinched as a burst of machine gun fire opened up, ominously close. The sentries took no notice. They stared at him silently as he bolted up the steps towards the imposing entrance.

A Staff Officer wearing red collar patches met him in the entrance hall and escorted him to a corner office down a long corridor. An elegant man with parallel tribal scars on his cheeks, wearing a white *jellabiya,* a turban and dark glasses, entered through a side door. Haydon recognised Ali Kabbani, who was followed by the squat, powerfully built shape of Colonel Abbas el Daoud, dressed in full combat gear.

"We've been expecting you, Haydon." The two men embraced. Haydon could smell his cologne. "I think you know Colonel Abbas, He is Chairman of the Revolutionary Command Council."

The army man nodded, then waited for the frail civilian to sit. The two men faced Haydon over a long wooden table. Kabbani gestured with his arm.

"Your French colleague has already been here." Kabbani smiled and swirled his shawl around his neck. "Pipped you, you see! You British are slipping."

"They've probably been reading your mail." Haydon laughed. "I've been out at the radio station."

"Foolhardy." The Colonel laughed, it came out as a bark. "The streets aren't secure yet."

"I noticed." He smiled at the Colonel, who stared back, stony-faced, hands resting on his knees.

"The Armed Forces have been obliged to do their duty to

protect the Constitution, which was being violated." Colonel Abbas leaned forward and waved his forefinger. "The Revolutionary Command Council, which is a military entity, intends to assemble an interim Government of National Salvation."

"My ambassador is keen to receive a formal statement of The Council's intentions, so HMG can consider early recognition."

"We intend abrogation of sharia law. Technocrats in key portfolios of government in the interim. A rainbow coalition." Kabbani bent forward and touched his arm. Haydon looked into his eyes, intelligent eyes, and wondered if he saw a hint of hesitancy. Maybe things were not so clear cut. "Elections will be scheduled as soon as the security situation permits. Our target is nine months."

"You'll make a public announcement?" Haydon ran his hand through his hair.

"As soon as mopping up operations are complete." The Colonel spoke loudly, his eyes had the disconcerting habit of seeming to look over his shoulder. "Several members of the leadership have eluded us, but we'll find them."

"Is control of the capital and security forces secure?"

"There's been fighting out at the radio station, you will have seen the damage. Tank units from the Presidential Guard arrived unexpectedly, but our forces saw them off." The Colonel frowned. "Some action around the Presidential palace and Security HQ. Which we quashed. Now we're clearing up the 'stay-behind' militias, cowards hiding in civilian dress."

"What does Whitehall require, in order to announce recognition of our government?" Kabbani pressed his fingers together in an arch and frowned. He looked worried, Haydon thought. Perhaps there'd been greater resistance than he'd expected.

"Commitment to a timetable for early elections, participation of major parties, a pledge to uphold the rule of law and human rights. The usual. You know the form, Ali."

"I think you'll find our statement will address all your requirements." He swirled his shawl again. "You make sure the Americans are onside. That is critical."

"Washington will be relieved to see the back of the *Umma* regime. They've been concerned about increasing anti-Western rhetoric. We'll be liaising closely with them." Haydon leaned towards Kabbani. "Are you a member of this Revolutionary Command Council?"

"No, I'm a civilian adviser." That's implausible, Haydon thought. Maybe he's the leader. His coup, his plan? Colonel Abbas clearly defers to him.

"What about your childhood buddy?" The deposed Prime Minister had been Kabbani's close friend at school. He'd served as his deputy until he'd publicly criticised the increasing repression of the regime.

"Don't worry, my friend. He's secure in a secret location."

"But he'll be tried. For his crimes." Colonel Abbas cut in. "Human rights abuses – torture, extra-judicial assassinations, theft of state property."

"Some might interpret that as revenge."

"The people will expect it." The Colonel rapped his knuckles on the table. "But he will receive due process. Which is more than he doled out to his victims."

Kabbani nodded, then he and the Colonel stood up. "When can we expect your announcement recognising the new regime?"

"Soon after your public statement of intentions. HMG will be reassured by what you've told me."

"We'll provide you an escort back to your Embassy." Colonel Awad turned to the Major who was standing rigidly by the door. "Arrange please."

"Thank you, Ali. Go well."

"You go well my friend."

Haydon told El-Haj to take the road running along the Blue Nile back to the Embassy. As they drove past the Kobar and Blue Nile bridges, Haydon snapped surreptitious photos with his Minox sub-miniature camera.

A strong army presence was visible on the bridges, steel fortifications erected in front of heavy lorries blocking the width of the road. He noticed the snout of an artillery piece poking out from a camouflage net and could hear occasional small arms fire in the distance, somewhere off towards the airport, but the centre of town was eerily empty. He sensed the coup was solidifying.

Hurrying up the stairs to the second floor, he entered the ambassador's ante-room. His secretary, Amina, waved him to go in.

The ambassador gestured him to sit. Haydon noticed the items on his desk remained laid out in perfect order, as if the man hadn't moved during the several hours that Haydon had been away.

"I gather you saw Kabbani."

"You spoke to him? The phones are back up?"

"No, my French colleague came through on the wireless link. His view is the coup is solid and Kabbani is saying the right things. The *Quai* is minded to recognise, as soon as this Revolutionary Command Council – why do they have to have these silly names? – has publicly committed to early elections and so forth, abandonment of *sharia*."

Haydon gave him a detailed report on his morning, the ambassador listening, expressionless, making occasional notes on a pad with a fountain pen, then placing it carefully in line with the blotter. He made an arch of his hands and looked intently at Haydon.

"You see. You were reticent of getting out there, but I

knew you would manage." Haydon felt a vein throbbing in his temple. "It's much as I expected. A change of government meaning change of extraordinarily little, someone's brother-in-law replacing someone else's cousin. The removal of *sharia* will be helpful, keep the secular community and the business elite quiet. Good, Haydon, I think I can now brief London with confidence. Any other observations?"

"I have some reservations about Colonel Abbas. The Americans like him, it's true." Haydon paused and collected his thoughts. "He deferred to Kabbani, but there was something unconvincing in his manner. I've been wondering whether Kabbani may be being played, in fact are we all being duped, by elements in the Army–"

"–there you go, Haydon." The ambassador beamed and leaned back in his chair. "Spoiling a good news story with unsubstantiated suspicions. Keep them to yourself please. We have had exhaustive private conversations with Ali Kabbani, going back months. This is our coup. We need to make best use of the opportunity it presents."

He picked up a red telephone and pressed a button.

"Put me through to the Permanent Secretary at the FCO please."

Chapter 9

Century House, London, March 1990

The Chief of SIS, Mark Glasson, sat at the top of the table, tapping his fingernails rhythmically on the wood. He looked a lot like Toad of Toad Hall, Haydon thought, wearing a checked tweed jacket that would have been appropriate for boar hunting with oligarchs in Kaliningrad. When he got his K he would become intolerable, and his wife Belinda would be worse. The two of them had been friends and colleagues for over twenty years. It was a peculiar thing about one's oldest friends, the longer you knew them, the less you liked them. *Was this the result of the greying of hairs?* That you became mean-spirited.

"At the time of the June coup, you reported that it was our team at the helm, yes?"

It came out sounding like *'yarse'*. Haydon wondered if his boss had been taking elocution lessons.

"I reported my concerns about Abbas el Daoud, whether we might have been played."

He looked down the long table in the book-lined office, the surface polished to a high sheen. Had Mark bought those leather-bound books by the yard? He never read office reports in detail, he got much of his news off the machine that tick-a-ticked ceaselessly in the corner of the room. Grisly irony. The head of one of the world's most respected intelligence services relying on a commercial news service.

"A *'revolution for democracy'* you called it, yes." Glasson shook his head, his face fixed in an ironic frown. "Our friends driving the tanks, roses in their gun-barrels. Pretty girls ululating. Citizens cheering. A generation of young leaders promising a return to happy times."

The Reuters machine emitted a staccato chatter, belched out a length of paper and fell silent. Haydon sat fidgeting, avoiding his boss's eye. Glasson stared down at him from a high-backed Vitra chrome and leather chair. Since Glasson had moved into the top job, he had become smoother. He'd changed his tailor and looked less likely to burst out of the seams. His hair had transformed, taken on a patrician salt and pepper hue. But his ability to deflect blame remained unerring.

"If I remember correctly, your in-tell-ig-ence reports," he emphasised each syllable, "which we circulated to our customers, predicted June's coup d'état, but incorrectly forecast it would lead to restoration of moderate democratic government within nine months. Better to say nothing than get it so crassly wrong, yes?"

"The coup leaders were crafty. The President, General Abbas is a genial man, he took us all in, playing the part of a patriotic democrat guiding the nation to early elections." Haydon flushed. He felt a desire to argue, but knew he needed to remain calm. The sideswipe was typical, disregarding his updates, setting him up as the target for criticism of SIS's analysis, which Glasson had almost certainly overstated to his political masters. "He detained the top people from the major parties – Umma, Communists, Trade Unionists, Islamic Front, Muslim Brothers and Unionists. A Full House. Swept them up in the weeks after the coup."

"Not the acts of a patriotic democrat. And you were taken in?"

"He shrewdly disguised the true complexion of the new regime. Had them all incarcerated together in the political wing in Kobar prison; that must've been a fun gathering. We got reports from inside the prison. No special treatment for any of them, particularly not the Islamic Front leaders. A ruse to camouflage the actual nature of the coup."

"But you're the man on the spot, how did you miss the signals?"

"I reported my misgivings."

"That wasn't my reading."

"Ali Kabbani, my best source in the new regime, assured me they were committed to early elections, that all major parties had agreed to take part. He was convinced that General Abbas was a force for good." Haydon crossed his arms. "It's taken nine months for the Islamic Front to emerge as the real power behind this regime, Abbas seeming to be somewhere between their puppet and their willing collaborator. They've carried out a slow, carefully disguised, internal coup. The Islamic front leaders are being released, one by one. The mask has been peeled off. It's now clear they've been driving the bus since Day One."

"Not good for the credibility of the Service, and it reflects badly on me personally. Kabbani put one over on you, yes?"

"Kabbani's a liberal technocrat. Technocrats were supposed to be the vanguard of the interim administration, plotting a course back to better relations with the West. He told me the detentions of party leaders were a short-term stabilisation measure. He was blindsided too. Now he's being sidelined. The technocrats are being plucked out of government and replaced by bearded religious nuts. Bright nuts, mind you."

"I need successes while I'm fighting battles over budget allocations. Costs of the new HQ building are running way over." He pointed out of the window towards the building site. "You're saying elections won't happen, yes?"

Haydon stood and paced up and down by the plate-glass window, looking down over the busy Thames. It was raining, looking down he saw the river streaked with dirty foam. He thought he could hear the bells of Big Ben striking midday. He felt weary, he didn't enjoy being Mark's punch-bag. A gaggle of cranes stood at attention by the river's edge, the Babylonian-looking building pushing its way skywards. People had nicknamed it The Pleasure Dome. He knew he'd never make it to a plush suite at the top floor at Vauxhall Cross, when SIS eventually moved out of Century House, which had been condemned as being wholly insecure.

"They parrot the line of 'guaranteeing' elections, but the grapevine is full of rumours that they'll proscribe all the traditional parties, then hold bogus elections, which they'll win, in Soviet style."

"My question is what key national interest do we have in any of this? A tin pot, bankrupt tract of desert with endless famines and no valuable resources. Unless you count mangy camels." He chortled at his own witticism.

Reaching down into a desk drawer, he pulled out a long cigar. Rolling it back and forth under his nose, he inhaled deeply, nostrils twitching. Like a rodent, Haydon thought, the rapid blink, the small eyes darting about, avoiding contact.

"Look Haydon, in this post-Soviet world, I see this organisation's principal role as supporting British commercial interests overseas. In the Sudan there are none. All major British companies were nationalised under Nimeiri's regime. Am I missing something?"

"With respect Mark, I think you are. There are new security threats to our vital interests, overseas, and potentially even here on our shores." Haydon sat back down and stared at Glasson. "Last month's Islamic Congress in Khartoum brought together a lexicon of pretty much all the most dangerous players from the Arab and Islamic worlds. George Habash, Zawahiri, Imad Mughniyeh, Gulbuddin Hekmatyar, Rabbani, Sabri el-Banna. Just to name a few. An alarming gathering. Even Carlos the Jackal is living in Khartoum as a guest of the state. These are flashing warning lights?"

"Our American cousins demonstrated in Afghanistan how easy it is to manipulate these radical Islamic groups, yes." Glasson yawned and looked at his watch. "Under Bill Casey's leadership, the Agency hijacked the lot of them to be US tools in bludgeoning the Russians. Suborned them as allies. Fundamentalist loonies. They were more useful, more effective, than B-52s, and cheaper too, they saw our Sov friends right off, fur tails dangling where their balls had once been."

"As the result of which these extreme groups now represent a greater threat to Western security than the Palestinians ever did, even at the height of the 1970s airliner hijackings." Haydon felt himself going red. He paused and took a deep breath. "Mark, we even trained them in bomb-making, an act of madness."

"The trouble with you Arabists is you're obsessed. You see suicide bombs under every *jellabiya*." Glasson swivelled his chair to face Haydon, hands arched, toe tap-tapping audibly under the desk. "There's a lot of *balla-balla*, I grant you, but these groups need money, without money it's just empty talk. And money comes from the Saudis and Kuwaitis, which means US influence. Let alone Uncle Sam's own sacks of dollars, which The Agency doles out in all directions. No, those guys dance to Langley's tune. Hard to credit, I know, but–"

"Their victory over the Russians in Afghanistan has pumped them up, made them feel invincible. Now these same groups are strutting about in a hurry for the next conflict. Their new cause is to expel US troops from their holy lands. Mecca, Medina, Jerusalem. They want the Great Satan out."

"Haydon, I will not increase your resources, don't bother to ask." Glasson rubbed his chin, swivelling back and forth in his chair. "I've agreed to green-light continued funding for Operation SEAMLESS, so get on with running that. I like the prospect of a regular flow of intel from aid workers across the whole country. Grass roots insight into what dirt's appearing under those radical fingernails. Especially stuff we can share with Langley."

"I'm on top of that Mark, but–"

"–you have recruited a replacement Manager, yes?"

"I'm interviewing."

"Good, get on with it."

"Mark, I'm flagging my concern that Middle East terrorism is about to take a dangerous upturn." He stared out of the window, his eyes following the lights of the endless line of airplanes following the flightpath towards Heathrow. "We're not talking about the Joe Bananas gang in turbans–"

"Haydon, go run your fantasies past your buddy Pete Monkton, yes." Glasson picked up a file and started turning the pages. "He's in London for a couple of days, I had a pow-wow with him yesterday at Grosvenor Square."

"I worry he's letting himself get conned. These *Muj* have moved on. What they call the Far Enemy is their new target. That's the USA, that's us, and Europe."

He lowered his voice and continued. "Monkton's buddies from Peshawar and Quetta are living there in Khartoum, posing as farmers, several hundred Afghan-Arab fighters and their families. Emptying beehives and planting crops, supposedly. Living on a large farm somewhere towards the Ethiopian border. I doubt those Afghani warriors will want to spend their time growing yams and shovelling cow shit."

"Monkton understands those people better than you. He worked with them for years when he was Station Chief in Peshawar. Knows their secrets, yes?" Glasson put the file down on the table, took out a cutter from a drawer and snipped at his cigar. Leaning down, he began the rigmarole of lighting it, puffing away, his face disappearing behind a cloud of smoke. "His reporting to Langley is that they've a solid handle on this Sudan business. He has the money, he has the technical means to ensure he isn't being conned. End of. Anything else?"

Haydon rubbed his forehead. They had already banished him from the centre stage.

The next logical step was the exit door. *Did he really care?* His pension would be enough to underpin a reasonable retirement. Bore himself silly playing golf. He hated the game. White shoes with flaps and strangely patterned pullovers. Over the years, the endless need for compromise and manipulation had eaten into him. It had ended his marriage. *What is there left of your soul?* Ros had asked. A fair question. He didn't know the answer.

"Mark, if you won't listen to–"

"–look Haydon, I sent you to Sudan to be my eyes and ears in a war-torn backwater. That's it." Glasson puffed energetically on his cigar. "I get more useful reporting out of Langley. Abu Nidal and Hezbollah are top dead centre in their crosshairs. Go see Monkton. Listen to him. He knows his shit. You don't. Be kind to yourself for once. I can't keep on defending you in this building, yes? You don't make policy; you carry it out. Do the hell what I ask."

Haydon stood up and gathered his papers off the desk. He felt tired. Was he destined to end up as the Cassandra of Middle East terror? Prophesying catastrophe and being derided as a paranoid fantasist, a has-been clinging to outdated fears. Or was he underestimating Monkton's powers?

The Sheikh

Chapter 10

Buckinghamshire, April 1990

Two ponderous soldiers in camouflage uniform checked over Haydon's vehicle at the guardhouse before raising the barrier and waving him through. Driving up the long avenue of old chestnut trees, past the open parkland leading to the main house, his mind went back to the day he'd arrived at Oxley to join his own induction course. Over 20 years ago now, but the house was as ugly and institutional as he remembered it.

A textile magnate had built it in the mid-19th century, when England produced half the world's cotton cloth. A rambling, red brick mansion, outsized Gothic turrets gave it a top-heavy, gaunt look. Since the Second World War it had served as the training centre for SIS recruits, and, over the years, annexes, guardhouses, security fences and staff housing had been added.

The Hut was an ugly prefabricated structure set apart from the main house, used for activities which were 'outside the box', meaning not related to training of Britain's budding overseas spies. Haydon entered a green painted room furnished with tired chintzy furniture. Charlie Lomax was slumped in an armchair, leafing through a magazine. He looked languid, his tall frame unfolding as he stood up. The two men shook hands. Haydon held on to the younger man's hand and looked him in the eyes.

"Don't look a day wiser! Have you done a dodgy deal with Beelzebub?" He punched Charlie's arm. "You ran off in such a hurry after the Libya debacle."

"Sorry I didn't stay in touch." The sight of Charlie's cheeks blushing pink amused Haydon. "Five years rushed past."

"I've got grey hairs now."

"Life seemed to close in around me after the Libya business blew up. It hit me harder than I'd expected." Charlie took out a handkerchief and rubbed his temple. "Ines left me. I was in so much pain, I had to run. Then my father died."

"I know you were close." Haydon reached out and touched his arm. "What happened with Ines?"

"Ghastly trip to a ghastly clinic. I felt like a heel." Charlie turned away. "I wasn't prepared for how devastating the feelings would be. The look on her face on our way home. I knew–"

"–no need. I'm not surprised you took off." Haydon rolled his head back and forth, feeling the warm sun on his cheeks. "Why Colombia?"

"You know about Colombia? Oh, of course. You've been reading my file. Stupid of me." Charlie looked up. His expression was half smile and half grimace. "Two years in Cartagena, a fun city. Learned Spanish. Splashed money. Bought a monster dirt bike. Thought I was some kind of Easy Rider. Spread wild oats, drank too much, danced salsa, took bad drugs and lived in the moment. But I couldn't settle."

"You always were restless."

"I was full of rage, Haydon. Perhaps I still am. You led me by the nose into that miserable mess. Those eternal months in the Tripoli pokey. I was sure I was going to die in that hell hole." They sat down on a bench. "Incidentally, Haydon, I'm sorry about you and Ros. I heard it on the Oxley grapevine."

"The nature of a spy's life. Too many shadows. I could hardly live with myself, it must have been worse for her." That's the truth, he thought. So addictive, the secrecy. Adultery, manipulation, espionage: blood brothers. "I was surprised when I saw your name on the Oxley list. I thought I'd have put you off spying."

"Surprised me too. I can't explain why I applied. I seem unsuitable, even to myself."

"We'll discuss your suitability over lunch. I've squared it with the Major. He and I go back awhile." Haydon stood up. "Local pub. OK?"

They removed their jackets and loosened their ties, then sat down at a corner table under a large umbrella, nursing pint glasses of cold lager. The pub was quiet, early afternoon on a brilliant spring day. The veranda faced out onto a narrow river, a broad weeping willow casting long shadows over the grassy banks running up to a picturesque hump-backed bridge. Haydon watched a swan gliding along the calm water, her brown-feathered goslings following close behind her in a broad vee.

His eyes scanned the other diners, then he raised his glass and looked over at Charlie.

He's different, he thought, even has a few greying hairs at the temple. He could make out the loner in him; less the rebel, more the guy who doesn't quite fit in. Maybe that's what I like about him, it makes him so easy to steer.

"How's Oxley worked out for you? Tough?"

"Threw myself into it. I'd got bored of the easy life; I wanted a challenge. Oxley provided it – those instructors are a mean bunch of bastards." Charlie lit a cigarette and inhaled deeply. "Your friend the Major. Hard sod. Still, I was up and over the assault course as fast as most of the virgins. Gave me a kick. Came out on top on night exercises."

"You needn't have bothered. They make allowances for late entrants; they expect you to have the beginnings of a paunch by the time you're thirty."

"I wasn't good at the cerebral stuff, just about squeaked it." Charlie lit a cigarette and leaned back. "Hated cryptography, statistics and coding. All that maths gave me headaches."

"I've seen your reports, you're being modest."

"Sure?" He looked into Haydon's eyes, searching for irony. "Were you here?"

"In prehistory. After my short service commission. I was also a late entrant." He smiled. "Mind you, back then I was fit. In the Paras you don't get a let up."

"Still no sign of a paunch." Charlie jabbed his finger at Haydon's tummy and laughed. "The years have been kind to you."

"Flattery, Charlie. You always were an excellent liar." Haydon wiped froth from his upper lip. "A vital quality if you want to move up in the Service."

"Seems a long time since your flattery seduced me to work for you. I was so naive. You led me by the nose, intimidated me, though not as much as that torturer in the basement of Abu Salim. What was his name – oh yes, Moawia, the swine."

"No, no. Get it right Charlie! It wasn't flattery or intimidation, just bribery. Your eyes rolled around your head when you calculated how much money you were going to make. They were like Frisbees." He leaned forward. "Look Charlie, I was chuffed when I learned you'd applied for the Service. You're made for it, you've got a properly twisted mind! But why?"

"The money from the Libyan deals ran out, I blew it. Crumbs left, fun while it lasted. I bought a small flat in Paddington, pretty much all I've got left." Charlie rubbed his neck and fidgeted in his chair. "And you? Promotion?"

"The opposite. Posted to the rear end of the globe. For services rendered too well. Station Chief in Khartoum. Dead end." Haydon's face was deadpan. "I'm in exile. You know how that feels."

"It feels splendid." Charlie frowned. "I think. They forget all about you and leave you alone. You get on with your own thing."

"I've an assignment in mind for you. An important one." Haydon paused, then stared directly into Charlie's eyes. "I need someone I know well, that I can trust, who speaks Arabic and understands the Arab mentality."

"In Khartoum?"

"Yes, but not diplomatic. You'd be going into the hotel business."

"The hotel business in Khartoum?" Charlie laughed, his shoulders shaking, spilling beer onto his trousers. He brushed it off with his hand. "You are joking? There's no tourism, nothing happens and it's dry. A dead-end you just said, and unprofitable. A punishment posting. Why would I want that?"

"Haven't you been paying attention?" Haydon drained his glass and banged it on the table. "Communism's dead. Soon no more USSR. New era, ergo we need to come up with a new enemy. And quickly. Otherwise the Treasury will be after us, chopping our budgets. My boss doesn't like that."

"But Sudan?"

"We Arabists believe it will be the next serious menace. The Popular Arab and Islamic Congress held in Khartoum recently was an A to Z of radical Islam. Cooked up by the ideologue of the National Islamic Front - Hassan el Turabi - to confront the common enemy – by which he means the West." Haydon frowned. "His big idea is to unite the diverse Arab and Muslim grievances under a single banner, from Philippines to Palestine and from Nigeria to Syria and everywhere in between."

"Pretty enormous banner. Don't they mainly hate each

other?"

"Yes, up to now they've done a brilliant job of squabbling. But do you see the danger if he were to succeed?"

"Not really. And my knowledge of the hotel business is less than zero."

"Luckily for you it's a small hotel. Fourteen rooms. The Forum. We've owned it for a few years. Budget accommodation. The clientele is mainly NGO workers and journalists – straggly beards, dirty feet and no bras, and the odd deluded backpacker. We pick up stuff from around the remotest parts of the country, listening in at the bar. You're about to inherit it from your favourite Italian aunt. She's coming home to die." Haydon drummed his fingers on the table. "Your recent travel fits the legend, you like offbeat places. And, most importantly, nobody, anywhere, to connect you to SIS or the FCO. You'll need to brush up your Arabic, I'll arrange that, and get you trained in the rudiments of hotel management."

"I don't have an Italian aunt."

"You will by the time the legend people have finished with you."

"I need time off after graduating Oxley. I'm planning to go fishing. Iceland, taking my girlfriend up there for a week or so."

"You're not going back to Oxley."

"Sorry?" Haydon saw Charlie's face flush pink. "There's four weeks of the course remaining."

"I've pulled you. You've graduated. It's on your personnel file already. No ceremony, no prizes. Congratulations." Haydon reached forward and clapped him on the back. "That's the only plaudit you're going to get. We're putting it around you didn't make the cut. You've been thrown off the course. In fact, just what you deserve. You've been a bad boy."

"What stories has the Major been telling you. All nonsense."

"Nonsense is spelled S-T-E-F. That's the reason you're out of Oxley. The rules were spelled out to all of you. You broke them, blatantly. Not that I blame you, she's a doll. But you should have worked out she's our doll. You thrive on being insubordinate, it's a thing I like about you."

"You can't prove—"

"—actually, I can. Didn't you work out this place is wired to the teeth? Better learn the lesson before you're unleashed into the big, bad, world." Haydon spoke gently. "We need to know exactly who we're sending off to sensitive posts overseas."

"Jesus Haydon! You're a shit."

"Indeed. But I'm your shit. And you're going to be joining the illegals in Section X. The fighter command of the Service." He smiled. "Someone will collect your stuff and deliver it to your flat."

"Christ Haydon, you could have bloody waited for me to say yes." Charlie leant back and closed his eyes. "Libya was enough to put me off deserts for life. I joined the Service looking forward to prancing around the boudoirs of Moscow and Paris, being honey-trapped by gorgeous KGB agents, two at a time, not to rot in a forgotten corner of dusty nowhereland."

"Your choice is easy: work in Khartoum for me, or back on the streets in disgrace." He waved the waiter over and gestured for two more beers. "You should be overjoyed, no more classrooms, straight in at the deep end on an important covert op. Which is why you won't be going within a mile of The Office."

Haydon looked over at him and felt a stab of guilt. He was doing it again. Shoving a virgin into harm's way. The guy doesn't have a clue how to say no. Wind the bugger up and give him a shove, and off he'll go. *Caveat emptor*, he thought. Charlie needs to grow up for his own safety. The time he spent in that prison in Tripoli should have wised him up.

No, he's perfect for the job, Haydon thought. He's got the balls and he'll play the part of the innocent as if he were born to it. No time to get sentimental. He was too old for that.

Chapter 11

Haydon rang Monkton at the Embassy and fixed to meet him early that evening at the Fumoir bar at Claridges. Strangely, he felt no nerves or guilt about his affair with Lena. It was just like dealing with any joe, and with a joe you dealt in fables, constructs of the truth that fitted with whatever result you were seeking to achieve.

The small room was smoky and crowded. Soft jazz was playing in the background.

Monkton was sitting at a corner table, puffing on a long Partegas cigar and drinking neat Bourbon on the rocks. He waved Haydon over. Haydon noticed two tall girls in tight leather skirts sitting at the bar, sipping champagne. Impossibly long eyelashes flickered in his direction. Russians. He turned away and leaned in towards Monkton.

"Those are our new allies, Pete. Imagine. Making googly eyes at us! After all those years we chased them around, and they chased us. They were our worst enemy." He nodded towards the girls. "Now we're in some strange love affair. Mrs Thatcher and Gorbachev are best buddies. Do you reckon we're permitted to be honey-trapped in this new era of collaboration. Shall we give it a try?"

"Better get your boss's OK first, they look too expensive for you Brits." Monkton swigged his drink. "And I only just got done fighting their Russki asses for real, whilst Reagan was serving Gorbachev with Pepsi Cola in the Oval Office."

"Now we're expected to share intel with them. Things move fast when you're out in the sticks." He reached over and pointed at Monkton's tie. "Lords Pete? Are you the lone Agency cricket lover? I didn't know, or we could have gone, maybe taken some of your *muj* chums. Those Afghan *Muj* play cricket you know, they all look like W G Grace in a foul mood."

"Your ignorance is shameful Haydon, seeing as how much you Brits love tie-sniffing." Monkton smiled and lifted his tie for inspection. "See the little foxes heads, more exclusive than Lords. Myopia Hunt Club, North Shore. Old school."

"I heard you were best on camel back." Haydon grimaced. "Hunt foxes on dromedaries on the North Shore?"

"No, we use M-16's and hand grenades, yeah." He laughed, a deep belly laugh. "Patton lived right there in Wenham. He showed us the gentleman's way to hunt."

"Glasson instructed me to come and pay homage to you."

"Lookit Haydon. Your well-groomed leader tells me you've got yourself all ramped up about Turabi's Congress. It was just a gabbling raghead's orange-juice fueled love-in. The Ay-rab version of Woodstock. And we were there."

Typical, he thought, Glasson had got straight on to Monkton to make sure the party line got through. Haydon looked over at the older man, the bright yellow and orange tie matching the rugged, sun-bronzed face. He looked like a Boston Brahmin of the old school. Which was what he was. Well into his 50s, but he still exuded military fitness.

"I'm becoming concerned that Sudan may be about to become a haven for a new form of Islamic terror. The military junta is providing a fig leaf behind which a radical Islamic regime is taking shape. Hassan el Turabi is pulling the strings, behind his kindly uncle's face." Haydon sipped his bourbon. "The Congress had every *badmash* from Timbuktu to Mindanao in a single hall in Omdurman. Pity the roof didn't fall in, save us a mountain of trouble."

"Three days of long, self-indulgent speeches about eternal brotherhood and common cause. Boring each other to tears. Poor dumb sonsofbitches." Monkton's face turned serious. He sucked on his cigar and blew a column of smoke upwards. "The Congress was the perfect opportunity to have the whole goddamn lot of them on display, an intelligence treasure trove. My boys studied the fleas in their beards, their nose hair, their interactions, even their goddam faeces. Tech services had a wild jamboree."

"Who is on your worry list?"

"The guy that disquiets me is Imad Mughniyeh; he's a special case. Hezbollah security chief. We strongly believe he was behind Buckley's kidnapping and murder. And many others. We got his DNA off of a coffee cup outside the conference hall. Mossad practically creamed themselves. Got him right in their crosshairs, so, you better believe me, he won't be long for this world."

"OK, but what were the rest of them plotting." Haydon leaned forward and waved away cigar smoke. "When you weren't looking?"

"You don't understand these people Haydon. Why do you think they call us The Far Enemy? Because their real enemies are closer to home." He raised his glass in mock salute. "They spend their energies cussing each other and plotting to do each other down. And I can buy any of them easier than a discounted Walmart Hershey bar. That's what you need to get your head around."

"Maybe a new generation is emerging, Pete? One that follows a puritanical banner, can't be swayed by the mighty Dollar."

"Haydon, I know most of them, yeah. I've broken bread with them on dark nights in freezing mountain caves. Practically every one of them has taken my greenback, or several." Monkton smiled and punched Haydon's shoulder. "They gotta big themselves up for their domestic audiences, each one wants to sound braver and nastier than the other. Then they come to talk to me. About their real enemies, ask for my help to fix them. Puritans need money to pursue their causes just like other folk do, yeah."

His commitment wasn't to any doctrine, Haydon thought, but to a way of life founded in a belief in heroic adventure for its own sake. Waving brightly coloured stars and stripes was part of this tradition, but it wasn't his motivating factor. He glanced over at the bar. The two Russian girls had gone. The place was filling up. Mostly businessmen, Eurotrash, Arabs, Chinese. No Brits, they couldn't afford the place. Cigar smoke curled around the ceiling. An elderly man in a white dinner jacket sat down at the piano and started to play. Haydon leaned in to Monkton.

"It's just that I get whispers these guys want to bring the fight to Western capitals." He frowned. "Getting us to feel the same pain as them."

"That's camouflage. Lookit. Old man Bush. Died-in-the-wool New Englander wearing a ten-gallon hat. He's a goddam Yaley, just like me, not a trace of cowboy anywhere in his makeup, but he gotta play to the folks out West. Texans and Okies. Same goes for ragheads." He paused while the waiter served their drinks. They clinked glasses. "Turabi's doing us a favour, you better believe me, Khartoum is now the Vienna of the Islamic world, a perfect intel source on the lotta them. Neatly gathered in one place, like in a goddam goldfish bowl. They come to me quietly in the evenings, when no-one can see them, hands open for dough. That's why I'm there, burning my butt in this shitty posting. Like I'm some kinda kindly nanny to my ole buddies."

"Lucky you. I'm there as a punishment." Haydon rolled his head around and started massaging his neck. "So you believe the military are in charge, not the bearded ones?"

"I took you duck shooting with Abbas. He's my good buddy, you've seen it. The President's a straight shooter. Likes a drink too, when no one's looking. And while the fundamentalist bearded eggheads jabber, he gets things done. You gotta get to know him better, yeah. That will cool down your unseemly fervour."

"I'd like that." He knocked with his knuckles on the table. "My instinct is to be proactive, take some of those hardline guys out of the picture, frighten them before they pull any pins out."

"Bad idea. My advice to you, is – be wise, listen to your elders." He gave Haydon a steely look. "That's me. Not the time to go rocking boats, they have a way of capsizing. People on board you don't know about, maybe above your paygrade."

"But isn't that what we're there for? To sink bloody boats. Shut things down before they start?"

"Then we'd just have to figure out who's replaced the guys we just sank and start all over again?" He leaned forward and whacked Haydon on the arm. "Like I said we got a handle on this."

"Maybe you're right, Pete." Haydon narrowed his eyes and sipped his drink. "Perhaps I've spent too much time working amongst the Paddies."

"Don't look so glum about it Haydon, you're a gloomy critter. Be good to yourself, yeah. Lighten up! Lemme get you another bourbon, you probably can't afford one here, let alone three."

"Damn right. That's why I'm your good friend."

"And I thought it was my wife you liked." He puffed deeply on his cigar and leaned back contentedly. "When are you back to the camel market?"

"Weekend. BA. The prospect of returning to that godforsaken place is enough to make anyone gloomy."

The Sheikh

Chapter 12

Haydon had arranged to meet Johnny Doyle for supper at Romano Santi, a cheap and lively Italian restaurant in the heart of Soho, noisy enough to talk openly, without any risk of being overheard. Johnny was the one friend he could talk to about work, and he needed a neutral sounding board to blow off steam.

Leaving Claridge's, he set off up Brook Street at a brisk pace. At Regent Street he dashed precariously across the flow of traffic, pausing on the pavement, then turning to stare into the reflection in the window of a dress shop. He smiled to himself. No need for caution, not on the quiet streets of Mayfair. Tradecraft had been such an integral part of his life; it was good to feel the instinct was intact. He peered at his reflection: grey hair, a furrowed brow and a clenched jaw. A vaguely familiar middle-aged face. Behind his image, he saw the last pink rays of sunset fanning upward towards a darkening sky. He turned and walked on.

Mulling over Monkton's words, Haydon couldn't let go of his sense of foreboding. His instinct told him that Khartoum was becoming a crucible for a new generation of terrorist cells. Was this wishful thinking? For him to be centre stage in a new Vienna, a happier image than that of a sad outcast in a last post in an irrelevant backwater. Maybe his ego was beavering overtime and Glasson was right. The all-seeing Agency had everything pinned down.

He had a couple more days in London before he was due to fly back to Khartoum, and he needed the time to finalise details of Charlie's legend and training. He'd become possessive, thinking of Charlie as 'his' project, and was apprehensive about the vetting process. Charlie might well have done something so ghastly as to remove him from contention, which would kibosh his installation as hotel manager of the Forum. Those years in Colombia had suspiciously inexplicable voids.

Crossing Wardour Street, he found himself in bustling Soho. He turned off into a narrow alley, eerily silent. His footsteps clacked a rhythm on the pavement, and he felt a warm summer breeze toying with his hair. Neon lights flickered into life, and, as he emerged into Greek Street, he heard a growing hum of laughter and music. He felt empty. He needed a drink, and reassuring words from a trusted friend.

"Last time we met you were moaning on about being posted to a dead-end city, where you'd be marooned in a desert." Johnny Doyle tapped his temple with his forefinger. "Now you're telling me you're at the epicentre of a new hub of radical Arab terror. Nuts! If I wasn't your buddy, I'd recommend a shrink. I prescribed you sailing and divorcées, but you foolishly chose the monk's life in Khartoum and now you're suffering."

The restaurant was packed. They were seated at a banquette by the window, looking out onto the crowded street. Haydon sniffed the pungent smell of garlic. A waiter uncorked a bottle of Chianti and poured.

"Don't get me started." Haydon buried his hands in his hair. "The monk's life hasn't worked out well either. Another bad story."

"Miserable sinner. Tell me?"

"Forget it. Look, I'm getting the feeling we're facing the greatest danger since the dark days of the Provos. Brewing up right there in Sudan." He rubbed his forehead. "I read the signs, they're obvious. Another Warrenpoint is coming, this time worse. With *Muj* pressing the bang buttons. But I can't convince Mark to take it seriously."

"Have you considered he might know better than you? He is, after all, C."

"This is Bill Casey's posthumous legacy, Johnny. As CIA Director he ordered his guys to work closely with the radical Islamic militias in the Afghan war against the Russkies." He tapped his finger on the table. "No deals to be done with the secular *Muj* groups – Ahmed Shah Masood or the Durrani Pushtuns, the old royal line. We, and the French, tried hard to change American minds, but Casey was adamant. They were out in the cold."

"Why?"

"Why? Casey was a lifelong Catholic, a daily churchgoer, like 'Wild Bill' Donovan before him. He believed he could 'do business' with fellow, like-minded, believers in a God.

Any God. He saw the Afghan God-botherers as perfect counterparts, with their supposedly pure religious motives. Men like Hekmatyar and Rabbani. Clever, treacherous, brutal and radical.

Casey showered them with Stingers and dollars, sent his guys in to fight alongside them, then the Agency convinced themselves they owned those *Muj* maniacs."

"What have Hekmatyar and Rabbani to do with Sudan?" Johnny took out a packet of Rothmans and lit one, inhaling deeply and exhaling a satisfied sigh. "Far away from their mountain caves and tents."

"The regime in Sudan. I believe the military guys are puppets. Nice friendly faces. But controlled from behind curtains by the Islamic Front, led by Hassan el-Turabi. He's a law professor, bright, talkative and dangerous. No official position. His big idea is to unite all the different Muslim and Arab groups against a single, common enemy. The West." Haydon took out a handkerchief and rubbed his forehead. "He's been organising these so-called congresses. Several Palestinian groups, Iranians, Iraqis, Filipinos, Somalis, Kurds, Algerians and Egyptians, and yes, the 'Afghan-Arabs', Hekmatyar and Rabbani, and others. A full pack of militant cards."

"Aladdin in wonderland?" Johnny coughed, then sipped his wine. "Haydon, look we've seen all that jabbering before. Look at the Palestinians, every time they try a new tack they get royally smashed by the Israelis." He squashed his cigarette under a highly polished shoe. "It goes nowhere. What's different now?"

"True, in the past they've always been defeated. But the Afghan war gave them a taste of victory. They've had training and modern weaponry from the US, and from us, they defeated a well-armed Russian army. That's what's different." Haydon could read the scepticism on Johnny's face.

"At Five we had our concerns about fighters coming home from the Afghan war, radicalised, trained and ready to create mayhem. But none of our sources have picked up danger signals. The read from Grosvenor Square is they have the peril contained, and my office isn't flagging any hot threats. I think you're wrong."

"That's Mark's read too." Haydon shook his head. "My Agency counterpart insists he has a strong handle on it and warned me off. My gut tells me different."

"So, it's Haydon Talbot's sensitive stomach against the world. Again. Go for it tiger!" Johnny laughed, then started twirling spaghetti around his fork. "You're going to end up with a hell of a belly ache. You go up against Mark, you'll be gone. Better jump ship while he's still smiling. Get out with all possible goodies. Believe me he'll be generous, just to get rid of your sorry ass."

"I hope I'm wrong is all."

"Who's the Sheila?"

"The most taboo girl in town." Haydon leaned back and stretched his arms,

"Really that complicated?"

"You don't want to know. The perfect choice to wreck my career."

"My, you do like complications. We'd better order another bottle quickly."

After Johnny had left, Haydon ordered an Irish coffee and lit a cigarette. He realised he was pissed. Maybe he could think straighter when he was drunk? Maybe not. Johnny's advice made good sense, but he wouldn't take it. He was so sure he was right, and everyone else was wrong. This was a reliable warning signal. *Why couldn't he let it go?*

Of all the crazy things we've done, he thought, the craziest was training the Afghan *mujahadeen* in bomb-making skills. Under our instruction, the *Muj* perfected the art of building car and truck bombs. The same techniques worked for planes, roadside bombs and any other type of device that went bang. How long before they turned them back on the West?

Early days, he thought. Take it easy, smile nicely, and go slow. *Don't make waves.* He'd found no trace of a smoking gun, but the bloody thing was out there somewhere. He'd launch Charlie into the hotel op, haul in on all the nets and filter the intel. It would come to him. Meanwhile, he'd make nice with Mark and Pete and toe the party line.

The Sheikh

Chapter 13

Khartoum, August 1990

Haydon inched the heavy curtain aside and peered down from his first-floor bedroom window. The sharp colour of the villa's over-watered lawn contrasted with the brown, dusty street beyond, fringed by voluminous mango trees, which provided respite from the dry summer heat. He pitied colleagues who lived in stark concrete streets without a hint of vegetation to provide shelter from the brutal sun.

His eyes rested on a group of white-clad men squatting on the curbside, then he slowly panned down the line of vehicles parked in each shaded patch until he made out the shapes of two figures sitting motionless in an old white Datsun. Poor sods, they must be boiling. Serves them right. As he watched, one of them got out of the car and lit a cigarette. A skinny. They were all skinny.

Maybe it was the pay.

It brought back memories of Moscow in the bad old days; his first assignment, at the height of the cold war. He'd enjoyed it as one enjoys a schoolyard game. He got a buzz playing hide and seek with those KGB clods. There was never a letup. You had to be on your guard wherever you were. 24/7. You took it for granted your flat was bugged, probably even your bedroom. You had to get used to that. Sometimes he'd felt like some kind of porn actor. Most dips were even convinced the Embassy was wired up in some magical way. The Sovs were masters of the art. They'd even come across bugs in embassy cars. You treated them like loudspeakers, broadcasting misinformation and insults to the unknown listeners.

It was out on the streets that it kicked off for real. Dreaming up new stratagems to fool the watchers when you needed to make a covert meet, where the price of failure was some other sod's miserable death. Dips weren't likely to get whacked or tortured. They reserved that for the illegals. Moscow rules. Whilst he hid behind diplomatic status to cover his butt. Assistant Cultural Attaché. He liked that. He must read a poetry book sometime.

In Khartoum, you couldn't be so sure your diplomatic status would keep you safe.

Probably the skinnies were *Mukhabarat*, state security. But they might be PLO or Hezbollah, or even freelancers for hire. And there were other shadowy militias, somehow controlled by the Islamists, who seemed to be part government, part not. No one knew. They operated from so-called 'ghost houses', outside of any known jurisdiction. Famous for torture and 'disappearances'. He felt a frisson running up his spine.

Taking a pair of binoculars off the table, he focused in on the Datsun's registration plate and scribbled the number into a notebook. Flipping back a few pages, he checked earlier entries. This was a regular. No danger.

Nowadays he had Lomax to consider. SEAMLESS was back up and running, Lomax playing the role of offbeat hotelier. He had settled in and was doing a fine job of infiltrating the NGO community; smoking dope with the beardies, getting too close to girls from VSO and the Red Cross.

It made him feel old, envious even. Charlie allowed off the leash, licensed, even encouraged, to break the rules. But the guy was exposed, so Haydon needed to keep a discreet watch, and all their meetings involved careful tradecraft.

He went downstairs and poured himself a Scotch. He carried it out into the garden and sat in the shade nursing the glass, mesmerised as he watched the large ice cubes melting fast. He couldn't discern whether he was, for the first time in his life, 'in love'. What did it even mean? He knew he was out of control, obsessed. Was he suffering some guilty, masochistic mania, expiating for a life of dishonesty by balancing unsteadily on an unruly tightrope? Lena made him feel so vital. Which should herald a revival of his jaded soul. More likely it would bring his life to a shameful halt. Fucking the wife of a colleague, one who held his career in his Texan-sized hands, it was an act of wanton self-destruction.

His mind went back to those horrid sessions of coercive interrogation training at Oxley, all those years ago, striving consciously to derive masochistic pleasure from pain. Willing the agony on, hurrying towards it, towards the outer edge of the pain-barrier. It felt a little like that now, an ironclad and childish stubbornness, as if a vortex were sucking him in and threatening to consume him. He took a long swig of his whisky.

They had kept up the pretence for over a year now, much too long for safety. Playing parts from an old movie. Asking no questions, living for the rare times they could be together, reliving the moments in their heads during the many, blurry times apart. Their passion and mutual need was stronger than anything he'd ever experienced. They arranged their meets like sleeper agents, leaving phony messages in the pigeonholes at the Sudan Club. Bogus names on the envelopes. He signed his notes Paul, she Jeanne. *Fake anonymity that kept the deceit at arm's length*. He knew he was in a precarious trance, but didn't want to be released, and wondered if he might be experiencing a breakdown.

When they crossed paths on the diplomatic roundabout, Haydon found it easy to shift into friendly bonhomie. Peter Monkton and Lena. A close dip couple in a world of dip couples. A kiss and a slap on the back, avoiding looking her in the eye. Logic screeched he must bring it to a halt, a one-night stand that had run on for far too many nights. Still, he hurried off to every next encounter, heart thumping, watching his back, even though he knew he was walking too fast to run a proper routine. *Sucker.*

He'd been living in this malaise since he'd arrived in Khartoum, he had a sense of marking time, of playing an inescapably losing hand. It wasn't just loneliness – the end of his marriage to Ros hadn't been antagonistic or even traumatic. They'd faded apart, with rueful inevitability. He hadn't even told Glasson. Maybe she'd change her mind and come and join him one day, although he doubted it. If she did, would he be able to give up Lena?

They met in the afternoons at a Station safe house in the district of Khartoum 2, to which he alone had keys. Breaking all the rules, and relishing doing so. He felt a frisson of danger as he padded through the dusty streets, arms tingling as he fumbled with the lock to the metal gate in his urgency, leaving it slightly ajar behind him. They used the back entrance, accessed through a rubbish-strewn alley, behind an industrial site, which led to the flat through a desolate courtyard decorated with half-dead plants and a patch of brown, dead, grass.

He got there early and poured himself a drink, then darted around tidying up the small flat, brushing sand off the bed-sheets, turning on the fan, looking at his watch, drumming his fingers on the coffee table, smoking cigarettes, and sipping his whisky a little too fast. The flat was dusty and airless. A shabby place for shabby trysts, which added to the intensity of the forbidden pleasures. They met rarely, constrained in the narrow confines of the society in which they lived. He wondered how long he would continue to remain sane.

Finally, he heard the garden gate clicking shut. He stood up and walked towards the door. He could smell the gardenia before she came into view. She was wearing a simple light cotton dress, her hair flowing down over her shoulders and a thick red belt pulled in at the midriff. She smiled that angular smile. Not shy, just complicit. He started to say something, but she raised a finger in front of her mouth.

She walked on into the bedroom; he followed her in. He watched her take off her wedding ring and place it carefully on the heavy wooden dresser. She always did that. She turned towards him and pushed him down on the bed, reaching to touch his face. He closed his eyes. He realised he was trembling. She reached down and undid his belt.

Afterwards they lay spooning, the wetness of sweat and sex gluing them together, the sheet wrapped around them, the fan above them stirring the warm air and making mad panting noises. He smelled the freshness of her hair. His arms were around her, nestling her breasts, his fingers lightly feeling the hardened nipples.

"You're going to tell me something I don't want to hear. I felt it in you just now." Haydon murmured. "Remember, if you say your name you'll have to shoot me."

"I'm not Texan, *chéri.*" She pulled herself up and sat with her arms around her legs, staring at him. "For a closed-clam Englishman you're unusually prescient."

"Isn't that what's special?" He loved her French patois. Which became exaggerated when she was excited. He pulled himself up and kissed her. "Communicating with noisy silences?"

She turned her head away from him. He wondered if she was crying.

"*I invited that depressive limey over on Friday. Gotta*

make nice and talk shop, sorry. He's causing bumps in the road and I gotta keep the guy calm." She mimicked his Boston twang, which came out sounding Quebecois.

"Odd, we always meet for lunch at the Club and talk work."

"Better to know in advance, time for our eyes to adjust to the light." She leaned down and kissed him lightly on the forehead. "I'll do my best not to be there, *chéri.*"

"How do we go on? When–"

"Lock our dreams away in a pretty box. Hide the key." She turned back to him and reached for his hand, placing it on her breast. "But let's stay a bit in our dream, just a while longer."

It felt to him as if, by acting the roles of fantasy people, the schizophrenic relationship somehow pardoned their disloyalty. He wondered how much damage this dishonesty was wreaking deep in his psyche.

"Paul and Jeanne don't exist."

"They never did." She pulled him closer and nibbled at his ear. "My worry is I've started falling for the real you. Which is not part of the plan."

"There never was a plan." Haydon kissed her breast. "We just let fate take control."

Chapter 14

The bookcase in The Manager's office at The Forum Hotel concealed the entrance to a small recording-room. It swung open silently on heavy, well-oiled hinges. Initially, Charlie Lomax had taken childish delight in the covert set-up, but long hours sitting at the cramped metal desk in the poky room had dampened his enthusiasm. He took a gulp of water from a plastic bottle. It was warm. The air cooler emitted a clanking noise that heralded a welcome puff of dusty air.

Charlie rubbed his neck. He felt dirty. A pile of notebooks lay on the desk, each one marked with handwritten dates and times. A thin film of red sand covered the open pad, splodging the page as he wrote. In front of him, banks of *Nagra* tape recorders were stacked on shelves, each identified in black marker pen on a large sticker. Every now and then, one of the voice-activated microphones would set a reel spinning. He turned the volume control up and held the earphones tighter over his ears, feeling sweat running down his back.

This must be what it was like for a Franciscan monk, hearing daily confessions from ancient spinsters in a provincial cathedral. Prattling inanities and useless gossip. *Jeez, this is boring*. At least there was the occasional diversion into sex talk and animal grunting, although that felt like a horrid intrusion. He had not signed up to SIS to sit for hours in a small airless box, eavesdropping on the bedroom conversations of well-intentioned hippies. And nothing remotely sinister so far in any of those notebooks. He had to find a way out of this tedium.

He pressed the playback switch under a label marked 'Room 8'.

"Strewth the way that stuck-up Pommie bastard looks at my tits gives me the creeps. He's a perve."

"Me too, I don't trust the guy, there's something not right about him."

This was the worst bit. Playing back, masochistically, insulting references to himself, which were annoyingly frequent. The words grated as he watched the reel turn slowly around. He felt his face flushing. He tried his best to be personable with his guests, but it seemed his charm wasn't universally appreciated.

He had thought the Ozzie girl liked him. Maybe she did? He certainly fancied her. It was true the no-bra combo with tight tee-shirts turned his eyes into saucepans. Surely that made him a healthy male, not a perve? The noise of running water drowned out her reply. So far, in the three months since he'd arrived to take over his 'aunt's' hotel, this monitoring malarkey had not produced a whiff of what he thought of as promising intel. Maybe the analysts in Century House found something useful in the multiple reels he handed over to Haydon every week.

He looked at a fuzzy black and white video screen at the scene in the restaurant area, he watched a tall girl from a Canadian NGO sitting with Heinrich Ziegler, an agronomist from Hamburg who specialised in apiculture. He'd cornered Charlie at a cocktail party at the German Club and told him more about rural beekeeping than he wanted to know. He pressed a switch marked 'Table 3' and adjusted the sound. This would be dull.

"You been in the bush, *schatzie*? Haven't seen you in a while."

"I've been at the camp in Kassala, running a food audit. Got to town today." She ran her fingers through her long, black hair. "I need rest. And I need pampering, I feel like a scarecrow. The famine there is going critical. Rains failed.

Again. A catastrophe on its way. I'm shouting about it but nobody at home listens. Just another bloody famine in Africa, they say. Same, same, so what. You?"

"Doing a contract for this rich Saudi guy. House out by the Nile in Soba. Pays my bills in cash. Four wives, poor schmuck, can you imagine? Four! Covered up like for Halloween. Flocks of children."

"Maybe I become number five, go for the simple life."

"No one seems to know about him. Breeds horses. I see him cantering along the river in the early mornings. Maybe he just wants a quiet life?"

"*Merde*, a person comes to Sudan for a quiet life? Get out of here!" She poked his arm. "What does he do with bees?"

"Owns a gigantic farm out beyond Damazine. Grows ground nuts and *sim-sim*, they say he's a big trader in gum arabic. Towards the Ethiopian border. I go there every month, check on his hives. Big production of honey. Hundreds of workers. Humans, not bees."

"Sounds like a good news story for a change." She reached over and touched his face. "Rare in this place."

"His bees are kosher, and he knows his stuff. But there are lots of dodgy looking Arabs wandering around, toting guns. Razor wire, that sort of *scheise*. Rumour is they're fighters back from the Afghan war." Ziegler leaned forward. "Still, long as he keeps paying me, I don't give a damn. I enjoy going down there, spend a night in the guest house. Civilised enough."

Charlie checked the machine was recording. This might interest Haydon.

"We don't want swarms of revolutionary terror bees buzzing around the place!" She giggled. "Khartoum is dangerous enough already for Westerners. All these mad, bearded folk the regime is welcoming, ever since President Daoud announced all Muslims have the right to settle in Sudan."

They both laughed. The German reached over and took her hand, stroking it gently.

Charlie took off his headphones and ran his hands through his hair. He made a note on the pad to flag it up. Dodgy Arabs with guns. This Saudi might be up to something.

Charlie leaned back and smoked a cigarette. Flattery. It had done for him again. *Pathetic*. He'd keeled over and let Haydon haul him in like a gasping fish. The prospect of being the first of his Oxley cohort to be posted overseas, pulled off the course mid-stream and into the supposedly elite ranks of Section X, the illegals. Too alluring. He'd felt like the *victor ludorum* of his course when Haydon announced he'd been selected for this special role. Now he felt like a loser, shipped out to nowheresville and forgotten about. *A self-important fool!* A year of this and he'd be brain dead. Got to get out of this claustrophobic box. He'd tell Haydon he couldn't do it. He'd have to bring in a specialist to do this listening stuff.

Charlie was after adventure and glamour. Neither of which were to be found at The Forum. It was not only dull but also demeaning. Thanks to Haydon's obsession with some new and invisible enemy. That no one else believed in. So far, he had glimpsed no serious threat to the security of the West, whilst Haydon didn't seem to mind being far away from the action. It was like the guy was determined to revel in his banishment. Some kind of closet masochist? Meanwhile he was destined to listen to banal conversations, ingratiate himself with long-haired sandal-monkeys, all in pursuit of unknown Islamic phantoms.

The NGO world formed an underclass of bright young people who normally didn't intersect with the governmental, diplomatic and commercial worlds that were a spy's natural fishpond. Aid workers came to Khartoum for R & R, for contact with their head offices or embassies. Most of them lodged at the reasonably priced and clean Forum, bringing tales of happenings far from the capital – in Darfur and the Nuba Mountains, the Red Sea Hills, the Ethiopian borderlands and anywhere else in between where trouble might be brewing.

It reminded him of his life in Cartagena. Friendly anonymity in an alien colony, where he had no prior connections. He'd made friends in this offbeat community. Running a small hotel for hippies, supplementing his salary with a little dealing, spending his leisure hours peacefully stoned, not what he'd intended, but some kind of palliative for his growing disenchantment. His wheels were being oiled by access to decent quality dope that his friend Tom Ormond brought down from the north on his regular trips. And for those he really trusted, he had, carefully concealed in the recording room, a cache of embassy supplied, illicit, Scotch.

The worst thing about being an illegal was being cut off from the Embassy. He had no backup, no support, no colleague to share his worries with, no entrée into whatever society there was in Khartoum. His socialising was limited to his NGO clients, and the biweekly covert meetings with Haydon. These took place, after lengthy tradecraft protocols, in a seedy safe house that smelt of stale cigarette smoke and illicit sex. He was pretty sure that Haydon was responsible for both.

About the only buzz this job provided was running the dry-cleaning routines before those meetings, to ensure his back was clear of ghosts. So far, he hadn't flushed out a flea on his back. But he made a point of staying alert and on edge. In Libya, he'd learned his lesson about the price of overconfidence. He would not let it happen a second time.

Stubbing out his cigarette, he decided to tell Haydon at their next meeting he couldn't hack the listening lark anymore.

Chapter 15

"They look insufferably lazy. Like me." Tom sucked on the joint and inhaled deeply. "But I read somewhere that, unlike me, they can reach 30 mph in the water. At that speed you could water-ski behind one."

Their eyes followed as an enormous crocodile slid off a sandbar into the river, causing a ripple as it sank below the surface. The two men were enjoying their favourite leisure activity. Sitting on a sandy riverbank at a bend on the Blue Nile, feet dangling in the cool water, smoking quality grass and listening to Leon Russell croaking out '*Watching the River Flow*' on a cheap cassette player. It was Friday, and parties of week-enders occasionally putted past on small speedboats, some stopping to picnic on one of the many sandbanks that fringed the fast-flowing river.

"One of your dodgy facts, for sure, but it'll be you doing the water-skiing. That one's fifteen feet long, at least." Charlie took the spliff and puffed on it. "Take your hairy leg off in one bite, complete with the ski."

"I suspect he'd prefer yours. They're more white and fleshy. Like an ugly termite."

Charlie reached into his backpack for a large thermos marked 'Tea' and poured amber coloured liquid into two plastic beakers. He handed one to Tom. They each took a swig. Charlie took another pull on the spliff and coughed, wiping his mouth with the back of his hand.

"Explain something."

"Ask the oracle."

"Why does illegal booze taste better?" He pointed at the thermos. "This is ordinary Johnny Walker Red, but here, on the river, it tastes smoother than Black label. Surely everything should be made forbidden, *harram*, and life would be much improved."

"That's precisely why you're my friend, Charlie. You're not bright enough to understand life's deep mysteries, you buy my dope at a good price, and I drink freely of your forbidden booze. What's not to like?"

Tom had been one of the first people he'd met when he'd taken over at the hotel. Wild-haired and irresponsible looking, he worked as a VSO, teaching English at a school in the Red Sea Hills near the remote colonial summer retreat of Erkowit. On his visits to Khartoum, he stayed at the Forum, and the two had become friends.

"You may be seeing more of me." Tom picked up a small rock and threw it towards a white ripple on the slick water. A croc's tail emerged from the river and whipped around, the beast swimming away from them into deeper water. "I've had visits from aggressive security people from Port Sudan. They threatened to expel me. Bloody rude. I told them I'd be grateful."

"What crime did you commit?" Charlie laughed and waved his glass about. "Have you been pissing on the flagpole again?"

"They don't seem to like *hawajas* living near to this new compound they're building. Not far from the school, out in the sticks, lots of machinery, noise and shooting even. The rumour amongst the locals is it's Palestinians guerrillas, some new group calling itself Hamas."

"Why didn't they arrest you?"

"They came back a few days later and asked the same questions. I played dumb."

"Why do you think they were Palestinians?"

"I've met a few of them. Wild-looking bunch, friendly enough, they all carry AK47s; some of them smoke my dope.

But strangely, a few wear crucifixes."

"Many of those Palestinian hardliners are Christian."

"Doesn't explain why they're setting up there in the boondocks. Some kind of training camp as far as I can make out."

Charlie wondered if he could press his friend for more information. Better not. A small piece of jigsaw? Arab fighters with AK47s sprouting in far corners of the country, like dangerous mushrooms. He took a drag at the spliff and leaned back.

"Appeasement is feeding the crocodile, hoping he will eat you last." Charlie said. "Who said that?"

"Churchill said it, but it makes little sense. The bloody thing would bite your hand off before you got started with the feeding. Let's go home."

Haydon made himself a Turkish coffee and sat on the ledge by the grubby window in the living room. The shadows were lengthening in the wasteland below, and the dusk sky was orange and gloomy. He lit a cigarette and inhaled deeply. Why did sunsets in Khartoum make him feel so empty? He checked his watch. Charlie was late. He'd settled in well, Haydon was impressed by how fast he'd pumped SEAMLESS back to life. The hotel had gone downhill after Afra had got sick, but Charlie was schmoozing his way quickly into the NGO world. It hadn't produced any jewels, but it was early days.

It wasn't clever to use the safe house for two covert purposes. It doubled the risk of one blowing it for the other. Was he becoming jittery? He'd sensed the edge of a shadow on the hairs on his neck when he'd left the house that morning. He would task a team to run a cleaning routine around him, flush out any fleas on his back. Just in case.

He'd bumped into Salah el-Fateh a few days before. They'd both been lunching at the Engineer's Club. Since the coup, the security man had grown a neatly trimmed beard, as Yahya had predicted, which gave him an even more sinister look. He greeted Haydon warmly, but something in those strange, disconnected eyes rang warning bells. He'd set out to cultivate a working relationship with the man, but it was hard-going. Those eyes seemed to penetrate through him. He needed to up his protective shield of charm.

He shook himself back to the present, stubbed out his unfinished cigarette and started to tidy up, looking carefully for anything out of place. As he was washing up glasses on the sink, he heard the rattle of the gate and, looking out, saw Charlie strolling across the courtyard. His hair was longer now and he'd grown a straggly beard. Wearing a loud paisley shirt and bell-bottom jeans, he had a louche appearance. Perhaps this disguise was finally exposing the real man beneath?

"You're late. Skinnies at your back?" They shook hands. "Drink?"

"You got whisky?" Charlie shook his head. "I'm clean, I ran a wide routine. Took my time. As you instructed."

"Better safe. Be as late as you like. Keep it that way."

Charlie nodded. Haydon poured a long drink, added a chunk of ice and handed it to him. "Cheers. You're looking more and more the part. Mind you, you won't be getting invitations to Embassy functions, they don't like unwashed hippie types."

"I'm feeling more and more the part. I'm getting to enjoy being a hotelier. But I can't do this listening business Haydon, you've got to help me out there." He reached over and handed a plastic bag to Haydon. "Five reels. Nothing much."

"Tell me." Haydon looked into the plastic bag.

"Listen to tape four before you send it off." Charlie pointed with his finger. "Stuff about some Saudi guy. I've marked it on the log. Let me know if it's of interest."

Haydon raised his eyebrows.

"Maybe one of those guys back from Afghanistan. Farms at Soba and Damazine. Armed guards at the farm, sounds like they're fighters."

"OK, I'll check him out." Haydon raked his fingers through his hair,

"You don't sound interested."

"I'll look into it. Keep doing what you're doing." He put the plastic bag down on the table. "Anything else?"

"Maybe. My VSO buddy from Erkowit. Tom."

"VSO?"

"Voluntary Service Overseas. Our answer to the Peace Corps. He's my sort of beardie. Told me there's a camp under construction, a little way outside the town. He's had visits from the Port Sudan security nasties, freaked him out. A give-away there's something brewing." He leaned forward. "Palestinians. He thinks it's some group called Hamas. Training camp maybe."

"Hamas? He's sure?"

"That's what local people are saying. No other detail."

"See if you can get more. They're a new group out of Gaza, we don't like the look of them." Haydon interlocked his hands and cracked his fingers. "If it'll help, I'll authorise expenses."

"He went back yesterday. I'll let you know when he's due back in town."

"Good. You look worried. What's bugging you?"

"Listening to those *Nagra* machines is the dullest thing I've ever done." Charlie yawned and put his hand over his mouth. "I hate it. Can't you bring in a guy to manage the tapes and leave me to do the schmoozing, the active stuff, and recruitment?"

"Charlie, I hear you. But Afra managed it all, so I'd need to show London some golden product first to get them excited." Haydon rubbed his hands together. "When you've proved your worth, I'll push for additional resources. You have my word."

"But—"

"Look, the intel will come to you. Bit by bit." Haydon leaned back. "When it does, you'll become active. All of a sudden you won't be bored. Your first recruitment. That will be challenging, but it'll give you a boost."

And that will be the moment, Haydon thought, when I find out if he has the mettle for it.

The moral challenges of recruitment were inevitably tortuous. In training, it was anonymous, a fun game. Theoretical. In reality, it involved doing things you'd rather not do to other people's lives. Putting them in harm's way. He took a long sip of his drink. Peering outside, he saw that night had fallen.

Chapter 16

Haydon drove slowly along the river, glancing up as he passed the whitewashed Republican Palace, where General Gordon had met his end, speared like a pincushion by spears thrown by dervishes loyal to the ancestor of the Prime Minister overthrown in the recent coup. He parked by the Sailing Club and smoked a cigarette, the windows of the Land Rover open, his eyes following a small, wooden felucca as it drifted past, fishtailing as it encountered little whirlpools, nets and fluorescent buoys bobbing along behind.

What he needed was to keep his close working relationship with Pete Monkton on an even keel. And keep his forbidden life locked away tightly in the pretty box. *Focus!* Tossing his unfinished cigarette out of the window, he started the Land Rover and drove slowly off. He'd clocked the skinnies in their old white Honda as he'd left his house and watched in his rear-view mirror as they pulled out and settled a few hundred yards behind him. They were welcome to join him.

Lena's admission that she was beginning to fall for the 'real' him had unsettled him.

He'd felt safe in their fantasy world of Paul and Jeanne. He wondered if he were ready to own up to the truth that he too might be falling in love with a real person. He had been too well-trained by specialists in the art of dissembling, drilled already from childhood at successive boarding schools to camouflage his emotions, to smile with confidence while storm showers of guilt and fear were gnawing at your guts.

Now perhaps it defined who the hidden him was. A bit-part actor. Trained to prepare meticulously for meetings with the most tricky or drunken or nervous joe, deep in hostile territory. Going over outcomes, evolutions, escape tactics, keeping focus on exactly what would get the joe to do what he didn't want to do. To cajole or seduce or threaten or lead, to get the desired result at all costs. *This is just another meeting with a joe.*

Crossing the river on the Blue Nile bridge he turned east, past Kobar prison and into the exclusive suburb of Kafoury, a line of grandiose villas with ample grounds staring majestically south onto the Blue Nile. Every garden filled with colour, sprinklers sparkling in the sun, white shapes bending down to tend to lush flowerbeds. Monkton's villa stood out with its peculiar crenelated tower, craning out above a long line of tall royal palms. An unlikely wave to Walt Disney from this arid city?

He'd hoped there'd be a crowd, his best option for camouflage. Getting through two hours of sitting alone with Monkton and Lena without betraying himself would be challenging. *She was someone else.* Not the person he held, naked, in his arms during those long afternoons. But as he drove in through the tall gates, Lena was driving out, the roof down on her red sports car. Dressed in tennis gear, she waved cheerily and blew a kiss as she raced on by. Monkton was waiting outside on the porch and led him out to a bar on the shaded veranda. Walls topped with barbed wire ran down to the water's edge, fringed by lush flowerbeds overflowing with colour. A sleek speedboat was moored on a wooden jetty.

"Gonna take you on a trip down the river. "

"Fishing?"

"Someone I want you to meet." Monkton started filling a cocktail shaker. "Mint Julep wake you up?"

"Not more duck shooting. Too late in the day."

"Better than that. We'll see to killing ducks with Abbas another time." Monkton rattled the shaker vigorously, then slowly poured the cocktail into freezing silver cups, handing one to Haydon. "Mint Julep cups. Traditional. Copies of the jockey's cups from the Kentucky Derby."

"Mmmm. Delicious." Haydon wiped icy froth off his upper lip with his hand. "Is this some devilish Yankee plan?"

"To improve your education, yeah. You're coming along strictly as an observer, you do what you're good at. Staying quiet. Drawing your own conclusions."

"My guess is we're meeting your mountain-hiking mate? This so-called Sheikh."

"Clever boy. At his house by the river at Soba. Conveniently our hopeless watchers don't possess a boat."

"What's the context?"

"You shared your worries with me. Which are understandable, I gotta admit. You don't know the guy, so you can't trust him. I want you to judge for yourself and see the benefits of keeping these Arab-Afghans under our benevolent wing. So we can point them in the right direction and fire them off against the powers of evil."

"Isn't our job to mistrust everybody, look at them with a sceptical eye?"

"You bet it is. Goddam right, I'm as mistrustful as the next guy. Only a notch less paranoid than our resident madman James Jesus Angleton. But I've fought alongside these fellows, yeah." He raised his glass towards Haydon. "Cheers. Lookit. Guys like Mughniyeh, Carlos the Jackal, Abu Nidal. Super dangerous bastards. But they're not on the Muslim team, no – they are on the Palestinian team, the mad commie radical team, the Ayatollah's team. They are our always enemies and our worst nightmare. Implacable. Deep west-haters. Going after them, I do it all day long, and you too. But Hekmatyar and Rabbani, all these other Afghan-Arab guys, they gonna help me root out these evil bastards. They already give me reams of intel."

"What's the difference?" Haydon scratched his head.

"They're terrorists at heart, ready to plant a car bomb or six on someone else's street."

"This guy was born and raised in the capitalist cradle. More than you Haydon, I figure. Family oozes wealth, exec jets, power, and friends with big, big, figures. Cheney, Baker, the Bushes." He tapped the table with his fingers. "He could afford to support his Afghan brothers, lay out his own money and prestige, get his own fingers dirty. The Saudis worked hand in glove with us in Afghanistan. Prince Turki and Bill Casey. Hand in glove. They sent the Sheikh and his engineers to build the roads and cave complexes to support the *Muj*. They're our allies. You'll see."

The skies above the river seemed crowded with birds, part of an endless migration. Geese and ducks in profusion, long Vees in the sky following the mighty Nile south, sand grouse flighting in from the desert, plovers, cranes, sandpipers. Haydon watched as a fish eagle dived vertically into the water with a big splash, then reemerged a few seconds later with a small perch wriggling in its bill.

Pete Monkton stood erect at the wheel of the speedboat. A tall, imposing figure, swaying gently to the bucking motion. Haydon felt small beside him. Arcs of spray shot up either side of the boat like rainbows, the prow bouncing its way against the current. Twin Mercury 135 horsepower outboard engines powered them forward at 30 knots, carving white tails behind them. Their wake rolled and slapped against the steep mud banks of the Blue Nile as they sped by, the river fast flowing as it curved southwards at Jereif.

Distant figures waved as the boat shot past small groups picnicking on the sandbanks and islands that peppered the river. A typical Friday scene. Every few hundred yards, large old Lister pumps coughed away a deep chant, pumping water up to irrigate the long, thin fields that seemed to run endlessly inland from each bank. Cotton, maize, vegetables, groundnuts and palm trees lined up in different hues of green.

At a bend in the river past the small town of Soba, the American cut the throttles and let the boat drift slowly alongside a short wooden jetty, flanked by a high fence. The two men tied up the boat and clambered up the dry mud bank to a wrought iron entranceway, where two armed guards were waiting, holding a gate open. One of them, squat and broad, gestured them in. Then, pointing with his distinctive AK-47 carbine, he turned to lead them down a narrow path, which opened out into an irrigated grassy area.

A small stable block stood at the far end of a narrow field, in front of which two men in *jellabiyas* were examining a grey horse. They looked up as Haydon and Monkton approached. One of them was unnaturally tall, Haydon thought, perhaps 2 meters. The other man was stocky and broad-shouldered.

"That little thing wouldn't make it over the high passes, my friend!" Monkton raised his arm in greeting. "Spindly critter, yeah."

"No high passes in this country, brother. Everything is flat as a plate, you see." The tall man raised his arm to his heart and bowed his head. "Greetings, *sadiqi* - my friend. She'll fill out. You want to try her? She's fast."

"No siree. Given that stuff up. I'm still bow-legged after following you on those long rides through the Hindu Kush. Nowadays I prefer to sit and jabber."

A groom led the pony away to a stable. Monkton didn't make introductions, and Haydon understood his role was to listen, remain silent, and observe. Haydon and the other man followed silently behind, as the tall man and Monkton wandered through the stable yard and over to a modest one-storey mud house. The guard followed a few paces behind, his rifle slung over his shoulder. The two men were obviously close, speaking freely in English and Arabic. They walked together through an archway and into a shaded courtyard dominated by an ancient mango tree.

Flowers poked out of large earthenware pots, pools of water leaking from the bases. To one side, cushions adorned a patchwork of Persian rugs. The four men sat down, and a servant, preceded by the pungent smell of cardamom, entered carrying a brass tray from which he served each of them with Turkish coffee. Haydon felt unbalanced sitting cross-legged. He noticed Monkton had mastered the art and looked perfectly comfortable.

Chapter 17

The guard stood like a sentry by the entrance, facing outwards, rifle cradled in his arms. The bass thumping of heavy diesel pumps pushing water up from the river into the irrigation canals seemed to Haydon to be beating a martial rhythm.

They sipped their coffee in silence. Haydon glanced over at the tall man, sitting erect and immobile, his expression as if he were smiling at some pleasing inner thought. So, this was the infamous Sheikh, Islamic warrior, scourge of the Russkies, educated millionaire, ascetic cave dweller and CIA agent. He wanted to dislike the man, wanted him to fit into his preconceived image of a threatening Islamic fanatic. But he sensed no hint of aggression or animosity in his manner. If anything, he resembled a placid university lecturer, grey bearded and impecunious. After a long pause, the man turned his head slowly and addressed himself to Haydon.

"My friend Mister Peter tells me you worry about my presence here in Sudan, and about my comrades from the *jihad* against the Russians in Afghanistan. He says you suspect I have built training camps here for dangerous guerrillas." He shook his finger. "Let me explain you why you should forget these worries."

He spoke quietly. Haydon leaned forward, nodded his head, and was about to reply, but the Sheikh raised his hand and continued, pointing towards the other man.

"This is Mister Mohammed Saad. My colleague that Mister Peter knows also from Afghanistan. He has been my chief engineer for many years. From Iraq. He organised the bringing of my construction machines we used in Afghanistan, you see."

The stocky man smiled and bowed his head towards Haydon.

"When we defeated them, the Russians fled away. So, I brought to here the equipment I used to make tunnels and roads for the *mujahadeen* in Afghanistan. Then I also helped some of my old comrades from there to come to Sudan, that is true."

He paused and looked away. Haydon could hear the muffled click of prayer beads as they turned in his hand. I wonder if he's a chess player, Haydon thought. Everything he says is so measured and easy. He turned back to face Haydon and continued.

"The Islamic government welcomes all Muslims here," he said with a smile as he paused, moving the beads one-by-one in his unusually long fingers. "In return we wish to contribute to this country's development, you see. In the construction field yes, but also in agriculture and banking. Mohammed supervised the building of guerrilla trails and cave complexes in Afghanistan with Mister Peter, now he is in my charge to build the road from Khartoum to Port Sudan, which I am presently making for the government."

He stopped and murmured what Haydon presumed was a silent prayer under his breath, his lips moving, eyes closed. He opened them again and resumed speaking.

"What I lived in two years in Afghanistan, I could not have lived in a hundred years elsewhere." He smiled and cleared his throat.

"The rubbish of the media and the embassies, you see. I am a construction engineer and an agriculturalist. If I had training camps here in Sudan, I couldn't possibly do this job. This is what I can tell you."

He touched his heart with his hand, then continued.

"I wish to bring up my sons here. To be free with my family. Away from all fighting and disturbance. To breed the finest horses, make the best honey, build things up rather than blast them down." He made a sweeping gesture with his arms. "You see, there in my Damazine farm I have many cattles, I grow peanuts, sunflowers and white corn, sim-sim, soybeans and sorghum. This farming fills my heart with joy."

Haydon rubbed sweat off his forehead. He started again to reply, but Monkton cut him off with a sharp look.

"That is the truth, you see. There is nothing else."

The tall man shook his coffee cup. The servant came over and took it from him. He unravelled his loose clothes, then stood up and walked silently out of the courtyard and into the house.

"The Sheikh has nothing more he wishes to say to you." Monkton stood up. "But he has invited us to visit his road building project and his farm near Damazine, whenever we wish."

They followed the guard back up the dark earthen track towards the Nile. They passed a group of men kneeling on prayer mats, mumbling incantations in a base undertone and conducting rituals with their hands, then bending to touch the earth with their foreheads. Haydon heard the high whinny of a horse, the stamping of feet, and in the background that incessant thump of the heavy water pumps.

It had been like a political speech, Haydon thought. Written especially for him?

Probably at Monkton's urging. How much of it was credible? Had Monkton really been able to dig below the surface of this unusual man, sitting around campfires high in the Hindu Kush? Could the American be right that this man was genuinely committed to building up something in Sudan, putting the destruction and bloodshed of the Afghan war behind him?

The guard held the iron gate open for them; the bolts slamming shut behind them as they stepped down onto the wooden dock.

They sped downriver in the late afternoon sun, the strong current behind them hurrying the speedboat along. The rains had been heavy in Ethiopia that year, and the Blue Nile was flowing faster than usual. Drawing up by Alkwasir Island, Monkton threw the anchor over the side onto a small sandbank and cut the engines. The boat swung around to face the current, then jerked to a stop, the swish of water audible as it rushed past. A few hundred yards away, a couple of speedboats were anchored, small groups of people lying on rugs on the sandy shore.

Monkton opened a cool box and produced cans of ice-cold beer, handing one to Haydon.

They sat in silence, sipping and smoking. Haydon saw the evening rush had started. Thousands of birds flighting into the river, skirting just above the water. A fish jumped high out of the water, escaping from some unknown predator below. He heard the swoosh of wings as a group of pelicans flew past. He never got bored with this stunning evening parade.

"Well?" The American finally spoke.

"Outstanding. Did you arrange the speech just for me?"

"Cynic. But of course, I want you to make your own mind up, judge the man, not his reputation. Are you a little more comfy? That's the thing, yeah." Pete puffed on his cigarette and exhaled. "Assuaged some of your dark suspicions?"

"He doesn't give the impression of being a mad mullah, but he also doesn't look like a *muj* slayer of Russky bears." Haydon replied.

"Back in the day, on those bitterly cold trails crossing the Zazi mountains, that's what struck me most." Monkton finished his beer, crushed the can and threw it into the river, pulling two more from the box and handing one to Haydon.

"The guy was humble and restrained. I never heard him complain. Not once. Considering he's a little rich boy from Jeddah. Before I got to know him I expected him to be just another spoiled Arab brat."

"My sources say the *muj* feel betrayed by the West. When you'd won the war and seen off the Sov threat you walked away, abandoned them."

"That's pretty much true. We pulled out of Afghanistan lock and stock." He swigged at his beer. "Not a single Agency asset left in the country. Goodbye and good luck."

"Isn't it possible the *muj* want payback?"

"Why the hell you think I'm rotting in this sorry shithole?" The American grunted. "Yes, they feel betrayed. So, I gotta keep making like Father Christmas, doling out hundred-dollar bills, yeah. Like you're always reminding me - *'You can never buy Afghans, you can only rent them'* – well I'm the guy pays the rent. Turabi's congresses have been helpful, I get to catch up with some of them right here, then I go to Peshawar with my Christmas stockings full and come back with them empty. I need these guys onside, to feel my love. Friends don't just disappear. So they remain well rented, ready for my bird call the next time I need to whistle them up."

"I saw how close the two of you are." Haydon flicked water at him. "What did you tell him about me?"

"A tight and repressed *Ingleezi* making waves. That you can be helpful in the war against the Persians, as he calls Iran and Hezbollah." He swigged his beer. "But he already figured you Brits out from way back. From Peshawar days. You've no honey in your backpack, he said. He understands what a small black and white world you inhabit."

"Nice, Pete, thanks." Haydon rubbed his forehead. "I've something for you. I'm getting reports of a training camp under construction near Erkowit. Credible source indicates probable Hamas. Getting close to completion."

"Good man. Hadn't heard about that. Send me details, long and lat if at all possible. I'll get an NRO task set up. Get us sat photos, we got a KH-11 fly past due soon. I'll share the stuff with you, of course."

Monkton stood up and pulled up the anchor. They floated quietly downstream in the current for a while.

"Hezbollah, Abu Nidal and Hamas. Those are our priorities, Haydon. The gloves are all the way off; after the pain we've taken, we gotta bag those guys up wherever we find them. Help me out here. Squeeze your source."

"I hear you Pete. I'm on your side. I'll get back to you with any more on the Hamas camp."

Monkton started the engines and eased the throttles forward.

"And leave the Sheikh and his playmates for me. They're easy meat."

The sun was sinking below the fringe of palm trees that marked the riverbank as they tied up at the jetty at Monkton's house. There was no sign of Lena. Monkton walked him to the front door and waved him off. Driving through the gates, he saw the white Honda falling into line behind him.

Haydon drove slowly home, thinking about what he'd seen. It was difficult not to like Monkton. His infectious mindset was wonderfully free. Cowboys and Indians. Good guys and bad guys. Adventure and fun. As if he was licensed to live out his own fantasy world, where no one could gainsay him. A modern-day Superman, grappling with the forces of darkness and saving the world, mint julep in hand, Texas sized cigar in his Texas sized mouth, and New England courtesy to add to his charm. Not to forget the boxes of dollars under his bed, intended to ensure the story followed his desired narrative.

He thought about the Sheikh. There was something innately amateurish about him. A billionaire's son. Playing at guerrilla games. Could that be so dangerous? The two of them had staged such a picturesque tableau for his benefit, two actors staging their own play, sitting on an earth floor and telling tales. A play within a play. He laughed.

The Sheikh

Chapter 18

"Make a break of it." Haydon told Charlie at their biweekly meeting in the safe house. "The place used to be a summer hill station during colonial times. The Sudanese version of Simla. A romantic resort, perched 3,000 feet up in the Red Sea Hills. Spend a few days relaxing with your VSO chum."

"Have you been there?" Charlie asked. His boss had a perverse sense of humour. He seemed to take pleasure in sugar-coating uncomfortable destinations to which he dispatched Charlie, whilst avoiding going to them himself. Still, anything to get away from the mind-numbing boredom of the recording room, and the holier-than-thou beards at the Forum. And he liked Tom, they'd have some laughs, and he needed a break.

"No, I'd like to see it."

"It's just that I've never heard anyone describe Erkowit as romantic."

"Where's your sense of adventure?"

"And my friendship with Tom doesn't run to romance. We talk about football and boys' stuff."

The coffee percolator whistled. Charlie caught a whiff. Powerful stuff. He needed to get one of those. Haydon poured the thick liquid into small cups. Both of them lit cigarettes. Haydon inhaled deeply and smiled warmly at him. A sure sign he's about to lie. *He's going to ask me to recruit Tom.*

"Poke around the place, but carefully." Haydon ran his fingers through his hair. "Don't draw attention to yourself. Go for a hike in the hills behind the camp? Take a picnic. Stay at a safe distance. See if you can't figure out a discreet approach, where you can get pictures of the camp. From any angle. With the 600mm telephoto lens you won't need to get close. But remain unseen, that's paramount."

Haydon spread a large-scale black and white photo of the Red Sea Hills on the table. "This is from a satellite run three days ago. Here's the town of Erkowit." He stabbed with his finger at a small settlement some 25 miles inland from Suakin on the Red Sea. "The school is half a mile to the east here. This compound here, maybe 2 miles northwest, that's got to be this place your source suggests is the Hamas site. Which is what we're interested in. Look, this line here looks like a firing range. There is probably the parade ground. We can't identify that flag hanging there, we'd like you to have a good look. Might tell us something. See if you can get a shot."

"What's that straight line? Just by the dried up riverbed, south of the road." Charlie pointed. "There."

"Well spotted. That's the secret airstrip that Mossad built for the Falasha operation. They flew the Ethiopian Jews out in C-130s on covert nighttime missions." He tapped the photo again. "When you pass by, have a look around and check for signs of recent use. You're looking for wheel tracks. If there are any, take photos. Hamas would love to make use a secret Mossad airfield."

"I'm not comfortable involving Tom. I could get him into serious trouble."

"Wake up Charlie." Haydon's voice was sharp. "This is your first recruitment I'm offering you. Be subtle, be careful but damn well close the deal. The cultural attaché will fix things with those VSO people if Tom gets into any trouble. Your job is to minimise risks but to obtain the valuable intel."

Charlie hadn't argued. His mind went back to Oxley, the hours they'd spent discussing and chewing over the morality of agent recruitment. The centre point of their work. It was how their performance was measured. It felt creepy and dishonest, and he wondered whether he would ever get over the distaste. He hoped not.

"Did you have to overcome your scruples in your first recruitment?"

"Of course." Haydon sipped his coffee. "I'm human Charlie, although you may not think so. But I saw the results quickly, big time, and they saved lives. Which helped me overcome my misgivings. You'll see."

Erkowit, Sudan

The first five hours of driving were on smooth black tarmac. Charlie thought this must be the new road that Saudi guy was building. After passing Atbara, the tarmac ended, a heavy wooden barrier perched on oil drums blocking the road ahead. After maneuvering around it through soft sand, the road transformed into a series of parallel tracks of sand, stone and impressively deep ruts. His eyes hurt from staring at the monochrome desert view, his shades seemed impervious to the blinding glare. By the time he turned off the main Port Sudan 'highway' near Sinkat, he had been at the wheel for 10 hours straight.

He'd left the hotel in the cool, well before sunrise, and discovered the air-conditioning on the beaten-up hotel minibus was on the blink only after his shirt was sopping wet with sweat and stuck to the back of the plastic seat. It was so hot he doubted he'd survive until evening if the crappy vehicle broke down. He'd got through 5 bottles of water already. By midday, the heat of the sun was beating through the designed-for-somewhere-else 'sunshine roof' directly onto the crown of his head. *Why had he agreed to this crazy journey?*

As the road climbed towards Erkowit, Charlie caught sight of what looked like a large compound some way off to his left, snuggled below a rocky ridge. He saw an unobtrusive turning, aiming toward the site, barbed wire running along a sandy track, but no visible security barrier barring entry. He thought of doing an impromptu recce but couldn't think of a plausible excuse if he were stopped whilst driving up there. Too risky. He needed to get the job done without ending up lying on the ground with a rifle barrel in his ear.

Stopping the car by the side of the road, he focused his long telephoto lens on the guard towers he could see jutting up from a gatehouse, and pressed the button. He kept it depressed and panned the camera along the ridge line, the motor drive clicking off multiple shots. Unless Tom had some friendly way in, which he doubted, it was going to be an uncomfortable hike to edge around behind that ridge and get a clear view down over the site. And the flaw in Haydon's cunning plan was that Charlie couldn't let on to Tom that he had a special interest in remote guerrilla training camps. Or that he kept company with bogeymen at the British Embassy.

As he drove on eastwards, he found it amusing seeing the few broken-down ruins of old colonial buildings dotting the approach to the town. *A romantic resort?* Long ago abandoned, patches of brown, desiccated plants hinted at irrigation systems and planted gardens from colonial times. The surroundings were bleak. Rocky hills, dried-up river beds and jagged crags. No trees in any direction. He wondered if it had ever rained in that desolate spot. No shade. No greenery. How did people even live here? It was hotter than Khartoum; the altitude didn't make a jot of difference.

The village turned out to be a ramshackle collection of mud houses, dominated by a lime green mosque, paint peeling off all its walls. Mangy dogs rooted around garbage strewn around the narrow streets. A donkey, ribs poking out of its scrawny frame, stood motionless, its front leg tied to a stake by the edge of the small central square. The only sign of life was a scrappy coffee bar with a few outside tables. A group of elderly men sat around smoking and playing dominoes. As Charlie drove past, he heard the baleful call of the muezzin blaring through tinny loudspeakers installed at the top of the minaret, summoning the faithful to evening prayers.

Behind him a blood red sun was sinking into the foothills which ran towards the endless desert. He continued on, out of the village, which opened to a flat, dirt area, spindly goal posts signalling the village school. Away to the side of the cluster of school buildings squatted an ugly concrete building. Tom was sitting outside on a plastic chair, dressed in a *jellabiya* and a baseball cap, his long hair amplifying a scarecrow appearance. He was shaded by a small corrugated-iron porch and was smoking a long joint.

"Abandon hope all those who end up here?" Charlie shouted out of the car window. "You look like an inferior version of a Port Said street vendor."

"Welcome to my lost world, buddy. You look pretty shagged out yourself, matter of fact." Tom waved with his baseball cap. "See why I'm so keen to get booted out of this place?"

"Christ I need a beer." Charlie crawled out of the car and slumped into a chair next to his friend. "That was a tough twelve-hour drive."

"Out of luck, mate. Nearest beer is twelve hours away. Back in your Embassy bar. Better you hurry back there then." Tom passed the cigar-sized joint to Charlie, then opened a cool box by his feet. "Your choice is lemonade, water or *karkadeh*? I do have one bottle of locally distilled *araki*, illegal of course, made from dates and almost certainly lethal, but if you don't mind going blind. Fancy it?"

"*Karkadeh*."

Tom pulled out a bottle of cold reddish hibiscus tea and poured it into a pint mug.

Charlie leaned his head back and gulped down the drink, holding the mug out for more. "Christ how do you survive in this hell hole? I thought Khartoum was bad."

"Long hours of teaching, then I smoke a cartload of this local weed, and dream a lot. Principally about Cindy Crawford's tits." He refilled the mug and passed it back to Charlie. "I get a kick out of the local kids, they want to learn, they're full of bubbly curiosity and have proper reserves of mischief. Like me. They're from the *Hadendowa* tribe, we Brits used to call them fuzzy-wuzzies. You think my hair's frightening, take a goosey at theirs."

"Anything to do around these parts aside from smoking weed?" Charlie took a long pull on the joint and inhaled deeply, feeling the smoke burn in his lungs.

"I get down to the Red Sea whenever I can. Snorkelling, fishing. Jeez, the fresh fish tastes like elixir after my usual diet of roast goat and dried up vegetables. There's a small group of undergrads from Cambridge living in a shack on stilts built on the reef offshore Suakin. Marine biology students doing research. A fun bunch, they stay six months then rotate. There is even one, repeat one, piece of stupendous totty. As you might imagine, there's competition, and it's a schlep to get a ride down there. So I'm at a disadvantage."

The idea of suggesting a hike into the baking hot hills seemed ludicrous, but Haydon had insisted he should propose it. Charlie felt a dope-high coursing through his veins. This was potent stuff. Maybe, when combined with serious dehydration, it doubled the power. He felt weak. Sod it. He would do what Haydon asked. Anyway, Tom had no one to spill the beans to in this godforsaken place.

"Tom, I want to ask you a big favour. I want to go on a picnic tomorrow, a little walk through the hills."

"Sorry mate, it's the wrong place. We don't do picnics here." He waved his arms in the air. "You die out there in the desert. Are you hallucinating already?"

"I'd like to get over to the far side of that compound you told me about. A quiet spot above the ridge, where we could look down without being seen. A bit of boy scout stuff. Think John Buchan."

"Jeez, man." Tom paused, then stared hard at him. Finally, he threw his head back and laughed, spilling his drink over his white *jellabiya*, wiping it away with his hand. "You just made my day, hell. Boy scout. That's a fucking gas."

"You don't like picnics?"

"I always knew there was something screwy about you. I thought maybe your mummy hated you, or you liked to dress in women's underwear, or maybe you were some kind of closet stamp collector. But I never, never, not in a million years, dreamed you were a sodding, plodding, front line spook. Picnics in a hundred degrees!"

He slapped his knee and started giggling.

"Someone asked me to have a look, a friend of mine at the Embassy."

"Bully for you." Tom laughed and exhaled a stream of smoke. "Tell you what. You want me peeping into people's trash cans, then better you come clean on what's in it for me?"

"How about I drive you to Suakin the day after tomorrow?"

"That'll do for starters, and—"

"—and?"

"—yes, and my next stay at the Forum will be on you, or on your spooky bosses. Three nights, lets say. And you pay all the drinks at the Embassy Club. As many as I can reasonably consume before I pass out on the floor. Then you carry me back to the hotel. OK?"

"I agree but–"

"What but?"

"You don't tell a soul."

"Oh, well the price for that goes up. Four nights. Then I don't even tell myself. In fact it never happened."

Tom relit the joint and inhaled.

"I never dreamed a real-life bogeyman would look like you. You're too guilty-looking and far too easy to read. Well, there you go. Are you licensed to kill by any chance?"

"Fuck off already, bastard."

Chapter 19

"Bloody hell, it's worse that Scotland." Charlie shivered and stamped his feet.

"Wimp." Tom hefted a bag over his shoulder. "Let's move. We'll follow a dry riverbed along to the base of the bluff, then we'll have a steepish climb up to a rocky knoll, from where we'll have a clear view down over the camp. The sun will be coming up by the time we get to the lookout spot."

"Let's aim to be back to your hovel before the midday heat fries our brains." They set off at four in the morning. Tom had taken to the idea of this covert recce, transforming from his normal persona of stoned rebel to that of seasoned military guide. Charlie had to struggle to keep up with him, his backpack, filled with bottles of water, banging against his back with every step. A strong westerly wind was blowing from the desert, adding to the biting cold and pinching their cheeks with arrows of dust. Tom had given him a thick jersey to stave off the unexpected nighttime chill.

A crescent moon gave off enough light for them to follow the course of the riverbed, which meandered north away from the few lights of the town of Erkowit. Their footsteps were strangely muffled in the soft sand.

"There's about fifty meters just ahead where the river-bank fringes along the camp boundary." Tom talked in a low undertone. "We need to be cautious, just in case they have patrols out."

Charlie peered up and thought he could make out the out-line of barbed wire running along the top of the riverbank. He heard the distant thumping of a generator some way off, then, closer by, the sound of a vehicle approaching. Tom touched his shoulder then put his finger to his lips, sinking to his knees. Charlie pressed himself tightly behind a boulder. They heard the vehicle stop and a powerful searchlight swept along the riverbank. *Would they spot the footprints?* He slowed his breathing and closed his eyes.

After a few minutes the light extinguished, and the vehicle drove off. Charlie breathed a sigh of relief.

Tom's figure emerged from the shadows. "Sphincter working overtime, let's move."

They hurried on, looking up at the fence line until the river turned abruptly away eastwards, before curving back behind the line of rocky cliffs.

A red sun was bursting up from the horizon as they started the steep ascent, sand mixed with loose shale making it treacherous underfoot. Charlie slipped a couple of times and had to lie spreadeagled on the slope before finding a tenuous footing. After scrambling up for fifteen minutes, they emerged onto a flat area with a prominent rock outcrop, making a perfect viewing platform.

Charlie yanked off his backpack and set it down on a rock, panting heavily. As he was pulling off his jersey he glanced down and saw a brown-coloured scorpion scuttle away into a crevice in the rock. He jumped backwards in alarm.

"Hell Tom, that's a giant, three inches maybe."

"That long tail packs an unbelievably painful sting, so I'm told." Tom said. "Never tried it."

They moved cautiously towards the edge of the rocks and peered down. The camp lay splayed out beneath them, the dawn sun painting the area in a uniform orange. Half a dozen barracks blocks stood to one side of what was obviously the main administration block. Off to the right was a firing range. They could clearly hear the crackle of rifle shots. A column of men was exercising on a parade ground, the sound of barked orders audible.

Tom produced a small pair of Zeiss binoculars and started peering through them, while Charlie unpacked his Nikon and attached the bulky 600mm lens. Resting it steadily on a rock, he scanned from left to right across the camp.

"You see the flag, Charlie." Tom pointed. "On the flagstaff to the right of the main building."

"Precisely what I want." Charlie pressed the button. "With this wind the flag is perfectly outlined. It's a uniform green, with some kind of writing in white. They'll blow it up in the lab."

A long burst of heavy machine gun fire sent echoes rattling up from below. The two men flinched.

"It's an obstacle course." Through the long lens Charlie could make out figures dressed in black crawling under a barbed wire mesh. "They're firing live ammo above their heads. Those guys will be keeping their noses right down in the dirt. At least I would."

"They look like ninjas, dressed from head to toe in black." Tom focused on a group of men standing behind the machine guns. "Just their eyes showing. They're going to get sweaty any time soon."

The Nikon motor drive clicked away as Charlie kept the button depressed, panning the lens across the breadth of the camp. After a few minutes he stood back and started packing up the camera.

"I've got what I need, Tom. One reel done. Let's head back." They slid on their bottoms down the shaley slope.

"Watch your nether regions don't meet up with a scorpion's nest?" Tom laughed. "Nether regions would burn up if we did this in a couple of hours."

The temperature was rising fast as the sun transformed from orange to yellow. Both men had wrapped scarves around their heads. At the point where the riverbed curved south, Tom paused. "I reckon we shouldn't risk passing that boundary." He rubbed his face with his hands.

"It's a big risk. We'll go cross country, it's a safer route. We take a loop around to the east."

"Who is the wimp now then?" Charlie punched Tom's shoulder. "That'll add an hour or more. In this heat. We'll melt."

"You're sure?" Tom scratched his head. "OK, big boy, but we take it slow when we get close to that fence."

They walked on in silence, retracing their footsteps along the river. The sand seemed heavier underfoot now, Charlie was sweating, the backpack chafing his shoulders. The wind had dropped, and he could feel the sun burning his exposed arms. As they approached the boundary, they paused for a few minutes and scanned the tall fence topped by a roll of razor wire.

"Nothing. All quiet." Tom gestured and they moved off. "Stay close to the riverbank, we'll be pretty much out of sight."

"*Dongolawi araki.*" Tom lifted a dirty bottle of brown liquid out of his fridge. "Top stuff. Made from local dates and distilled in rusty machines. A hundred and fifty proof, packs a rougher punch than the dirtiest Russian home-made vodka you ever imagined. If it doesn't kill you it will probably send you blind, deaf and dumb."

"We deserve to get royally drunk regardless." Charlie was lying on the sofa in Tom's tiny living room. It was stiflingly hot, the roof fan seemed to have no effect, it just went round and round and distributed sand into the air. They'd showered in the hot outside shower, but had continued sweating even as they dried themselves off.

"In this place you deserve to stay permanently drunk."

"Half and half with *karkadeh* is the secret." Tom mixed the drinks reverentially and handed a plastic beaker to Charlie. He took a swig and grimaced.

"Truly disgusting, but by God it'll serve its purpose."

"How come you get to play this James Bond person?" Tom raised his glass. "Is it a recent thing?"

"It's a long story. It began with the allure of big cash." He rubbed his cheeks. "I was starting off my business in Rome and I got myself seduced into doing something really stupid. And nearly fatal. More recently my life was so dry and empty I craved excitement. Like an idiot."

"So today is just another day of fun and games for you?" Tom took a gulp, then refilled their glasses.

"Today was properly adrenalin rich." Charlie laughed. "Thank you, Tom, it was a gas. Sharing life's adventures with a good friend. It's what it should be about."

"And your patriotic duty?" Tom's words came out slurred. "I hadn't figured you for that one."

"Mainly it's just boredom, and often shameful." Charlie could feel the alcohol coursing through his veins. "Peeping through keyholes. I've got to admit it to you, Tom, I feel dirty. Coming down here, trying to con you. Even when I knew you'd figure it out pretty easily. It was a betrayal of our friendship."

"So what? Our relationship is cool. We smoke dope, we laugh, we like each other's company. In this desolate place that doesn't come easy. Look around you!" Tom squinted, then shook his head. "You being spook central, that's cool with me. Forget shameful, just surf the giant wave and I'll be waiting on the shore with a big man's spliff. You could have been straight with me, Charlie, that's what friendship is about. Being honest. Well mainly. Not when you're trying to fuck your friend's girl, of course. That's different."

"My boss reminded me this was the job. Manipulating others to do dangerous things that serve a higher purpose." He clasped and unclasped his hands. "*'You'll get used to it'* is what he said. That was the moment I knew I was sinking down a rat-hole."

Tom pulled himself off the bed and went to refill their glasses. He emptied the bottle and lifted it in the air.

"Live on the edge! Die on the edge! That's the way I like it." He raised his arms in the air. "We've made it to our twenties. Who the fuck cares if we live to thirty? Thank you, buddy, for your deeply dirty visit. It brightened my depressing week, in a long line of depressing weeks. I'd already concluded I was never going to make out with the Cambridge girl on the reef, which, frankly, is all I care about after half a bottle of *Dongolawi araki!*"

He sank back on his bed and shut his eyes.

"Thank you, Tom." Charlie made a fist. "You're the first *joe* I've recruited. I suggest we light one motherfucking big spliff to celebrate the event. Live on the edge rules, OK?"

Chapter 20

Khartoum September 1990

Everything had been so rosy when he arrived at the Embassy early that morning. Although it was a Saturday, Glasson had called him from his office secure line.

"Satisfying to see a positive result for once. See what comes from following my instructions, yes?" His voice was strangely distorted by the scrambling device. "Everybody happy. Everybody except Hamas and the Sudanese, which is how we like it."

"We've got SEAMLESS to thank for this Mark. If we keep scouring the country, listening in to those NGO voices, we're likely we find more of the same."

"Worthwhile op, Haydon. Hamas is a dangerous threat. Our American friends are turning the heat up on the regime: they've demanded the Erkowit facility be closed and the Hamas militants expelled."

Haydon knew Glasson would bask in plaudits from Grosvenor Square and was surprised to detect faint praise. "I'm keeping a loose watch on these Afghan-Arabs. Nothing yet, but their presence makes me nervous."

"Leave the Afghan-Arabs to Monkton. His area of expertise. I understand he's keeping you looped in?"

"Yes. I'm about half-way to being convinced."

"Keep your focus on our primary threats, Haydon." His voice was tinny from the scrambler device. "Hezbollah, Abu Nidal and Hamas, yes, and the Iranians."

Charlie's report, carefully sanitised of any clues as to the source, together with photos of the Erkowit camp, had been heralded as an important success. Evidence the Islamic regime was providing facilities and direct support to Hamas. Glasson had promptly shared the material with Monkton, who had traded it with Mossad in return for God-knows-what. London was cock-a-hoop because Langley was knocking on the door asking for more. A sad reflection on his patriotic career choice, Haydon thought, that the Service now measured their success by whether or not Grosvenor Square was pleased with them.

The US ambassador had lodged a démarche with the Sudanese Foreign Minister, enclosing a large colour photo of a green Hamas flag flying large over the camp, as well as several zoom-ins of armed guerrillas, dressed in the hallmark Hamas ninja-style uniforms and green headbands, clambering under an obstacle course, assault rifles to the fore. Haydon noticed with dismay that the photos were date and location stamped, which showed a shocking lapse of operational security. The Sudan Government, as expected, responded indignantly, denouncing the photos as fakes, and the démarche as another Western provocation.

Immediately after the call, during the Embassy's regular morning 'prayer meeting', the Consul had piped up and spoiled Haydon's day.

"I've sad news to report. A British citizen is dead in a road traffic accident near Erkowit. The details are sketchy, and I've instructed my Port Sudan honorary consul to get up there and report back. The corpse was found lying by the roadside, just outside the town. No sign of the vehicle involved, it's likely to have been a hit and run. God knows that's unsurprising, what with the appalling standard of driving in this country."

"Anything on the deceased? That's a remote location." Haydon's heart sank. How many Brits travelled to Erkowit? Could this be a hostile act? Hamas? Sudanese security? Had they already figured out how those date-stamped photos had been obtained? If so, Charlie would be next in the firing line.

"Police have reported details from a British passport found on the body. In the name of Thomas Cartaret Ormond. 23 years old. Seems he was a VSO chappie – that's Voluntary Service Overseas – teaching at a primary school in Erkowit." He dropped a file on the table. "Faxed copies are in here. Anyone heard of this man?"

Anita Proudlock, the second secretary who dealt with NGO and multilateral relations, raised her hand.

"I know Tom. Knew him, I mean." She stuttered and blushed. "We had drinks sometimes when he came to Khartoum. I think he was the only English person living in that area, it's quite a lonely posting. There are those Cambridge postgrads, marine biologists, based near Suakin, they will have known him."

The Deputy Chief of Mission, Peter Kelmscott, chairing the meeting, scratched his head. "Look, let's keep this simple. Find the next of kin, arrange transport for the remains. Do the paperwork. Anita, you contact VSO. And keep it out of the press for Christ's sake. Agreed?"

An hour later, Haydon was sitting with his elbows on his desk, head in his hands, the phone on his desk ringing. He ignored it. Eventually, it stopped. The air conditioning was blowing ice-cold air down at him, but he was sweating.

Maybe, if he did nothing, the whole thing would go away? His mind went back to when he'd been caught smoking, out by the fives courts at school. He'd denied it, even though the cigarette he'd dropped was still burning on the ground in front of the steely-eyed master. He supposed he'd learned a lesson from the painful beating that followed, but what? He'd mastered the art of dissembling, but deciding when to admit guilt? That remained an uncertain judgement. So far, the ambassador hadn't asked questions. He knew nothing of SEAMLESS or of Charlie Lomax.

If the whole thing unravelled and Charlie was blown, or worse. He wouldn't get away with pointing the blame upwards towards his boss, who was guilty as hell: passing unsanitised raw intel to his American friends. No, the bird shit would splatter on his head. Tom's death was no coincidence. Two Englishmen in that remote area, as out of place as if they'd been wearing top hats and tails. What were the chances of a ground surveillance of a hot facility, in a secluded spot, going unnoticed?

After the démarche, someone would have provided the Sudanese security goons with the date-stamped photos and ordered them to investigate how the lapse had occurred. They would have hurried to Erkowit, seeking anomalies from the day in question, waving their weapons around and interviewing terrified villagers, who would have reported seeing two long-haired, strange-looking white men. *Shit!* But he wouldn't tell Charlie that.

He'd warned Charlie to be cautious, but never imagined there'd be such an immediate and harsh response. Anyone in the village could have noticed his presence. They wouldn't have a name, but the hotel vehicle would be a dead giveaway if anyone was able to read English. And had the vehicle's registration details been noted at any of the roadblocks on his way there or back? It might not be long before the *Mukhabarat* took a keen interest in The Forum.

What to do? Order Charlie back to London? Shut down SEAMLESS? That would be the prudent course. But Tom's murder confirmed what Haydon already suspected: that Sudan was becoming a dangerous crucible for radical Middle

Eastern conspiracies. He needed to balance the risks to Charlie's safety with potential yields from continuing the op. Illegals faced the greatest dangers, with no diplomatic protection. He would increase protection and surveillance around Charlie and the hotel, but he needed to play a long game, flush out the smoking gun, which would enable him to confront Glasson. Thinking back to that burning cigarette, he picked up the red phone on his desk.

Haydon signalled Charlie to a crash RV at the safe house.

"I roped Tom in, Haydon." Charlie covered his face with his hands. "Bullied him to go with me and show me the path behind the ridge. Where I could have a clear view over the camp."

"Our consular guy reported he was walking at the edge of town, not far past the school. Hit by a small truck travelling at over 50 mph. Died instantly."

"I feel like his blood is all over my hands."

"You mustn't think that way Charlie. It was me who asked you to use him." Haydon shrugged his shoulders. "It's what we do. There's always risk in our work, you know that. We do it to protect lives, and you achieved a major success against a dangerous adversary. Sometimes, often, there's collateral damage." He reached out and touched Charlie's arm. "It might – might, just be a tragic coincidence. We can't be certain. Not yet."

"Come on Haydon–"

"–any idea if you might have been spotted?"

"Never saw a soul looking in our direction. But maybe there were cameras we didn't clock, motion sensitive, concealed somewhere around the perimeter."

Haydon had thought of that. When the security people had seen the date-stamps on the photos, they would have gone back and replayed whatever CCTV they had running. With these latest video cameras, you could zoom right in. Easy enough to identify two figures dressed in European clothes. That would have been enough to set off the chase.

"Possible. No way to know. Our contacts in the *Mukhabarat* aren't letting anything drop. Look, we have to decide about your situation. London sees no reason to pull you out. Their view is that we up your security envelope and stay on maximum alert. But the decision is entirely yours." Haydon felt a pang of guilt in his chest. "There's an element of risk, and I won't hold it against you if you decide to pull out. You'll have my full support."

"That would make a waste out of Tom's death. I'd rather see it through." Charlie rubbed his chin. "Do what I can to get back at the bastards."

"If it was Sudanese security or militia, we may get a run at them. If it was Hamas, they'll be gone by now." Haydon stood up. "Charlie, I'm tasking a couple of my security guys from the Embassy to run counter-surveillance around you. For a few weeks, until we're sure there are no hostile eyes on you. Any danger signs and I'll pull you out. Coordinate with them closely please, so they know anytime you're on the move. They'll monitor the hotel's external cameras daily, searching for anomalies."

"Make sure they fix themselves up to look like aid workers. Unshaven. Unkempt. Rude even! Otherwise, they'll draw attention. Especially if they look too much like hunks."

"There are plenty of tough guys running security in the NGO world nowadays. They'll fit right in, legend will be security advisers for this Operation Lifeline Sudan organisation. Made up from UN, WFP, UNICEF and others, it's pretty new." Haydon pulled a packet of cigarettes out of his pocket and lit one. "Let them know anything that seems out of place, however insignificant it might seem. And keep your eyes peeled. Please."

"No problem, I can live with nannies for a few weeks."

"Whenever you're coming here, agree a routine with them in advance. Double your precautions and take as long as you need. I don't want this safe house blown."

The Sheikh

Chapter 21

Omdurman, Sudan

The Kabbani family compound sat, concealed behind tall mud walls and high palm trees, in the centre of the old city of Omdurman. It was comprised of several traditional houses, each one set back from a large central garden and dominated by water channels and gushing fountains.

Outside the walls, the streets were heaving and noisy. Yellow taxis, mules, donkey carts – their drivers whacking them with sticks – smoking, buzzing motorbikes, porters carrying loads on their heads, rushing merchants, and women in colourful *tobes* competed to force their way through the jammed alleyways. Car horns hooted incessantly as drivers struggled to make headway. Angry, white-clad pedestrians banged their fists on car roofs and shouted insults.

Dinners in Omdurman rarely got going until after ten in the evening. It was September, and the weather had cooled from the impossible summer peaks, sand hanging heavy in the air, a reminder of the long, hot months. Groups, all male, sat around tables scattered about the courtyard, palm fronds whispering accompaniment to the dull murmur of conversation.

Brown paper bags decorated every table, each one concealing an illicit bottle of Johnny Walker whisky, purchased from employees of various embassies. Diplomats considered this trade a reasonable way of supplementing their incomes. Discovery of alcohol by the religious police frequently led to imprisonment and, occasionally, to public floggings, although this was rare amongst the elite class. Sometimes heated arguments or jealous husbands, or clashes with difficult neighbours, led to anonymous phone denunciations, resulting in embarrassing and noisy late night police raids.

Haydon arrived at the party late. He knew that food wouldn't appear much before midnight. After passing through the heavy wooden entrance gate into the courtyard, he paused and scanned the tables, conducting a mental inventory of notable guests. He smelled a powerful aroma of roses, and his eyes followed a mass of creeping flowers snaking over the red mud walls, breaching the symmetry of ancient Islamic architecture.

He walked over to a corner table where Ali Kabbani was sitting with Pete Monkton and Yahya Abdelaziz.

"*Yaaaa Salaaam!* Here comes the man of the hour!" Kabbani stood up, and the two men embraced. "They're saying your expulsion is imminent. That would be seen as highly prestigious, you see. We should drink to it."

"Who is forecasting my departure? I'd–" Haydon laughed.

"My strident colleagues in government are demanding a forceful response to yet another British colonialist provocation. That means you, you see."

"But it was my American colleague who complained to your foreign minister about a Hamas military training facility. Monkton here is the one. There's surely no reason to blame the British?"

"You are the donkeys for your American masters. Everyone knows that. And what you call a Hamas military training facility." Kabbani wagged his finger at Haydon. "My people revealed it to be instead a centre for international religious retreats. Peaceful and philanthropic."

Haydon poured himself a large whisky and added chunks of ice from a bowl. He took a sip, grimaced, then added some water.

"Ali, you don't believe that regime crap." Monkton was

elegant in a blue blazer, white linen trousers and boat shoes. "This city is increasingly a jamboree for bad guys, yeah. Carlos the Jackal was seen playing poker at the Syrian Club last week. Apparently, he's a poor player, but he brought whisky, so the other players were happy especially as he didn't shoot any of them."

"But, listen. You're all looking in the wrong direction, my friends." Yahya spoke quietly. The others had to lean forward to hear him. "Even the regime is. Hamas, it's true, is a minor irritant for the Israelis, although recently they rounded up most of the top leadership. Decapitated them. The radical groups we see here are all parochial, their interests are limited to their own little local gripes."

"So where, according to you, my learned friend, should we all be looking?" Kabbani smiled.

"The real danger confronting us, you see – we Muslims as much as you westerners – is from these *takfiri* lunatics that are rumoured to be embedding themselves, like parasites, all over the place. We don't even know who they are. Like ninja, they even permit themselves to break Koranic codes in pursuit of their 'higher goal'. They shave their beards, sometimes they drink alcohol, if it helps their disguise."

"So what's their higher goal?" Monkton asked.

"*Takfiri* see the world in black-and-white. There are true believers and non-believers, no shades in between. Non-believers – *kuffar* – they class all of you as apostates. Apostates deserve death. A *takfiri*'s mission is to re-create the old Islamic Caliphate, according to a literal, old-fashioned, and simplistic interpretation of the Koran."

Yahya reached up and rewound his turban around his head.

"That Manichean approach sounds oddly similar to Reagan's much heralded world view." Kabbani frowned. "The Evil Empire."

"That's going it a bit." Monkton coughed and raised his eyebrows. "So, this lot of lunatics don't figure in Turabi's broad church?"

"Some *takfiri* see our Islamic regime here as insufficiently committed to pure Koranic principals, so they consider them rightful targets for attack." Kabbani sipped his drink. "Even Hassan el-Turabi is reportedly on their list. Difficult to imagine."

"Why does the regime tolerate them?" Monkton said.

"Like the Muslim Brothers, *takfiri* hide themselves, operating in cell structures. The *Mukhabarat* will be on the watch out for them. And you should too. Even your friend the Sheikh has increased his personal security. He's received direct threats. Most likely *Wahhabi* zealots from Saudi are after him, and many of those are *takfiri*."

"We're living in the Berlin of the 90's. Smoke and multiple broken mirrors." Laughter seemed to bubble from Monkton's belly. "It's far from black and white. Our world is dusty red. Still, Ali, I'm pleased to learn that you and your bearded colleagues have to look under your vehicles in the morning. Like the rest of us gotta do."

There was a blast of noise. The music had started. Kabbani had invited a popular troupe of musicians, led by a jovial one-armed singer, Osman Sharfie. Haydon watched him playing a flute-like instrument with his good hand, rhythmically conducting the band with the stump of his missing arm, breaking into wailing song from time to time. Guests stood up and moved around desultorily, shuffling rather than dancing, arms above their heads, fingers snapping, drums beating a pentatonic tempo, the audience clapping enthusiastically in time.

Further conversation was impossible. Haydon wished the food would come. He leaned back and gulped his drink. He realised he was drunk. Where was it all leading? Sudan was a melting pot of Islamic, Palestinian and Arab groups. Was it going to be a repeat of the proxy wars of the 70s? Korea and Vietnam, Cuba and central America. This place was getting more dangerous, like a confused sea, waves breaking from all directions.

An orange moon had pushed its way above the walls, highlighting the tall palm trees and adding a strange glow to the party. Perhaps Pete Monkton was right, he could control his Afghan radicals, by judicious application of money, arms and intelligence. But could he really turn them and launch them against other Muslim or Palestinian groups?

The music stopped. A smell of roast lamb preceded a line of waiters carrying heaped trays of food to a large table. As Haydon and Monkton wandered over to join the line of diners, Monkton squeezed Haydon's arm and held him back.

"Word of caution, buddy." He said in an undertone. "What Yahya told us. He's right, we need to take heed, increase vigilance, up counter-surveillance."

Haydon pricked up his ears. There was something hard in the American's tone. He felt pressure on his arm.

"Specifically?"

"Erkowit. It's gonna lead back to your guy, if it hasn't already." He lowered his voice.

"Which guy?"

"Don't play funny with me Haydon. If I know, the chances are others do, or they will. He's gonna get a spotlight right up his ass."

"You didn't do us any favours Pete."

"Our bad. My guys fucked up with the photos. Sorry. Now we all gotta watch our backs."

"Who's the main threat?"

"The skinnies, but they may not be the problem. Hamas will want payback. Maybe they farm out the job to come other group, yeah. Hard line Palestinians, we've seen it before. Even these 'ghost' militias, whoever they are. And Yahya may be right, these *takfiri* may become a hidden threat."

"I've put some beef around him."

"Good. Another thing." Monkton sucked in his cheeks, then whispered. "Your safe house. The one off Al Mufti Street. Better make real sure it's clean. Same story."

Monkton released the pressure from Haydon's arm, and they walked together over to the buffet. Monkton reached down for a plate and shovelled food onto it. Haydon shivered. He felt stone cold sober. He reached over and rubbed his arm where Monkton had held it. Was the warning really about SEAMLESS? So he knew about Charlie, maybe he knew about the hotel. But the safe house? Was this a personal warning? The safe house? Had Monkton had eyes following Charlie? Or Lena? He felt his chest contracting.

"Thanks for the heads up, Pete. I'll be on high alert. I don't want to lose my source."

"It's what friends are for, Haydon." Monkton turned and carried his heaped plate back towards the table. Haydon winced.

Chapter 22

Khartoum, October 1990

During the weeks after Tom's death, Charlie was hyper-vigilant, passing on the slightest suspicion to his minders. The two of them, Des and Harry, turned out to be easy enough company, although Charlie had no desire to be nursemaided, or to have his personal life cramped. Haydon had provided him with a bleeper, enabling him to page them at any hour, to summon them in an emergency. Around the hotel, they slotted into their allotted legend as NGO security consultants.

"We was called 'bird-shit' back then, Charlie. Straight up." Des announced, straight faced.

"Not sure I heard you right, Des?"

"That's what lesser mortals calls us paras, you see. A term of proper respect. We comes out of the sky, unexpectedly like, causing mess."

Des was tall and stick-thin, with carefully brushed hair and a ponderous demeanour. Harry was stocky and balding, with a straggly ginger beard and lavishly tattooed arms. The two of them exuded quiet toughness, and their presence was reassuring. However, having them looking over his shoulder and providing Haydon with details of his every movement felt intrusive. Haydon had also been a para, and Charlie wondered how far back the relationship went.

The Forum had a rooftop terrace on the 3rd floor, with views down over the surrounding area. The 'Summit bar', open only in the early evening, had tables scattered around, and a dirty canvas awning to provide shade. Creepers planted in ceramic pots provided a little welcome colour. Concealed

CCTV cameras were installed at each corner parapet, angled down towards the streets. Occasionally, when the bar was closed, Charlie had noticed the two men peering through binoculars, looking for any odd signs, drivers staying in their cars unnaturally long in the boiling heat, pedestrians looking uncomfortable. Nothing suspicious had showed up.

After they'd been there for two weeks, Charlie asked Haydon to change their routine, have them shadowing him only when he was moving around away from the hotel. Haydon demurred, told him he wanted them in place a little longer, until he was quite certain that Charlie wasn't being shadowed.

The Forum Hotel was full, as was every other hotel and guest house in Khartoum. A three-day Organisation of African Unity summit was taking place, convened to discuss the catastrophic refugee crisis in the country's south. Government delegations, journalists and NGOs flooded in. Black Mercedes limousines with white-clad police motorcycle escorts, sped down the main road from the airport, sirens blaring and lights flashing, scattering oncoming traffic. Security around the capital was tight, with roadblocks operating at bridges and on main roads out of the city.

Charlie sat in his office and looked through a pile of hotel registration cards, scrutinising them, running down the entries with his finger. He'd let them pile up. He had been preoccupied and disliked this part of his job. As of that morning, the Forum had fifteen guests, including Des and Harry, who described themselves on their form as *'UN Security detail (OLS) Juba.'*. There were two copies of each card. The security police came every morning to collect their copy.

He wondered what happened to the thousands of forms they amassed.

One room was occupied by two Spanish backpackers, a tired and sick-looking couple, both of them with unkempt, frizzy, hair; they looked like brother and sister. Their card stated they had travelled by bus from Ethiopia and were intending to continue by train and boat to Cairo.

Intrepid. Four cards were of western journalists, one of them Charlie knew from his incisive articles about radical Middle Eastern groups. The remaining seven were employees registered as being with various NGOs.

One of those caught his eye. Filled out in Arabic. Two guests: Hassan el-Mahgoub and Abdelrahman Yassin. Due to check out by midday. Their employer was entered as the 'Al-Quds Centre for Islamic Development', Amman. Room 7. He'd noticed the two men at breakfast that morning, probably in their early thirties, well dressed. Unlike the usual front-end field guys, who were typically scruffy, irreverent, and unkempt, these two were neat looking, more like Ivy League types, the sort that might work for the World Bank or Coca-Cola. He'd chatted to them when they'd arrived. Impeccable English. Jordanian passports, although he thought their accent sounded more Egyptian.

Charlie locked and bolted the door to his office from the inside, then walked over and clicked the hidden catch to release the tall bookcase, swinging it open on its heavy hinges. Stepping into the recording room, he sat down at the metal desk, leaned forward, and covered his face in his hands. He thought about Ines. What would she have said about this intrusive peeping? He felt the slash of self-hate burning in his gut. It was as if he had no will of his own. And yet he thought of himself as selfish. Ironic.

It had all gone to shit, and so quickly. Tom's death had highlighted the unforgiving nature of the world he'd chosen.

Forget about glamour. This was horribly grubby. He was a professional manipulator. That was his job description. Just as Haydon had manipulated him to take on this dead-end job, he'd used his learned skills to pressure Tom to do what he'd wanted, providing him with no warning about the existential risks involved.

To what end? One VSO worker dead, before his time, one Hamas training camp moved away to some other, now presumably unknown, location. Immaterial. And he was sitting in an airless box eavesdropping on guiltless strangers' bedrooms. How low could you get? Was there even a way back from what felt to him like perdition? He'd started to obsess about retribution. Would that solve his deep sense of guilt? He pinched his cheek and felt the sharp pain. Focus on the now, no time to sink into self-pity.

He switched on the desk lamp and, opening a notebook, wrote in the date, drew a line with a ruler down the page, then put on the headphones. He was relieved to see from the visual tape markings that the voice-activated mikes had not been too busy. Less than a quarter of the cassettes had run through. That was something. And he was reasonably sure he would not have to listen to any sex groans. But these two fellows would almost certainly talk in Arabic, which would slow him down.

He'd take notes of all the dialogue he could understand; the boys in London would get the tapes and provide full, accurate transcripts later on. He toggled the selector switch for 'Room 7' and pressed play.

It was a little over 6 minutes of voice. He couldn't identify which of the two men was speaking. No names. They referred to each other as 'brother' or 'friend' and their accents in Arabic were similar. They probably weren't security service trained, Charlie concluded, or they'd have turned on the bedside radio, as a matter of habit, to frustrate possible ears.

They spoke quietly, but the mikes were modern, with high sensitivity. There were gaps, when the room seemed to go silent. He supposed they might have been whispering too softly for the mikes, perhaps standing by the window, and there were passages he couldn't catch. He replayed the tape several times, noting the counter reading of key phrases. The veins in his temples throbbed as it had dawned on him, as he replayed it, that he had stumbled across a potential gold mine of intel. Now they'd have to find a way to mine the seam.

He lit a cigarette and inhaled. He read back his notes one more time, then carefully rewrote them on a duplicate carbon pad.

00.07
Voice 1: "The door, check the door. Look outside, brother."
Voice 2: "Nothing."
Voice 1: "We haven't much time. Pack quickly then we go. The flight is in 3 hours."
Voice 2: "You saw the man himself?"
Voice 1: "He calls himself Harun al-Rashid. No names. He is to be our only contact. Closed cell. You and I and him only."

01.33
Voice 1: "*(Inaudible)*... no contact with our Islamic brethren. We are to be *makhfia*, hidden ones. Business executives. Coca-Cola lovers."
Voice 2: "We go to the mosque?"
Voice 1: "Perhaps. But important is we create no suspicions. We are to stay clean skins. Not on anybody's list, of

radicals or fundamentalists. The leadership selected us to lead a new *jihad*. Our job is to attack the Far Enemy in his own house, God willing. But for us we will have lives of pretence."

02.56

Voice 1: "He will provide all necessary moneys. Always using *Hawala*. We will live like wealthy men. Travel in business class, stay in top hotels. The *kuffar* will not expect operatives dressed like successful Harvard business managers and clean-shaved like them."

Voice 2: "They require our special skills, friend?"

Voice 1: "Yes. Lorries mainly. We make the devices. Prepare them for others to conclude. *Shaheed*. Possibly also aircraft, delayed fuses, timers or pressure switches. We hit targets that will shock them."

Voice 2: "So their people will suffer the same that we suffer."

Voice 1: "Like when the Jews bombed the King David Hotel. They created horror among the population."

04.28

Voice 1: "The first operation. He says it will be bigger than anything done before. Bigger than Beirut. When we hurt the Americans badly. We will be heroes."

Voice 2: "Heroes or martyrs, my friend?"

Voice 1: "Whatever is the way God wills it."

05.16

Voice 1: "Westerners are softer than Israelis, my brother. London, New York, Paris, Brussels. Easier for us. They will not be expecting it, believe me."

Voice 2: "Where will be first?"

Voice 1: "*(Inaudible)* ...famous building. But we will be

told when the time is right."

Voice 2: "I am proud, friend. It will be our time to shine, for Allah."

Charlie unlocked a cabinet and took out a tray of metal canisters, each marked with a date. These contained the photos of guests, taken at check in by a hidden camera concealed above the reception desk. He found the most recent canister. Removing the reel from the *Nagra* machine, he dropped the original into a padded envelope, together with the roll of film and a copy of his notes. Lifting the phone, he sent a pager message to Des. He would deliver it immediately to Haydon.

The Sheikh

Chapter 23

London, October 1990

Haydon paused halfway over Lambeth Bridge and leaned over the parapet, staring down at the dirty Thames and feeling the bracing autumn wind on his cheeks. His eyes followed the wobbly progress of a squat tug, its bow swaying from side to side as it struggled to pull several heavy barges against the flow of a flooding tide. A parable of his endeavours, he thought, struggling against the swell of muddy group-think. An easterly gale was blowing, the clouds racing over Big Ben were charcoal dark. Shivering, he pulled his overcoat tight around him, then strode on, following the walls of Lambeth Palace.

He'd flown back overnight on British Airways, carrying the SEAMLESS material, which he believed was explosive and convincing. Standing still for a while, he looked at the huge naval guns in front of the Imperial War Museum, remembering his father bringing him there as an eight-year-old. How romantic war had seemed to his schoolboy self. The tanks, the mock ups of WW1 trenches, the biplanes hanging from the ceiling, the audio noises of air raid sirens, the colourful soldier's uniforms.

The romance hadn't lasted long. Not after he arrived on the grim streets of west Belfast, where people threw rocks at his Land Rover and shouted insults at him wherever he went. Or the threatening hedgerows of South Armagh, where the silence itself was deadly. He crossed over the busy road and turned up Kennington Road.

Arriving at Century House, he passed through security

and took the lift to the 20th floor. He'd been over the arguments in his mind. He aimed to get approval for establishing a special team that would focus on this new cell, identify links in the chain, and dismantle the organisation before any attack could be launched. Manpower and funding. Authority to travel in pursuit of the suspects. He was confident that Mark would support immediate action. They had uncovered a dangerous threat in time to nip it in the bud. A political win for them all if they pulled it off, a catastrophic intelligence failure if they didn't.

The lift doors opened. Julia was waiting for him in the reception area. Dressed in her usual conservative attire of Jaeger woollen suit and white silk blouse, with a Hermes scarf looped loosely around her neck. Seeing her brightened his mood; she emanated warmth and positivity, regardless of circumstance. She smiled at him, a slightly quizzical smile, then shook her long hair back over her shoulders and offered her cheek.

"Julia. Greetings from the nether regions."

"Good to see you, stranger. You look tanned."

"Sandblast, not tan." He pecked her on the cheek. "C is expecting me?"

"Asked me to deliver you into the hands of Director Ops. Mark will catch up with you later. In conference this morning. He asks you please to brief Greg."

Greg Harbut was the new SIS's Director of Operations. He'd got the job ahead of Haydon, the job he'd aspired to since early in his career. A flash of envy stabbed at his chest. He took a breath and composed himself. Julia ushered Haydon into an anteroom. A grey-haired secretary looked up, still tapping away at a typewriter, smiled, and gestured with her head towards an inner door. Julia led him in and then left, closing the door behind her.

"Sit, Haydon, make yourself at home. Coffee?" Greg

stood up, beamed, and waved an expansive arm towards the panoramic widows facing out over the House of Parliament and St James's Park. "You probably know this room better than I do."

"A few happy months I swivelled around in that chair, Greg. And I liked it."

"Me, I can't get used to this job. Bugger all sleep. Always a flap somewhere. People ringing me at three in the morning. You're a lucky sod. Getting your feet up, down there in Africa?"

He let out a friendly laugh, which came out as a snort. Haydon sat down and glanced out of the window. Low, grey clouds rushed past. He had been so naive back then. Sitting in that chair had convinced him the job was destined to be his. He tried to will away the bitter feeling.

Greg was a China specialist, one of the high-fliers of the Service, who believed the West's next threat would come from the Orient, and all other hazards were secondary. An affable and collegiate man, with an unruly grey beard and an easy laugh, he had the bulk of a rugby player, or a ruddy-faced farmer. It was hard not to like him. Haydon thought it shouldn't be difficult to get him onside, although he tended to over-elaborate things, seeing the world as an intricate Chinese puzzle.

"So, tell me about your flap, Haydon. At least you didn't wake me up with it." Greg sighed and picked up a file from the desk. "You're exercised about yet another cell of fanatic *jihadis*."

"You've seen my reports. What we've uncovered in this latest haul is one cell of one group that has been established specifically to attack Western targets in Western countries. And for sure there's more we haven't uncovered yet."

"Our linguistic johnnies have given your SEAMLESS tape a once-over, made minor adjustments to the translation. First impression is it's light on substance. A conversation between two unknown men with Jordanian passports, of unknown allegiance, one of whom talks about meeting a man with the unlikely *nom de plume* of Harun al-Rashid, location unknown. That makes for a lot of unknowns."

"It fits in with what I've been warning. Turabi's push to unite diverse Arab, Palestinian and Islamic causes to confront what they refer to as the Far Enemy – by which they mean us – The USA and Western democracies."

Harbut smiled and tapped the table with his fingertips as if he were playing a piano.

"I'm familiar with your argument." He crinkled his nose, then flattened his hands on the wooden desk. "The counter-argument, which seems to be the majority view in this building, and at Langley, is there continues to be a lot of talk, but no action. Which is what we expect from these groups, and indeed it's exactly how we like it. We don't want to waste limited resources on whispers."

"Beirut wasn't talk–"

"–Beirut was Hezbollah. Beirut was Imad Mughniyeh. It was Iran. And above all it was a Palestinian story. Which has nothing to do with these new boys you're describing."

"What stands out on the tape is the cell members are to be *makhfia* – sleeper agents – disguised and well-funded." Haydon leaned forward, continuing. "Funding will be untraceable via the *Hawala* system. They are to pose as wealthy, well dressed businessmen and permitted to break strict Koranic rules in order to maintain their disguise."

"That is not new, Haydon. We've seen multiple non-Muslim actors in this fray, even in the most radical Palestinian groups. Your neighbour in Khartoum, Carlos the Jackal for one.

He's a Venezuelan catholic. George Habash and Wadie Haddad of the PFLP, both Christians. The leader of the Black

September group that carried out the Munich Olympic massacre, Luttif Afif, he was reportedly half-Jewish and half Christian."

"But my sense is we're dealing with a new generation of adversaries, no longer intrinsically linked to the Palestinian cause, which has in the past been the fulcrum for Middle-Eastern terrorism." Haydon sensed he was losing this argument. "The Afghan-Arabs, *salafist* groups, more recently *takfiris*, all present in Sudan. Greg, I need manpower and funding to dig down and get to the heart of it, flesh out coming dangers."

"I hear you, Haydon." Greg made an arch with his hands and frowned.

"Look. What I can do to support you right now. Hmmm." He drummed his fingers on the desk. "I'll task our tech boys to conduct a comprehensive search of databases, looking for matches for the faces and voice prints. On a priority basis. Which will take time and use up considerable computer capacity. If we get hits, it will provide usable context. Adding to what I consider to be your 'preliminary intelligence'."

"Thank you Greg, that will be helpful." Haydon played with his shirt cuffs.

"And I've forwarded the passport information to Amman Station, with instructions to liaise, as a matter of urgency, with the GID." He stroked his beard. "We'll get good collaboration from them. If those passports aren't kosher, we'll be off and running with firm leads and photos."

"The thing that worries me most on the transcript is the hint that these two are experienced bomb makers or engineers. The reference to 'special skills'. Lorries, aircraft. And they don't seem the types to be martyrs."

"Got you Haydon. So, let's get meat onto this bone." He adjusted his tie. "Come back to me when you have detailed intel on the bad guys, their affiliations, plans and targets. You can rely on my full support."

Haydon looked into the cheery face. This was going nowhere. He could sense C's unhelpful hand pulling the strings behind Greg's jolly smile.

Chapter 24

Back in his office in Khartoum, Haydon sat behind his desk, leaning forward, his head in his hands, cold air from the air conditioner blasting onto his bald patch. He felt goose pimples on his arms and sensed the beginnings of a headache.

His meeting with Glasson had been brief and unrewarding.

"D Ops has spoken. I shan't overrule him, Haydon. No increase in funding. You never stop trying, do you? If the computer runs or the passport checks produce gold, we'll look at it again." Glasson had fixed him with an owlish stare. Or was it an attempt at a smile? "Get back to Station, report when you've made substantive progress. Substantive, yes. Your work on the Hamas facility, more of that, yes, excellent. Less of the flights of fancy."

Haydon pulled a file from a stack on his desk and sighed. He opened it and leafed through the dailies. There had been a marked up-tick in surveillance on embassy personnel and vehicles. Perhaps the *Mukhabarat* were harassing them as payback for the Erkowit incident. In one particularly aggressive move, a watcher's Toyota Hi-Lux cut up and nearly forced the Consul's car into a ditch. The ambassador was going to make a complaint to the Foreign Minister.

He read through the dailies from SEAMLESS. Des reported they might have spotted foot surveillance of the hotel, but couldn't be sure, it might just be a shadow. They'd gone on heightened alert and were monitoring the exterior cameras, looking for signals. Charlie had hooked up with some French girl from the UNHCR. No sign that she was anything other than what she purported to be. An NGO worker in Singa had talked at the bar about seeing vehicles filled with armed men passing through the town, taking the road south towards Damazine. He'd said 'thousands' of local people had been employed at this 'Saudi owned' farm near to the Ethiopian border. Haydon made a mental note to chivvy Monkton, to get him to take up the Sheikh's invitation to visit the farm.

The prospect of hostile surveillance of the hotel gave him the willies. It might be nothing. Or, if he were lucky, it could be Monkton's people keeping an eye. He needed to check. If the *Mukhabarat* suspected Charlie's involvement in Erkowit, what action would they take? A raid on the hotel? That could be catastrophic. If it became clear SEAMLESS was blown, he'd need to act fast and shut it down, cleanse the property of bugs and cameras, hope like hell he could avoid major diplomatic blowback. He'd task the lads to prepare for that eventuality, get an evac and destruct protocol set up. Even if he had to sacrifice Charlie, deny all knowledge, the Sudanese might still concoct evidence and blame the Embassy.

He'd better call on Salah el-Fateh, clear the air, sniff out what the man knew. If he knew. He buzzed his secretary and asked her to set up a lunch appointment.

His door opened and a puckish head poked through, followed by the smartly dressed figure of Yahya Abdelaziz.

"Quick trip, Haydon. Can't stay away, my friend?"

"Come in Yahya. I need advice."

"You people pay me for it, although not bountifully." He had a quiet laugh. It sounded like a stifled sneeze. "How can I help?"

"Help me challenge my own instincts." Haydon gestured him to sit, then scratched his head vigorously. "I feel weary and unappreciated."

"Perhaps you need a learned psychiatrist, rather than a simple lawyer?"

"The other night you warned about the *takfiri* threat. I

need to understand how these radical groups operating here are interwoven."

"Ah Haydon, yes, but first define what is radical?" The lawyer stroked his wispy beard. "Almost all of us, even the most reasonable – whether Muslim, Christian or anything else, except perhaps for the two Jewish brothers who remain living in Khartoum, you see – we all feel sympathy for the plight of our Palestinian brothers. So would you consider us all to be radical?"

"Let me rephrase, Yahya. Dangerous armed militia. Fundamentalists, Palestinians, Afghan-Arabs, Iran and Libyan and Syrian backed militia groups, Egyptians, Algerians, others. Could they feasibly coalesce into, let's call it, a united pan-Arab threat to the West?"

"That is Turabi's dream, and your nightmare." Yahya paused, his eyes narrowing. "But it's unlikely. There's too much internecine competition, you see. They all compete for funds, for sponsors, for militant supremacy. The Egyptians despise Qadaffi. Qadaffi loathes Fatah. The Algerians hate everyone. And so on."

"The Afghan-Arabs?"

"Unpredictable." Yahya closed his eyes and leaned back. "The Americans were their paymasters in the war against the Soviets. But Saddam's invasion of Kuwait has complicated that relationship. A lot depends on what George Bush does next. But I wouldn't worry about them for the time being."

"Helpful. Thank you Yahya."

The lawyer raised his arms and stretched.

"What frightens me, Haydon, you see, aside from those *takfiri* lunatics, is the unofficial regime militia. Maybe related to the *Mukhabarat*, or answering to some anonymous group within the Islamic Front leadership. They operate these so-called Ghost Houses, unaccountable and brutal. I have clients who have just disappeared. No one can find out anything. It's as if they don't exist."

"The atmosphere in this city is becoming sinister, and normal rules don't apply."

"The rules are now made in the name of Islam. I never thought my fellow countrymen would return to the days of the Mahdi and his Khalifa." He laughed again. "So you see, we Sudanese probably understand even less than you."

Haydon strode out of the Embassy, waving his driver away and setting off down Othman Digna Avenue. He needed to clear his head. He stopped at Nile Street, which ran along the banks of the Blue Nile. Waiting to cross the busy road, he saw the battered white Datsun bumping along behind him at a distance, two skinny faces visible in the front seats. His usual lot. Following him assiduously to a meeting with their boss.

He took the sandy track along the river to where *The Melik* was moored. One of Kitchener's fleet of gunboats. She'd seen action at the Battle of Omdurman in 1898 against the forces of the Khalifa. Since 1926, she'd served as the headquarters of the Blue Nile Sailing Club. He wandered along the flank of the old vessel, running his hand down the peeling paint. Rust had made holes in her steel hull, which rested on a high sandbank, to where she'd been pushed, over years, by wind and tide.

He carried on along the river bank, glancing up at the Republican Palace. It felt like recent history, Haydon thought. He felt some strange sort of nostalgia. It was more than a century since General Gordon had been killed, on the stairs of that whitewashed, colonial building. His adversary, The Mahdi, had died just six months later. Hassan el-Turabi and The Mahdi, both of them militant Islamic leaders, made in the same mold, a century apart, each of them leading a poor benighted people to disaster in pursuit of bizarre fundamentalist prophesies.

He crossed the road and glanced back. The Datsun was still there, crawling along the edge of the road. Why didn't they switch to walkers? Shortage of personnel? Laziness? He hurried on. He suddenly felt alone. Not a feeling he was used to. There was no one at the Embassy with whom he could share his concerns. And since Monkton had given him that cryptic warning about the safe house, he'd only seen Lena in passing at diplomatic functions. He'd read the hesitancy in her eyes, confirming to him that the warning had indeed been personal. Right now, he needed Monkton onside.

It took him an hour to walk to the Hilton Hotel. At the confluence, where the fast-flowing Blue Nile came up against the brown and muddy White Nile, the two rivers swirled around the teardrop-shaped Tuti Island, perched in the middle of a watery competition. Its green, irrigated fields, mud-brick walls and braying donkeys were much as they would have been in Gordon's time. Not a vestige of urban development. River traffic, lateen sails bulging, laboured gracefully against the flow. Far to the northeast, upstream of the conjoined Nile, the city of Omdurman sprawled away, melding brown in the haze towards the endless desert beyond.

Haydon sat down at a corner table in the nearly empty dining room. An elderly servant was desultorily sweeping the wooden floor by a piano covered in a dust sheet. Haydon saw dirt stains and holes in the tablecloth. He needed somehow to make an ally of Salah. At minimum, a silent ally, neutral. Or might it be possible to recruit him? That would be a tortuous process. The best line of argument would be to focus on the potential for support, survival even, in the event of sudden retirement, an unexpected fall from grace. An occupational hazard during times of political instability.

Sudan was undergoing rapid change, carefully camouflaged but revolutionary. The old guard was being pushed out, a new breed of Islamic firebrands was taking over. Salah would have considered this. He drummed his fingers on the table and checked his watch again.

Salah el-Fateh arrived half an hour late, raising his arm in apology and plumping himself down with a sigh. Wearing tortoise-shell spectacles, with deep tribal gars on his round face, the head of the feared *Mukhabarat* had an academic appearance.

"Endless problems, friend. The price of vigilance, you know." He picked up the menu as if it were a book and started to read it.

Chapter 25

Khartoum, October 1990

The long dining room was almost empty. A tall waiter, in a red and gold uniform, stood by the kitchen door, picking his teeth. The hotel had been built in the 1970s in anticipation of a gold rush of American companies pouring in to invest, but they had all long ago departed. Now the few guests were official foreign government delegations.

"I spent happy times in your country, you know." Salah sipped a small glass of tea. "I was there for a training course in Camberley. I was young. I learned to drink lukewarm beer, watch dull cricket matches. Other bad habits. Listening at keyholes. You English taught us that well, you see."

"I'd like to invite you back, as our official guest." Haydon rested his hands on the table. "No keyholes. To harmonise our respective interests, seek out avenues to benefit both sides."

"I doubt my masters would be enthusiastic." He slurped his tea. "They don't possess the pragmatic streak necessary to keep adversaries talking."

"Our profession requires us to walk on unstable ground, trying to avoid tumbling into concealed potholes."

"Mister Haydon, believe me, the ground does not shake as fast for you as it does for me." He laughed, then took out a packet of Benson and Hedges and lit one. "Not at all. You can be sure of who your boss is, who it is that you need to obey. I don't have that luxury. And here the potholes are deeper. If you fall into one, you may never reappear."

After ordering their food, the security man rubbed his

hands together and leaned forward, talking in a whisper. "Don't worry, my friend. You're concerned that I hold the Erkowit affair against you, but it's one less armed group I'm required to monitor. I have manpower problems, you see."

"But I don't–"

"Although, of course, this government, and its predecessor, fully supports the just cause of our Palestinian brothers."

The waiter brought their food on a large tray. Haydon inhaled the scent of barbecued lamb chops. Salah stubbed out his half-smoked cigarette in an ashtray. The two men sat in silence whilst they were served. The old man shuffled off back towards the kitchen.

"I'm reminded of the historical bonds of friendship between our two nations, even during periods of conflict." Haydon picked up a lamb chop and held it up. "The Mahdi and General Gordon being a case in point. Mutual admiration and understanding is evident in their personal correspondence. I am hoping that you and I can be of similar help to each other."

"That relationship didn't finish well for Gordon." Salah laughed. "And friendly relations rely, in the end, on the parties avoiding hostile acts, you see."

"I don't want–"

"–look, my friend. I'm tasked with reacting to acts of aggression towards our regime. I've overlooked Erkowit, but don't take it as a sign of weakness." His eyes narrowed, sharp and dangerous. "Remember, I can do more harm to you than you can do to me. So let's have no more surprises, no strange coincidences."

"Should we not build on areas of common–"

"–remember we supported your policy in Afghanistan, opposing the Soviet occupation of that country. We will continue to support those groups who fought loyally by your side."

"My government has no doctrinaire opposition to Islamic regimes, we just fear of attacks by militant groups. Recent history has been painful. Hijackings, kidnappings, bombings."

"Some of your fears I share. These new *takfiri* and *salafist* cells are a danger to us both. I will share intel on these groups with you, and will expect you to do the same."

A uniformed officer approached the table and saluted. He handed a note to Salah, who opened it and frowned.

"I'm sorry Haydon. A summons. I have to leave." He stood up. "One crisis after another. I don't even get to finish my lamb chop. That's the price we pay. My apologies."

Haydon watched him stride off. What was up, he wondered, that was that urgent?

He bit into his steak.

Waiting for his car outside the hotel, Haydon went over the lunch in his mind. The man was sharp and treacherous, but he'd made a point of stating that he had forgiven Erkowit. Which was a relief. SEAMLESS should be safe from any repercussions from the *Mukhabarat,* although they might keep a closer eye on the hotel. But there'd been a warning. Not so veiled. Was it a threat to his person?

He hadn't expected a positive reaction to his advances. He'd dangled a fishing line, seeing if there might be a nibble. Salah would want to keep channels open in all directions. His invitation to collaborate against the *takfiri* cells would please London. He would report it as being the first step of a potential recruitment operation.

On his way back to the Embassy, Haydon stopped off at the Sudan Club, telling his driver to wait. Recently, he'd been checking the Club's cubbyhole obsessively. For a month now, there'd been nothing, and his own envelopes had remained uncollected. In the box marked P, he found a stiff envelope addressed to Paul. Inside was a single typewritten sheet.

Paul: It's me again. Jeanne: It's over.

Paul: That's right. It's over and then it begins again.

Jeanne: What begins again? I don't understand anything anymore. Paul: There's nothing to understand.

He recognised the lines. They'd watched *Last Tango* together, in bed. It had revolted him. Brando was so gross, so beastly. Their own secret seemed besmirched by having those faces attached to the names. He wished he'd never agreed to watch it. The preponderant theme, isolation and loneliness, plucked at some inner chord in his chest. He hoped Lena saw nothing of him in Paul's character, but he thought Jeanne could have been Lena twenty years ago, before her girlish innocence had sharpened into that profound intuition she now exhibited.

Was it over? Or was it her coded message for *'I'm still here?'*

Arriving at his office in the Embassy, his secretary told him that Monkton had rung to say he was coming over. He slipped Lena's note into a desk drawer.

Haydon felt a shadow cross his desk and looked up from his papers. Pete Monkton seemed to occupy the entire room, his bulk advertised his strength, although he didn't take any exercise as far as Haydon knew. He just was one of those men with 'presence'; dominating an empty room as completely as he did a full one. Lena had told him this external charisma betrayed an absence of inner depth. Haydon thought it probably disguised darker elements. Monkton wandered over to the window and looked out across the unnaturally green lawn towards the ambassador's residence and pointed with his arm.

"Bad shindig at al-Mashtal Street this morning. Worrying."

Haydon raised his head, nonplussed. In the distance, he could see a plume of grey smoke rising, melding into the rust-coloured haze. Monkton swung around and plumped himself into a chair facing Haydon's desk.

"Several gunmen attacked a mosque this morning, it's still on fire. Then they drove to the Sheikh's house and shot it up. Several dead. He wasn't there, he's in Damazine. I don't know if the authorities caught any of the attackers."

"I hadn't heard. What would be their motive?" He wondered if Salah had known.

Perhaps that was why he'd hurried off from lunch.

"The mosque? Perhaps the Mullah was perceived as too liberal, or he made some injudicious remark, insufficiently medieval. The Sheikh. Gee, they probably didn't like he collaborated with Uncle Sam in Afghanistan. That would be enough to qualify him as an apostate, punishable by excommunication and death."

"A spanner in the gut for Turabi's Muslim love-in unity drive?" Haydon chewed on his biro.

"Perhaps." Monkton pulled a cigar out of his pocket and ran it back and forth under his nose. "He'll have his work cut out, keeping all his so-called allies from killing each other. Yahya warned us about fundamentalist loonies going on the rampage, and this is just a start."

"Alice in Wonderland would have a field day with those crazies." Haydon rolled his eyes. He hadn't briefed Monkton about the SEAMLESS tapes. Glasson didn't take the threat seriously, so he might not have let slip the details to Monkton.

"I'm gonna ramp up counter-surveillance, bring in more muscle, bodyguards, marines. Careful security protocols. Better you do the same. My ambassador's going to complain to the Foreign Minister. Too many followers, too aggressive. Several incidents with unknown vehicles. We're handing him a list of car registrations we want identified."

"It's getting sinister, Pete. Shades of Beirut. There are too many factions."

"But no kidnappings. Yet. Gotta be thankful for small mercies. And Hezbollah nowhere to be seen, so far, but we're watching." He held a lighter under his cigar and twirled it around, then started puffing. "We use this attack on the Sheikh to our advantage."

"How so?"

"Steer his people to fight against these new threats. You gotta figure our interests are aligned after this shoot out. You see that? Same enemy."

"I don't trust any of these raghead groups, Pete, but I'll take your word for it."

"You and I. We'll go to Damazine, I'll fix it. Figure out what the guy's doing to protect himself, and how he's gonna hit back. See if he can identify who these bad guys are, how we can do harm to them, yeah."

"Fly there? There's a strip?"

"We'll go on safari. Camping, like the good ol' days. Remember? Build ourselves a fire under empty skies. Sing songs to drive away the lions. Ever been to Dinder?"

"The National Park?"

"No tourists in this godforsaken country to go there. Forest, scrub and savannah, plenty of game and no people. Too remote even for grazing, few villages." Monkton inhaled a long cloud of smoke. "We shoot for the pot. White eared cob. Delicious. We go to his farm after dark and jabber. No one sees us."

That would be fascinating, Haydon thought. An opportunity to figure out if Pete really had a handle on these Afghan-Arabs.

The Sheikh

Chapter 26

Haydon drove out of Khartoum in the exquisite pre-dawn cool, taking the tarmac road running south to Wad Medani. He'd fixed an afternoon rendezvous with Monkton at the point where the track leading from Sennar and heading towards Dinder crossed over the Rahad River. About 300 miles, he calculated. A ten-hour drive, maybe more, most of it on unpaved tracks. Making the long loop to the east would add several hours to the journey to the Damazine farm, but taking the road to the Game Reserve was a good legend to explain their presence in the remote area.

They'd decided not to travel in convoy. Two diplomatic vehicles travelling together on main roads would be conspicuous. He felt pumped up by a sense of impending adventure, excited to be freed from the confines of the Embassy, alone and self-reliant. His Embassy Land Rover was loaded with camping equipment, spare tyres, gas cylinders, boxes of food and jerry cans of fuel and water. Above the flat, monotonous brown of the desert, he caught glimpses of an orange sunrise reflecting off water, and long lines of migrating birds flying south.

He mulled over what Monkton had told him. The CIA man had a deeper understanding of the region than he did. He'd spent most of his career in the Middle East, while Haydon had been off chasing paddies in grubby West Belfast. The American was confident enough to take him along to Damazine, and the Sheikh had agreed, so he had a chance to glimpse into the heart of the Afghan-Arab movement and sniff out whether the farm was a front for anything sinister. Or not. If Monkton was right, Haydon could get on with working out which of the other nasty groups was behind the plot exposed by SEAMLESS. And avoid a disagreement with Glasson he was never going to win.

The landscape changed. The brown desert gave way to green and white cotton fields, as far as the eye could see, white cotton buds seeming to pour out from the bushy plants. The Gezira scheme, the largest single-run farm in the world, thousands upon thousands of miles of irrigation canals, transforming the desert into a hugely productive agricultural enterprise.

There was little traffic on the road. Once, a packed bus grew fast in his rear-view mirror and, with a long blast of its loud musical horn, swept past him, black arms waving from the open windows, the rear of the bus fishtailing dangerously towards the edge of the tarmac.

He skirted past Wad Medani, the whitewashed, colonial Gezira Scheme HQ building dominating the town, and on past Sennar, where the 1920s dam held back the water that irrigated millions of acres of cotton. By eleven o'clock the temperature had passed 100 degrees and the Land Rover's air conditioning was fighting a losing battle with the elements.

He crossed the Blue Nile over a rickety colonial era iron bridge south of Sinja, then turned east onto a sandy, rutted, track. Now there was no more agriculture, just dry savannah, criss-crossed by sand rivers and dotted with scrubby thorn trees and occasional copses of thick woodland. Occasionally, he passed small flocks of raggedy goats; once a small boy on a mangy donkey waved a stick at him and shouted as he bumped past. Coming round a corner, he surprised a large herd of white-eared cob which dashed away, their little white tails twitching as they disappeared from view.

He arrived at the RV an hour early. Parking under the shade of a thick acacia tree on the banks of the sand river, he took out a thermos of water and drained it, then leaned back and closed his eyes.

The honking of a car horn close by woke him up with a start. He shook his head and wiped beads of sweat off his face with the back of his hand. He looked out. Monkton was leaning out of the back window of a white Land Cruiser, smiling.

"Wakey, wakey. Time to get our sorry asses moving on. We've still a way to go."

Stepping down from the Land Rover, Haydon felt a welcome zephyr of a cool breeze on his face. He stretched his arms and scratched his head. The sun was sinking behind a line of tall acacias that fringed the riverbank. He heard a sound which, at first, he thought was tropical birdsong, but then saw branches swaying high above and realised the strange shrieks were from a troop of vervet monkeys swinging from tree to tree.

Monkton got out of the Land Cruiser and looked up. "Clever sons of bitches those. They shit on their enemies from a great height, staying well out of reach of goddam reprisals."

"We could learn from them, Pete."

"No, buddy, our battle is down here at ground level. We gotta bare our teeth and make like predators, ready to bite." He opened the Land Rover passenger door and climbed in. "I'll come go with you. Jed and Hal will lead ahead. They gotten one of these new DOD gadgets. Satellite navigation system. We follow. Maybe two hours driving to the farm, sand tracks mainly."

"Jed and Hal?" Haydon got into the driver's seat and started the engine. "My muscle. Who change tyres if necessary."

"Our campsite?"

"God knows how long we'll have to hang around tonight. Sipping goddam over-sweet coffee. It'll take me back awhile, long hours by a campfire. Telling war stories. I'll suffer from nostalgia. And boredom." Monkton groaned. "Patience, now that's a required quality around our Arab brethren. These guys will pitch our tents, someplace on the farm. But don't expect a lot of sack."

"Look Pete, can I be straight up with this guy, get my concerns out in the open?"

"We come all this way. I don't wanna do it a second time. But show some English public-school charm." Monkton punched Haydon's arm. "Look it, I'm as keen as you to know a hundred per cent these guys are on my side. Doing my bidding. You go right ahead, just don't get into a gunfight, you're gonna lose. Don't be in any hurry. Tomorrow we'll get a tour of the farm, check out the feed lots, make sure they contain maize cobs and not Semtex."

They drove off down the sand river, passing occasional stagnant pools of water.

Skirting around a small lake, they saw a light-coloured lion dashing away as they approached. As it grew darker, the headlights picked up reflections of eyes staring at them. The skittishness of the game surprised him. Maybe there were poachers in the area. After driving for an hour, they turned up a steep riverbank and onto a narrow track, heading southwest. They bumped along, the soft sand giving way to hard, deeply rutted, black cotton soil.

"Gotta be damn nigh impassable in the rainy season." Monkton pointed. "Track leads thataway to the Ethiopian border."

"How far?"

"Not more than 20 clicks. Perfect smuggler's rat-run."

They bumped along for another hour. He'd driven for over

twelve hours since leaving Khartoum; it seemed like an eternity. Haydon yawned. His arms ached, he felt a cramp in his legs and his back was sticky under his shirt. A full moon rose into a misty sky, painting the trees on either side of the track with an eerie glow. Somehow the scene struck Haydon as desolate, the headlights from the lead car highlighting leafless trees, seeming to form a wall that threatened to close in on them. He experienced a sinister sensation of being watched. He imagined this was how Marlow had felt, travelling up that dark river towards the Heart of Darkness.

Turning a corner, the cars' lights lit up a thick pole placed across the road between two large rocks. Monkton spoke into a walkie-talkie. Jed and Hal stayed in their car, Monkton got out and walked towards a makeshift guardhouse. Two guards shouldering AK47 carbines emerged and addressed him in Arabic. They pointed with their rifles, then walked over, lifted the heavy pole, and waved them on.

"Guys." Monkton talked into the walkie-talkie. "Follow the track round to the left, past the first lot of buildings. Park up when you see a white Jeep. Find a suitable spot and get the tents up. Then get some shut-eye whilst we are obliged to crouch on the floor and eat unmentionable things."

They drove along a white wooden fence; Haydon saw outlines of cattle grazing in a field. There was no sign of electric light. Some way past the farm buildings, a campfire was blazing, and he heard a faint sound of muffled voices. His heart was pounding, curiosity wrestling with a feeling of trepidation in his chest.

They got out of the car and walked towards the fire. A stocky figure, wrapped in a blanket, stood up and walked towards them. He put his hand over his heart and bowed.

The Sheikh

Chapter 27

Haydon recognised the Iraqi engineer who he had met at Soba. The stocky man smiled and motioned them towards the fire, where three figures stood, their hands over their hearts, murmuring greetings.

"Welcome, brothers, welcome to Damazine Farms. *Fadel*. Mister Peter, good to be meeting you once again, Sir. Welcome. Mister Haydon perhaps you remember me, they call me *Al-Muhandis*, the engineer, but my name is properly Mohammed Saad."

He nodded his head and motioned with his arm towards a thin man wearing a red-checked *keffiyeh*. "This Mister Zaki Bayazid, farming manager from here in Damazine. And this Mister Ahmed Mahjoub, land reclamation person."

The two men bowed. Monkton and Haydon bowed back.

"And Mister Rashid al-Duri, secretary to the Sheikh." Haydon looked at a slender man, light-skinned, with wire-framed spectacles and an intelligent face. He looked away, seeming to avoid meeting Haydon's eye.

An elderly servant appeared and handed them small cups, pouring for each of them from a tall brass *dallah*. Haydon inhaled the powerful aroma of coffee and cardamom. He realised how hungry he was. He hoped they wouldn't have to wait until midnight to eat. The hazy moon was high now, flames from the campfire illuminating the faces huddled around in a small circle, the burning wood crackling and sending out sparks.

"So, what are you constructing here, Mohammed?" Monkton asked.

"Mainly I am working there on building the Port Sudan

road, but sometimes I come here and plan so many works. You see, we have nearly four thousand square kilometres of land, that is one million feddans. So there are many things to do. And here I can relax, sometimes we shoot animals, there are so many gazelles in this area."

"One million feddans. How much of it do you actually farm?" Haydon said. "Mister Ahmed. Will you explain please."

"*Janni*, perhaps we use now one hundred thousand feddans productively, but we are always increasing, you see, building more irrigation canals, fencing, clearing bush, making access roads. We have plentiful water from the lake at the dam." Ahmed spoke slowly, enunciating each word, as if he had learned English from a book. "I am agricultural engineer and am required to reclaim at least ten thousand feddans each year."

"We have many livestock, so many cattles and horses. We grow white corn for animal feed. Also ground nuts and *simsim* – you call that sesame – sunflowers and sorghum." Zaki beamed. "We–"

He fell silent. Haydon turned and saw a tall figure walking slowly towards them with a slight limp, a bodyguard with a rifle slung over his shoulder following some paces behind.

"*Ahlan. Ahlan wa sahlan*, my brother Peter. Welcome to my farm. I am delighted to have you as my honoured guests." The Sheikh bowed his head towards Monkton and touched his heart with his hand. He motioned towards cushions positioned around the fire. "Please to sit. I have been with my falcons today, on horseback. A wonderful day."

Mohammed handed him a blanket, which he wound around his shoulders before sitting.

The bodyguard remained standing behind him. "We hunt here for bustard, you know. This area is famous for these. They are bigger than those we used to hunt in Pakistan, not so easy for my falcons. But I had wonderful success."

They sat in silence for several minutes while servants brought small tables and placed plates of food on each. The smell of roast meat was heady. The evening was still, a slight breeze visible from the smoke.

"Eat, my friends. You must be hungry, I believe."

"Sure am. It's a heck of a drive from Khartoum." Monkton said. He lifted a large drumstick off his plate and munched away. "This is delicious. Fruit of your hunt?"

The Sheikh nodded his head and lifted the wicker lid off his plate.

"We consider bustard to be a delicacy, tastier than chicken, you see. You will try for yourselves. You took a long way around by Dinder, they told me."

"Scenic route. Looking at wildlife." Monkton laughed. "Wiser that our presence remains concealed."

"Yes, wiser. In these times, even innocent meetings may be misinterpreted. For me it is the same."

"I heard you've had unwelcome visitors at your office in Khartoum."

"I was not there, *Alhumdilillah*. My day has not yet come." The Sheikh touched his hand to his heart. He sat quiet and motionless for a while. Haydon saw he was murmuring silently under his breath and heard the click of prayer beads moving rhythmically in his long fingers. Then he spoke in low, soft tones. Haydon had to lean forward and strain to hear him. "I had thought my time of fighting was behind me."

"What happened?"

"They stormed into my office, shooting and throwing grenades." His voice was calm and unemotional. "Thanks be to God my guards were alert and immediately fired back. Three of the attackers were killed. Security forces captured one other. Hopefully from him we shall learn the reasons and who was the culprit behind it. For now, I must take measures to ensure my security."

"But you are an Islamic hero. A modern Saladin I've heard they call you." Monkton stroked his face. "Your efforts in Afghanistan, expelling the infidels from a Muslim land?"

"Please. I was a simple office administrator. Not a warrior like yourself."

"The *muj* saw it differently in Tora Bora. So, which of your enemies did this?"

"There are many who object that I collaborated with you people Monkton in Afghanistan." He beamed and nodded his head. "For this they see me as apostate, traitor to the Arab cause."

"Who?"

"Ah, my old friend, you who know so much about us, who speak our language so well." He chuckled. "Haven't you gathered into how many jagged pieces we are fragmented."

The Sheikh hesitated, then held his hands up, pointing with his fingers.

"Look at us. Sunni and Shia. Sufis, Muslim Brothers, Wahhabis, Salafists, Kharijites, Ismaelis, Alawites. Many more than all the divisions of your Christian religions – and how so well you killed each other over many centuries." He counted again with his fingers. "Then, you see, the nationalist antipathies amongst us – Palestinians of different sorts, Egyptians, Algerians, Iraqis, Libyans, Indonesians, Iranians, each with their own concerns, let alone the Palestinian Christians, Egyptian Copts, Syrian and Iraqi Baathists, Druzes, Yazidis and Kurds, and then the simple-minded madmen like Colonel Qaddaffi."

"For me it's uncomplicated. There are good guys and bad guys." Monkton stamped on a burning ember by his feet. "Black September, Hezbollah, Mughniyeh and Abu Nidal. These are bad guys. They seek to do us harm. Bombs in

Beirut, kidnappings, hijackings, assassinations. Commies and Soviets, those are bad guys. For me it's easy to understand who my enemies are. But who are yours?"

"My guess is one of those Palestinian splinter groups, probably Abu Nidal, those lunatics who are based in Baghdad."

"But your friend, Hassan el-Turabi, it was he who invited Abu Nidal to visit him here. He is striving to bring these disparate groups you talked about together under one flag."

"Such a thing would take a holy miracle, and even Turabi himself is not safe in his own capital. You invite a hyena into your house, you must expect to be eaten."

A servant collected the dishes and plates. They sat in silence, listening to the crackling of the fire.

"My friends. Enough talk of such things." The Sheikh stood up and held his hand over his heart. "Here all is peace and quiet, and we shall enjoy a sound sleep. Tomorrow, I shall drive you myself to see everywhere around my farm. Then we shall discuss more."

Jed and Hal had erected the tents in a grassy area and built a roaring campfire. Haydon lay awake, fully clothed, on a cramped canvas camp bed, listening to the nighttime sounds of the African bush. The cackling of jackals close by, in the distance the deep grunting of wild pig, the hoot of an owl which seemed to reverberate around his tent, other strange sounds he couldn't identify. He'd always enjoyed nighttime army exercises, although his memories all seemed to involve pouring rain and drenched and mouldy clothes, socks and kit. Here he could taste the dry dust from the long drive in the back of his throat.

Monkton was so confident in his relationship with the Sheikh. Haydon couldn't explain the subliminal itch that warned him the American's control was not as solid as he thought it was.

Especially as there wasn't a shred of evidence that the worm had turned. It was every agent runner's dream: launching your enemies against each other. That was an enormous opportunity. Glasson was right. The clear and present danger came from the traditional Palestinian groups. Probably Turabi and his big idea of forging the disparate groups together against the 'Far Enemy' was just a pipe dream.

Still, he'd keep his eyes peeled on their trip around the farm for any signs that weren't in keeping with the Utopian dream of a retired fighter out to grass.

Chapter 28

They bumped along rutted farm tracks and over hump-back bridges traversing irrigation canals for most of the morning. The shock absorbers of the old farm vehicle were shot, so Haydon held himself up off the seat by the door handle, avoiding the worst of the spine-jarring jolts. Monkton sat with the Sheikh in the back, who was seemingly oblivious to his driver's failure to avoid even the largest potholes. The air conditioning was not working, but they kept the windows closed to keep out the mosquitoes and the baking heat. Sweat was pouring down Haydon's back, which dried into salt almost immediately. He scratched at mosquito bites on his neck.

Getting out of the car, they inspected a modern dairy building, evidently a source of pride to the Sheikh. A herd of Friesian cows grazed in a nearby irrigated grass field, the improbable green in stark contrast to the stick-dry bush past the wooden fencing. The scale of the enterprise was impressive. According to Zaki, they utilised only ten-per cent of their land, but the flat green fields seemed to run on for tens of miles.

Haydon's eyes searched for signs of unusual construction. They passed fields of groundnuts and healthy-looking sorghum, then came to a long line of low wooden buildings, the size of a small town. They looked like barracks, he thought, noting barbed wire coils running around the periphery.

"At harvest time we employ 4,000 workers, you see. Giving work to so many peoples of Blue Nile province." The Sheikh smiled. "Now I shall show you my most beloved project."

Emerging from a large arcade of planted eucalyptus trees, they followed a track down the middle of a long field of sunflowers, their blazing faces pointing skywards. Water gushed down broad irrigation channels snaking through the field. Haydon heard water pumps thumping in the background.

"Helluva sight." Monkton shaded his eyes. "Where do you get that ferocious flow of water from."

"No, no, that is not the thing." The Sheikh pointed ahead. "Wait, you will see."

They emerged into a broad clearing. Long rows of tall, wooden hutches of widely differing shapes stretched along its length. They drove slowly along the line of hives, each one topped with a large and impenetrable black cloud of bees.

"This is my special wonder, you see." He pointed. "I have brought to here different types of beehive from so many countries. To discover which ones will flourish best here. My wish is to produce 100 tons of sunflower honey every year."

As they sat in silence and watched the clouds move and reform, Haydon listened to the mesmeric hum, which seemed to him like the sound of a cello tuning up.

They carried on down a trail leading to a small, thatched building on the edge of a long expanse of water. A wooden dock ran out into the water, a small speedboat moored alongside. To one side, a heavy diesel pump thudded away, pumping water up to a canal. Getting down from the car, the Sheikh led them to a shaded shack, where a spindly servant in a white *jellabiya* waited with a tray and offered them tall glasses of cold water. They sat in wicker armchairs in the welcome shade, looking out over the lake, draining their glasses and holding them out for refilling.

"The Roseiras reservoir, my friends. Fed by the waters of the Blue Nile. God's grace."

"Look at this peaceful scene. It could have been the same a thousand years ago."

Monkton shaded his eyes with his hand and stared.

They watched a long fishing boat floating slowly past, nets strung out behind making the smallest ripple in the flat calm water, two fishermen standing motionless side by side.

The Sheikh turned to Monkton and smiled.

"Tell me, my friend. I think you have not taken a sudden interest in farming. Why have you made this long trip to visit me here?"

Monkton rubbed his face and leaned forward.

"We've picked up chatter about plans for attacks in Western countries. In Europe, maybe even against the USA homeland." Monkton frowned. "I need your help. Where are these threats coming from? Are they credible? You hear many things from your contacts amongst these groups in Khartoum."

"Might it be the same people who attacked my office? They shot up a mosque earlier that day, so I think them likely to be secular. Abu Nidal, as I told you last night, or Hamas. But soon the *Mukhabarat* will discover these culprits, they are interrogating the man they captured at my office. Just a few days, then I shall know. Meanwhile, I will increase my security, build higher walls, post more guards, install more cameras."

"If the same group that went for you is now aiming to attack us," Monkton said, "then once again we will share a common enemy."

"Perhaps. How can I judge? I don't know your source."

"The chatter is about plots emanating from this country."

The Sheikh paused and sipped his water, then placed the glass down and remained silent for a while, the click-clicking of prayer beads audible. Haydon watched his lips move silently. Then he turned to face Monkton and smiled.

"There are many who disapprove of my work together with you in Afghanistan. They call me a collaborator. They see America as the master that guides the strings of their Israeli puppets, you see. They think that without you, Israel would lose their power. And with President Bush's buildup of troops in my homeland, your so-called Desert Shield, these people are saying this is the same as it was with the Russians in Afghanistan. Worse even, for ours is the land of the holiest sites of Islam. And if these troops invade Kuwait and Iraq from my country, well, for this reason I am feeling uncertain, you see. Yes, uncertain."

"What causes us nightmares is we believe these people intend to use teams of clean-skins," Haydon cleared his throat, "ordered to break Islamic strictures if they need, to avoid detection, to shave their beards, even to drink alcohol. We would be blind to such people."

"My brother." The Sheikh raised his hands, as if in prayer. "We know each other so well in these years and have broken bread under the stars. We have taken risks with our lives together. But we are each of us constrained. I told you, I am living here to make a new life with my family. What I have shown you today is my dream that I am now making it real. They send people to kill me, but my love is for my sons and my honey and my horses, and for these fields and this river."

"But you will warn me, if you come across intel about this threat to America, to help us avoid another Beirut on my watch?" Monkton stared into his eyes.

"You should not doubt it, friend." The Sheikh stroked his wispy beard. "We will face these dangers together, as we have faced them side by side in the Zazi mountains."

They spent the night camped on the shores of a small lake in the Dinder Game Reserve. Haydon relished the isolation of being in the bush, out of contact with the world. Jed and Hal had built a fire, and he could smell the alluring aroma of roasting meat. Monkton produced a bottle of Bourbon, and the two men sat quietly drinking and watching an orange sun setting over the water. Sleek antelopes and grunting warthogs grazed side by side on the shores of the lake, and large flocks of ducks and geese flighted in, settling with splashes on the brackish water. At one point, the animals raised their heads in unison and stayed motionless, before rushing away into the undergrowth, fleeing some unseen predator.

It had been so much simpler in Belfast. High walls separating two warring parties, the so called 'Peace Wall' which kept the Catholics and Protestants apart. A few splinter groups, true, but two identifiable sides. No mistaking who the enemy was. But the complexity of the Middle East was baffling. Endless options of multiple opposing motives to consider. Monkton reached over and filled up Haydon's drink. He filled his own, and they clinked glasses.

"Signs that cause you sticky-ass, buddy?" Monkton said.

"I can't decide." Haydon scratched his head and waved away a persistent mosquito. "The guy gives me this odd impression of naivety. But perhaps it's that he's super clever. I saw no discernible signs of anything sinister, although we saw the bits of the vast property that he wanted us to see."

"The war against Saddam to free Kuwait is coming soon, and there will be loud bangs. This is causing him angst." The American rubbed at his moustache. "But I figure he needs our help in protecting himself from whoever went after him last week. I buy the idea that a lot of radical groups, Islamic and Palestinian, hate that he collaborated with us in Afghanistan. He's not the most popular guy in the class we thought he was. He's not Saladin reincarnated after all."

"So who went after him?"

"My money is on Hezbollah." Monkton scowled. "Iran

hates the Saudis. That makes most sense. And I'd be surprised if I'm not high on their list. God knows what they learned from poor Bill Buckley. But maybe The Sheikh is right, Abu Nidal are crazy, it could have been a contract hit."

Haydon took a slug of his drink, then leaned towards the American.

"I feel duly reassured Pete. That this guy is on the back foot, I don't see him causing us trouble. I'm more concerned with Hamas seeking payback." He smiled. "I don't like to admit it, but I'm coming round to the view that you and Mark may be right."

"There. That didn't hurt so bad, did it!" Monkton slapped his arm. "Hey, let me fill you up."

Chapter 29

A stocky bodyguard, his khaki waistcoat holding spare magazines tight over a white *jellabiya*, stood facing outwards by the entrance flap, carbine slung over his shoulder. His red checked *kaffiyeh* marked him out as a Gulf Arab. On a large Persian rug in the centre of the tent, five men sat cross-legged in a circle, their faces lit by oil lamps hanging from tent poles. Their palms faced upwards as they mumbled a long prayer, then they fell silent.

The Sheikh sat motionless, except for the elegant fingers on his hand, which turned the ebony beads on a long string with an audible clicking sound. He breathed slowly and recited a mantra under his breath. Pausing, he turned his head and stared, one by one, at each of the four men. He talked in a soft voice.

"You are the closest to me of all. We are as brothers. Therefore, I am troubled that one of us may have breached our sacred bond. Then I think this cannot be possible, for you are each as if a piece of my heart."

He fell silent again. *How could it be so?* That even in the smallest group, operational security could not be assured. Through the canvas, he heard the faraway barking of a hyena.

People said hyenas laughed. Maybe they did. Were they laughing at him? Could one of these friends really have betrayed him?

"I have learned from our visitors today that our enemy has obtained details about our latest planning." He paused and closed his eyes, then continued. "These *kuffar* told me that the attacks will employ only *makhfia*, hidden ones, for the operation, which they had learned will be attacks on their own countries – Britain and America. How could they have discovered this? We discussed amongst ourselves only at our last meeting, and we have not yet set off on this new direction."

Again, his eyes rested one by one on each of the men, searching their eyes for signs of fear or guilt. Each man held his gaze and shook their head. It was impossible that one of them, comrades from the war in Afghanistan, blood-brothers, could be an informer. But what other explanation could there be?

"Firstly, I ask each of you. Have any of you disobeyed my order and talked of these things by telephone, or by radio, or by satellite phone? Or have you spoken in a public place where you might have been overheard?"

"Ya Sheikh, as you ordered, I, myself, recruited the first cell of operatives." His secretary, Rashid al-Duri spoke in measured tones. "I met only the one man in person. In Omdurman, after Friday prayers, in a crowded and noisy place. That is in front of the tomb of Sheikh Hamed al Nil. The man called himself by the name Saif al-Adel. We could not have been overheard there. Impossible."

"How did you encounter this man? Could he be an informer?"

"I believe not, *Inshallah*. Our friend Mohammed Atef sent him to us. The two served together in the Egyptian Army, and he proved himself to Atef during important actions for *al-Jama'a al-Islamiyya*. An explosives expert, he has a degree in engineering. He is under sentence of death in Egypt and has declared himself openly to be *takfir*."

"If he was sent by Atef then we can trust him."

"He came to Khartoum together with another man, that will make up this first cell, he is also a bomb expert. Jordanian. Ex-special forces. Who calls himself Bebiker al-Urduni. These two worked together wiring vehicles in Kabul. Successful and secure, they operated like ghosts. They came here attending the OAU Conference for an NGO, that is their cover. They departed for Amman the same evening, hours after I had met the man."

"Might they have spoken by phone?"

"The man is operationally experienced and conscious of security. I insisted we must avoid all communication by phones or radios. The two men stayed together at the Forum Hotel, unlikely therefore that they spoke by phone, but, *janni*, perhaps there might have been a lapse." Rashid took off his spectacles and started to clean them.

"You see, that may be something." The Sheikh made a gesture with his hand, as if flicking away a mosquito. "My contact in the *Mukhabarat* recounted to me about an operation by the Americans. To pressure the Government here to close a Palestinian Hamas training base near Port Sudan. They suspect the involvement of an Englishman. And so it is interesting this Englishman is the manager of this hotel Forum."

This is a signal, he thought. The Divine lays us clues to follow, righteous arrows pointing towards our destiny, and we must listen for that inner voice. He had been right to be open with his friend Monkton, to invite him as a guest to inspect the farm, showing him what he wanted him to see. The American was undoubtedly clever, but he was also imperious, and could not bring himself to believe that anyone could oppose the might of the USA. So he had fallen into the trap and revealed what he knew. Handing over the initiative and providing a warning before any damage was done.

"My brothers. Let us consider carefully what should best be done. We need to find out whether this leak has to do with this Englishman. Perhaps we should mount an operation to infiltrate the hotel. Rashid, consider the options and advise us."

"Yes, Sheikh, I will produce options by tomorrow."

"We must keep focus on tight security. Rashid is correct. Cells must be small. No one must have the complete picture." He stroked his beard and smiled. "Soon the Americans will invade Iraq. Their armies in our holy land will then desecrate our soil with Arab blood. That will be the righteous moment to strike them in their hearts. We will move stealthily, but quickly with our plans."

"*Inshallah, ya Sheikh*" the men intoned.

"I thank you, my brothers."

He stood up, wrapped his shawl around his shoulder, and walked slowly out of the tent.

Chapter 30

Khartoum, November 1990

Charlie had a nuclear-scale hangover. When he woke up, he was alone; the sheets were damp with sweat and the air conditioning unit was clanking out a metallic throb, losing an unequal struggle with the burning heat. He tried, but couldn't remember the girl leaving. In fact, he couldn't remember much at all after they'd got back to the hotel. He recalled giggling and kissing in the stairwell. He pressed his fingers into his temples and closed his eyes.

They'd hooked up the evening before at the Grand Hotel, a feisty Australian aid worker called Shelley. Flaming red hair and a tattoo on her belly button. Sitting next to each other at the bar overlooking the Nile, each of them sipping lemonade and looking morose. They'd ended up consuming a bottle and a half of his secret supply of Johnny Walker, wrapped in brown paper bags, back on the Forum's Summit Bar terrace. She'd been worth the hangover, he thought, but it wasn't clever. Dirtying his doorstep and then some, drawing attention when he was supposed to be staying under the radar and on high alert.

If a guest had reported him to the Religious Police, they could have sentenced him to 50 lashes. In public. At least there had been kudos from beatings back at public school – you could walk a little taller, limp around a little, exhibit some chutzpah. Here you were, correctly, regarded as a buffoon if you allowed yourself to get caught in a public display of drunkenness. The regime took particular pleasure in catching out westerners. And he had no diplomatic cover.

He took a cold shower and dressed. Looking in the mirror, a tired and aging face glowered back. He felt a gnawing ball in the pit of his stomach. The omnipresent weight of boredom and anxiety was increasingly overpowering, the resultant hangovers too frequent. How to get out of this rut? He'd tell Haydon he needed to be replaced. That he wasn't going to make it. His guilt about Tom's death bit at him, fiercely, and he no longer believed what he was doing would atone for it.

Intel reports indicated Hamas was long gone, and there had been no signs of hostile surveillance.

Shuffling down the stairs, he crossed his office and entered the recording room. He'd been avoiding this chore and had fallen behind with logging the tapes. He was to meet Haydon the next day, so he couldn't prevaricate. Luckily, the hotel was nearly empty, just four rooms occupied, plus his guardian angels, Des and Harry. Haydon had agreed that if there were no security concerns by the next week, he'd withdraw them. Charlie didn't really care, their presence didn't bother him any more, they were amiable enough company. He didn't even worry that they were probably reporting to Haydon about his increased cavorting. It would give credence to his request. It suited him if Haydon came to believe he was losing his marbles.

He fast-forwarded each recorder in turn, stopping to check sections at random, finding nothing of interest to log. Sloppy work. He selected the machine for 'Room 3' and pressed play, then heard the telltale hiss-clunk that indicated a mike was malfunctioning. He called through to Harry's room and asked him to go and check out the setup. After finishing with the audiotapes, he did a quick run through of the video feeds.

While he was fast-forwarding the reception area video recording, some instinct led him to press the pause button. He rewound and played back a section. A man's distorted face peered at the camera, a hand seeming to reach out to touch the lens. Sallow face, black beard, somehow threatening. He must have been leaning right over the reception desk. Charlie recognised the face of a guest who had checked into Room 3 two days before, just for one night. Unusual, he'd thought; their guests typically stayed for several nights at a time.

He went into his office and pulled out the box of registration cards. Rifling thought them, he found the card for the last occupant of Room 3. *'Mohammed Idris. Manager. Company for Levant Trading. Beirut.'* There was a knock on his door. Harry's round face appeared.

"Odd thing, Guv." Harry slumped into a chair opposite Charlie's desk, scratching his head and then brushing dandruff off his shoulder. "Looks to me like someone gouged the mike out of its hidey-hole, then tried to stuff it back in. Did it badly, and the wire got detached. Should work now. Maybe I'm paranoid—"

"I agree but." Charlie fidgeted in his chair, then put his head in his hands. He felt ghastly. He looked up. "A random discovery of a well-hidden mike? I don't think so. The last occupant. Look, here's his card."

He handed the registration card to Harry. "Might he have been casing this place? Look at this."

Charlie played back the clip from the reception camera.

"He's scoping the camera all right." Harry peered at the screen. "But who is he? He obviously doesn't care that his face is being recorded. Maybe he's thick. Did he check out already?"

"Yesterday. We need to look at the feeds from when he

arrived. I'm seeing Haydon tomorrow and he's going to have to decide." Charlie leaned back, linked his hands behind his neck, and yawned. "Where's Des?"

"Day off. Picnic with svelte British Midland stewardesses on the river. Lucky sod. He'll be pissed by now, might even get eaten by a croc."

They sat side by side, listening to recordings and viewing tapes. Nothing. After ten minutes, Charlie realised he couldn't focus. The screens had become a blur. He had an awful headache and was feeling sick.

"Let's take a break. I'll finish them later."

"Guv, this could be important. Might be an imminent threat."

"I'm on to it. Will you report to Haydon. Tell him I'll bring him the tapes and logs first thing tomorrow morning."

"I don't think we should–"

"–ask him to run an urgent search on Mohammed Idris and the Company for Levant Trading in Beirut." He got up and waved Harry towards the door. "For sure they're phony names but you never know."

Charlie locked his office door and headed upstairs. He really needed a siesta, and he could finish logging the tapes in the evening. Entering his bedroom, he turned the air conditioning to the maximum. He set the alarm for six, then threw himself down on the bed. After a while, he sat up and reached into the bedside table drawer and pulled out a bottle of sleeping pills. He took two and put the bottle back. After a couple of minutes, he reached in again and took a third. Then he pulled the pillow over his head.

It was pitch dark. He had no idea where he was. Images

from a dream flashed across the screen of his mind. He was running through a muddy field, his bare feet struggling with every sticky step.

Someone was chasing him. *Who?* He untangled himself from the sheet, then used it to wipe sweat off his cheeks.

The only light came from the eerie red numerals of the alarm clock. 01.13. *Could he have been out for the count for nearly 12 hours?* He must have slept right through the alarm. He reached over and fumbled for a bottle of water. Sitting up in the bed, he swigged it until it was empty, then lay back on the pillows, gasping. He felt wide awake. He'd better go and do the logging. What a drag. He took a torch from the bedside drawer and got out of bed.

He heard a door slam on the floor below. Probably that Swiss couple from UNHCR having another of their explosive rows. They always looked so placid, but the girl was forever baiting her long-suffering partner, a quiet man with a drooping moustache and a morose face. He heard the noise of footsteps running, like in his dream, and then a high-pitched shout. Better go over and quieten them down, summon his non-existent diplomatic skills, before other guests started complaining. He pinched himself, got up, and wrapped a sarong around his waist.

Pulling on a tee-shirt, he was about to switch on the light when he heard the unmistakable *pop-pop-pop* of small arms automatic fire. Followed by screaming. Another burst and the screaming stopped. He remained stock still and listened. Cracking open his bedroom door, he thought he could hear someone moaning. The sound seemed to come from the floor below, close to the hotel entrance. He picked up his bleeper from the bedside table and carefully composed a message – '*CODE RED ALL FLOORS*' and pressed send. It would go to Harry and Des.

He kept his service weapon, a Browning 9mm Hi-power

automatic, locked in a drawer in his office desk. Maybe he could get down there, but he'd have to pass through the reception area. He crept down the stairs, one at a time, and turned into the foyer. His shoe-less feet stepped on something warm and sticky. Shining his torch, he realised with horror he was walking through a trail of blood.

Peering cautiously around the counter, he found himself staring into the distorted face of Harry. The security man was lying on his back and tried to raise his head, his mouth moving but no sound came. Charlie read agony in his eyes, then his head fell back with a crump and he was still. Charlie leaned down and touched his neck, feeling for a pulse. Nothing. He prised a pistol gripped in Harry's stiff hand, noticing the word 'LOVE' tattooed in a red heart on his forearm. Checking it was loaded, he crouched down under the reception counter and listened.

Chapter 31

There was a loud explosion that sounded as if it came from the first floor, where most of the bedrooms were situated, followed by the noise of glass smashing. A hand grenade? *Shit!* The gunmen must be going down the line of rooms and checking them individually. More shouts and screams, then a long burst of automatic fire. The phone started ringing loudly on the reception desk. It rang and rang, just above his head. He feared it would attract the attention of the gunmen and willed it to stop.

With the sound of explosions and gunfire, someone was bound to raise the alarm with the police or security services. *How long would it take them to react?* He checked his watch. 01.22. If he could get to his office and conceal himself in the recording room, he could use the direct phone there to ring Haydon and summon help. Closing his eyes, he made a conscious effort to slow his breathing. He had to stay calm.

Moving in a low crouch, his shoulder pressing into the wall, he felt his way along the corridor with his fingertips. He didn't dare to turn on his torch. He thought back to the exercises at Oxley. *Reaching the target unobserved.* Minimum movement, like a Japanese *butoh* dancer. He could make out his office door was ajar. He was certain he'd left it locked. He double-checked the pistol was cocked and the safety catch off. The sound of a bullet ricocheting off the walls behind him screeched past as he edged his body around the door frame. He switched his torch on, rushed in, finger on the trigger, swinging round to cover the back of the room. Nothing.

The room was in disarray, his desk and filing cabinets were overturned and paper was strewn everywhere. But the bookcase was still in place. Thank God they hadn't found the concealed entrance to the recording room. There was the sound of soft footsteps on the landing above. They must be close to his bedroom now. Was this Hamas payback? *Was he the target of this attack?* He reached down and unclipped the hidden catch, pulling back on the heavy bookcase. He slipped inside and pulled it closed behind him, making sure he heard the audible click of the steel latch falling into place, securing the door fast.

He rushed over to the desk, grabbed the receiver and dialled Haydon's home number. It rang and rang. *Pick up! Pick up!*

"Yes. What–"

"–Haydon, Charlie." He talked urgently over the sleepy voice. "Code Red. Repeat Code Red. Gunmen in the hotel. Unknown number. Automatic fire. Grenades. Harry is down, repeat Harry is down. Other casualties. Number unknown. I'm in the safe room. Request immediate assistance."

"Des?"

"I don't know, he's been out all day. Day off."

"Keep the line open, Charlie. Stay where you are, you'll be fine in there. I'll ring you back within ten with further instructions." The line went dead. He checked his watch. 01.27.

He reached over and turned the light switch. Nothing. Maybe the fuse had blown. He felt his knees trembling. He'd been so bored with life that morning. From boredom to horror in the flash of an eye. He sat down, hands pressed flat on the table, staring ahead fixedly. He tried to meditate, breathing deeply and focusing on his breath. How long was it going to take for Haydon to rally the security forces to get to the hotel?

He tried turning on the video screens to see if he could identify the position of the gunmen, but there was no power. Had they found the main fuse? He drummed his fingers on the desk and waited for the phone to ring. There was a muffled explosion. Close by. It sounded as if something had exploded in his office. Different in tone from the others, more of a whoosh. He felt a bass aftershock thump him on his chest.

He felt a powerful urge to get out and try to rescue his guests, if any of them had survived. But Haydon had ordered him to stay put and wait for his call. He checked his watch for the umpteenth time. 01.33. It was quiet outside, no sound of gunfire, *Had they gone?*

The phone rang. Charlie reached over and grabbed it.

"Security forces are surrounding the hotel." Haydon's voice was calm. "Witnesses have reported seeing gunmen driving off in a truck. Des is close to the hotel and is coming to escort you out. Don't open the door until he tells you. How are you holding up there?"

"How the fuck do you think, Haydon?" Charlie slammed his fist on the table. "Harry's dead. God knows how many of my guests. *Christ!*"

"Stay on the line. I have incoming comms."

The line went silent. Charlie sniffed the air. There was a pungent smell of burning plastic.

"Des has entered the hotel. He'll be with you shortly. Hold tight."

Charlie noticed thick, black smoke seeping from the gap under the bookshelf door and simultaneously heard a crackling noise. Then came the realisation they must have set fire to his office. Probably tossed in an incendiary grenade. Maybe they set the whole hotel on fire before pulling out. He needed to get out before it took hold; if he stayed put, he'd suffocate. There were no windows, no ventilation in this 'safe room'. The only exit was through his office and out into the corridor.

"Haydon, they've set fire to my office. Smoke is leaking into the safe room. I need to evacuate right now."

"OK, go ahead and make it out to the corridor, Des will meet you there in a couple of minutes."

Not more than four strides through his office, he thought, at most. He'd race through the flames and hope like hell that gunmen weren't waiting for him at the end of the corridor. Taking a half empty bottle of water, he took off his sarong and soaked it, winding it round his face to make a damp mask.

"OK, I'm leaving now. Wish me luck."

"Get on with it. See you shortly."

He reached over and pressed down on the metal door catch. It didn't move. The mechanism seemed stiff. He pulled the door towards him and tried again. Nothing. He gripped hard on the metal handle and leaned back with all his strength. The door didn't budge. He looked around for something to hammer at the catch with. Finding a bronze paper weight he smashed it repeatedly at the mechanism. Eventually the catch snapped right off, leaving only a small stub. He tried rushing at the door with his shoulder, but he knew it would be a fruitless fight against a steel door.

He grabbed the phone receiver.

"Haydon, the door won't budge, the catch on my side is bust. I'm trapped."

"Hold on, Charlie. I'll stay on the line with you. Breathe slowly, conserve your strength. Des has a fire extinguisher and he'll be attacking the fire from the other side. He's going to get you out. The important thing is not to panic. Fire engines are on their way. Slow your breathing, remember."

The acrid smoke was thick and rising. Pointing his torch across the small room, he could hardly make out the far wall. He heard a muffled voice from the other side of the door but couldn't make out what it was saying. Des was going to get to him. He'd get the fire under control. Charlie coughed, feeling a burning sensation in his throat.

He sat down on the floor. It struck him as ridiculous to be trapped in a 'safe room'. It was only a matter of time before he passed out, unless Des was able to open the door from the other side and pull him out. He looked at his watch. 1.37. Time was going so slowly. He lay flat on the floor, holding the wet sarong over his face and eyes, phone receiver glued to his ear. There would be more air down there. Slow breathing. He closed his eyes and started to say the Lord's Prayer.

"You've got to stay alert Charlie." Haydon's voice echoed through his head. "Remember when I saved you from getting on Vispoli's jet? At Ciampino."

"Yes, I was pissed with you for doing that."

"Yes, I was pissed with you too. But it worked out. I saved your skin."

"You put my skin in danger in the first place." Charlie laughed, then started to cough uncontrollably.

There was a sound of hammering from the other side of the door. "He's coming for you Charlie. Hold on."

"Charlie. You hear Des there?" Haydon's voice was faint. The muffled voice beyond the door sounded distant. "He's nearly with you. He's working on the door."

Charlie could no longer hear Haydon's voice. He had closed his eyes and saw a vivid image of Tom standing above him, a large spliff in his hand, looking down and reaching out a free hand, gesturing to pull him up. Behind Tom, a uniformed drummer was banging time on a large regimental drum.

"Live on the edge! Die on the edge!" Tom laughed, and the drum banged. "That's the way we wanted it, buddy."

"But I like it here, Tom." Charlie smiled. "I'm the manager, you know. Sorry about the mess up. We didn't play the game well; we should have done it better. But at least we weren't eaten by crocs."

"Charlie, you have to stay awake. Pinch yourself hard

please." Haydon's voice was a faraway rumble.

He started to shake. He couldn't breathe any more. His hand went to his throat, then he lost consciousness.

Chapter 32

They sat staring out of the car window at the smoldering ruin. Monkton handed Haydon a cigarette, then reached over and flicked open a Zippo lighter.

"Don't blame yourself, buddy, focus your energies on fixing the scumbags who done it."

"I spoke to Salah el-Fateh this morning." Haydon sighed. "He says he has leads. I interpret that to mean he'll nab the buggers if he feels it's in his interest. Which is improbable."

"We'll find 'em." Monkton slammed his fist into the palm of his hand. "Then we'll make 'em pay."

The two men stepped out of Monkton's Land Cruiser and walked into the wreckage of what had been the Forum Hotel, picking their way through smoking ash and lumps of fallen masonry. The stench of burning meat caused Haydon to gag.

"Nothing to see." Monkton nodded. "It's completely destroyed."

"Bastards tossed incendiary grenades all around the hotel then scarpered." Haydon puffed on his cigarette. "A while later the police rolled up, all flashing lights and sirens and flabby salutes, pistols drawn, like real heroes."

Monkton touched Haydon's shoulder. "Got any doubts this was anything other than Hamas payback?"

Haydon nodded, then kicked at a burning ember. He reached down and picked up a blackened fire extinguisher, then tossed it aside.

"After half an hour fire engines rolled up, more flashing lights and loud bells, but they didn't have any water and there was no hydrant nearby. So they lounged around and watched as the hotel burned. The fire left no signs of incriminating items, which is the one positive." He gestured. "Let's go over there, I want to find that steel door that jammed and trapped my guy."

They walked around mounds of fallen masonry and twisted metal, glancing at strange misshapen objects, impossible to recognise. Stepping over a pile of burnt bricks Haydon pointed to an oblong metal shape, twisted and scorched.

"That's the bloody door. My security man Des did his utmost to force it open, but was driven back by the intense heat. He got badly burned in the process, we've flown him to the UK for specialised treatment." Haydon started picking through the rubble.

"What did they use?"

"Phosphorous grenades. Russian made. Des found an unexploded canister by the hotel entrance. They burn at 1,000 degrees."

"Other clues?"

"If there were any, they went up in smoke with the recording machines." Haydon scratched his head. "You know Pete, I was on the line with Charlie Lomax all the way until the end. He died of smoke inhalation. Faded away as I listened to his coughing getting louder and louder. That was so painful, so painful. Nothing I could do, just tell him platitudes, reassure him that Des would rescue him shortly. Even when I knew it was too late, and he was done."

Haydon pulled on his cigarette and inhaled. When he'd been shaving that morning, the hollow face and rheumy eyes that stared back at him from the mirror had shocked him. He felt shrunken by what had been the worst week of his life. It had been his call to keep SEAMLESS in play. Now his operation had sunk without trace, and Charlie's death weighed on his conscience. He felt a stab of pain in his heart.

In some strange way, he'd loved the guy. He'd been irresponsible to a degree that Haydon had never dared to be, with an abundance of picaresque charm. For him life was one continuous adventure, the answer to any opportunity for mischief was inevitably 'Yes'. The anvil of guilt banged at his temples.

"The Embassy is treating it as a consular matter. I'm out of the picture. Two Brits dead. Three other nationalities. Two Sudanese staff. Forensics are having difficulty identifying remains. We haven't found enough to send home in a box; we're collecting random ashes from around here." He pointed, then banged his hand against his head.

"Survivors? Witnesses?"

"A French couple, NGO workers staying at the hotel. They were out on the veranda by the roof bar. God knows what they were doing in the middle of the night, the bar was closed. Lucky them. They hid under the bar counter, stayed there until flames forced them out. Somehow they managed to clamber down the side of the hotel, they must have been rock climbers? A calm pair, I met them at the French Embassy. They had nothing to offer, didn't see a thing. They just heard the shooting and the screams and explosions and stayed hidden."

Haydon struggled to hear as a police car siren accelerated down the street.

"We've heard chatter the op was contracted out. A sort of operational swap." Haydon coughed, then brushed ash off his trousers. "Like the PFLP did with the Japanese Red Army in the Lod airport massacre. Hamas will repay the compliment later, in some other bloody venue."

"I buy that. I have sources reporting it was the same fanatics that went after the Sheikh. Hallmarks of ex-military special forces, most likely Egyptian. Well planned, ruthless, well executed. Quick and out."

"Any idea of which group they belong to?" Haydon ran his hand through his hair. They wandered back through the rubble towards the car.

"The Sheikh – I spoke to him yesterday – says it has the tell-tales of the Abu Nidal Organisation, the ANO. They're *takfiri* and use multiple cover names – The Palestinian National Liberation Movement, Black June, the Revolutionary Arab Brigades, Revolutionary Egypt, to name a few." Monkton opened the door of the car and stepped in. "The most brutal of the Palestinian groups, Libyan based. Their leader, Sabri al-Banna, is a psychopath, a killer, a drunkard and a master of disguise and concealment."

"Palestine. Always Palestine at the epicentre of terror. How the hell are we ever going to solve it? Decade in, decade out. Endless iterations of Palestinian radical groups. One goes, another comes. Whack-a-mole, but with calamitous consequences. Meanwhile I'm under fire from all sides, London, my ambassador. I feel like a deflated punch-bag. Honestly, Pete, it's like I don't understand anything any more."

"These are dangerous times, my friend. We need to up our embassies' security to the max. You and I could be on any of these group's lists."

Next morning, at his office at the Embassy, he took a call on the scrambler phone from Greg Harbut. "We've got a 'possible' on one of the guys you queried."

"Go ahead Greg." He reached for his notepad and pen. The whirring sound of the crypto mechanism made it hard to hear. Leaning forward, he pressed his ear to the receiver.

"One name – Abdelrahman Yassin. The Jordanian passports flagged nothing for that name, but our GID liaison reckons, with high confidence, the photo resembles an ex-Egyptian special forces colonel named Salah Ahmed al-Din. Explosives expert, Soviet trained. Nothing on the other man, er, Hassan el-Mahgoub."

"Recent sightings or history on the guy?"

"Our GID guy was posted in Cairo back then, which is why he recognised the photo, or thinks he did. He says this Salah al-Din fled Egypt in a hurry in 1988, after a failed plot against Mubarak. No subsequent sighting, no flags, never a reason for us to know about him or follow him."

"Affiliations?

"GID reckon likely Egyptian Islamic Jihad. He may also use another *nom de guerre* – Saif al-Adel. That intel origi-nates from chatter, comms intercepts, picked up on our computer run. One report has someone of the same name in Libya operating with ANO."

"Saif al-Adel translates as 'sword of justice'. A common enough pseudonym amongst these radical fighters."

"Any progress on the identities of the attackers?"

"The ANO reference dovetails with intel I've picked up. American cousins are getting similar. I'm looking for local connections, and for a guy calling himself Harun al-Rashid. It's crazy, they use so many pseudonyms you wonder if they even know themselves who they really are."

"There's been a lot in the tabloids here about Lomax. Dip-lomat's son burnt to death, pictures of photogenic playboy in dark glasses. Are Brits safe abroad?" Harbutt's gruff voice took on a jovial tone, which put Haydon on his guard. "The pressure is building in Century House, Haydon. A view is circulating that SEAMLESS has been a costly disaster. Ques-tions being asked. With your name attached."

"Fuck them!" Haydon's face flushed. "I've lost an impor-tant agent and you can be sure I'm going to find the bastards."

"Haydon, getting results quickly is going to help us all out."

By lunchtime, he had a splitting headache. He locked up

his office and took the back stairs down to the underground car park at a trot. He would go home and sleep. As he reached out to open his car door, a hand reached out and gripped his arm. He swung around. It was Yahya Abdelaziz, standing by a pillar. The usually urbane lawyer looked shaken and disheveled.

"I've been waiting for you Haydon. I needed to speak to you, you see, away from the office."

"Can it wait please, Yahya. I need to get going."

"You won't want it to wait."

"Speak louder, I can't hear you."

"You must tell no one what I say, Haydon. Not your bosses, especially. I know you will wish to rush to your American friend. But if you do so, it will become catastrophe for me and my family, and for others. And you will learn no more." Haydon saw anguish on the man's face and read fear. "I need your promised word."

"Go on." Haydon's mind was whirring. Where was this coming from?

"I will, but you must then not ask me how I know it, or why, or anything. It just only is for you to know. *Mazboot?* Agreed?"

"Agreed, but why?"

"It is so dangerous a matter. Therefore, I require your word of honour." Haydon leaned forward to catch what he was saying. "I shall not speak of it again, even if it may cost my relationship with the Embassy."

"Yahya. I hear you." He looked the lawyer in the eyes. "My friend, you have my word I will never repeat what you tell me to anybody, and we will not talk of it again, unless you raise it."

"Listen. One thing. It is so." His face seemed to twitch as his eyes darted back and forth around the garage. "The man who gave the order for this attack on the hotel is by name

Rashid al-Duri. He is private secretary to the Sheikh."

Haydon felt a sharp intake of breath. He realised that on a subliminal level, he had already known this.

"How certain are you?"

Yahya released his grip on Haydon's arm and put his hand over his heart. "I know it surely to be true."

"I trust you Yahya, and I value this information." Haydon said. "One more thing. These three names – Saif al-Adel, Abdelrahman Yassin and Salah Ahmed al-Din. They may even be the same man or not. If you hear of any of them, please tell me."

"I will remember these names."

"And if there is something you require from me, believe me, I recognise a debt of gratitude to you."

The Sheikh

Chapter 33

Haydon sat in a chair set back from the bedroom window and scanned the street through binoculars. Nothing out of the ordinary. The skinnies in their usual spot, lounging in their dented white Datsun saloon in the shade of a mango tree on the far side of the road. No other inhabited cars or unusual people lurking suspiciously. A *haboob* was starting to blow; the wind was rising and red dust clouds swirled around the line of trees that fringed the road in front of his house. The frequent dust storms often lasted three or four days and covered hundreds of miles.

He'd tried to sleep, but his mind was too busy. What Yahya had told him had turned things upside down. Did Rashid al-Duri use the pseudonym Harun al-Rashid? That would be poor tradecraft, juxtaposing names so closely. But, if so, what was Abdelrahman Yassin's connection to the Afghan-Arabs? And what motive could the Sheikh possibly have to order a major attack on a small hotel in Khartoum, where the only known connection would be to Yassin, who had stayed there briefly, and only once?

So the Sheikh was not, after all, the retired *mujahid* and wannabe farmer he wanted them to believe, but was directing armed operations in country, and also likely to be the one planning attacks on western capitals. None of it added up, but there was no reason for the lawyer to mislead him. Yahya had been nervous, more than nervous, he'd been downright scared; he hadn't faked that. He was betraying someone dangerous, but who? The only motive for the attack that made sense was that Hamas, or elements of the Sudanese security establishment, had traced Charlie back to the Forum and held him responsible for the closure of the Erkowit camp. Payback. Simple.

Walking over to the fridge, he took out a beer, then sat sipping it, staring down over the street. He considered breaking his word to Yahya and reporting the conversation to London. He could do his best to protect the lawyer's identity, hiding behind informant confidentiality, but Glasson would squeeze him, and he'd end up having to reveal Yahya's name. And if he got rough with Yahya, Haydon judged the lawyer would clam up, or worse still, do a runner. It wasn't the right move. He needed him to remain in play, hoping he'd provide further pieces of intel to help build the solid case he needed to present to London.

Glasson had bought into Monkton's story that the Agency effectively controlled their Afghan-Arab allies and could deploy them at will. The mighty dollar ruled. No way was 'C' going to cross the Americans, not without unequivocal proof they were wrong, and even then? He would have to provide corroboration from other sources. He had got lucky with this intel, but it would be wise to keep it to himself until he could make such a strong case that Glasson had no option but to act.

Meanwhile, he'd treat Yahya with a soft touch. Recruiting him wouldn't be straightforward, but he'd get it done.

He noticed a flash of movement in the street. He picked up his binos and focused in. A jogger caught in the storm? Unusual. Then he saw that it was Lena, hair tied back and wearing a pink sweatband. He got up, jogged down the stairs, and hurried out into the garden to open the side gate.

They lay silent, side by side, spooning, Haydon hugging

her tightly, eyes open. He watched the violent storm knocking against the windowpanes, red sand pattering insistently as if demanding entry. He felt cut off from the world, stroking her hair gently, smelling the scent on her shoulders. There was nothing he needed to remember, no sharp thoughts or admonishments pushing up from his subconscious. He felt fully in the moment. The ball of anxiety he'd felt painfully stabbing at his chest this last week had vanished.

He'd opened the gate, and she'd rushed into his arms. Slamming it behind them, they'd run the gauntlet of the storm, sand stinging the backs of their legs as they entered the house. He'd pulled her by the hand up the stairs to the bedroom. She'd ripped off her clothes and they'd made love immediately and greedily. The months apart had intensified the subliminal force that pulled them together like powerful magnets.

He wondered if he represented a missing corner of her marriage, a bit she needed just to keep her relationship with Pete whole. Would their love retain the intensity if it were not for the forbidden ether that pervaded their times together? In his fantasy world, where he dreamed they lived in a cottage on some empty beach, how long would it be before the ache of urgent need dulled, and the aridity of the ordinary crept in, with it's destructive power?

She made a little purring sound, then started to snore. Was she dreaming the same dream? He got out of bed and padded downstairs to make a pot of coffee. When he carried it into the bedroom, she was sitting, arms around her legs, her face drawn in a feline smile. She took the coffee and sniffed it.

"Cardamom. So bitter but so alluring. A little seed that lies but is the necessary catalyst to make the coffee perfect. A metaphor for our lives of deceit." Her voice was husky. "The destiny of spies. And of spies' wives. Diplomats and their wives too, for that matter. Trained to live in a world of crazed mirrors and unspoken truths. And spoken untruths. Which is why our silences are so comforting. They don't require any code words."

Haydon laughed. "Are you making a case for the lives of spies?"

"I understand your silences more completely than I do the things you say." She pushed her hair back off her face. "We could never be happy together in the long term. We would start to hide from each other as soon as we emerged into the sunlight."

Even exposure wouldn't bring freedom, and anyway, he wondered if Pete hadn't known about them all along. There's no escape, he thought. It's too ingrained. The three of them were like rodents in a dark room, experiencing behavioral sink, little noses twitching and synapses bursting with unwanted knowledge.

She'd balanced an ashtray on her tummy. He watched it rise and fall with her breathing, saw the downy hair down below. They lay side by side, smoke curling above them. He tasted sand in his mouth. Somehow, it was seeping in through the closed windows. She stroked his arm.

"Nickel for your naughty thoughts." She reached over and kissed him. "You seem sad."

"I lost one of my agents in that fire at the Forum." Haydon puffed his cigarette. "He was like my protégé. We were close, I knew him from Rome days, and I feel directly responsible, like I let him down. We were talking on the phone as he was dying."

She pulled him towards her and hugged him.

"Pete told me you were cut up. It's bound to take time to

process."

"Pete doesn't suffer from self-doubt. He's lucky."

"Why do you two dislike each other, *chéri*? After all, you're really so alike."

"Alike? He's an extrovert, I'm the opposite." He grinned. "A miserable depressive."

"So is he. It's just you hide it behind different coloured masks. He laughs and tells jokes, bangs on about being a straight shooter. You retreat into a shell and put on an alluring aloofness. Both of you only unmask when you're doing what you really like to do – disguising yourselves, dressing up in native robes and heading off behind enemy lines."

"Danger and intensity are splendid tranquillisers."

"He says you see the worst in everyone."

"He's probably right. It's my job. He's got dollars to dispense, people treat him differently, they smile a lot and tell him what he wants to hear."

"It's not about us. It's something else, as if you're blocking his path." She pulled him towards her. "Are you?"

Haydon shut his eyes and scratched his head. Was she delivering a message? He raised himself on his elbow and gazed at her. Their lovemaking had been so intense. Now she looked innocent, trustworthy? Yet he trusted no-one. He felt a flash of anger at himself.

"I can't abide the way my superiors crave Uncle Sam's love." He kissed her shoulder. "The smell of greenbacks, and more alluringly still a route to preferment. Not that I don't like dollars, I would like plenty, but it leads to skewed decisions."

"Are you saying he's right?"

"Maybe I'm growing old. That would be a shock." He looked into her eyes. "I have something going badly wrong and I'm not handling it well."

"So you're not being a stag with his antlers down?"

"If I left, would you come with me? Leave everything behind and start anew." She turned away, inhaling deeply, blowing the smoke upwards.

"That came out of nowhere, *chéri*." She stubbed her cigarette out and sat up. "You have to give a girl warning when you're about to drop an A-bomb."

Chapter 34

Khartoum, November 1990

Yahya was walking to his car after Friday prayers in Omdurman when he found himself pinioned between two burly men, who grabbed his arms and manhandled him into a van. A sack was thrust over his head and his hands were secured roughly behind his back. He felt himself shoved down onto a badly sprung seat, and the van driving off jerkily. It was difficult to breathe. His heart was pounding so hard he thought it would burst apart.

He had been overcome with a sense of dread ever since his wife Ayesha's cousin, Zaki Bayazid, had visited him the week before at his office on El Baladiya Street. Zaki greeted him with smiles and warmth, but soon turned sour and threatening. He had not seen the man in more than a year; the last he'd heard was that he'd been working on some irrigation project in Pakistan.

They had first met at Khartoum University, Zaki studying agriculture, whilst he'd been reading law. Zaki had been active in the Muslim Brotherhood student association. He was ambitious and intelligent, but Yahya sought to avoid him, not wishing to get entangled in radical student politics. His wife had never been close to her cousin, and they had seen little of him over the years.

After a short drive, the van bounced to a shuddering halt, and the sack was removed from his head. He was sweating profusely, but, with his hands tied he couldn't wipe his face.

Stepping down into a dusty courtyard, his first sight was of barbed wire rolls topping a high wall. He breathed in deeply and blinked as he emerged into bright sunlight. Looking up, he saw a derelict sign high up on the tall adjacent building – 'Citibank'. His heart sunk. He realised he was in the most infamous of the dreaded 'ghost houses'. It had taken its name from its proximity to the office building where, in the good old days, the American bank had maintained plush offices. The large sign had never been removed after the bank had closed its doors and left the country.

The secret detention centres, of which there were several scattered around Khartoum, were rumoured to be controlled by a covert security militia of the National Islamic Front, the political party led by Hassan al-Turabi. Leadership of this militia was a closely guarded secret, senior government figures denied all knowledge of any such militia or of any black sites.

Several of his clients had passed through Citibank's doors. One of them had never been seen again, even though Yahya had been to the High Court to file a writ of *habeas corpus*. Which the High Court promptly struck down, and Yahya had been summoned to the Chief Justice's chambers and warned to 'show proper respect for the courts' or risk having his law license revoked. Another of his clients had described, in lowered tones, the torture, deprivation and terror meted out to inmates, and the rumours of nighttime hangings in the courtyard.

His guards ushered him into a two-storey villa to the side of the compound and down a flight of stairs to the basement. They shoved him into a large room, empty except for a desk and two wooden chairs. A small window, high up, almost blacked out with dust, was barred by a metal cage.

"Sit." The guards gestured him towards a chair. He sat. One of them freed his wrists, then retreated to stand by the door. Yahya was shivering, although he could feel sweat under his armpits, He knew he had to stay clearheaded. He started murmuring a prayer under his breath. They must know about Zaki's visit. That must be why they'd picked him up. He felt trapped. Zaki had threatened him, warning that his associates would mete out extreme retribution if anything he told Yahya leaked out.

The door opened and Salah el-Fateh swept in, dressed in a dark blue safari suit. He sat down behind the desk, looking directly at Yahya. Taking out a cigarette, he tapped it on the table before inserting it into a black cigarette holder and lighting it. He nodded to a guard, who brought him an ashtray. He took a puff and inhaled.

"I've always thought you to be a bright young man, who understood where the red lines are." He spoke with a slight lisp. "I believed you'd be an eminent lawyer one day, because you don't cross those lines, you see. Was I mistaken, brother?"

"Salah, I'm not aware of any red line I've crossed."

"I can see that clever head of yours is whirring around, trying to work out how to play this conversation. You don't know what I know, and that puts you at a disadvantage. Believe me, I know a lot." He pointed with his cigarette holder. "You must be aware why people call these places 'ghost houses', yes. It's because they don't exist, you see. It must be a shock to be picked off the street, to realise that no one in the world knows where you are."

"Yes, I am shocked. I don't understand."

"Let me be clear." He smiled, as if at a private joke. "There are two ways this interview ends. In one version you walk out of here smiling this afternoon. A short stroll to your smart law office, a little brisk exercise is good for your health. You'll have lost a few hours, but gained a powerful ally."

"That's an ending I favour."

"Or you may seek to be reticent, to conceal things and to try to deceive me. I can't forecast how that version ends, but certainly not well for you."

"What–"

"–Yahya, my friend, you know it's my job to be informed about all sources of power and of all threats operating in this country. Not necessarily to act on such knowledge, but to possess it."

"I can't–"

An awful scream came from somewhere in the building and seemed to reverberate around the room. It went on and on. Salah didn't move a muscle. Yahya wondered if he'd timed it on order to raise the fear factor.

"You needn't worry that I'll pass your information on. I realise that would be dangerous for you. It's not in my interest, you see."

Salah leaned back and put his hands behind his head, splaying his elbows. With his round face, horned rimmed spectacles and neatly trimmed beard, Yahya thought he looked like a jovial professor. A look that deceived.

"Can you be specific. What is it you wish to know?"

"You know exactly what I wish to know, and I suggest you tell me, before I take steps to oblige you to." Salah lit another cigarette and watched the smoke curling upwards. "So work out what's best for you and get on with it."

Yahya sat motionless in the chair, his mind whirring, his breathing heavy. He must appear collaborative, not get caught in any outright lie. He felt no loyalty to his relative. And no-one could know what he'd told Haydon. Unless Haydon himself had been indiscreet. He doubted that.

"You are interested in the visit to my office from my wife's relative Zaki Bayazid last week?"

"Go on."

"He told me he works for the Sheikh, a Saudi man, down south in Damazine, and that this man leads a new organisation called Al-Qaeda, established to defend the rights of

Muslims worldwide."

"How do they plan to achieve that laudable goal?"

"They intend to take action against the 'Far Enemy' and ally themselves with militant groups throughout the Islamic world. Similar to the policies of Hassan el-Turabi here, with his Popular Arab and Islamic Congress."

"But what did he want from you?" Yahya looked over at Salah. His tone was threatening. Perhaps he shouldn't have mentioned Turabi.

"He knows the British Embassy is one of my important clients. He wanted me to help obtain visas for his associates, hurry their applications."

"What else?"

"He was trying to recruit me, he lectured me about my 'Islamic duty'. Said it would bring me a lot of new clients. And he threatened me. If anything leaked, they would kill me and my family." He paused and rubbed his neck. "I told him I'd think about it."

Salah gave a dismissive wave of his hand. "You can stop with this *ballaballa*. Now tell me what you're holding back."

Yahya took a deep breath. It was as if the man was reading his mind. How much of this did he already know?

"He told me it was his boss who ordered the attack on that hotel. They'd learned that it was an intelligence front of the British, who'd used it in operations against their Palestinian friends."

"I want to know why they wanted these visas so urgently." He banged his fist on the table and shouted. "Stop fucking with me. Tell me what I want to know."

"They are planning operations against USA and UK, Europe also." Yahya whispered, head down. He knew he had just crossed a dangerous line, from which there was no return. "But their operatives are all on watch lists. So they are supplying them with Sudanese passports in false names.

Then they want me to provide references for the visa applications. The consular section will trust my recommendations."

"*Yasstma!* Listen! I want you to agree to his requests. Let him recruit you. Play it shy, you know how, like a virgin. Take his money, show yourself to be a greedy one. All lawyers are greedy. Help him with the visas." His eyes narrowed, and he pointed a finger at Yahya. "You are going to be my eyes and ears. I want names, I want the passport numbers and I want dates. Photocopies. Give me these things and you shall thrive. Cross me and you'll wish you'd never been born."

Chapter 35

Khartoum, November 1990

It was an odd sight. An elderly Sudanese limping back from the wicket, leaning on his bat for support and panting. He stopped to raise his bat in acknowledgment of scattered applause from a small group of mainly British spectators, seated in a row of deck chairs on the long, shaded pavilion veranda of the Khartoum Cricket Club.

"Well played, Ali." The bespectacled scorer raised his pencil in recognition. "What did I get?"

"19. Top scorer."

The temperature was well into the 40s. Several donkeys were standing motionless in the outfield, sheltering under broad acacia trees out by the boundary rope. Ali Kabbani wandered to the edge of the veranda and seated himself in a deckchair next to Haydon, sighing with relief. He leaned down and started undoing his pads.

"I'm too old for this, Haydon." He laughed. "I can't run down the wicket any more."

"You Victoria boys have a uniquely elegant style." Haydon laughed. "I can only manage an ugly slog, and inevitably miss the ball. I was out for another duck today; I'm aiming for a record."

"It was Mister Ramsbottom, you see." Kabbani wiped his forehead with a silk handkerchief. "He was a stickler for the straight bat. Hours in the nets. It sticks with you, you see, all your life."

"How are you enjoying your leisure time?"

"Honestly, serving in government didn't suit me at all. It

was a relief when I heard on the lunchtime news on the radio that I'd been fired." He turned to Haydon, whispering. "You see, I'm not a natural plotter. I gave it my best go but was out-maneuvered by all sides. I'm much too simple. The military boys, particularly that chameleon Colonel Abbas, as well as these Islamic fundamentalists, well, none of them wanted us softy liberals getting in their way."

"So how come you avoided ending up down the road in Kobar prison," Haydon chuckled, "like a few of your colleagues?"

"Proof of how unimportant I am, you see. It's a bit of good fortune!" He cackled. "They see me as such a lightweight they allowed me to slip away. Now I'm safe enough, so long as I keep my trap shut and stay away from the wrong people. People like you, especially!"

He'd never seen him looking so relaxed, Haydon thought. Maybe it's time for me to follow suit and go fishing. He felt the sun reflecting off the wooden floor, burning his cheeks.

"Your absence from the diplomatic circuit has been the subject of whispers." He pulled his cap down over his face.

"You may be next." Kabbani rubbed his beard. "I heard about your recent debacle. If you're not careful the government will demand your expulsion."

"Two Brits dead last week in the hotel outrage. It's a warning of worse to come." Haydon's brow furrowed. "I have this foreboding something really bad is brewing, but no-one wants to hear what I have to say."

"Makes two of us." Kabbani chuckled. "But it is better you keep your suspicions to yourself."

There were loud shouts from the square. The umpire raised his finger and a tall, gangling figure in a striped school cap loped off the pitch, twirling his bat. "You know Ramesh Patel, my assistant?"

Kabbani nodded. Haydon saw Ramesh wandering

towards them and signalled with a wave of the hand for him to stay away. He looked around to make sure there was no one listening, then leaned forward.

"I am worried about this man, the Saudi, the one they call the Sheikh."

Kabbani gave him a sharp glance and replied in an undertone. A donkey started a loud braying and kicked out at another one. Haydon had to struggle to hear.

"I wasn't involved in security conversations, it's a reserved area. Military intelligence pursuing one policy. The *Mukhabarat* doing something else. The party – the NIF – with its own security unit, up to who knows what. Turabi pulling some strings, but not all. A mushrooming of foreign groups making Khartoum their new home, each with their own sponsor and posing a distinct danger."

"I've met him twice." Haydon grimaced. "His story is good, and he tells it well, but I don't trust him. I'm convinced those Afghan-Arabs are planning attacks on the West. They've operational experience in Afghanistan, even in making car bombs. Ironically, some of them were trained by us, can you believe it? Which we're going to come to regret. I seem to be a lone voice that sees them as an imminent threat. My bosses view them as natural allies, their loyalty proven in Afghanistan."

"The Sheikh is Salah's personal project." Kabbani talked in an undertone, his eyes flicking about. "They meet frequently, mainly at night. Rumours of Saudi money sloshing about. After the Sheikh's office was attacked, Salah went on the rampage and swept up a bundle of random extremists in his net. Who knows if any of them were the right ones. No-one really cares."

"Salah is in his pocket?"

"You may have made a dangerous enemy of Salah, and other regime hardliners, with your Erkowit antics. I've heard rumours the hotel attack was set up by him and The Sheikh as payback. Who carried it out? No-one is saying."

The Sudanese stood up and started gathering his equipment. He turned and put his hand on Haydon's shoulder.

"Tread carefully, my friend. We may be unimportant, but we're also mortal."

The unenviable task of dealing with the aftermath of Charlie Lomax and Harry's deaths fell upon the Consul and his team. Nursemaiding grieving relatives, arranging for the handover of remains and all the other bureaucratic necessities. Charlie's sister arrived from Australia and Haydon tasked Ramesh to look after her. The idea of telling her a fictitious cover story grated. He'd liked Charlie too much for that. Better that someone who knew neither him nor the truth got to do that job.

The world's press had descended on Khartoum in force and were sniffing around. Several front-page stories in British newspapers covered Turabi's congresses, and the possible dystopian consequences for the West. One broadsheet suggested Sudan had become a 'wasps nest of Palestinian terror groups', a phrase picked up and repeated by other dailies.

There had been no challenges to the official story, and, fortuitously, a rogue Palestinian group, calling themselves the 'Revolutionary Arab Brigades', had claimed responsibility for the attack, which they said were against 'Zionist elements and their colonial imperialist allies'. Haydon knew this was a cover name used by Abu Nidal, but he remained unconvinced. It was typical for groups to claim responsibility for terrorist attacks, keen to earn kudos for any successful outrage even if they'd had nothing to do with it.

The Embassy Press Office had gone to great lengths to emphasise the Italian heritage of the Forum Hotel, focusing on its long-term owner, Aphrodite Ratchett, and providing glamorous photos of her with different international human-itarian figures. Charlie was described as having recently arrived to help his ailing aunt during her sudden illness, and Harry was referred to as a dedicated aid worker. The Italian Embassy commented that there was no reason that an Italian owned hotel, known for attracting NGO clients, would have been a target for a Palestinian terrorist attack.

With increasing press and diplomatic focus on the hotel attack, Harbut recalled Haydon to London, to keep him away from any risk of unwelcome attention. The Embassy was in a state of high alert and additional security personnel arrived and instituted stringent protocols, rendering all but essential work impractical. The ambassador departed on a trip to the remote archaeological sites at Jebel Barkal.

Haydon went to meet Monkton before leaving. He found him sitting under a multi-coloured umbrella by his swimming pool. For a man in his early 50s, he was still wiry and trim. His hair was greying, he had slight lines on his forehead, but there was no sign of a paunch. Haydon felt a twinge of envy. He lacked the self-discipline, and the years of fitness in the Paras were a distant memory.

"Sit." Monkton reached down and extracted a can of Budweiser from an oversize freezer box by his feet. "Ice cold. Tastes better on Fridays in a Muslim country."

"I'm off to London. Been ordered to stay out of sight. Too many eyes around here at the moment." Haydon tilted the can and felt the cold liquid make its way down his gullet. "God that's good."

"Taking leave? Good move. Anywhere fancy?"

"Pre-Christmas London. Catch up with family. Drink too much. Eat too much. Multiple hangovers, upset the relatives.

Countless regrets. Catch frostbite. Die."

"Just the way you like it. Lena's opinion is you're some kind of closet masochist."

"Pete, I've been hearing chatter." He gulped at his beer and sought to keep his tone light, but knew it wouldn't work. He was going to infuriate Monkton, but he needed to try one last time to convince him. "Separately. From reliable sources."

"Here we go again. How is it I know already what's coming?" Monkton rolled his eyes. "Like I'm some kind of goddam gypsy fortune teller."

"That the Sheikh gave the order for the hotel attack." He knew he mustn't mention Rashid, in case that leaked and pointed the finger back at Yahya.

Monkton frowned, reached down and took out another beer, popped it open. "Know what I figure?"

"You figure I'm obsessed."

"Damn right I do. In fact, you piss me the hell off. I do my best to be collegiate, bring you in close to one of my key intel sources, spend hours driving you around the boondocks, so you can see for yourself. Listen to your boring fantasies."

He stared at Haydon, jaw set and eyes narrowed. Haydon noticed his cheeks reddening.

It was the first time he'd seen anger in the normally cool American.

"I don't want to hear any more of your shit. Your op went south. I'm real sorry for that. Great idea, just like our Berlin tunnel that your nice Mr Blake blew. But it's dead as a barbecued hog, and Hamas have taken their revenge. End of. Move on. Go do something useful for Chrissake."

"Just consider—"

"Enjoy you leave, Haydon. Maybe you should spend time figuring out why nobody seems to like you. Apply for a transfer to Mongolia, or somewhere further if there is anywhere. You can bang on endlessly and bore the yaks to death."

Monkton stood up and picked up his beer. "You can see yourself out."

He picked up his towel and strode off towards the house without looking back.

The Sheikh

Chapter 36

London, December 1990

A dense fog hung over London. It was already dark at 4.30 pm. Redolent of childhood Christmas memories. Haydon pulled his scarf tight around his neck and rubbed his gloved hands together. He watched his breath emitting what seemed to be icicles into the air. Striding down St James's, his footsteps were muffled on the almost empty pavement. Blurry yellow street lights gave the city a timeless hue, he almost expected to hear the echo of a horse-drawn carriage approaching out of the mist. Passing the Reform Club, he caught sight, through the tall window, of a garish Christmas tree with flashing coloured lights, spoiling his Victorian fantasy.

When he'd received the summons to meet Glasson away from the office, he'd known his boss must be preparing to sugar coat nasty news beneath a veneer of Christmas conviviality. He didn't care. Part of him had known his career at SIS was drawing to a close. He'd prolonged it out of a stubborn desire for self-justification. That he was right, and they were wrong. That was never going to be a clever long-term strategy.

He trotted up the steps and pushed open the door to the Travellers Club. Curtis, the long-serving porter, greeted him from his cubicle.

"Mister Glasson is in the Smoking Room, sir." He turned and rifled through a wooden alphabetical pigeonhole. "No messages, Mister Talbot."

Haydon put his shoulder to the swing doors and entered

the Smoking Room, strolling over to the fireplace. Glasson was hunched deep in a leather wing armchair, holding a balloon glass in one hand and resting a long cigar in a cut glass ashtray on a side table. Haydon sat down opposite him and warmed his hands in front of the roaring fire. An aroma of burning oak and cigar smoke enveloped him.

"Mark." He smiled down and nodded in greeting.

Glasson offered him a lemon-sucking stare. A politician's smile. His well-cut grey double-breasted suit added to a self-satisfied appearance.

"Haydon. Compliments of the season, my friend. Vintage cognac?" He waved his arm expansively. "Delamain. Exquisite bouquet."

"Why not. I'm not going back to the office."

Glasson pressed a bell on the wall. When the waiter appeared, he pointed to his glass and gestured.

"I thought it more civilised to have this conversation away from the office." He picked up his cigar and puffed away, exuding a plume of smoke. "How long since we joined the Service you and I? Quarter of a century? More? We've come a long way since then, yes. Further than we ever imagined, when we were clambering up and over that fearful assault course at Oxley eh, covered in filthy mud and horse shit."

The waiter handed Haydon a glass.

"You conquered an even tougher assault course. Politics. I always knew you'd make it. Cheers to you, 'C', and your rarefied green ink!" He raised his glass, took a long gulp, and enjoyed following the burning sensation down his throat and into his tummy. "A brilliant achievement."

"It is principally a question of fitting in along the way. Fitting in, yes." Glasson emphasised the words. "Never your strong point, Haydon, it's where you always get stuck. You're laudably resolute and incisive, but rarely accommodating. The trouble is, the higher you climb, the more people you are obliged to accommodate."

"I never mastered the art. I'm stupidly attached to my opinions."

"Funnily enough, that hasn't gone unnoticed around the office." Glasson picked up his long Cuban cigar and began the lengthy rigmarole of lighting it. Finally, he started puffing furiously. That's his disguise set up, Haydon thought. Hiding behind a thick smokescreen, he'll now fire off his volley.

"You've compounded the toxic fallout from the demise of SEAMLESS by seriously antagonising our closest ally." He pointed at Haydon with his cigar. "You're an irredeemable loner. We went over this before. I was quite clear, yes? I had thought you might come around. That you would figure out that being the only one to espouse a point of view, when all your peers and superiors have an opposite one, might best be revised, but–"

"–what was it Ibsen wrote? *I am in revolt against the age-old lie that the majority is always right.*"" Haydon leaned his head back and laughed. He felt wonderfully relieved. Was it the brandy? Did he really not care that he was being fired? "Although I have to admit it didn't finish well for Doctor Stockman."

"My friend. You and I both know it hasn't finished well for you either, yes." He puffed again, then had a mild coughing fit. He banged his chest with his hand, then laid the cigar down in the ashtray. "But I'm going to help ease your way out, offer you every support. I've spoken to Personnel; they understand they're to make it as painless as possible, grant you every benefit."

"Time-frame?"

"Go back to Khartoum in the New Year. Wind things up. There's nothing major running that your deputy can't manage, yes?"

Haydon nodded.

"Turn it around in a couple of weeks. Put it about there's a new posting coming your way, can't say anything about it. Do not." He squinted at Haydon, then tapped repeatedly on the table. "Repeat, do not, play games. Just that one thing I ask. Initiate nothing. Say your goodbyes, sad to go, sob sob, and be back here by the end of the month."

"No point trying to convince you? That our American cousins have really got this thing upside down?"

"Leave it, Haydon."

"We're facing a dangerous new threat from the Afghan-Arabs. The Yanks no longer control them."

"Go bother Greg if you must." Glasson frowned, then rolled his eyes. "Mind you, Greg won't be sympathetic. Haydon, leave off. Don't spoil this celebration. Let's enjoy our cognac, please."

He sniffed at his glass, then continued.

"You know, back in the day, our cousins used to look up to us. The earlies of OSS, halcyon days, yes. '43 and '44. Then came Philby and Blake and all the rest of them, and the paranoia of Angleton's tenure at the Agency. After which we were always on the back foot and obliged, as an absolute priority, to keep cultivating our American friends. Their unlimited resources and power. Monkton is a key ally. We won a big victory together, against the Soviets in Afghanistan. So you," he pointed a finger at Haydon and scowled, "messing him up personally, as well as professionally, that's inexcusable. I was hoping I wouldn't have to spell it out to you, yes."

Haydon felt a stab of guilt in his chest. So Glasson knew about Lena. Then that was that. There was no point arguing. He'd committed a cardinal sin and was on the road to perdition. With no way back. He drained his glass.

"Maybe you're right, Mark. I'm too old and tired, probably too obsessed." He rolled his head and closed his eyes. "A dinosaur in a frayed tweed jacket. Better take up golf and *Tai*

Chi."

"Surprisingly Pete doesn't hold all this against you. Truly." Glasson had visibly relaxed, uncrossing his legs and leaning back. He had obviously been expecting a more antagonistic encounter. "He asked me to pass on an offer. Ops Director at Lance Group. Middle East Security consultants. Big ticket items. You wouldn't starve. Based in Dubai."

"The *quid pro quo*?"

"None. Like me, he values your implacably dogged nature. When it's put to good use, that is."

He reached over and pressed the bell.

"Drink up man. One more, then I'm to Covent Garden. Bohème. Divine, yes."

She'd recently moved to a flat off the Albert Bridge Road in Battersea. He wanted to hear her voice, tell her his news in person, share the prospect of a reinvigorated life, the shedding of a heavy burden. He felt a pang in his chest.

He found a phone box by the Ritz and dialled Ros's number. After two rings she picked up, he pressed a coin down into the slot.

"Ros. Haydon. I'm in London."

"This is unexpected." The husky voice he knew so well. He felt a wave of nostalgia breaking over him. "What's up?"

"Can I pop over? Cup of tea?"

"Now? It's not convenient. I'm just on my way out."

"I'm quitting the Office. Facing a new phase of life. I wanted to chat it over with you."

"At last. Well done you. I never, ever, thought you'd get around to taking the plunge."

"It wasn't entirely my choice."

"How did I guess? Well done anyway." She paused. "Haydon, I read about Charlie's death in the papers. I was shocked and saddened."

Haydon felt a stab of guilt in his belly. He sensed she knew the truth about Charlie. Her female intuition was so strong.

"It was such a tragedy."

"He was too young to die. I was fond of him, you know. I think back to all those times, the four of us, in Rome." She coughed. "Was he working for you?"

"I can't talk about that."

"I hope you didn't take advantage of him, Haydon. Not again."

"Could I pop by tomorrow? Clear the air."

"I've moved on, Haydon." He heard resignation in her voice. *Damn*. The phone started beeping and he hurried to push another coin into the slot.

"But–"

"–Listen Haydon, there's someone new in my life. But I'm pleased for you. You're free at last, from what had become such an unhappy place. I'm sure you'll find it easy to adjust to a new life. Freedom to start again."

His heart sank. On some subliminal level, he'd been hoping for some kind of reconciliation, at least an opening. *I've moved on*. How final.

"How about lunch later in the week?"

"Not a good idea Haydon. I've spoken to a lawyer." She paused. "It would be better if we get that stuff out of the way before we meet."

"Nothing I can say?"

"I have to go now. Good luck to you Haydon. I mean it." The line cut off.

Chapter 37

"Pissed again?" Johnny Doyle held the front door open. He was wearing a dinner jacket and holding a whisky in a tall cut-glass tumbler.

Haydon wobbled unsteadily and smiled. Pulling off his overcoat, he tossed it over the banister. Throwing an arm around Johnny's shoulders, they walked together into the living room.

"I've been sitting in a gloomy pub in Shepherd Market. Ogling Ukrainian barmaids and spilling my beer. Huge tits. Seeing double. Actually seeing double double."

"Celebrating or grieving?"

"Drowning unfathomable miseries."

"Better get you a stiff drink then. Unfathomable miseries sound ominous."

"Drink's bound to make them worse, but who cares."

"Six months since I last, your best friend, had to listen to you groaning about your lot. Not much warning, eh. No time to prepare my psyche. Better pour myself a large one."

"You're made of titanium, you can take it."

"Need to be, as your unpaid shrink." He made a serious face. "Luckily my hot date had a headache. At least she said she did. Otherwise I wouldn't have opened the door, however many times you pressed the bell. Serious totty. We were at Covent Garden. First night."

"La Bohème. So depressing. Like me."

"How come you know that, you uncultured sod?"

"Glasson told me he was on his way there. As soon as he'd finished firing me." Haydon plumped himself in a deep armchair with a sigh and took the proffered glass.

Johnny stood in front of the fireplace. They raised their glasses. Haydon could hear the grandfather clock in the corner ticking away. Old friendships were balm, he thought, no need to say anything. Not to explain, not to justify, or to be funny. You just picked up where you left off.

"I know you so boringly well." Johnny's torso shook with laughter. "You've an entire bee's nest under your inflated bonnet. I bet you convinced yourself, again, that you're right and the rest of the world, especially your bosses, are all wrong. And you told them so straight up. Right so far?"

"But remember, I'm usually proved right." He realised he was slurring his words. "In the end."

"To the annoyance of the powers that be, who don't like being proved wrong. It wouldn't put them off firing you. Congratulations!" He sipped at his drink. "I hope you're leaving by the front door, with your reputation intact?"

"Meek as a lamb." He put his hand over his heart. "Job offers dangled. All will be forgiven. So long as I fuck off a great distance and remain achingly silent."

"Made an enemy of our American cousins, did you?" Johnny lit a cigarette and puffed on it. "Poor judgment."

"Pete Monkton. He made an official complaint." He made a dismissive gesture with his hand. "Insisted I was frustrating important ops. Imagine Glasson's delight. It is true he warned me, and that I failed to take the hint. Oh and worse—"

"How could there be worse?"

Haydon shrugged his shoulders. "That Sheila—"

"—you didn't?"

"He was on my case before that. A difference of opinion. But the Sheila, it may not have helped."

"Better take those job offers while they're still hot. You're living dangerously."

"Then I've just learned, from her mouth, that Ros has a new man. Divorce papers and expensive lawyers *en route*."

Amman. Written up for you here." He handed over the sheaf of paper. "Please destroy after digesting, or if you decide not to use it."

"Should I even be receiving this, Haydon?" Johnny pressed his fingers against his temples. "Are we not crossing thick red lines."

"Probably. But if HMG is not prepared, then we are in peril of serious outrages, here on home turf. We already have the IRA setting them off, can we really afford a new bunch of bombers? This is my final act of service before I exit the stage."

"I may decide to do nothing, destroy your notes and forget this conversation."

"If it's in your hands there's a chance. Glasson, Harbut, Monkton and others have all discounted my reports."

"Get on with it." Johnny leaned back, put his hands behind his head, and closed his eyes.

"One, plans are being developed in Sudan for attacks on high-value targets in Western capitals, planned to be on a scale similar or larger than the Beirut barracks bombing in '83. Two, The Sheikh and his Khartoum based Afghan-Arabs are controlling this op and the key mover seems to be his private secretary Rashid al-Duri. This new group goes by the name of Al-Qaeda. Reportedly, according to a reliable confidential informant – I have noted him there as Zulu – Rashid ordered the attack on the Forum Hotel. He also uses the alias 'Harun al-Rashid'. Three, two members of the first active cell identified have previously travelled on Jordanian passports – numbers are there on my document – under the names Hassan el-Mahgoub and Abdelrahman Yassin, supposedly representatives of the *Al-Quds Centre for Islamic Development'*, in Amman, if that even exists. Yassin may be an ex-Egyptian special forces colonel named Salah Ahmed al-Din, previously affiliated with Egyptian Islamic Jihad, an engineer and explosives expert. Yassin may, or may not, also use the *nom de guerre* Saif al-Adel, which translates from Arabic as 'sword of justice'. He may have links to the Abu Nidal Organisation in Libya. One last name that has come up is the operative who scoped the Forum in the days before the attack. Mohammed Idris, claiming to be the manager of the *'Company for Levant Trading. Beirut.'* Lastly, Monkton, and therefore Glasson, is convinced the Sheikh and his Afghan-Arabs are continuing to work for him, as his proxies, like they did, successfully, in Afghanistan. I could not convince them otherwise. Monkton is getting ready to pay them big bucks to organise a hit on Imad Mughniyeh."

"That's it?"

"I'll be in Khartoum, winding up and handing over, for two or three weeks in January." Haydon covered his face with his hands, then breathed deeply. "I'm warned off from taking any actions that might frustrate Monkton's interests. I'm limited to tidying up and saying my goodbyes."

"Old friend, I hear you. Or rather I didn't hear you. I can't do anything that could send up a flag or lead to awkward questions." Johnny frowned. "So far none of this is domestic. Ergo, it belongs legitimately to Six."

"Is there any way that it could become domestic, and therefore actionable by you people?"

"If a CI appeared here on British soil, with this same information, then that informant would belong to Five." He stood up and turned to leave. "I trust your instincts Haydon. I'll do what I can, which may not be much. You need to tread carefully."

Chapter 38

Khartoum, January 1991

Yahya hadn't slept at all. He swivelled from side to side in his leather office chair, unable to concentrate on the files piled on his desk. He felt trapped, helpless, shoved around in other peoples' chess games, and no obvious route off the chessboard. Striving to keep three balls in the air meant deceiving each of them, whilst putting on a brave face. He looked at his watch. Zaki was late.

Everyone was always late.

Until now, his progress through life had been smooth, with few moral quandaries to wrestle with. He'd cruised through law school and on into his own legal practice. His easy-going personality, good connections and confidential manner had won him a growing and prestigious clientèle. When the British Embassy had appointed him as their external lawyer, that had been the icing on the cake. He had arrived. Now this had come along and threatened to blow it all up, and put him in personal danger, squeezed between Zaki and Salah, both of them as dangerous as angry black mambas.

Facilitating the visa applications for Zaki had been easy. He'd written personal letters of recommendation, stating he'd known the two men well at Khartoum University, that they were travelling for short family visits to the UK. He chatted up Rasha, the senior clerk in the Visa Section, and she in turn put in a good word with the Vice-Consul. A week later, she'd rung to say the visas had been approved. He'd taken several photocopies of the passports and application forms and locked them in his office safe.

He hoped that having got them the visas, it might end there, but his pragmatic side knew that was improbable. Once these people got their claws in, they would never let go; a mole inside the British Embassy would be too valuable to them. And he didn't intend to become their mole.

Glancing out of the window, he saw a yellow battered Hillman Minx taxi driving through the gate into the courtyard.

He stood up and walked over to the door as his secretary ushered Zaki in. A lithe man with a hollow face, Zaki was light-skinned. Perhaps he had Turkish blood in his background. As they embraced, he could feel the bulging muscles stretching at his shirt. He looked every bit the working farmer he claimed to be. There was little evidence of the smooth and ruthless Machiavellian plotter who wanted to enmesh him in his deadly operations.

"Cousin, welcome. *Fadel.* Sit, please. Welcome." He waved at his secretary. "Bring coffee please."

They sat side by side on a sofa by a small table. After the secretary had served the coffee and left the room, Yahya leaned towards Zaki and smiled.

"It is all done. The visas are ready. Your friends can collect their passports from the Embassy."

"Thank you, cousin, that is good. Submit to me an invoice for your time. Make it out to Damazine Farms." He rubbed his hands together and grinned. "You mustn't think we ask you these favours for free, no."

"It would not be easy to repeat." Yahya frowned. "There would be suspicions if I were to ask again, at least for some time."

"Security is the first thing, yes, I understand, we keep everything compartmentalised, don't worry. You have shown you are with us, we will make it worth your while. We intend to take the fight to their lands." There was something threatening in his tone. "It will not be we Muslims only who will suffer. No."

"I am pleased to have been helpful. Is there anything else, cousin? I have another meeting now."

"Listen. This man Mister Haydon, you see. I have met him. He visited Damazine Farms with the American and met with the Sheikh. A creepy-faced spy. We would like you to put your eyes on him." Zaki leaned forward and whispered, his eyes darting around the room. "He is clever and watchful. It may become necessary to take action against him. I am awaiting orders. We would like you to find for us the address of his house. You will be well rewarded for your time again, of course. Report anything you find about his movements."

"He is in London, I think. I don't know when he will return."

"Could you get into his office while he is away, perhaps? Look through his files?"

"His Section is in a special secure area. I do not have access."

"See if you can find a way."

After Zaki had left, Yahya pulled a small tape recorder out of his pocket and switched it off. He felt relieved. He would prevaricate. That was the thing. Keep looking for an exit and pray for salvation. He sighed. Now he had the nasty prospect of reporting on his meeting to Salah.

Typical, Yahya thought, a glaring reminder of where power resided.

"Come to me on foot. To the place where we met last time. My man will be waiting for you at the gate."

He'd left it two days before ringing Salah. A minor act of rebellion. Why? He assumed he would already know about

Zaki's visit to his office. Still, he couldn't bring himself to dance to the security man's tune, even if he'd have to do so in the end. He picked up his pace. It was January, the coolest month, and it felt good to be padding the empty streets of the old capital. Aside from barking dogs, the area was quiet.

Looking ahead, he saw the landmark building with the wonky Citibank sign. What an irony. Poor wretches, locked in their cells with no windows, allowed an occasional view upwards from the walled exercise yard to an endlessly dusty blue sky, with the skyline dominated by the sign of a broken American dream.

A scrawny man, deep scars on his cheeks, a pistol sticking out from under his shirt, was waiting by the gate, smoking a cigarette. He beckoned Yahya through and led him past the guardhouse and across the dusty courtyard to a corner office. Salah sat behind a rickety wooden desk, reading a file. He waved Yahya to sit. A nasty smell of disinfectant permeated the room.

"Next time we'll meet at an anonymous safe house. I'll send a car to collect you." Salah looked up. "If anyone sees you entering this place voluntarily, it would ruin your reputation. You'd be presumed to be a regime collaborator, and that would spread around the business community like wildfire, you see. You'd lose most of your clients."

Yahya removed a sheaf of papers from his jacket pocket and placed them on the desk. "Here are copies of the visa applications. Showing the names of the two men, photographs, their addresses, passport numbers and proposed dates of travel. Who knows whether any of these are real."

"Unimportant, you see. Your cousin. How did he react?"

"He appeared pleased. Asked me to bill him for my time. A little bribe. A hint of what might be coming."

"So what more did he ask for?" Salah's eyes narrowed. "He will have wanted to maximise product from his new agent inside the British Embassy."

"I do not see myself as his agent." Yahya felt weary. "He asked me to keep a watch on Haydon Talbot, find out his home address, get into his office and look at his files. He hinted they may take action against him."

"Can you fulfill his requests?"

"Haydon is in London, I don't know his movements." Yahya breathed in deeply. "I can find out his home address, learn some of his movements after he's returned. But I could never obtain access to the secure area where his office and files are. I told this to Zaki."

"Good. An excellent start." Salah stroked his wispy beard. "But I think better for now that you do nothing about Talbot. If Zaki pressurises you, stall him. Then speak to me, we will decide how best to respond."

Salah wrote a number on a piece of paper and passed it over. "This telephone is manned around the clock. When you have information for me, call the number and say these three words. 'Sorry I misdialled'. I will then send a car the next day to your office at seven o'clock in the evening. If your message is urgent, then instead say 'I dialled the wrong number' and I will send a car to your office immediately. That is your emergency signal."

The sun was sinking fast as Yahya set off at a fast walk towards his office. A cool evening breeze was blowing and in the twilight sky, he watched great flocks of birds, geese, sand grouse and duck, circling down for their evening flight to the river.

He'd kept the two poisonous tarantulas happy. For the time being. But he knew both of them represented malign forces, and before long, one or other would ask him to do something that he could not do, but they would not let him slide away. A sense of dread ran through him and he stopped still and shivered. It was as if someone had trod on his grave. He had to find a way out, even if that meant abandoning his best client, or even leaving the country. He needed a wise head to share this conundrum.

Chapter 39

Yahya drove through the main gate into the Khartoum Racecourse and on past the grandstand, before crossing over the race track towards the Polo Club. White and red goal posts loomed ahead of him, and, in the background, the tall minarets of the Al-Burhania mosque dominated the city skyline.

The distant wailing cry of the *muezzin*, calling the faithful to afternoon prayers, competed with a thundering sound of horses' hooves, and, as he approached the pony lines, a dust-cloud rushed towards him. Emerging from the cloud came riders at full gallop, urging on their ponies, and he heard the sharp report of a wooden ball being struck, followed by loud shouts, as a player in a red shirt stood up in the saddle, raised his stick and whooped, the goal judges waving little white flags to signify a goal.

He drove on to where a line of cars was parked, canvas chairs in front of each of them, polo sticks laid out on coloured rugs. The eight players cantered back to the middle. The umpire blew his whistle, threw the ball in and a melée ensued, before a player in red broke away and galloped off towards the far goal, creating another thick cloud of orange dust. Yahya drove to the end of the line and parked next to a white Mercedes. He opened his window.

"Why you aren't out there on horseback whacking the ball, or trying to?" Yahya waved at the dark-skinned man, sitting by himself on a safari chair, peering through binoculars. "Aren't you the Club Chairman?"

The man set down the binoculars, turned and smiled.

"Nowadays it's a walking stick I require, not a polo

mallet." Ali Kabbani was wearing a pristine white *jellabiya* and dark glasses. "Occasionally they invite me to umpire, I just about manage that without falling off. Come and sit with me, Yahya. *Shai?*"

Without waiting for an answer, he reached over for a large thermos. He poured milky tea into a small glass and handed it to Yahya. It was hot and oversweet, but he was thirsty.

"What are you doing out here, my friend? It's not your sport, and you're missing your valued siesta."

"I need your counsel, Ali. Urgently. You are the only person to whom I can talk to about the terrible mess I've got myself into."

Two riders galloped past close by, riding each other off and shouting. The dust irritated his eyes. He took his handkerchief out and tried to rub it away.

"You look tired, my friend." He clapped Yahya on the shoulder. "And I always think of you as having such a clever nose for avoiding trouble. Tell me. It is a woman then?"

"I wish." Yahya grimaced. He recounted everything that had happened since Zaki Bayazid's surprise visit, leaving nothing out, describing his encounters with Haydon, Salah and Zaki.

If he had misjudged Kabbani, then he was doomed. He knew he was staking his life on a deep sense of trust.

The umpire blew his whistle, and the players trotted to the sidelines to change ponies. A boy stood by the scoreboard and raised a sign '4' indicating this was the last chukka. The two men sat silently and watched as the sweating figures panted and towelled their faces, before remounting their ponies and cantering back to the middle.

"You have only one gambit, my friend, and you must play it while the information you have remains of any value. That means quickly." Kabbani linked his fingers together and frowned. "The visa details are of critical importance for the

British, right now, to enable them to thwart an attack. But the details have a limited life, so you must exact your price in advance. That is your only safety. They will want you to remain in place here, at substantial risk to you, hoping that you will get them more. But you must refuse. You must leave this country Yahya. It is the only way."

"Leave everything?"

The older man nodded his head. "Haydon trusts you, I think?"

Yahya nodded. "As much as any diplomat trusts a foreigner."

"Listen, friend. Salah and these Al-Qaeda people are going to keep on squeezing you from both sides, you see. Each step you take, for either of them, makes you more vulnerable to their continued pressures. Both of them can destroy you at will. The chances of you surviving in the middle are zero. You need to play your one and only card well and leave Khartoum quickly."

"What do I ask Haydon for?" Yahya realised his voice was trembling. Kabbani reached out and touched his arm.

"The British ambassador came to see me, when I was still in government. He briefed me about these new Foreign Office scholarships. He asked me to consider and put forward candidates. Not just for postgraduate and doctoral studies in UK, but secondments to firms and even to government departments. They can be for, *janni*, perhaps, as long as three years. Targeted at talented people, those considered potential future leaders. That's you. It is called the 'FCO Scholarships and Awards Scheme', remember to ask for it by that exact name."

He coughed as another cloud of dust enveloped them. Yahya saw he had his eyes closed. "They are in the grant of the Foreign Office. Insist on this if Haydon tells you it's not within his power. Demand to leave on a scholarship immediately, on the understanding that you will provide him with the information immediately your application has been approved, and you are safely arrived in London."

"But he'll insist on having the information in advance." Yahya rubbed his forehead. "Yahya. Did you not tell me he said he owed you a debt of gratitude? Now you must cash in that debt. You've got to be tough. I know that's not in your nature, but I tell you it's vital to wield this stick now. Let him understand your desperation. Otherwise, you're doomed, you see."

A loud hooter sounded. The players walked their ponies off the field. The sun was turning red and sinking towards the White Nile. Kabbani stood up and embraced Yahya.

"The best of luck to you, my young friend. You and I know this conversation never ever happened."

He offered Yahya an enigmatic smile, threw his scarf over his shoulder and turned away, walking towards the gaggle of players.

Yahya sat with his feet up on his office sofa, drinking from a large tumbler of whisky. It was neat, with just a block of ice, and it tasted bitter. Suiting his bitter mood, he thought. But he could feel it having the desired effect. He'd never experienced such intense anxiety in his life. Tears of self-pity welled up at the corners of his eyes. He'd turned off the air conditioning in the winter cool, but now was sweating, and realised he was breathing unnaturally fast. Earlier, he'd bought some Librium from his friendly pharmacist and taken two. Both the sharp migraine and the tension he'd felt throughout his body had eased.

How had it come to this so quickly? Finding himself on the

verge of abandoning all he'd built up since those years at law school, fleeing his homeland for an uncertain life as a refugee, away from his family, in the UK. He could find a colleague to take over his practice; he'd just have to hope there'd be a place for him when he came back. If he came back.

Was the scenario as dire as Kabbani had suggested? He'd lived through enough political revolutions in recent years and knew he could read the trends, manoeuvre around unpredictable changes, work out where uncrossable lines lay. He thought of himself, above all, as a survivor. This Islamic regime had been increasingly showing its brutal face. He'd seen plenty of evidence of their capacity for violence – the ghost houses, the arbitrary arrests, the torture and even extra-judicial executions. If he crossed Salah, even unintentionally, he had no illusion as to the likely outcome.

And Zaki? With his mysterious boss and their new organisation dedicated to global *jihad*? The attack on the hotel was evidence they didn't think twice about the brutal slaying of innocent civilians. And he wouldn't be seen as innocent.

And if he survived, betraying his prize client and keeping the extremists and Salah at bay? Then, when politics changed, which they surely would, he'd be tarred with the extremist brush and there'd be no way to hide the stain or escape retribution. If they killed Haydon, he'd have blood on his hands, or if they carried out attacks in the UK. No, he couldn't live with himself, even if he could ride it out. Kabbani was right. He had to get out now, and Haydon had to provide the means.

He picked up the telephone and rang Haydon's house number.

The Sheikh

Chapter 40

Eyebrows had been raised around the chancery, which was only to be expected. Haydon had only been in post for 18 months, and it was unusual for a Station Chief to be moved after such a brief stint. His assistant, Ramesh, kept him informed of the gossip, mainly that it was rumoured that he was being blamed by London for the fiasco at the hotel. He'd replied, finger raised to his lips, that, to the contrary, a plum posting was coming his way. He was sure this would circulate around the Embassy before the end of the week.

"I'll be out of here within a fortnight, I've just got to say my goodbyes and pack up. You'll be running things in the interim, so we'll do a detailed handover next week." He smiled at Ramesh. His youthful enthusiasm was infectious. He reminded him of prep school. "You know all the ropes, Ramesh, there's just a couple of sensitive issues we need to talk through carefully."

He was curious to know why Yahya wanted to meet him so urgently. The lawyer had rung him at home, which was unusual. He'd sounded panicky, possibly drunk? Out of character, he was normally calm and composed. Something told him he had come up with more golden intel from inside the Sheikh's circle. That would be a boon. He needed it.

"May we meet at the same place?" He'd spoken fast, almost staccato. "Urgently, you see, tomorrow morning, please? You remember?"

"I remember, but I have a better idea. Come to my office and we'll go somewhere."

"But–"

"–I understand you, Yahya, don't worry. Come at eleven

sharp."

This would be his opportunity to close on Yahya, make use of the man's distress to get him signed up. One last recruitment in his long career in the field, it might prove to be the most consequential of them all. He would have to reassure him, offer him practical support, and money, certainly. He'd have to figure out and agree on a protection and extraction plan, but keep him in play until he had a firm handle on the threat.

He'd propose that Yahya wear a wire when he met his contacts. He'd show him one of these new tiny devices, which couldn't be detected in a quick pat down. Later, he'd bring Ramesh into the loop and pass him on. It would all have to happen in a tight timeframe, and he'd need to be at his sharpest to coax him over the line. He tapped his fingers on the desk.

His secretary buzzed him on the intercom, then opened the door for Yahya. Dressed in a black suit, pristine white shirt, and thick aviator glasses, Haydon thought he looked like a jazz musician.

"Greetings friend." He stood up and smiled. "Have you heard my news?"

"Of course. You're leaving Khartoum later this month for good." Yahya's eyes darted about. He fidgeted and remained standing by the door. "Where can we talk?"

"Come, I'll show you." Haydon stood up and beckoned with a finger.

He led the lawyer through a door at the back of his office and up a narrow stairway to a small, windowless room. Pulling the heavy door shut behind him, he pressed down on a long metal lever. There was a muffled hum of air conditioning. Grey pyramid shapes covered the walls and ceiling, giving it a futuristic atmosphere. A plastic table, with integral benches running along each side, was the only furniture. Haydon slid onto one bench and motioned Yahya to the other.

"This is a Farraday room, Yahya. Electronically imper-meable and semi-anechoic, those foam pyramids absorb the sound of voices. You can say whatever is on your mind with zero chance of it being recorded or overheard. We call it The Cage."

"I have further information." Yahya removed his dark glasses and placed them on the table, touched his throat, then coughed. Haydon noticed redness around his eyes.

"About?"

"The subject we talked about. Cover names, passport details, photos and numbers, dates of travel to the UK. These are Al-Qaeda people, part of a larger team. I think they are planning an attack, or scoping for one. My information is time critical."

"That is important news, my friend. I won't ask how you obtained this." Haydon smiled broadly, but Yahya was look-ing down at his fingernails. Haydon noticed a growing sweat stain on the front of his shirt. "May I have the details."

"I need to leave Sudan. Right away." His voice quavered. "You must get me out on a scholarship or secondment, with a visa and an air ticket to London. Before you leave. Preferably in the next few days."

"Yahya, we don't do scholarships. That would involve dif-ferent government departments, application procedures and so forth. I can't whistle one up just like that." Haydon leaned forward and placed his hands on the table. "I'll introduce you to the head man at the British Council, put in a good word. Why? What's the hurry? You've built a decent practice."

"But you can 'whistle one up', Haydon." Yahya scowled. "Why are you lying to me? You know that is untrue. You have control over the 'FCO Scholarships and Awards Scheme'. It is in your gift, and I am a perfect candidate."

Haydon was stunned. Yahya was seriously intending to

abandon his career and practice and leave Sudan just like that. Something drastic must have occurred for him to be so terrified. And he was right. If it was considered vital to national security, he could easily arrange to fulfil Yahya's demands.

"What I can do is agree an increase in your monthly legal retainer. A significant increase, to reflect the undoubted value of this information, and more to come in the future."

"I took a big risk for you before, when I gave you information that could get me killed. Killed Haydon. When I told you about Rashid al-Duri, you promised then to repay what you said was a 'debt of gratitude'. You surely remember that promise, so recently made?" He shook his head and cleared his throat. Looking directly into Haydon's eyes, he said. "You see it is this debt I am now asking you to repay."

"That is a conversation for another day, friend." Haydon leaned forward and pointed his finger in an aggressive gesture. "Right now, if you have actionable intelligence about a threat to the UK homeland, you are duty bound to share it with me."

"It is not for another day. It is for now or it is for never." He took out a handkerchief and wiped his forehead. "My life is in jeopardy. I must flee my country. For you. I have no alternative. Well there is one only, which would not be in your interest, and it would be my last resort. And not what I wish for."

"Is that a threat? Are you threatening me? Think carefully what you are saying, Yahya?" Haydon's voice hardened. "Suggesting you will withhold information? In return for a place on a scholarship scheme? You are a man of honour, more worthy than that."

"You talk to me about my honour?" Yahya's dark face reddened, and he slapped the palms of his hands on the table. "What would Mister Charlie Lomax or Mister Thomas

Ormond say about your honour. If they were here? Their cases are on your account Haydon, not on mine. You think I'm some sort of fool? It seems to me as if all of us are expendable to you. Listen to me, I don't wish to finish like them."

"You are our Embassy lawyer. You can't speak to me like that."

"If we cannot agree, then you shall have my resignation letter this day, and you will not see me again."

"I cannot give in to what amounts to blackmail."

"Blackmail. Honour. What savage and hypocritical words." He mopped his forehead with a handkerchief. "Which will not solve either of our problems."

They sat facing each other across the narrow desk in silence. Haydon felt his heart beating fast. He knew rage was showing on his face. He leaned back, closed his eyes and took slow, deep breaths. Charlie and Tom. A hard reminder. A worm inside his head whispered that Yahya's accusation was close to the truth.

"You are a pragmatic man, Haydon." Yahya broke the silence, rubbing at his temples in a rapid, circular motion. "I am offering you a trade. You understand? Essential for both of us. Let me be clear. The moment I am arrived safely in London, with an FCO award to enable me to live reasonably, and a visa to allow me to settle in UK, then I will provide you, personally, with the details I described, as well as further intelligence and names."

Haydon leaned back and stared at the ceiling. Right now, he needed to focus. *Obtain the desired result.* Yahya had vital information, probably the key to thwarting a terrorist attack planned against London, and he would not budge. Which surprised him. He'd thought he could massage or bribe or threaten Yahya over the line. Money wouldn't do it, and the man was too scared for his safety to give in to his threats.

"I hear you, Yahya." Haydon raised his arms as if in surrender and smiled. "Yes, I am a pragmatist, I think I can see a way to make this work. But there are complications. I need approvals from above. Which may not be straightforward. I will do my best. Is there any way I can convince you to provide the information now, on the understanding–"

"–I have told you my requirements Haydon." He crossed his arms and stared sternly back at him. "I have seen the price others have paid for their trust of you."

His dream of convincing Yahya to remain as a penetration agent within Al-Qaeda was dead in the water. And this information was time critical. Getting a visa and the FCO award would not be difficult, and would cost nothing. He could swing it, provided that Harbut and Glasson signed off on it.

"Make your preparations. Be ready to travel." Haydon leaned forward and clasped his hands together. "We'll meet here tomorrow same time. I'll hope to have obtained clarity for you by then."

"One thing more, Haydon." Yahya's voice fell to a near whisper. "These people are seeking to find out your home address, perhaps they are planning an action against you. Like me, you need to be careful until you leave."

"I will."

He shuffled down the bench and stood up. Pulling up the lever, the door unsealed with a sucking sound and swung open.

"Thank you, Yahya."

Chapter 41

It felt like being a soldier again. Butterflies flapping in his tummy, he hadn't felt those since Belfast. Never knowing if you were slap bang in the cross-hairs of some invisible rifle sight, an unknown enemy concealed in a tenement roof. In some odd way, he felt elated to be facing an existential threat. It eased the painful sense of failure in all areas of his life. He unlocked the door of the safe house and walked into the living room.

Yahya's warning had sunk in. He was a hunted man. Two weeks to survive in this place, to stay on alert, a step ahead of predators. Usually, he was the one providing reassurance to his agents, and they were the ones at risk. Much good his reassurances had been for Charlie. Assurances given in this same room. It seemed like karma that he should face the same dangers, and from the same people. Pouring himself a large scotch, he took a gulp, then sat down on a rickety wicker armchair. He ran his finger along the edge of the coffee table. Dusty and filthy. How come he'd never noticed? *What a tawdry and depressing place.* He'd have to use it as his bolt hole for these next ten days, then wash his hands of it and hand the keys to Ramesh.

He thought back over afternoons spent here with Lena, silent or laughing, embracing quietly, or chatting softly after making love. Those memories, which had seemed so special, now seemed sleazy and bleak. How long had Monkton known? Had he had him followed? Possibly. Or had she told him in a fit of anger, or worse, had he known from the start? Some skewed marital arrangement, perhaps she reported back after each illicit encounter, like a mole in an enemy camp, and he'd been the dupe all along. He let out a mirthless laugh.

They'd framed their fantasy around *Last Tango in Paris*. It had seemed apt, clever, at the time. Now, in his imagination, he saw images of the last scene of the film. Jeanne telling Paul her name. Then shooting him. He'd always known there'd be a tragic ending to their love story. If it had ever been a love story? It didn't matter now. He'd see her this one last time. They'd say goodbye and she wouldn't shoot him, although she might sneer, and that would hurt. He might have to endure a couple of uncomfortable encounters at diplomatic farewells, but he could steel himself to put on a dishonestly cheerful face.

They'd exchanged messages via the pigeonholes at the Sudan Club. He had written– *'Paul propose la denouement vendredi 18h00'*. Two days later, he found an envelope addressed to Paul. Opening it slowly, he detected a faint smell of gardenia. He read– *'Il vaut mieux ne rien savoir.'* Would she come? Her reply was ambiguous. He looked at his watch. Five o'clock. He lit a cigarette and inhaled, holding the smoke in, relishing the burning sensation in his lungs. He'd lost everything. So quickly. His job, his marriage, his self-respect, his reputation, now his mistress.

Maybe the Al-Qaeda people, or Abu Nidal, or whoever the hell was chasing him, would find him and do the job for Jeanne. A fitting ending.

He exhaled, leaned back, and closed his eyes. What to do about Yahya? The proper course of action was to inform Glasson of both meetings and request approval to move him to London. He should have done so before, at the time of the meeting in the garage, although what Yahya had said about Rashid and the attack was unsubstantiated, and he didn't even know now who the source was.

Glasson would be bound to interpret such intel as a continuation of his personal crusade against the Sheikh, which he'd made abundantly clear he was to cease and desist. Most likely he'd order him to extract the information from Yahya without agreeing to any terms until after the intel had been sifted and judged valid, but he was certain Yahya would not agree to that. He'd go to ground and disappear, and the intel would become valueless. Worse still would be if Glasson passed the product straight to Monkton, and, even if he held back Yahya's name, the intel would be enough for the Sheikh to identify the leak, with potentially fatal consequences for Yahya. Three on his conscience, that would be more than he could take.

He considered reporting on today's exchange but holding back details of the garage meeting and of Rashid's name. He could concoct a narrative that fitted Glasson's pre-existing belief that the culprits were Hamas or Abu Nidal. Palestinian anyway, not Afghan-Arabs. But that story would not hold if they later interrogated Yahya in London. Part of any deal was bound to include a thorough CI debrief. Then the truth would out, and with it any hope of a comfortable retirement would go splat.

The third option involved breaching every rule in the book and would be an act of gross disloyalty to the Service, with untold consequences for his future. The enmity and competition between Six and their colleagues north of the river was legendary. But it seemed the best course of action, offering a realistic chance of uncovering, and possibly thwarting, a major attack. Which was his paramount duty, not the comfort of his retirement, nor his personal safety, nor his loyalty to a politically motivated boss.

He lifted his briefcase onto the table and opened it, extracting a large satellite phone. He pulled out the long retractable antenna and powered the apparatus up. It took some time to establish a handshake with the satellite. Stubbing out his cigarette, he opened a notebook and put one finger on a line of numbers, which he punched into the satphone.

There was a long delay on the line, while the signal bounced off the Skynet 4 satellite some 22,000 miles up in space and came back down to earth. The ringing tone was distant and oddly muffled.

"Doyle."

"Warrenpoint."

"Go ahead."

"Requesting expedited reception for Zulu with urgent trade."

"Trade validity?"

"Confirmed."

"Details?"

"Your separate post tomorrow. Within 48 hours."

"Change of ownership."

"Unapproved."

"Understood."

He hung up. He'd put his friend on the spot. If things went beserk, he'd have destroyed Johnny's career as well as his own, but he knew his friend would understand things must be critical for him to have made this call. Once Yahya had safely arrived in the UK soil, MI5 could recruit him as a domestic confidential informant. They would manage him and agree to terms. He'd have to sell this to Yahya. It was imperfect, but the best he could achieve.

He sat by the window, chain smoking, staring down at

the unkempt garden. Rubbish was strewn around the small patch of brown lawn. He thought she wasn't going to come, but, just after half-past six, the outer gate clanged open and she strode across the courtyard, her face hidden behind a checked shawl, the metal gate slamming shut behind her. He waited by the door and held it open as her footsteps approached, uncertain of what to expect.

She walked past him into the room, placing her handbag on the table, and unwound the scarf from her face. She looked tired. Her lipstick was smudged. Tossing her head back, she let her hair fall down behind her neck. She sat down, crossed her legs, and stared up at him.

"*La denouement*. That's when the lady gets to sing, *chéri*?" Her voice was husky. She paused and took out a packet of Marlborough and lit one. "Can I have a Scotch please. With plenty of ice. No water."

He went to the fridge and pulled out the ice tray. He poured the drink and handed it to her. She narrowed her eyes and looked at him. He sat down opposite her. She didn't reach out to him.

"His work defines what he is. Since his injury, it was a grenade fragment, you know. In Afghanistan. He's never been the same since." She sipped her drink. "We were a happy couple back then, I was the perfect military wife, we Lebanese know how to play a subservient role. Since then, it's been his successes that count. It means everything to him. Maybe you never understood that."

"But what–"

"I nursed him through it. The depression. Drink. Then his friend Bill's grisly death in Beirut. A big blow, knocked him over." She lit a cigarette, then turned away. "Afghanistan gave him a new lease of life, brought him out, lifted him up. He became the all-American hero again. Bill Casey congratulated him personally, from his hospital bed, just before he died. He was so proud of that."

She smiled at Haydon, a kind smile, he thought. He'd never seen her look so vulnerable. "Then you." She sucked on her cigarette. "Not about stags with antlers, he'd be OK with that, some sort of Hemmingway thing. But worse. You threaten to upend his whole story, his narrative, his biggest success. Surely you can see that?"

"I didn't–"

"I hear you're leaving." She blew a smoke ring towards the ceiling. "When?"

"Couple of weeks, less."

"You'll always be a loner, Haydon. For you it's anonymity that's all important. Like you want some kind of magic cloak." She glanced at him, then turned away again. "He and I have shared a life. An imperfect one. But you aren't able to let your defenses down and expose yourself to the light. You asked me that question, I don't even know if you meant it. But I wouldn't come with you. You knew that. We'd just be drifters, sharing a bed, estranged in our hearts from the get go."

"*Il vaut vraiment mieux ne rien savoir?*" He felt drained. It couldn't get worse. He felt like a beaten up rag-doll. He grinned. A stupid grin. "Maybe, like for Paul, it really would have been better not to know."

"We lied and we knew we were lying. That's God's truth, *chéri.*"

"Trouble is, lying is what I do for a living."

"I hope you find your way to emerge into the light Haydon. I do. You British public schoolboys are like mushrooms. What the heck did they do to you in those places?" She reached over and touched his cheek gently, then glanced at her watch. "I've got to go."

She wound the scarf around her head and stood up. She gave him a light kiss on the lips and was gone.

The Sheikh

The Sheikh

Chapter 42

Damazine, January 1991

The two men strolled along the line of beehives, the field of sunflowers glowing brightly in the background. They wore no protective clothing, although the swarms around each hive formed thick, black clouds in the mid-morning heat and hummed a threatening note, like the sound of a cello tuning up. They were both dressed in white *jellabiyas* and sandals and looked like any of the farm workers busying themselves around the fields.

"Perfectly organised societies, Rashid, you see." The tall man pointed. "So long as they have abundant nectar, they are never aggressive. *Abadaan*, never. Not to us, not to their neighbours. I have provided them with so many feddans of sunflowers, they live a beautiful life with plentiful nectar. If only we humans had such simple needs."

"Ah, ya Sheikh, but it is the women that rule over all those male bees. Imagine it."

"The queen remains always in the hive. Her purpose is to mate and produce offspring. The men work, they build, and fight to protect the hive."

"I will never feel safe with them, as you do."

They walked on towards the reservoir, the expanse of water stretching into a distant haze, then turned and climbed the steps up to the veranda of the small farm building. The Sheikh sat down, Rashid went inside and returned with tall glasses of cold lemonade on a tray, and plates of dates.

"I listened to the radio." Rashid poured out the lemonade, then sat. "President Bush is calling it '*Operation Desert*

Storm'. Yesterday they bombed Kuwait and Iraq heavily and there are many dead. It is as you warned, ya Sheikh."

"Now there are so many infidel troops despoiling our land of the holy places. Maybe one million of American soldiers, English and French and Germans. And more of other *kuffaar,* shaming our people and those slaves of America, the blasphemous and corrupt Saudi princelings. The Americans want our oil, they need our oil, and that of Iraq too, and of Kuwait. They will never leave away from our lands again, believe me, unless they are driven out, like we drove those Russian ruffians fleeing away from Afghanistan."

The Sheikh extracted a *subha* from a pocket and chanted under his breath. Ninety-nine ebony beads. Each one representing one of the ninety-nine names of God.

"*Allah, al-rahman, al-rahim, al-malik, al-quddus, as-salaam, al-mumin-*" He mumbled.

Rashid sat motionless, staring out over the water; it seemed to stretch as far as if it were a sea. He took off his spectacles and cleaned them with his handkerchief. The Sheikh seemed to look straight through him, eyes blinking, as he moved the little beads, which clicked as he chanted the words.

When he finished, he lowered his head and sat quietly for a while.

"They will smash up everything in Kuwait and Iraq, then they will demand from them payment in oil to rebuild it up again." The Sheikh turned his head from side to side. "It is good for business, you see. War. It drives the economy but also technological innovation in America."

"But Afghanistan–"

"That is my meaning. Afghanistan has no oil. It has nothing of value. Everything is smashed up. But there will be no rebuilding. Those Afghanis do not have wherewithal to pay." He replaced the *subha* into his pocket and folded his hands on his lap. "When the Russians left, the Americans left also.

Those of us who had done the fighting were abandoned and forgotten. The moneys the Americans and the Saudis had paid us to fight ceased with the peace. It made the *mujahadeen* feel like they were mercenaries, or prostitutes. We thought we had been fighting for a cause, for Allah, but we found we had been serving the devil."

They sat in silence, sipping their lemonades. A long line of birds flew overhead. They could hear the swish of their wings as they passed, heading south, away from the northern winter.

"Shall I proceed with the action. Against the Englishman?"

"Yes, but with caution. I do not wish to tell our Sudanese friends, but Abu Nidal will be so happy to take credit for a strike against a Western spy. Pay them well please, as before, in cash." The Sheikh folded his arms. "The American told me this Englishman opposes our discussions, and he blames us for the operation against the hotel. Have you discovered his house address yet?"

"No. I have asked the lawyer to find it. I will pressure him if necessary."

"He arranged the visas?"

"Yes. The operatives are ready to leave in one week."

"We must await confirmation that all items are in place. How are they to be delivered?"

"It is agreed with our friends, together with Ibrahim Huwayji, Syrian Air Force Intelligence. The items will go by diplomatic bag to the attaché at their Embassy in London." Rashid took out a notebook and flipped the pages. "Perhaps within ten days."

"*Alhamdililah*. Thanks be to God." The Sheikh narrowed his eyes. "You see, this will be the first of many blows. A mighty strike to awaken them to our sufferings."

"And the American, ya Sheikh, are we safe?"

"He wants me to act with him against Imad Mughniyeh

and Hezbollah. For which they will pay us five million dollars." He wound his *keffiyeh* carefully around his head and tucked it in. "We shall continue with our past collaboration, as it was when we were in Peshawar. He believes the *Shia* to be our common enemy. I have agreed with him that it is so. They scare him most, that godless Mughniyeh, and Hamas and Abu Nidal. These make so much noise inside his head."

"This is *Taqiya,* ya Sheikh. Deceiving an enemy for a pious goal?"

"Yes, Rashid, my friend, it is *Taqiya*. Please tend with care to all details and risks. Especially the commitment of the operatives, we have to be certain of each one of them."

Haydon slept badly. He was on edge, his hearing alert to barking dogs and extraneous noises, his Service pistol resting on the bedside table beside him. His pursuers wouldn't have much difficulty discovering his home address, maybe Salah had already handed over his details to the Sheikh? He was going to have to spend his remaining nights holed up at the safe house. Meanwhile he'd raised the security level at the Embassy, circulating an alert that, after the hotel attack, warnings had been circulating of the possibility of further attacks on westerners.

Burly Des had driven him home, following a circuitous route, and was staying in the spare room. Haydon had kept his eyes on the rear-view mirror, watching the skinnies following in their battered Datsun and finding their presence oddly comforting. Would it be, like in the Godfather, their sudden and surprising absence that would herald an imminent attack? He groaned. He couldn't wait for it all to be over, to look back and see this desert land disappearing behind him.

Getting to the Embassy early, he sent a FLASH urgent dispatch to Johnny by diplomatic pouch. He started working his way through handover papers, but as soon as he'd initialed the last page, his secretary produced another bunch of files and dumped them on his desk. There was a knock on the door, and Yahya entered. Haydon nodded, stood up and wordlessly led the way out of the office and up the stairs. They sat opposite each other in The Cage. Haydon could smell sweat on the lawyer, who kept wiping his forehead with a handkerchief.

"Yahya. I have a solution." He leaned forward and looked directly into the other man's eyes. "It's imperfect. I have to navigate rocks, but it's what I can do. But it has to be this way, for your own safety, it must seem as if I'm not involved in this at all."

The lawyer stared at him. Haydon could read the mistrust in his eyes. "That does not make any sense to me, you see."

"Listen to me. Here is cash for you to buy a return ticket to London, and for your immediate expenses." He placed an envelope on the table. "Apply for your visa with Rasha, giving the reason as a badly sick relative who you must visit hurriedly before they pass away. I will ask her to expedite the application as soon as you have submitted it. With luck you could travel tomorrow. Then give me your flight details."

"But—"

"When you arrive in London. Take a taxi to this hotel." He passed a sheet of paper across. "You will be contacted by phone by Mister Jackson. If you do not hear from him within a couple of hours, ring this number on the paper."

"But the visa to stay, the scholarship?"

"Mister Jackson is a senior man in our domestic security service. He is not part of my organisation. It is important you understand your future relationship can only be with them.

You must, this is crucial, tell him you would not provide this information to the Embassy here, because you have reason to believe it not secure. You have to say that you learned that I met secretly with the Sheikh. You insist you will only speak to people in London." He made a steeple with his hands, as if he were praying. "He will be aware, and you will agree your terms with him. He knows of your needs, and that you will provide the information only once you are satisfied you are safe and can stay in UK until any danger is past."

Yahya slapped his hand on the table.

"Why can't you agree with me here, Haydon? I know you."

"Please, believe me, Yahya. I am not playing games with you. This is what I can do. I understand the dangers and pressures and I want to hear your information, but it would be dangerous for you, for reasons I cannot tell you."

"And if he doesn't help, what am I to do?"

"I have spoken to Mister Jackson, Yahya. You have my word that I trust him completely. He has the power to arrange everything you asked me for. This is the best way forward. But it must be that our discussions together never happened. You understand? This is vital for both of our sakes, and for this to work."

Yahya seemed to shrink. He put his hands over his face, then shook his head.

"It seems I have no choice, Haydon. I so much hope you are not signing my death warrant."

Chapter 43

Khartoum, January 1991

It was to be the last of a ritual line of dull diplomatic farewells, a final send off on the evening before his departure. Ali Kabbani had insisted, although Haydon had implored him.

"Ali, my good friend. Can't we have supper the two of us, laugh and enjoy each other's company." He pulled a face. "I've said too many goodbyes, I feel like a squawking parrot, desperate to sound genuine as I embrace people I don't like."

"*Abadaan.* Never. Diplomats are seldom genuine, you see, we all know that, and we forgive you for it. I demand this honour. I shall slaughter a sheep to salute the departure of an English gentleman and his tame parrot alter ego. And I'll take it as an unforgivable insult if you refuse."

"Please, as few guests as possible."

"All right, all right."

January was the best month in Khartoum. Cool evenings. Mid-twenties during the day. Clear skies, without the usual layer of orange sand suspended in the sky. El-Haj was driving, with Des in the front passenger seat, his M-16 carbine on his lap, eyes scanning around the vehicle. There had been no sign of followers, but Haydon could sense the security man was on edge. Since Harry's death, he'd become withdrawn, his propensity for banter blunted. He'd put in for a transfer, and Haydon had approved it.

Omdurman was heaving, the traffic more anarchic than ever. Undisciplined buses and lorries spewed black smoke and honked loud multi-tone horns, forcing bicyclists, pedestrians and mule carts onto the pavements. A fruit stall had been knocked over and disgorged oranges and bananas onto the road. Giggling children darted in front of cars to pick up the unexpected bounty and hurried off. A scrawny dog darted past with a live chicken in its mouth. Haydon watched the chaos with a frisson of pleasure. He'd miss it, the colours, the windblown white garments, the multifarious noises and smells, and yes, the outright confusion.

The heavy wooden gates of the Kabbani compound opened as they drove up. The party was in full swing, a low hum of conversation drowned by the drums of a troupe of musicians, seated cross-legged on a dais. Entering the courtyard, Haydon saw Kabbani seated at a table by the central fountain. His host stood up and opened his arms.

"Welcome, welcome to my honoured guest, *marhaban*." The two men embraced. "A small gathering, as you wished, you see. A few of our good friends only."

"Thank you, Ali." Haydon sat down. A waiter handed him a large tumbler of scotch. He raised his glass and drank. "Brrrrr. How can your livers survive these endless neat whiskys?"

"It's the ice, you see, it's made from Nile water. It does something to it, it fortifies the constitution."

"Is Yahya here?"

"He phoned to say he couldn't come. He has a work thing, I think."

"Hey, limey!"

An arm slapped him on the back. He looked up. Monkton had his arm around Lena and was smiling down at him. Haydon stood and kissed her on the cheek, smelling the gardenia, avoiding her eyes. He hadn't found it awkward to run into her at social events, it was as if none of it had ever happened. He felt no rush of excitement nor guilt, nor even anger. It seemed like an easy encounter with a colleague and his wife. A relief. He had enough to worry about, watching his back for bearded gunmen. Probably being sent courtesy of Monkton's friend.

"Gotten tired of farewell parties yet?" Monkton punched him on the arm.

"I'm ripe to go, Pete. Retirement beckons. Cobwebs. Boredom. Golf. Bodily descent."

"We just dropped in to say our goodbyes, then we're off to another grisly dinner." Lena sighed and gave him a hug, then turned and wandered off into the crowd. Monkton put his arm around him and guided him to a table away from the band. Tall flares lit up the courtyard, casting orange shadows on the high walls. A thin moon had risen, and with it a cool breeze. Haydon shivered. In the orange light, the American's face seemed carved of stone, absent of emotion.

Monkton pulled his chair closer.

"Listen buddy. I wanted to clear out the air before you go. Straight up."

He leaned forward, face close. Haydon could smell his aftershave. "We've been on different sides of a bunch of stuff, we don't need to talk about it. But I want to hold on to you as a friend, help out if I can. Put the stinking shit behind us."

"I'd like that, Pete. I'll be gone tomorrow. You'll have no more bumps from me."

"Look it. You know that Buckley was a close friend of mine, best man at my wedding to Lena. We went back a long way, did a lot of stuff together. For me it's deeply personal, and he single handedly destroyed most of our mid-East networks."

"I know how important this is to you."

"I never came across a guy as dangerous as Imad Mughniyeh. No other terrorist killed as many Americans. He's way at the top of our list. By a Texas mile. So I gotta put him right out the picture. My life's work is to terminate Mister Mughniyeh. But he's a chameleon, we've never been able to keep a bead on him."

"What's your point?"

They paused as a tall man stooped to greet them, touching his hand to his heart and bowing, before moving off, sensitive to a private conversation.

"Payback is overdue, and this right here in Khartoum is the time and the place. Turabi has kindly put these guys all together in one spot, a full bag of tricks." He placed his hands on the table. "They come and go and meet each other and we watch them. There ain't nothing in my in-tray but Mughniyeh, and I'm not letting go until he's done and six feet under and in small pieces and I've seen them buried."

"Pete. I understand this. I'd feel the same in your shoes."

"That's the reason you and I have been hitting at each other." He scratched his head. "It's been tough for you that the top cards are all in my stack, but that's the way it is."

"I'm out of here on Friday. File closed." Haydon ran his fingers through his hair, then paused and took a sip of his drink. "My contrarian views will be yesterday's fish and chips. Mark will send out a pliant replacement who will toe the line. End of."

"I admire you, Haydon, we're two of a kind. Fellow Arabists and fellow soldiers. You're tenacious and when you got something in your teeth you don't let go. Plus you're a natural rat-catcher. Just is that our interests don't coincide. Pity."

"So, you're going to sink Turabi's pet project, bringing the Sunni and Shia together in one happy family."

"Yeah. We've got a decent handle on that." He took a packet of cigarettes out of his pocket and placed it on the table.

"You going to meet up with the Lance people?"

"In a couple of weeks. Thank you for the intro." Haydon reached over and helped himself to a cigarette. He lit it, inhaling deeply, feeling the smoke down into his lungs. He needed one.

"So, we're good, buddy?" Monkton stood up. "We'll hook up in London. Drink more of that old bourbon."

"We're good Pete. You go well."

The two men shook hands, Monkton looking him in the eye.

Haydon sat down and enjoyed his cigarette. He was trying to quit smoking, but that didn't work when triple strength whisky was coursing through your veins. He noticed Monkton had left the packet on the table and pocketed it. Probably had a bug in it. He laughed. Probably Pete had bugged him long ago, perhaps even at the safe house. He'd not said a word about Lena. Maybe she was right, his ego was tied up in his work.

For the Americans it was all about the Iranians, about the mad Ayatollah, Hezbollah and Mughniyeh: these were the bogeymen. The Shia. The Embassy siege and the failed rescue attempt had done for President Carter. Then the Beirut bomb that killed 240 Marines. The kidnappings. And the bombing of the US Embassy in 1983. For them, the Sunni Afghan-Arabs were a friendly bunch that had fought alongside the Stars and Stripes in Afghanistan. If you overlooked Hamas and ANO, of course. Maybe Monkton was right to focus on the immediate threat and not the coming one.

For his part, he'd done everything he could. Warned his bosses, repeatedly. Alerted Five to a specific threat. Now it was out of his hands. He stood up and walked unsteadily towards the crowd.

He felt a stab of nostalgia as he hugged Ali Kabbani and waved goodbye. Would he make it back to this bitter-sweet city again? He stumbled as he walked through the gate and had to steady himself against the wall. The party had passed in a blur. He realised he had a headache coming on.

Des was standing by the car. The tall man looked agitated. Haydon checked his watch.

Two thirty. He shouldn't have kept them up so late. Thoughtless of him. "Sorry Des. Lost–"

"Lucky you stayed out late. Someone just lobbed an RPG round through your bedroom window. Came through on the security net just now." Des held the car door open for him. "Boss, we're going to the safe house. From there directly to the airport in the morning. Ramesh will collect your cases and bring them."

"My staff?"

"The bang will have woken your guard up. No injuries reported."

"The house didn't catch fire?"

"Not reported." He shut the door and jumped in the front. "Haj, take the Shambat bridge. We need to avoid obvious routes, then take the Blue Nile bridge."

They drove in silence, Des scanning the empty streets, his weapon cocked. Haj staring straight ahead, steering jerkily. Nothing like going out with a bang, Haydon thought. He'd sobered up quickly. They hadn't been smart enough to check that he was home and nicely tucked up in bed. They wouldn't have entered the compound, anyway, just fired the thing off from across the road. He wondered how they'd got his home address. *Salah?* It had become personal for Monkton, so he'd admitted. Now it was for him too, he'd received a message directly from The Sheikh. Yahya had warned him of the danger, but he hadn't thought they'd dare.

Haj dropped them at the safe house. Des settled down in the living room. Haydon knew he wasn't going to get a lot of sleep.

The Sheikh

The Sheikh

Chapter 44

The atmosphere in the Office was upbeat. Haydon's imminent departure had set off a cascade of musical chairs. The attack on his house seemed to be viewed as a comic parting shot, the powers that be didn't upgrade the threat level to the Embassy or to Western interests in Sudan. There were more farewell rituals, although these were markedly less sincere than his Khartoum send offs had been. He wondered how you could spend decades in a workplace and end up without a single colleague you could call a friend. He relished the countdown of days to his departure.

He felt curiously detached, and busied himself with the bureaucracy of retirement, crossing swords with Personnel about his pension and holiday pay, knowing that it would all end up on Glasson's desk. His meeting with Glasson, when it finally happened, was predictable. There was something valedictory in his overt chumminess, generous with the smartie jar but condescending in other ways. He had become ever squatter, as if success had puffed him up like a Michelin man. His well-tailored double-breasted suits seemed to amplify his square, frog-like shape.

"Scotch, Haydon?" He stood by his office bar and handed him a large, cut-glass tumbler. "Let's raise a glass to past shenanigans and to your new career. Said yes to Lance Group yet?"

"Seeing the MD next week."

"Peter Joliffe. Good man. I'll put in a word. Boodles chap."

"Not sure what that looks like."

"Take the job. Lance is going places." Glasson rolled a long cigar between his palms, then leaned down to sniff it. "You can understand why I've had to keep you waiting all week. The IRA mortar attack on Downing Street has kept us at it all hours."

"Their most audacious outrage since the Brighton bomb. Do you remember that day?" Haydon rolled his eyes. "The atmosphere doesn't seem as sinister and dark now as it was back then. We even questioned whether we might be losing the war against the IRA."

"This one was impressively meticulous planned. Again. The boyos worked out exact angles and where the van with the launcher had to be parked for optimum accuracy. We were dead lucky. The war cabinet was in session in the cabinet room. The Prime Minister was looking out of the window when the first mortar exploded in the garden. He saw it go off. Middle East terror is in the undergrowth this week."

"Now I understand why an RPG round through my bedroom window got drowned out."

"Haydon, I'm sending Archie Stevens down to take your place. He knows the form. He's to focus on immediate threats. Hezbollah. Hamas. Abu Nidal. He has exceptional knowledge of these bad actors."

"A solid man. I'll meet up with him for a handover session."

"Do that. But don't stir up trouble. Really."

Haydon splayed his palms out on the coffee table.

"As if!" He chuckled. "The atmosphere in Khartoum has become increasingly tense, different radical groups popping up all over the place. It's worrying. The rocket attack might not be an isolated incident."

"Not your concern anymore, old boy." Glasson started the lengthy rigmarole of lighting his cigar. "Let's look forward, not back. Cheers."

He raised his glass and drank, then puffed furiously at his cigar.

"Oh Haydon, I've sorted out your bits and pieces with Personnel. Squashed their pettifogging complaints. It's the least I could do for you."

"Thank you, Mark. And I want to flag up that my number two there, Ramesh Patel, has been doing a fine job, he's due for a move up soon. He's competent and disciplined. I've submitted my review."

"Noted." He released a column of smoke. It hung in the air and curled upwards. He took Haydon's arm and led him to the window. They clinked glasses.

"It's taking forever, you know." He pointed to the building site by the river, numerous cranes pointing upwards like giant's arms. "Do you think I'll move in before it's my time to follow you out of the door into the private sector?"

"I used to dream of an office there, looking down over the river." Haydon laughed. "At least it'll be bomb proof."

"We've come a long way, old friend. From being Oxley pipsqueaks together." Glasson turned back abruptly and went to sit behind his desk.

"Come down to my country place one weekend, Haydon. Don't be a stranger. Belinda would love to see you. What am I going to do without you to butt heads with? You're a cussed sod, but by God, I'm going to miss you."

Haydon stood in front of the mirror in the bathroom and squeezed at the copious middle age spread of his waistline with disgust. He needed to run again, to join a gym, get back to playing squash. Now was the perfect time. There was no excuse. He had arranged to meet Johnny for supper and decided to walk along the river as far as Greenwich, then catch the new Docklands Light Railway back and walk on to Soho.

The snow that had fallen heavily the week before had melted, leaving dirty patches on the pavement. The hazy winter sun peeking through the mist didn't warm his cheeks. He walked fast, his panting another reminder of how unfit he'd become. Looking up, he glanced at the endless ranks of cranes. He'd read somewhere the docklands redevelopment was the biggest building project anywhere in the world. He could believe it. But who was going to buy these gigantic quantities of new flats?

He paused and glanced over his shoulder at the reflection in an estate agent's window, then realised that, for the first time in ages, he didn't need to worry about watching his back. No need for tradecraft. No dangers were lurking in the shadows. It would not be difficult to leave all that behind. Living a life away from the shadows might make him whole again, although there was no way back for his marriage. He was staring at a blank sheet of paper. He must make good use of it.

He thought about Yahya. If all had gone to plan, MI5 would by now have netted him and registered him as a 'walk-in' – a source that had voluntarily approached the security services in country, with valuable information about domestic terror. Had they offered him what he needed, in return for his information? If not, then the lawyer would face a horrible situation, returning to Khartoum to find himself in a fatal trap between Zaki and Salah, and with no support from the Embassy.

Johnny was sitting at their usual corner table when Haydon arrived. He was wearing half-moon reading glasses and peering at the stiff menu card. It was early, and the normally noisy restaurant was quiet. Haydon ordered a strong Bloody Mary. The two men studied each other with quizzical expressions.

"This is the furthest off books I've been in three decades of service." Johnny's face was deadpan, the reading glasses giving him a professorial look. "Imagine, I'd been looking forward to enjoying my pension."

"You'd loathe a dull life, Johnny. If we end up in Ford Open prison together, I'm told there's a fine cricket team." He wagged his finger at Johnny. "Huge Jamaican fast bowlers, violent drug dealers in the main, with bald conmen acting as unbiased umpires."

"We're over the first hurdle." Johnny leaned forward and spoke in an undertone. "He's been accepted as a walk-in. His story checked out. He wished to share information with us but didn't dare to do so at the Embassy in Khartoum. He's told us about his concerns, specifically about you, how he'd been told by his source that you'd met covertly with the Sheikh. Clever that. Putting yourself in the frame as a decoy."

"Gave you names?"

"Better. Gave us copies of the visa applications and photocopies of their passports. Which are now on every border watch list." Johnny drummed his fingers on the table. "Sudanese passports in the names of 'Hamid Bebiker Nur' and 'Hamza al-Bushra'."

"You cross check them with the names and photos from the hotel list?"

"Your people shared those with us a while back, routine distribution. Our liaison man handed over these new details and asked for any matches, names, photos, preferably both. There are high confidence photo matches with your

'Abdelrahman Yassin' and 'Hassan el-Mahgoub'. We now know we're dealing with two serious ex-military explosives experts."

"These people use so many aliases. They're like bloody ghosts."

"Maybe they confuse themselves too." Johnny smiled. "I'm pretty sure the first one is, in fact, an Egyptian colonel whose real name is Salah Ahmed al-Din."

"What's next?"

"The applications gave an address in High Wycombe, which we've had in our sights from other enquiries." He scratched his head. "God knows why High Wycombe attracts so many Islamic lunatics, I thought it was a quiet, rural place. We're starting to surveil it, setting up a unit across the road."

"How is Yahya bearing up?"

"Terrified. He can't see any safe way to go home." Johnny tapped his fingers on the table. "But we've got him a student visa for a year, and we're working on a fellowship at the Middle East Centre at St Antony's Oxford. Luckily, it's practically cost free, so approvals shouldn't be difficult to get."

"Did he reveal his source?"

"A certain Zaki Bayazid, relative of his wife. You know of him?"

"I've met him. He's the manager at the Sheikh's Damazine farm, part of his inner circle."

The waiter came and took their order. Haydon's mind was racing. They both lit cigarettes and sat in silence. The key thing was to keep Yahya in play, at least until the bombers had been identified by their passports and tracked on from a border. But if Zaki sensed Yahya had been turned, they'd dump those passports and consider the High Wycombe address to be blown. Then they'd find another way, under different names.

"Are you creating a legend for him to play back to Zaki?"

"Medical. His wife is joining him this week. Yahya told her he has a series of urgent tests. Cancer. That'll buy us a few weeks. His medical condition can get worse if necessary." Johnny turned away and blew smoke towards the wall. "We're considering whether he should send a message to Zaki, or whether that might seem out of character."

"Better wait and see if Zaki contacts him. Might bring more fish into our pond."

"Look Haydon. We've dragged this smelly one across the line." He rubbed his fist into his hand and frowned. "Five have taken on a walk-in from what used, once upon a time, to be your patch. This man has information about a serious domestic threat that may dovetail with other ongoing investigations. Our imperative is identifying their target, when and how they'll act."

"You want me to butt out?"

"It would be wiser for both of us, and for the investigation. You get to breathe a sigh of relief and let things follow their proper path. Better you know nothing and stay far away. You can focus on your retirement package and enjoy sleeping in."

The waiter placed plates of pasta in front of them. Johnny leaned down and sniffed. "*Tartufi!* Heavenly." Both men stubbed out their cigarettes.

"*Inboccalupo.* Good counsel. I hereby duly butt out." Haydon twirled spaghetti around his fork. He felt relieved. He'd passed the parcel and that was that, he didn't want to hear any more.

"If I need your help, I'll request it from Six. Through official channels."

"You know I'm up for a highly paid job in Dubai."

"Horrid place, you won't like it." Johnny made a face. "Security company. Money for old rope."

"Crooks, tarts and accountants. Which one are you?"

The Sheikh

"Piss off. I'll be better paid than you."

Chapter 45

Salah Ahmed al-Din stood motionless in a long queue at passport control at Terminal 3 at Heathrow Airport. He had flown from Istanbul, choosing a flight that would be crowded, preponderantly with Muslims. He felt anonymous, concealed in this cowed and shuffling line, each passenger seeming to approach the passport officer in their turn as a humble supplicant.

He thought they must all look equally nervous to the white officers, frowning down from their high stools. Unlike most of the men in the line, he wore western clothes, a blue blazer and chinos, dark glasses tucked into his breast pocket. He'd looked every bit the businessman that his passport claimed him to be.

Hamid Bebiker Nur. He had repeated the name enough times, seeking to convince himself it was his real name. He'd counted up the number of identities he could remember travelling under in these last years. Fourteen. You had to train yourself to adapt and grow into each identity, each nationality. Today he was Sudanese. That wasn't difficult. He'd been born in southern Egypt, in Asyut, not so far from the Sudanese border. According to his passport, he'd been born in Dongola.

He'd never been to the place, but he'd done his research; enough to manage a casual enquiry. He shuffled forward a couple of steps. Another 15 minutes, he calculated.

Looking over at the adjacent line, he caught sight of Hamza – well, that was the name on his passport – approaching the booth. His line had moved more quickly. He turned away and looked straight ahead, keeping the tall figure in his peripheral vision. Behind the immigration officer's booth, he noticed the large rectangular windows made from darkened one-way glass. He sensed eyes peering out from behind them, focusing on each of the faces in turn, searching for a match with the lengthy watch lists they'd have at their fingertips. We probably all look the same to them, he thought. Unless you had an obvious scar or facial disfigurement. He noticed Hamza had been waved through the booth and saw his back disappearing towards the exit.

This was going to be a quick one. He'd make sure of it. Do the job and get out of the country before the bang went off. Be back at Heathrow within five days and gone. Job done. All the gear was in place, Harun had told him. Their job was to rig the truck, which wasn't complicated, so long as you had a proper workspace and the right tools. In Kabul, they used to rig a truck in less than two hours; it had been a sort of assembly line for suicide vehicles. What happened after they rigged the truck was not their problem. Some fantasist who believed that becoming *Shaheed* would earn him 72 virgins in heaven would drive the truck to the target, gripping hard to the dead-man's-switch. As soon as he let go of it, he'd discover whether his improbable prize was real or imaginary.

"Next."

He stepped up to the booth and handed over his passport, breathing slowly and relaxing his facial muscles. The officer opened it and held it up, comparing the photograph and the face.

"Purpose of your visit?"

"Visiting relatives. New-born. Nephew." He smiled. "Length of stay?" The officer's face was unsmiling. "Ten days."

"Staying where?"

"With my sister in Canterbury."

The officer stamped his passport and waved him through.

He'd braced himself not to look at the darkened window, staring ahead as he walked towards the exit. In the baggage hall, he found his suitcase already circulating on the belt. After clearing customs, he followed signs for the underground and bought a ticket to Marylebone.

Descending the escalator, he found Hamza standing by the exit, looking up past him. "Clean?"

"Nothing." The tall man rubbed his cheek, then turned and walked ahead of him towards the platform.

As the train pulled in, Hamza stepped in quickly, while Hamid waited by the door of the next carriage, jumping in once the doors were closing. Every few stops, they stepped out and repeated the routine. At Earls Court Hamid followed Hamza up the escalator and onto the street.

Hamid hailed a taxi and gave the driver an address in Southall.

"We're black." Hamza said. Seating himself next to Hamid. "We can relax."

"Never. Why the change of destination?"

"Harun said the High Wycombe cell may have become insecure. We're to stay at the workshop and await contact."

"Should we be worried?"

"Alert, my friend, we stay alert, not worried."

Johnny Doyle sat, scratching his head, at the head of the long table in the Ops room of MI5's HQ near Euston Station.

"Report please."

"They're operational. We've seen them at Arrivals pretending not to know each other, yet here they are running dry-cleaning routines. Look at this CCTV from Heathrow tube station." The operator scrolled a black-and-white image forward on a large screen and pointed. "Here, Hamza is watching Hamid's back as he descends the escalator. They're aware."

"We have them entering Heathrow tube at 11.07, and then again walking away down Warwick Road at Earls Court at 11.43." The image showed the two blurry figures walking out of shot. "After that nothing."

"And High Wycombe?"

"Our lookout post has a clear view of the front of the semi-detached house." Perkins ran the followers section. His face was sombre. The screen showed a nondescript two-storey house, paint peeling off around the windows. "No movement. No sign of life."

"Strange. Or was that address always intended to be a bum steer?" Johnny rubbed his chin. "Keep watching. Raise the priority level. We don't want to send out their faces and risk tipping them off. Agreed?"

The men around the table nodded their heads. This was not a great start to a major op.

Haydon was made to wait for more than an hour in a dingy interview room on the second floor of Century House. In all his years at SIS, he had never ventured into the territory of the Internal Directorate. The room was windowless, empty except for a cheap metal desk and six wooden chairs, and lit by ugly fluorescent strip lights. Odd that they'd tipped him off by this obvious sign of intimidation, instead of trying to catch him off his guard in a more friendly forum.

He thought back over the past months, looking inside and scanning his conscience. Again and again he'd warned his bosses of the danger, and repeatedly been warned off. Now the country he'd sworn to protect faced a threat that could have been, should have been, countered and neutralised. He would not roll over and help them out of a political mess. No, they'd have to squeeze it out of him, although they'd find some way of skewering him, behind the almighty fig-leaf of 'National Security'.

Paul Cheeseman, Director of Internal Security, swept into the room, followed by Greg Harbut and Anthony Plant, the Service's in-house lawyer. Impressive. The three men sat down and stared unsmilingly at Haydon, staying silent for a long couple of minutes. Had some psychological consultant advised them on methods of coercion? Haydon smiled. The three men remained coldly impassive. He'd crossed paths, over the years, with Cheeseman. Pathologically humourless, he was typical of an aggressive little man, pink cheeked and with a terrier's quivering stance. Well-suited to the job of Glasson's attack dog. Attack poodle more like it. Cheeseman leaned forward and tapped his fingers on the table.

"You think it's funny, do you?" Tap tap tap.

"I'm sorry. But you resemble a panel of hanging judges."

"This is no laughing matter." Cheeseman scowled. "Did you think the Office wouldn't find out?"

"Good morning to you too, Greg." Haydon turned to his usually affable colleague.

"Might you ask him to explain the subject before recounting riddles. Find out what exactly?"

"Haydon, you're up to your neck in muck." Greg maintained a gloomy face. "It appears you've gone rogue."

"No idea what you're on about Greg. You've been listening to the wrong people."

"Better you come clean." Cheeseman's face flushed. "There may be serious repercussions, and if it's found that you've violated the Act, the terms of your departure will obviously be reviewed. Harshly reviewed."

"Greg, I'm halfway out the door. I'm hardly likely to wish to immerse myself in pig shit right at the end of my career. I'm focused on peace and harmony and a quiet sunset."

"Where is Yahya Abdelaziz?" Cheeseman's face seemed to go from pink to red.

"In Khartoum I presume. Why?"

"Did you facilitate his escape?"

"Escape from what? He's the Embassy's lawyer for Chrissake. He's no need to escape from anywhere."

So, they know he's gone. Gone with potentially dangerous information. Someone tipped them off. But who knew? Salah? Monkton? How? Unless they got Yahya in their claws, they could never establish his role. And right now, they don't know where he is. Although that's a matter of time. They'll work backwards from his visa application, although that came under the Home Office. As did MI5. Then there'd be an almighty dust up between the two security services and their respective ministers. Which would finish right at the top. But if Five got the bombers? He realised Cheeseman was talking.

"You are under investigation for breaches of the Official Secrets Act."

"On what grounds?"

"I have revoked your pass." Cheeseman's fingers were tapping away. "Return it at the desk on your way out. You will have no further access to this building. Return here within 24 hours with a written statement detailing your recent interactions with Yahya Abdelaziz. Travel outside of London is prohibited without approval in writing from my department. Do you understand?"

"Well no actually, I don't."

Cheeseman scowled. The three men stood up, turned and walked out. Haydon remained seated. The lawyer hadn't opened his mouth. He was there as Glasson's eyes. That was a second-rate try-on. Nothing of substance, bluster and threats. He would produce the report on his meetings with Yahya, but miss out the meetings in The Cage and in the garage. He needed to see Johnny urgently. Picking up his coat, he removed a small recording device from a side pocket and pressed the stop button.

The Sheikh

Chapter 46

Haydon emerged from an alleyway of bookshops and darted between the lanes of fast-moving traffic on the Charing Cross Road. He jumped up onto a moving bus heading north, holding on to the safety bar at the rear deck and, looking backwards, his eyes scanned for any unusual movement. After half a mile, the bus stopped at a red traffic light and he stepped off. Donning a flat cap from a bag, he pulled it low over his eyes and walked on.

It was odd to think he would now be thought of by his colleagues as a traitor to the Service. Many of them would shun him for crossing a forbidden line and betraying them to 'that other Agency north of the river'. He'd deliberately turned his back on the organisation where he'd spent so much of his working life, where his youthful idealism had become increasingly burnished, until all that was left was the body-armour of cynical contempt. He hoped his new allies would help him escape from the road to perdition. Turning into a scruffy coffee bar on the Tottenham Court Road, he made his way directly to the back.

Johnny was sitting, back to the door, in a corner booth. Wearing a blue suit and yellow tie, he looked out of place in the moth-eaten establishment. There were two cappuccinos on the table in front of him.

"It's like old times." Haydon smiled. "I haven't run evasion routines around London since basic training. Not that I was much good at it back then."

"Six are perennially stretched for followers; they've got a small unit. Not like our army of thousands. I doubt you're important enough to warrant them flooding you."

"Maybe, but it's getting nasty." Haydon told Johnny about his summons to Cheeseman and the veiled threats. "They'll soon be knocking on your door, demanding access to Yahya. Claiming he's one of theirs and you've been caught poaching. And I'm going to need rescuing from everlasting darkness."

"They can go whistle." Johnny grunted. "My Minister is briefed that we've two hostile bangers on our soil, and a substantial risk of a serious incident, probably in central London. After the IRA mortar attack on Downing Street last week, the government might not survive a major Islamic outrage in Westminster. He's aware we have a walk-in who exposed an imminent attack, and this man is our best chance of getting further intel on the bombers and their target. He's a robust politician and will bat Six right off. I'll appraise him of your situation."

"News on the marks?"

"They landed at Heathrow two days ago. We got photos of them at the airport, and a positive ID on the ex-Egyptian colonel Salah Ahmed al-Din, who travelled under the name of Hamid Bebiker Nur. The other one is a presumed Jordanian, the other guy at the Forum. His Sudanese passport is in the name of Hamza al-Bushra." Johnny rubbed his chin. "They flew in on the same flight from Istanbul, posing as strangers. From the airport they took the tube to Earls' Court, where we lost trace of them. They did not go to the High Wycombe address. We need to find them. Quickly."

Johnny massaged the back of his neck, then pulled a face. "Look, I didn't want to rope you back into this mess, but we're fresh out of ideas. It's a risk for you, even talking to us. I'll do my best to mitigate it, but if things go sour, you and I are equally doomed."

"Are GCHQ scanning comms out of the Sheikh's addresses?"

"All channels in and out of Sudan are targeted."

"The focus needs to be on Damazine, his Khartoum office and the Soba farm."

"Satphones and HF traffic out of those locations are prioritised. They're the easiest to geolocate and decrypt." Johnny frowned. "Haydon, we have to establish the target and the date."

"Zaki would never give Yahya that information; he may already be suspicious about his absence, which could explain why the bangers didn't go to High Wycombe."

"Although that address might always have been a blind."

"True. Look, the only person outside the Sheikh's inner circle who might have any handle on this is Salah el-Fateh, the head of the Sudanese *Mukhabarat*. He's aware of the op, and of the bomb-maker's identities, Yahya gave him copies of the visa applications and told him their general intentions." Haydon sipped his coffee, then pinched his nose between his fingers. "His hands are good and dirty. He meets quietly with the Sheikh and doesn't like things happening on his patch that he isn't aware of. He may have knowledge of the target, although it's unlikely he would know the bangers' whereabouts."

"What might induce him to talk?"

Haydon thought about the security man. He was, more than anything else, a survivor. He'd swerve around regime changes, he'd alter his opinions and beliefs to enfold any new political direction. His mantra was to be in contact with every strand of politics that might one day end up in power. He was the very definition of realpolitik. Which was why he would deal with the West as easily as he dealt with the Sheikh.

"If he believes that we have evidence implicating him, and therefore his Government, in a major outrage in London, he'll want to neutralise the risk of blowback." Haydon scratched his head. "Anything that might threaten his survival. Providing us secretly with the means to thwart a major bombing would be a cheap win for him. Of course, he'd demand assurances that his involvement would remain unknown. And he'll squeeze us for other stuff, it's in his nature to bargain. He'd probably demand cash, maybe something else."

"Could you speak to him?" Johnny stared at him.

"I'd have to go back to Khartoum. With a following wind, I might be able to meet him at the airport and travel back on the same plane." Haydon rubbed his lips with his forefinger. "But I'll need a clean passport, and your guys to spirit me through the airport unseen, both ways. In direct breach of Cheeseman's order, so I'd need a written request from your boss or better still from Chairman JIC."

"I'm going to bring you in to HQ, keep you hidden in cotton wool, well away from Cheeseman's clutches. There's going to be a reckoning with Six, but right now there's only one priority, which is to stop the bombers."

A brutalist concrete building, 140 Gower Street had been constructed during the post-war building boom. A ten-storey block standing near to Euston Square tube station, the dull, anonymous edifice had served as HQ of The Security Service since they moved there in 1976. Haydon was shown to a small room on the ninth floor, simply furnished with a desk, a computer terminal, a chair and a camp bed.

"We'll keep you here, wrapped up tight, until we're ready to go and butt heads with Six. They'll have to play nice so long as we've a malign active unit within our borders." Johnny had told him. "I've briefed the DG, he's ordered that you be attached to assist us in this investigation. You'll be provided with a letter to that effect. He will speak to his Minister, appraise him of the potential conflict with Six, and they will decide when the matter should be raised with Chairman JIC, Sir Anthony Withers."

Haydon nodded. The Joint Intelligence Committee was based in the Cabinet Office, the Chairman acting as the coordinator of the intelligence 'clearing house', which brought together all the security services, including MI5, MI6, GCHQ, Defence Intelligence and others, and was the ultimate arbiter of internecine squabbles.

Haydon called Ali Kabbani on a secure line and asked him to arrange a meeting with Salah. Kabbani didn't ask any questions. He rang back an hour later to confirm a late-night airport meeting was on. Haydon and Johnny brainstormed options and agreed on what could be dangled to Salah in return for the information they needed.

A black Range Rover with darkened windows drove him to the airport. It started to sleet as they emerged from the underground garage. Perhaps it would turn to snow, Haydon thought. Which could delay his flight and scupper the plan. A silent man in the front passenger seat handed him an envelope containing a passport in the name of William John Hartley. For the rest of the journey the two men were quiet and unsmiling.

Arriving at Heathrow, the driver flashed a pass at the security guards, and they were waved through, driving directly out onto the tarmac. They pulled up next to a British Airways Boeing 767.

"We'll be parked up right here when you return. You'll be disembarked first, just turn left down the steps."

Haydon climbed the steps and boarded the plane. He felt heavy and tired. Sitting down in his first-class seat, he closed his eyes. He was used to playing puppet-master and didn't enjoy the feeling of being the puppet. Or more accurately the bait. The plane would only be on the ground for ninety minutes at Khartoum, but that could turn into eternity if things went the wrong way. What was the risk that Salah might decide his interests were better served by letting Haydon fall into the hands of radicals? He wondered if Monkton knew about his trip, whether the NSA had been listening in to his call to Kabbani? And what if he'd told Glasson? Glasson must surely understand that closing down the bombers was the only thing that mattered.

Groaning inwardly, he rubbed his eyes. Two days ago he had been almost out of the door, his pension intact, his future assured. Freedom. Now, he knew, he could end up as the fall guy, the lightning rod, taking the rap if a bomb went off in central London. He lacked the political agility to remove the target from his back. He opened his eyes. The heavy door was being pulled closed. He listened to the whine of the engines spooling up.

Chapter 47

A white-uniformed police officer leaned around the aircraft bulkhead and beckoned to Haydon with his finger. As he passed by, the flight attendant gave him a look that seemed almost piteous. What did she know that he didn't? Did he look that defeated?

Haydon sniffed the air and caught a whiff of that desert dust that was so particular to Sudan. He shivered. It was two in the morning, and it was cold outside. He'd thought he'd never set foot in this place again, but here he was, and so soon. But if all went smoothly, it would take less than an hour and he'd be gone.

A small minibus was waiting at the foot of the air-steps, the police officer holding open the door. Bright airport lights illuminated an empty apron. They drove a few hundred yards to the VIP building, where the policeman led him through several anterooms, each furnished with the same oversized white leather armchairs and heavy wood coffee tables. The air conditioning system was blasting away. Haydon felt goosebumps on his arm and was grateful to have on a winter jacket.

Entering another long room, a burly bodyguard stood by a set of double doors. Haydon saw Salah sitting almost concealed in a deep armchair at the far end of the room. The stocky man struggled to his feet and opened his arms for the customary bear hug.

"My brother, welcome, *marhaban*. Welcome back to Khartoum." His face contorted in an angular grin. "After the shocking attack on your home, I feared we might never see you again. We were shamed that those people made it past our protective cordon, my security personnel have been severely reprimanded. We have been pulling in suspects and our first thought is these people were mercenaries, but we will get to the bottom of who was responsible."

Haydon sank down into the too-soft chair. He realised it wasn't leather but plastic, and had a sticky feel, as if previous occupants hadn't benefited from the present freezing temperature.

"Do you know who the paymaster was?"

"We shall know that soon and will report to you all our findings." He stroked his wispy beard and grinned. "I had heard rumours it was your American friend that chased you away. Could it be so?"

"It was my time to leave, Salah." A uniformed servant brought a tray of coffee and poured a cup for Haydon. "Thank you for seeing me at such short notice, and so late in the night. That is kind of you. Our time is limited, before I take the flight back to London. Perhaps I can get straight to the subject?"

"Ali Kabbani impressed on me the urgency of your visit." He frowned. "But he cast no light on the reasons, you see."

"We need your help, Salah, and we will be so grateful for it." Haydon leaned forward, his hands pushing on the back of the soft chair. "We have intelligence that a major terror attack in UK is imminent, probably a sizable truck bomb, on our mainland. The bomb-makers arrived in London on Sudanese passports, and I understand you have seen copies of these passports. We are trying to establish, with urgency, three things: the whereabouts of these men, their target, and the date for the attack."

"That is indeed worrying, I can see that. It is this wretched invasion of Iraq which is causing so much instability around the entire region. There is so much anger amongst Arab peoples."

He will not react about having seen the passports, Haydon thought, but he knows why I am here, and his mind is grinding away, calculating the odds. Will he play poker with me? Salah continued rubbing his beard, his eyes narrowing, then continued.

"I don't know how I could obtain these informations to help you."

"You are always perfectly informed, Salah, about everything that happens in your country. Which was why I thought it wiser for us to meet face to face and quietly. I believe your private conversations with the Sheikh may have cast light on the matter." Haydon rested his hands on the coffee table. "Also, I am concerned about the possible severity of repercussions. If this attack were to take place, and evidence of collusion found its way into the international arena."

"Evidence." Salah frowned and sipped his coffee. "*Janni*, perhaps you meant hearsay? Which is often found to be inaccurate, you see. Especially if two parties only were present at a meeting. Recollections vary, human memory is so faulty."

"Oh yes, true indeed, I agree. Hearsay would not cause any concerns." Haydon ran his fingers through his hair. *Time to shovel my chips onto the table and call his bluff.* "But tape recordings, well that would be a different matter. Recordings, together with a participant's public statement, that would make for worrying evidence. Especially if it were, for example, unveiled on TV, or at the UN Security Council. Hard to imagine how damaging the blowback to that could be, internationally and domestically."

"I don't consider that likely."

"Another thing to consider, we live in this new world, Salah. Nowadays electronic intelligence is all pervasive. You're familiar with Echelon? It sweeps up all sorts of fascinating things from space."

Salah's eyes had narrowed to slits. He sat motionless; his face slightly flushed. They faced each other in silence, like a kind of staring competition. Sphinx-like, Haydon thought, breathing slowly. The hum of the air conditioners seemed deafening. *Was he going to make it back onto that plane?*

Salah would have calculated that the lawyer must now be under Haydon's control in London. His hunch was that he would believe it credible that Yahya had been brave enough to tape the two meetings at his office. That he might have been seeking *kompromat* to protect himself.

Haydon had been assured by Yahya that he had not been patted down before either meeting. So, it was just possible Salah had been overconfident, lazy. In his own lair. With these mini cassette recorders that were widely available, you needed to be alert to that risk. As to Echelon, that was an unknown threat, he couldn't know what Haydon might have learned about other secrets that Salah had thought were safe.

"I would need to be reassured that details of our exchanges would remain confidential, and, of course, deniable."

"You have my word, Salah." Haydon bowed his head. "My solemn word."

"And in return how would you be able to assist me, with the so many of worries that I have?" Salah spoke quietly, squinting from behind his glasses. "If I were successful in using my influence and connections to find answers for you. I would expect reciprocation for this. And also I would need to cover my outgoing expenses. I may need to expend funds to buy such information."

Haydon felt his neck muscles relaxing. Salah had blinked. It was a negotiation. "We would, of course, offer financial recompense to defray your costs. One million dollars in cash."

"That would cover incidentals, yes. But also, you see, I have similar problems to yours, I seek information on the whereabouts of enemies of the state, who are hiding out in your country, causing me difficulties. May I expect your collaboration on this."

Haydon nodded. He'd need to put a clothes peg over his nose. Salah shifted in his chair, reached into his pocket and took out a piece of paper, which he placed on the coffee table. Haydon picked it up and bowed his head to read it.

"It is good we should begin a collaboration this way." Haydon checked his watch. "I see mutual benefits, and we will show you gratitude in future support."

"You will find the names of interest to me written there. Also account details. I will ring you later today. If I have the answers you require, of course. Ali passed me the number that you gave him. I assume that is a secure line?" Haydon nodded. Salah smiled and stood up. "You will then promptly action your side of our agreement. Let us pray for a satisfactory ending for both of us."

The two men embraced. Haydon realised he'd been sweating, his shirt felt sopping wet but was freezing on his back. The police officer escorted him back to the plane.

His monosyllabic minders spirited him back through Heathrow Airport in the same black Range Rover. Heavy rain spattered the windscreen and obscured the view as they struggled up the M4 in dense morning traffic. He snoozed for most of the journey and woke as they bumped down the ramp into the underground car park at 140 Gower Street. His escorts ushered him up the elevator to Johnny Doyle's office on the sixth floor.

"Tell me good news." Johnny scratched his head. "I'm praying for a breakthrough." Haydon reported on his meeting with Salah.

"My gut is he knows something, and we'll hear from him today." Haydon rubbed his chin. He needed to shave. "He knows his information has a limited life and he wants the money. He also wants our future protection, and intel on his dissidents in UK, in that order."

"You trust him?"

"I trust his commitment to self-preservation."

"We're flat out. GCHQ snared an Inmarsat transmission out of Damazine. The call was made to a handset located as moving around the Southall area of west London. One way, although the Southall unit responded briefly, but the call was too short for accurate geolocation. Probably a burst transmission." He pinched the bridge of his nose. "The proximity to Heathrow is worrying, and that is, as from now, our primary focus and the presumed target. We've upped security to the highest level, flooded the perimeter with mobile units and roadblocks, deployed some army units, which is a first. Special focus on trucks and commercial vehicles. There's bleating from the airlines and airport authorities, but right now we need to build a ring of steel around the airport."

He stood up and started pacing the floor, waving his arm from side to side.

"We must consider the attack to be imminent." He looked unusually disheveled. Haydon presumed he hadn't slept. *That makes two of us.* He felt dog tired. "Meanwhile, Six has lodged a formal complaint, stating that we are holding one of theirs. The DG replied via Sir Anthony that you are being held for questioning as part of an urgent internal security investigation."

"Your people won't throw me to the wolves?"

"If we find the bomb all will be well, if not–"

Haydon briefed Johnny on his meeting with Salah.

"That number is a dedicated line. Any incoming call will be

patched straight to the ops room. We'll operate from there."

"Study this." He said, handing Haydon a folder. "Our analysis of Salah Ahmed al-Din's *modus operandi*. The principal source is data shared by Six out of Kabul Station. Well-trained in explosives during his military career in Egypt. But in Afghanistan, with instruction from Monkton's people, and our own, he ran what was effectively an assembly line for IEDs and car and truck bombs. He caused a lot of Soviets and regime deaths. It couldn't be worse. He's a thoroughgoing pro."

"Signatures?"

"His IEDs were typically remote or contact activated." Johnny sighed. "Car and truck bombs, mainly ANFO, ammonium nitrate based, big blast stuff. Usually, the driver would be holding a 'dead-man's switch'. When released, deliberately or when he was neutralised. Bang."

"If we manage to identify a suspect truck, we need to shepherd it away from populated areas."

"Ideally, we need to find it before it sets off on its journey. But yes, we are drawing up contingencies to try to force it into parkland or woods or into the bloody River Thames for that matter." He shrugged his shoulders. "I'm placing every available mobile on standby. Hereford is briefed, two squadrons are standing by to move on command. One at Heathrow, one in Hyde Park."

The Sheikh

Chapter 48

Southall, February 1991

The warehouse was one of many anonymous buildings on a run-down industrial estate in Southall, a flaking sign outside advertising *'Elite Engineering Services'*. A high wall, topped with barbed wire and broken glass, surrounded the compound, and a continuous stream of airliners passed low overhead, the incessant screech of jet engines causing Salah al-Din a thumping headache.

When the taxi dropped them off and he pressed the bell, he could hear it ringing in a faraway part of the compound. After a long wait, a small, sliding 'Judas window', set into the heavy metal door, squeaked open. To his surprise, the bespectacled man who he'd last seen in Omdurman, and who had called himself 'Harun al-Rashid', opened the gate to let them in.

He led them to an accommodation block set off to one side of the compound. They passed a small office with desks, phones and fax machines and upstairs to two offices which had been re-purposed as bedrooms. The two men left their small suitcases, then Harun showed them to a dingy sitting room with a sofa and an old TV.

"Wear gloves at all times, we don't want any fingerprints left." He handed over several packets of kitchen gloves, then said in a quiet voice. "And don't answer the bell, ever. Nobody will disturb you."

"Where do we shop?"

He showed them to a small kitchen and opened the fridge door.

"Here are enough supplies to last until you leave." The man resembled a professor, he thought, with his thin wire-rimmed glasses and tentative manner. "You said you need two days to complete the rig up?"

Salah al-Din nodded his head. "Yes. If we have everything that we require."

They retraced their steps and walked through the small courtyard and over to the warehouse, which took up most of the compound. Harun pulled open the heavy sliding door.

"The items you requested are all there."

He pointed, then took off his spectacles and cleaned them with a handkerchief.

"Check please and tell me if there is anything else you need. Otherwise, I will not return again until I bring the driver with me on Tuesday. We must avoid the worst of the morning traffic, so I will launch him in the early morning. As soon as you have fitted him, and the truck has left the yard, we shall leave together to the airport. We will separate there in the car park and board different flights. It will take the *shaheed* one hour to reach his target."

Harun had been as good as his word. All the items Salah al-Din had asked for were stacked along one wall of the warehouse. Fifty-kilogram sacks of urea-nitrate fertiliser, five-gallon cans of nitric acid, canisters of hydrogen gas, jerry-cans of diesel, a wooden box of blasting caps, bottles of nitroglycerin, wires, batteries, mobile phones, all the paraphernalia and tools needed to build a powerful bomb. The truck, a white 7.5 tonne Isuzu, was parked alongside with its tailgate open. The interior lighting in the warehouse was good, he noted, with relief. Good lighting was critical when you were wiring up a complex IED.

"There is everything we need," Salah al-Din said.

"Is the target above or below ground, in a basement or not?" Hamza asked. "That will influence how we build the device, you see, how we channel the blast."

"Above ground. If it can be directed towards the left of the truck, that would be most effective." He gestured with his arms. "The target is between ground level and, say fifty feet."

"We can do that. Left and above."

"This driver, the *Shaheed*. We will stay masked while we fit him; it is wiser, yes?" Hamza enquired.

"Correct. It is wiser." Harun stroked his beard.

"You are sure of this man?" Hamza asked. "Is it not better he is observed, and the device can be remotely activated if he undergoes a last-minute crisis? That happens sometimes, even with the most unexpected of them."

"I am sure of this man."

"I will anyway rig the device with remote mobile phone activation, as well as a dead-man's hand," Salah al-Din said. "That is my usual method, it allows for redundancy and flexibility if your plans change."

"So long as it goes off at the target, your work is done," Harun said. "This will be the biggest shock to the Far Enemy since the Beirut bombing of the Marine Corps. This time it will be in their own house, the first of many strikes to come."

They walked around and examined the truck.

"Better than the beaten-up old rubbish we used to rig in Kabul." Hamza laughed. "You've had a mechanic check it out?"

"Fully serviced, yes. Now, listen. Memorise this number. Only for emergency use. No names if we speak." Harun passed over a slip of paper. He looked at his watch, then continued. "My friends, it is the time for *Salat al-zuhr*. Let us join together and make our prayers."

Three small prayer mats lay on the floor. The men followed the ritual of the midday prayer, murmuring the words, before prostrating their heads to the ground in obeisance. Salah al-Din wondered whether Harun could see the irony, the absurdity, of praying right next to the pile of ingredients for the building of a huge and destructive truck bomb.

After prayers, Harun stood up.

"My brothers I shall leave you now. Thank you for your efforts for the cause. Please do not leave the compound. We meet again on Tuesday, *Inshallah*."

Rashid al-Duri parked his white Vauxhall Corsa hire car in a lay-by under a motorway bridge in Ealing, set between derelict buildings and overgrown allotments. He reached over to the passenger seat and opened a briefcase containing a Nera Worldphone. A bulky machine, he used it sparingly, and always from a different location, suspecting the Americans had a way of tracing satellite transmissions. They'd told him it was encrypted and unbreakable, but he doubted that. The Americans were too clever with electronic devices.

He powered it up, extended the short telescopic antenna, then lifted the handset and punched a long number into the instrument keypad. He waited while the machine went through a sequence of whirring sounds, followed by a distant, indistinct ringing tone.

"Peace be upon you, my brother." There was a delay as a ghostly voice travelled to space and back. "You have finalised preparations?"

"My Sheikh, all is in hand, yes." He waited for his own voice to stop bouncing back. "My last act will be to collect the driver on Tuesday. May I have your order to proceed?"

"We will punish these infidels who defile our holy lands. Their armies are even now moving towards Baghdad. Yesterday they committed a terrible massacre, on what they are proudly calling the Highway of Death. It is correct that we respond with one of our own. I order you to proceed, and wish you success, *Inshallah*."

The connection ended. Harun hurriedly removed the battery and packed the machine back into its case, then drove off towards Wembley. He intended to spend these next 36 hours calmly, in company with the *Shaheed*, praying with him and shepherding him through the spiritual path of his last two nights on earth, until he departed on his final, lonely, journey.

This new *Jihad* the Sheikh had declared against the Far Enemy was bound to have dramatic consequences. The stated aim of targeting carefully chosen and symbolic targets in Western countries would lead to dramatic repercussions. The American, so far, believed the Sheikh to be his ally, even his tool, to be deployed for attacks against his own enemies. But it wouldn't be long before the CIA man realised he had nurtured, so close to his bosom, a most dangerous foe.

He wondered whether he would end his days on this earth as *Shaheed*. Living so close to death, for so long, in Afghanistan, he'd long ago made his peace with his maker, and felt entirely ready for the next world. He was unmarried and had no children. This made him sad, but in another way, it allowed him greater freedom, releasing his mind and his soul.

He wondered whether the Sheikh's dream was possible. To force the West to address the inequalities his people suffered, to atone for the ordeals of the Arab race and the Muslim world. To order their vassal Israel to come to terms with the occupied Palestinians. Perhaps if they obtained WMDs, he thought, then that would be the game changer. Anything less and they'd be steamrolled by the Great Satan, wherever they hid in the entire world.

The Sheikh

Chapter 49

Haydon paced up and down the windowless ops room. The fluorescent lighting and air-conditioning were oppressive, giving him the sensation that he was deep underground. Johnny frowned and beckoned him to sit beside him at the long table.

Different coloured phones and wires were scattered along the length of the table. One wall comprised multiple TV screens, most of them showing black and white CCTV relays. Phones were ringing at workstations set around the perimeter of the room. People wearing headphones were talking in undertones, others were scurrying in and out of the room carrying papers.

"Look at those queues backing up on the M4. Jammed for miles in both directions." Johnny puffed out his cheeks and pointed to several screens where Haydon could see a six-lane motorway clogged with motionless traffic. "This level of security is unsustainable. Almost all flights are delayed, there's unrest in the terminals at the long lines at security. The presence of Army vehicles is being reported on the radio. It's only a matter of time before the press blows up the story. By the end of today we'll be under pressure to loosen the roadblocks."

"Perhaps all that visible security will have deterred the bombers?"

"And headed them off towards some unknown secondary target?" Johnny shook his head. "Nightmare. I hope not. We can't cover all of London, our best hope is to snare them approaching Heathrow."

Haydon was exhausted. He pinched his cheeks and

breathed deeply. They'd been stuck in this airless room for hours. Waiting for what? He'd started to doubt that Salah was going to ring. Maybe he had been playing him all along, in order to find out how much he and his bosses knew, then reported it back to the Sheikh? He nodded off, then woke with a jerk, warm saliva dripping down his cheek. The blue telephone was ringing. That was the dedicated number he'd given Salah. Johnny lowered headphones over his ears and waved his hand urgently for quiet. The room fell silent. Haydon lifted the handset.

"Your people have agreed to what I asked?" There was a delay on the line. Salah's voice reverberated from an overhead loudspeaker.

"Yes, it is all agreed." Haydon's voice bounced back. "We will fulfill all your requests."

"That is good. I have answers to two of your queries." Salah's breathing was wheezy.

"The target is to be Big Ben. Tomorrow morning. That is Tuesday. You have little time. I could find out nothing about the whereabouts of the two men."

"Big Ben?" Haydon jolted upright. "That's hard intel?"

"Solid." There was a pause. "Can you confirm you will proceed your side of the deal immediately?"

Haydon turned to Johnny, who nodded his head.

"It will be actioned first thing on Monday morning. The other element will take more time. We'll contact your man at your embassy, yes?"

"Yes." There was a pause. "If I find out more, I will ring again."

Haydon replaced the receiver. *Thank God.* The guy had come up trumps. Johnny stood up and banged his fist on the table.

"Listen up everyone. New intel. Target is reported as Big Ben, high confidence. Tomorrow morning. Pull up the contingency plans for Operation Watchdog. We will work from that. We have maybe twelve or fourteen hours to get everything in place. Assume the suspect vehicle will be coming from the Southall area. Blue Team draw up lists of approaches and routes to Parliament Square, particularly from the west. List all open spaces suitable to kettle suspect vehicles away from the most heavily populated areas. These will be designated 'Safe Zones'. St James's Park? The river even? Green Team draw up a plan for gradual redeployment of watchers and vehicles from Heathrow. Remember that the bombers will be watching, so we want them to keep thinking that's where our focus is. All available vehicles need to be positioned to intercept and drive the truck towards the most suitable Safe Zone. Red Team start planning impenetrable blockades around the entire area of Big Ben, Parliament buildings and Whitehall. List which streets and bridges we can close. It's a working day, so the area will be busy with workers as well as tourists. I want all the choppers we can get our hands on available on standby."

Haydon watched groups forming and huddling together. Big Ben. The Houses of Parliament. He thought of the implications. A strike at the epicentre of Britain's democracy. The audacity was breathtaking. This was a new brand of Middle East terror. They'd got used to IRA attacks in that small area of London, which would now stand them in good stead. Operation Watchdog was a detailed, planned response map to counter any bomb threat in the Whitehall area, drawn up after the recent IRA mortar attack on Downing Street.

Johnny's voice broke into his reverie.

"Come, Haydon, now. DG wants an update; he's been summoned to the Cabinet Office. Cobra. Home Secretary chairing."

They strode out of the Ops room and took the stairs to the sixth floor two at a time. A secretary ushered them directly into the book-lined corner office of the DG, the panoramic window facing down towards Regent's Park. The Director-General of MI5 was a tall man with a squarish face and a boxer's nose. He had worked his way up through the ranks of the Colonial Service, where he had served in Malaya and Uganda before joining the Security Service. He exuded solidity. He waved them to sit.

"Quickly, please." He spoke in a bass monotone. "I need a sitrep, options and recommendations, prognoses, and any requirements that I will need to extract from the Cabinet Office."

"Haydon's informant, Sudan's security supremo, has reported, with high confidence, that the target is Big Ben and the op is planned for tomorrow morning, time unknown." Johnny paused and rubbed his cheek. "The bomb-makers are trained ex-military personnel, skilled in building truck bombs in Afghanistan. They may, or may not, drive the vehicle. Their photos have been circulated."

"What actions are you proposing to intercept the vehicle?"

"We are working up options to seal off the area from the Palace to the river, closing Vauxhall, Lambeth, Westminster and Waterloo bridges. Our assumption remains the vehicle is being assembled in West London, likely Southall. Today GCHQ intercepted a third satphone connection between Damazine and a mobile in the general area of Southall. Again, too short to geolocate. We have maybe twelve hours to prepare."

The DG turned to Haydon. "You trust this informant? Could it be a blind to distract our focus away from Heathrow?"

"This operation is the opening salvo from a new group

calling themselves al-Qaeda, of whom the Sheikh is the presumptive leader. My informant, Salah el-Fateh, maintains a close relationship with this Saudi man." Haydon laid his palms on the table. "He fears we have evidence to expose his fingerprints, and blowback would be damaging to his government, and potentially land on his head. He's focused on his own survival. So yes, I trust his intel."

"What do you need, Johnny?"

"We need to take the lead with no interference. *Carte blanche* to shut down Westminster, from Hyde Park to Victoria and Trafalgar Square. Flood the surroundings with mobile units. All available manpower. Sniper teams. SAS are on stand-by. Choppers overhead and in Hyde Park." The DG scribbled on a yellow legal notepad. "If we identify a suspect vehicle, we seek to funnel it down pre-delineated routes and into open spaces, unpopulated areas. I'm thinking parks. I have a team working on this. We'll have a huge personnel and vehicle requirement to enable us to block off side roads."

"Johnny, run this op out of COBRA. Get over to the Cabinet Office as soon as you can." The DG stood up. "Set things in motion here, then move over. I'll brief Sir Anthony and the Home Secretary just now. You'll get everything you need. Build a trap of steel and catch the buggers in its jaws."

He waved them to leave and started gathering papers off his desk.

Johnny headed over to the Cabinet Office to run the op from JIC. He ordered Haydon to get some sleep and be ready to join a patrol car at 03.00.

"I need your eyeballs out there. On stalks, scanning every truck driver. You'll be in a surveillance van with darkened windows and stabilised light-intensifying binoculars. Your starting position will be on the Hammersmith flyover. That's the best possible choke point, covering most likely routes from the west towards Westminster. We'll close off the inside lane and stack it with road works, ghost cars, motorway maintenance signs and vehicles. With only one lane, traffic will slow to a walking pace. Mobile units will radio you of possible bogies coming your way. You'll scan them from a distance. Any sign of recognition and you move off, staying ahead of them, and we begin the operation to kettle the vehicle towards one of the Safe Zones, with a rolling closure of side roads intended to keep him bottled up. If we're lucky, and he takes the direct route up the A40, he may not click until we're funneling him into Hyde Park, just before Apsley House. We're already sealing that area, fencing it off."

The plan sounded good, but it was based on several assumptions, any one of which might be wrong. That Salah's information was accurate. That the truck was in the Southall area, and that it would take a direct route towards Big Ben. That Haydon would recognise the driver. And if not? And the bomber detonated in a crowded area while he was twiddling his thumbs on the Hammersmith flyover?

This op was now in the storm's eye, turf wars paused whilst battle-axes were sharpened, the protagonists poised to reach for a share of the glory or distance themselves from an abject failure. Haydon glanced at his watch. 01.30. He lay stiffly on the narrow canvas camp bed in the corner of the small office. It brought back memories of Belfast in the bad old days. Back then, his body was used to discomfort and exhaustion. Manoeuvring himself out of the bed, he walked over to the kettle. He knew he would not sleep. He felt a stab of elation. Was Cheeseman experiencing the same predator's buzz, a grubby bully's anticipation of bringing him down? He sipped his coffee and felt the hot liquid advance down his throat.

His instinct had been right about the new Al-Qaeda organisation and the bee-farming Sheikh. Much good that was likely to do for him. Being right often turned out to be a brutally self-harming quality. Glasson was bound to find some Alice-in-Wonderland way of turning it upside down, and mountains of bird-shit would spatter on his head, regardless of the result of the op.

Cheeseman would skewer him, with a nasty scowl. Haydon realised he didn't care. The imminent kick-off of a major op enervated him. It had always been that way. The addictive buzz of setting off in the dark of the night, facing an unpredictable outcome. He took a few deep breaths and felt the excitement grow.

The Sheikh

Chapter 50

Salah al-Din shivered as he held the torch unsteadily in his left hand, struggling to get the key into the heavy padlock and remove the chain. They had both shaved off their beards, and their faces felt pinched by the frost. It reminded Salah of winter in the Zazi mountains, south of Kabul. The two men donned balaclavas, covering their faces, as had been agreed, then pulled open the heavy steel gates.

Harun al-Rashid was driving a small, white Fiat, but, to his surprise, when Salah shone his torch into the car, he saw that Harun was alone. He got out of the car, and the three men walked together to the warehouse.

"Where is the driver?" Hamza said, peeling off his balaclava. "Are we delaying the op?"

"This man slipped away last evening, whilst I was out buying supplies. I did not expect that from him. It seems he was fearful, and his faith was weak." Harun's voice was unnaturally high-pitched. He took off his spectacles and cleaned them mechanically with a handkerchief. "But that is the will of God, and the plan will proceed. Here, take this. You will need it to make your way. Contact Atef once you are safe. He will report back to the organisation."

He handed Salah an envelope. Looking inside, he saw a bundle of twenty-pound notes. "Drive the car directly to the airport, that will take you fifteen minutes. Leave it in any car park and walk away. You will have plenty of time to get past passport control before any alarm is sounded. Drop the keys and your gloves into a trash can."

Salah and Hamza exchanged glances. "You will seek martyrdom?"

"I shall drive the truck myself, yes. It was my mistake, you see, I trusted the depth of the man's faith and commitment to our cause. So, it seems I am the chosen one, and I shall serve my comrades and my beliefs. It is my time written now. There is no other way." He reached down and laid out his prayer mat. The two men followed suit. "Friends, let us say our *Salat al Fajr*, in fellowship, before the sun has arisen. Then you shall finish with your work quickly and I shall depart on my journey."

After praying, Harun embraced the two men, then climbed up into the cab of the truck. "Proceed with whatever it is you must do." He smiled at them. "I would, if it is possible like not to use the dead man's hand. I should prefer to take the decisive action by myself, to show my decision, my obeisance and my loyalty."

"I honour your courage and faith, Harun," Hamza said. "We will rewire it as you wish."

Salah and Hamza worked on either side of him, uncoiling and connecting wires running back to the bomb lashed down in the back of the truck, securing him into his seat harness with snap fasteners. Harun had taken out his ebony *subha* and started to chant in an inaudible murmur. After some minutes, Salah tapped him on the shoulder. Harun opened his eyes and turned towards him. Salah pointed to a mobile phone secured to the dashboard with duct tape.

"Just press the green OK button. It is now armed and ready."

"If, for any reason, that fails, the dead man's switch is here. I have adjusted it." Hamza said, handing him a small device. "Hold it and press the button. When the button is released it will activate."

"That is all?"

"That is all."

"My brother." Salah and Hamza each kissed Harun, then

stepped down from the cab. "Travel well on your long journey. We shall join with you again in paradise, *Inshallah*."

"*Inshallah*." Harun reached down and started the truck. The diesel engine smoked, and the truck vibrated. The two men pulled opened the gates and watched silently as he drove off, jerkily, down the road and out of sight.

The Sheikh

Chapter 51

Haydon sat, uncomfortably bent over, in the back of an MI5 surveillance van, peering into the rubberised eyepieces of a pair of long, stabilised binoculars facing out through the 'intelligent' one-way glass. The magnification was eerie. He could practically see their pimples. Crouched in that same position for hours, he scanned each of the commercial vehicles that crept through his eye-line. He had a clear close-up view of the faces of each driver.

The metal seat had obviously been designed for smaller people, causing him stabbing pains in his lower back, but he knew that one lapse in concentration could be disastrous. It was bitterly cold. The acute discomfort gave him a strange, nostalgic buzz.

It was now after dawn on a winter week day morning, and the closure of one of the two lanes of the Hammersmith fly-over had already created a tailback from the early morning traffic.

Continuous chatter on the radio played into his head-phones, mobile units on the different approach roads to the west reporting in on any suspect commercial vehicles headed in his direction.

"MOBILE 40 GREEN FORD TRANSIT M4 JUNCTION 3 EASTBOUND LONE DRIVER MIDEASTER APPEARANCE REG FOXTROT ROMEO TANGO 202 BRAVO OVER"

"TRAFFIC BRAVO 20 A316 SHEEN EASTBOUND WHITE BEDFORD LORRY REG CHARLIE JULIET ZULU

119 LIMA TWO MALES DARK COMPLEXION OVER"

It seemed an absurdly long shot. About one in every ten vehicles was a commercial vehicle of some sort, so the chances he would recognise a known face amongst this tide of traffic was slim. Occasionally, a stream of passenger cars gave him a brief respite, allowing him to cover his weary eyes with his palms and rest his incipient headache.

He wondered what narrative Glasson was concocting, whether Cheeseman was, even now, seeking permission to bring Special Branch on board and set in motion charges against him under the Official Secrets Act. Would they detain him? That depended on the outcome of the next few hours, he thought. If the bomber got through and catastrophe occurred, the search would be on. The search for some dumb scapegoat to pillory and punish. Right now, that felt awfully like it had his name on.

"STATIC ZULU ALFA HOGARTH ROUNDABOUT WHITE ISUZU VAN REG ECHO ROMEO TANGO 387 NOVEMBER ERRATIC DRIVING NO SEE DRIVER OVER"

He glanced through the eyepiece at the line of traffic. After a few minutes, he noticed a white van slowing down at the back of the queue, a few hundred yards back. The driver was alone in the cab. Adjusting the focus screw, he sharpened the image, then felt a jolt of recognition run down his spine. He'd last seen that face at the farm at Damazine. He reached down and toggled a knob on the control panel to switch the radio to the dedicated command channel.

"RAPTOR TO GOLD COMMANDER BINGO REPEAT BINGO BOGEY WHITE ISUZU VAN REG ECHO ROMEO TANGO 387 NOVEMBER POSITIVE CONFIRMATION DRIVER RASHID AL DURI REPEAT RASHID AL DURI PRIVATE SECRETARY TO THE SHEIKH DRIVER ONLY VISIBLE REQUEST ACTIVATE WEATHERVANE IMMEDIATE REPEAT ACTIVATE WEATHERVANE IMMEDIATE OVER"

There was a long pause before the radio crackled.

"CONFIRM WEATHERVANE ACTIVATED PROCEED OVER" Johnny's voice boomed in his ear.

He watched a man in a high-viz jacket step out of a van parked behind them and reach down to remove a traffic cone. Then, holding up his arm to stop the traffic, he waved a Motorway Maintenance vehicle out into the outer lane. After 20 yards it stopped, orange roof lights flashing.

Haydon turned his head towards the driver.

"Jerry, move off now and stay to the left. They'll keep this road closed for some minutes, enough time to enable unmarked cars to move into position, blocking turn offs onto main arterial side roads." He coughed and cleared his throat. "Pull up before the end of the flyover and wait until I tell you the traffic is moving again. Then we'll aim to stay a few hundred yards ahead of the target van, all the way. I'll keep calling it."

There were a lot of moving parts to this op. More than a hundred vehicles maneuvering over the next four miles. They'd pulled in every available unmarked car from the Security Services and neighbouring police forces. But they'd still only be able to seal off the principal thoroughfares, and if Rashid suspected anything was up, he might turn off onto back roads, and that would be a nightmare to manage. Haydon's hunch was Rashid couldn't know London well enough to risk it. His instinct would be to stick to the main roads. And the most direct route to Parliament Square was straight ahead, all the way to Hyde Park Corner.

The purpose of Operation WEATHERVANE was to corral the suspect vehicle towards the southeast corner of Hyde Park, where marksmen, special forces operatives, bomb disposal experts, electronic warfare teams, ambulances and fire-engines had been hastily deployed behind a three meter high, mobile blast-proof wall, beefed up with sandbags. If there was an early detonation, well, he wouldn't know anything about it. Apsley House would take the bulk of the blast damage; perhaps the Iron Duke would look sternly down from above and approve of such an important defensive operation taking place under his drawing-room window.

"PRIMARY ROADBLOCKS IN PLACE PROCEED PHASE 2 WEATHERVANE OVER"

The Motorway Maintenance van started reversing back into the inner lane and the impatient traffic pressed forward in the outer lane.

"Stay in the left lane and drive slowly." Haydon rubbed his face with his palms. He needed to concentrate. "Keep at least six or eight cars between us and the van. We need to keep eyeballs on him."

It started to sleet. The van's heating was blowing fitfully, and the rear window had started to fog up. Haydon used a handkerchief to keep a patch of it clear. He felt his pulse speeding up. He spotted an unmarked 'ghost car' shadowing too close behind the van. There was nothing he could do about it.

His mind went back to that day at Warrenpoint. Twelve years ago. An 800 pound fertiliser bombs had unleashed the two giant explosions he'd witnessed. The devastation they had wreaked over such a wide area, the giant craters, uprooted trees, the human bits and pieces scattered over hundreds of yards. He couldn't imagine anything more destructive. But he'd read up on recent truck bombs: the bomb that Hezbollah had used against the Marine Headquarters in Beirut in 1983 had contained 12,000 pounds equivalent of TNT. If this suspect vehicle contained anything similar, it would take out not just Big Ben, but much of the Houses of Parliament as well. And if he was within a hundred yards of it when it blew. He shook his head. He'd be vaporised. Not a bad way to exit, really. He shook his head. *Focus!*

"I have the vehicle in sight." He called out to the driver. "Stay at the same speed as the outer lane traffic."

He peered into the eyepiece and suddenly had a perfect view of Rashid's face. The man seemed to be smiling to himself, his lips moving. He was praying. He was surprised that such a senior figure had been tasked with driving a suicide vehicle, but perhaps The Sheikh considered this attack so important that it justified the death of one of his closest associates. If it reached its target, it would be one of the most calamitous terrorist outrages of all time. He wondered about the two bomb makers. Where the hell were they? There had been no reported sightings. Could there be more than one truck?

They jerked to a halt. Haydon had to put out his hand to stop himself from falling backwards. Peering through the windscreen, he saw they were at the traffic lights at Warwick Road.

Maybe two miles more to go. That would take them ten

minutes. An eternity. The most nerve-wracking ten minutes in his life. He realised his knees were knocking together. He closed his eyes for a few seconds and inhaled deeply, trying to empty his head of extraneous thoughts.

The target vehicle was steady, about thirty yards behind. Rashid's face seemed calm, almost beatific, his mouth still moving in prayer. Perhaps he was repeating the same mantra over and over? Haydon wondered about the strength of belief required to lead a balanced, even humble seeming person to commit such an awful atrocity. Blowing up random civilians. On a busy weekday morning, many of the victims would be ordinary people, for sure some would be Muslims. He pressed the mike button.

"RAPTOR TO GOLD COMMANDER BOGEY APPEARS UNAWARE CONFIRM HYDE PARK CORNER ENTRANCE GATE CLEAR OVER"

"ENTRANCE CLEAR AND ALL ASSETS IN POSITION RAPTOR ON ARRIVAL DRIVE QUICKLY THROUGH GAP IN WALL ONTO SOUTH CARRIAGE DRIVE CON-FIRM OVER"

"RECEIVED AND CONFIRMED OVER"

They were moving quickly now. The Cromwell Road was empty of traffic. Even after the road narrowed to two lanes again as they drove into Knightsbridge, the traffic was light, and when they passed the top of Sloane Street, the suspect vehicle had pulled up right behind them. If Rashid noticed anything now, it was too late. He had no remaining options to turn off. They'd have successfully bottled him up. The entrance to the Hyde Park Corner underpass was closed with the barrier down and a 'ROAD CLOSED' sign.

He tapped the driver on the shoulder and pointed. There was sweat on his forehead and he wished he had a sweatband.

"Stand by to follow the signposted diversion ninety degrees left through that first arch. Then speed up quickly and aim for a narrow gap in the blast wall. It will be straight ahead of you. As soon as you are through it, swing sharp left and stop as close to the blast wall as you can get. When the guy figures out that he's been kettled, he may decide to detonate. And if he's holding a dead-man's-switch and he's incapacitated in the blast area, it will blow immediately. We need to be behind the protection of the blast wall before it goes off."

He turned to look back at the van. Rashid's head was swivelling from side to side, the van weaving wildly as he tried to figure out which way to go. Haydon realised he had finally sussed something was wrong. He must know that he was trapped. Haydon felt the vehicle swerving and then as they bumped crazily over a pavement, he was bounced into the air.

The Sheikh

Chapter 52

His mind was a kaleidoscopic blur, the near-death sensation he'd read about in books, his life flashing by in front of his eyes, images spooling past his retina like a film replayed at high speed, but time was standing still, his senses were frozen. He wondered if this was the end. He heard a muffled sound, like a record scratching super slowly. His breathing had slowed to a flutter.

He opened one eye, then the other, and worked out he must be lying on the floor of the van, staring up at the roof. It felt as if a layer of dust had covered his face, irritating his eyes. He tried to haul himself up, but the steel mounting of the stabilised binoculars had fallen across his chest and was pinning him down. Then light poured in, and he thought someone must have opened the rear doors. He turned his head and a face under a beige coloured beret peered down at him, the mouth moving, but Haydon couldn't hear what he was saying.

His ears were ringing when he opened his eyes again. Probably only a minute had passed, but it felt an eternity. Long grass was tickling his neck, and he knew he must be lying on the ground. He was shivering in the winter cold. His head was pounding and there was a harsh, acrid smell in the air. He became aware of a warm stickiness on the side of his face and neck. Blood, he thought with alarm. Gritting his teeth, he pushed himself up into a seated position, blinking as he gazed around him. He looked up at the side of Apsley House, its windows were all shattered. There were chunks missing from the facade, like missing Lego bricks.

As his memory trickled back, he remembered holding on

tight; the van speeding up through the arch, tyres screeching as it swayed and threatened to turn over as they sped towards the small gap in the blast-wall. That was the last thing he remembered. No deafening boom, no immense explosion. He looked down and saw that his hands were shaking. Reaching up, he felt around for the injury on his head. His fingers came away sticky with blood, but the gash didn't seem deep.

He turned his head, surveying the surrounding scene. Trees had been uprooted, a park bench was standing on its end, ambulances were parked nearby, lights flashing, people milling around. He felt fortunate to be alive, battered and dazed, but breathing. Others might not have been so lucky. Where were Jerry and the other man who'd been in the van with him? He said a silent prayer and hoped this was not Warrenpoint all over again. Rescuers picking limbs out of trees. He tried to stand up but sat back down.

He suddenly realised that he felt elated and happy. *How odd.* The anxiety and pressure of these last weeks had disappeared. His tummy felt warm and calm. He'd cheated death. Again. He smiled. It was over. Big Ben would be chiming out those famous tones, Parliament was still standing, a national catastrophe had been avoided. He realised that someone was talking to him. Looking up, he saw a tall nurse wearing green scrubs. She reached her hand out and helped him to his feet.

"You look happy." She had a Glasgow accent and flashed him a teasing smile, then ushered him over to an ambulance. "We need to look at that cut on your temple, clean you up a bit. There's an important looking car waiting for you over there. They won't want you frightening the general public more than they already are."

She put alcohol onto a cloth and wiped the blood off his face, then examined the cut. "You'll live."

"My good looks unaffected?"

"Scary enough to frighten small children, yes."

She applied a large bandage to his forehead and stepped back to examine him. "That's rude of you."

"You're pretty much undamaged. Unlike your colleagues in the front of the van, they'll be spending a few days in hospital, couple of broken bits, nothing awful. Lucky, you are, the three of you. You squeaked through that gap with seconds to spare. Our hearts were in our mouths when we saw your van leap into the air like a drunken jack-in-the-box. Luckily for you it landed on its feet."

Johnny's car and driver were waiting to drive him back to Gower Street. From the underground car park, he was escorted up in the lift to the 6th floor. Johnny was swivelling his chair back and forth behind his desk, phone handset tucked under his chin, cutting the end off a Cuban cigar. He nodded to Haydon to sit.

"Yes, Sir. As well as it possibly could have. Very little damage. Mainly to the Arch and the facade of Apsley House. Our EW guys jammed the GSM spectrum, to block any remote activation. We think an SAS marksman took out the driver, one shot. Dead-man's hand must have activated. No. A few minor injuries. Blast barrier did its job."

He lit the cigar and started puffing furiously.

"One of the bomb makers has been taken into custody at Heathrow. Hamza el-Bushra. We think it's the Jordanian guy. Special Branch nabbed him at passport control. The other one - Hamid Bebiker Nur - is on every border watch list. Hopefully we'll snare him soon. Current thinking is the cell was made up of the three, including the driver, Rashid el-Duri. But we're full on searching for other connections, there will surely have had to be support elements. We're going to bust open the High Wycombe house today."

Haydon's ears were still ringing. He wondered how long before his hearing would return to normal, if ever. He couldn't hear the voice at the other end of the call.

"Back here with me. In one piece, yes. I'll tell him." He laughed. "I can manage that, Sir. Oily smiles over a club lunch. Peace talks. But this is bound to rebound on Glasson, there are too many people that know the truth."

He leaned back and blew smoke towards the ceiling.

"Good idea. A gong would take the sting out of it. No fuss, no."

"Yes, Sir, that would put it to bed. If you could let me know when that has taken place." He winked at Haydon. "Thank you for your support."

He replaced the handset and laid his cigar in a cut glass ashtray.

"The DG. A relieved man. He put his trust in me, and I went a long way out on a limb. He asked me to pass on his thanks to you."

He stared at Haydon with an amused expression.

"Our friendship is tough on my central nervous system."

"Who said friendship should be cheap?"

"A few seconds later and your pieces would have fit in this box." He offered the mahogany cigar chest to Haydon, who waved it away. "I could have kept you on the mantelpiece. You'd be less trouble there."

"It was a close call, Johnny." Haydon lit a cigarette and, staring at it, realised his fingers were trembling.

"Bloody lucky you recognised Rashid." Johnny tapped the table.

"Who gets to question the bomb-maker? He could be a treasure trove of intel on this new group." Haydon leaned forward. "There can't be any cover up of The Sheikh's involvement, and of the growing danger from Al-Qaeda."

"Picked up on British soil, so it's a domestic terrorist threat." Johnny shrugged. "No contest. He belongs to Five. He's in a holding cell at Paddington Green, being held incommunicado under the Prevention of Terrorism act."

"So now I get to wander back south of the river and face the music. Cower in the visitor's waiting room like some kind of vermin, awaiting that creep Cheeseman's pleasure." Haydon flushed. "A miserable prospect. Glasson will find a way of turning it all on its head."

"Don't get overheated. It's all been arranged, you depressive sod." Johnny wagged his finger at Haydon. "The PM has been briefed on your role. He's going to call Glasson, ask him to pass on his personal thanks to you and tell him he's putting you forward for a gong, *entre nous*.

Which will shut him up." He chuckled. "Sir Anthony is gunning for Glasson. Mark will waggle his arse, try to claim credit. But the story is known around those jagged corridors where adders lurk."

"So I head back to Century House and face down Cheeseman?"

"No, once the PM has made his call, Glasson will be on the blower to the DG, gushing like a schoolgirl, claiming success and offering you anything you want. He won't want you outside the tent with your flies open. He'll be in defensive mode, hoping to save his job. Probably give you Moscow if you ask him nicely."

"And you think I'd want that?"

"I no longer have any clue as to what you want. You're a man of mystery. The DG is going to suggest to him that you two meet for a 'clear the air' drink. Neutral ground. It'll take a couple of days to organise I reckon. Meanwhile you'd better catch up with sleep."

"Can I stay with you?"

"As long as you like. So long as you don't interfere with

my love life. Get debriefed upstairs, then head back for some kip. I've got to brief Sir Anthony. Start of a 'lessons learned' exercise. That should be fun."

Chapter 53

Haydon sat in a leather wing armchair in front of the fire, nursing a Scotch, leaning back in his chair and basking in the warmth. He'd walked the cold February streets, not even a crocus smiling to offer a hint of spring and got to the Travellers Club early. The sense of utter freedom he'd experienced since the explosion, or perhaps it was more since his near-death experience, had stayed with him during the days that followed. He couldn't recall ever having felt so insouciant, so entirely free.

From what?

He picked up a poker and shoved a large burning ember back into the fire. Although his part in this story would never be known, he deserved to wallow, just a little, in the thought that he'd played a central role in thwarting the most dangerous threat to Parliament since Guy Fawkes.

Looking up, he saw Glasson crabbing his way into the smoking room, smiling a fixed smile.

"Dear boy, so good to see you safe and sound." He plumped himself down opposite Haydon and pressed the bell on the wall to summon the waiter. "This has been a tough one."

He was wearing a grey double-breasted suit, amplifying his width. A red, polka-dot handkerchief flowed out of his breast pocket. He looked suspiciously tanned. Haydon wondered if it came out of a bottle.

"We must congratulate ourselves on a job well done, yes. And you are unscathed, boyish face unblemished. Well done, yes." He rubbed his hands and licked his lips. "What say you we share a bottle of Château Cheval Blanc?"

"I'll stick with my Scotch, thank you." Haydon drained his drink. "But tell me, Mark, might Special Branch not burst in at any moment and purloin my whisky? Am I not under urgent investigation for breaches of the Official Secrets Act, banned from the grimy portals of Century House?"

A white-jacketed waiter appeared from a hidden side door and took their order. Glasson signed a chit then leaned forward, talking in an undertone.

"Look Haydon, we both know there have been misunderstandings, better not to dwell on them. Colleagues interpreted your off-patch conversations with friends north of the river as disloyalty. I've had to bat those away. Yes, yes, we had differences in perception, about how best to confront a great peril facing the nation. But together we managed it. Brilliant success, we should all take pride, yes." He sipped his drink, then tapped his nose with his finger. "Strictly between me and thee, the Prime Minister rang me to offer his congratulations and asked me to pass on his personal thanks to you."

"You haven't answered my question."

"Of course, my old friend, yes." He rubbed his hands together and beamed. "The accusations levelled against you were found to be entirely without merit. No-one is coming to take away your whisky."

"But I thought you were opposed to my intelligence indicating an imminent Al-Qaeda attack in this country?" Haydon raised his eyebrows and frowned.

"You're conflating timing with substance, Haydon. In my job I'm required to navigate political obstacles, parochial and international. I don't have full freedom to act." He brushed away dandruff from his lapels. "But look here, together we got there, yes. That's what counts."

"Mark, we urgently need to ensure Yahya's situation is sorted. His fellowship at St Anthony's, funding, immigration status and so forth." Haydon leaned forward and tapped

Mark's knee. "Without him, the London skyline would look different today. He can't go back to Sudan, but will continue to provide us with useful advice, and the possibility of keeping a line of communication open with Zaki Bayazid, which might one day prove critical."

"Agreed. Come and see me in the office with the details. You have my word I'll resolve his requirements."

"Another thing requiring your attention. I've been advised to submit an official complaint to JIC, requesting a referral by the Chairman to the security tribunal."

Haydon took out a packet of Rothmans and lit one, leaning back in his chair, holding the smoke in his lungs.

"Your Director of Internal Security threatened to adversely revise the terms of my departure from the Service. Harshly was the word he used. Interestingly, I have the entire conversation recorded on my little tape machine. Which your lickspittle failed to check for. A little amateurish."

"Hold on, Haydon."

He watched Glasson's face go through multiple contortions, his cheeks reddening.

"It's me you're talking to. We sort these matters out over a drink, yes, that's the way we do it. We don't expose rifts outside of the office. You have my word I'll deal with your concerns, I'll even look at the panorama of weighty posts, if that's what you wish. Don't concern yourself with your departure terms. Cheeseman exceeded his remit and he will be admonished."

"What I would like is for that pint-sized bullyboy to be posted to South Georgia, where he can lord it over flocks of long-haired sheep. He can bugger them for all I care."

Haydon drew on his cigarette. He was enjoying being naughty, pricking Glasson's over-inflated bubble.

Glasson scratched his head, rubbed his neck, then clasped and unclasped his hands. "Haydon, let me be clear. I admit I failed to heed your warnings. I was too much in

thrall to our American cousins. My bad. Will you accept that?"

"That is the most gracious apology I've ever received from you. Actually, the only one." Haydon laughed, a deep rumble. "I want another large whisky. I'm still in shock from my narrow escape and I need to get properly soused. Personnel would recommend it."

Glasson rolled his shoulders, as if re-inflating his bruised ego, then stiffened. "You didn't mean what you said, Haydon, did you?"

"Ah Mark, what a question." Haydon smiled. "No more so than you meant to have me arrested by Special Branch and locked up in an underground cell. Let me enjoy my drink and we'll leave those weighty matters to another day."

They raised their glasses in a silent toast.

Chapter 54

Mayfair, March 1991

Linda stood by the lift door and welcomed Haydon back to Century House. She winked at him and offered him a warm smile as she installed him in an office just down the corridor from C's. Glasson oozed comradeship, putting his arm around Haydon's shoulder and ushering him along the corridor into his inner sanctum. He enjoyed seeing the perplexed faces of colleagues who only days before had been revelling in his vertiginous fall from grace, as they sought to comprehend his unexplained reincarnation from villain to hero.

"No decisions yet please on anything Haydon. Time for things to settle down, yes. I'll fix matters whatever it is you decide." He sat, cocked his head and made an arch with his hands. "Look, your friend Pete is in town. Wants to see you and make things right, yes. Do me a great favour and avoid upsetting him."

"Nothing to worry about, Mark. I'm a changed man." Soon after, Pete Monkton rang.

"Gotta see ya, buddy." The friendly voice boomed down the line. "Shit to knock about, bourbon too. Same place? Five on Thursday. OK?"

He walked to Claridges, although the sky was dark and threatening. A harsh north wind was blowing small darts of snow almost horizontally, stabbing at his cheeks, the river a rough grayish blur. He bent forward into the wind as he hurried across Westminster Bridge, his gloved hands pulling the lapels of his overcoat tighter around his neck.

Pausing at the end of the bridge, he stared up at the friendly face of Big Ben, imagining in his mind's eye a white truck swinging around over the road and mounting the kerb. Would it really have knocked the entire edifice down? The explosives team said the bomb blast had been rigged to aim slightly up towards the tower and would have toppled it. He shivered.

Walking on through St James's Park, the leafless trees stark and ugly, he remembered sitting here with Johnny, trying to figure out whether to leave the Service or to accept the insult of demotion to the backwater of Sudan. Only to discover it wasn't a backwater at all. This was just the beginning. He had a premonition the world was going to hear more from The Sheikh and his Al-Qaeda organisation. They should deal with the bastard right now, he thought, whilst they had evidence of his complicity and knew precisely where he was.

The Fumoir Bar was empty. It was too early for the Mayfair crowd. Pete Monkton was sitting at his same corner table, dressed in his favourite uniform of fawn sports coat and striped, seersucker shirt. He waved to Haydon, stood up, and opened his arms to greet him.

"Son of a bitch!" He held Haydon at arm's length and smiled, deep crow's feet around his eyes amplifying his sincerity. "Didn't know you had it in you Haydon, you're still a soldier deep down, damned good show. You sure got lucky, moments away from being spattered all over Hyde Park, the crows would have had a field day."

They sat. He pushed a cut-glass tumbler over to Haydon. The liquid was deep brown, almost red.

"Drink, buddy. And enjoy. On me. Twenty-five year old Michter's bourbon. The best. Don't ask how much it costs." They clinked glasses. "To narrow escapes, to many of them, the way we like 'em. Sure gives you one helluva thirst."

"You're right." Haydon felt the smooth bourbon burning down his throat. It tasted like elixir. "We made it behind the blast barrier seconds just before the thing blew. Big sod, they reckon it contained 1,200 kilos of ANFO. The Grim Reaper cut me serious slack. I owe him. But my hearing isn't too good."

"You did your bosses a major service. Gets my vote any day. You're like me, Haydon. Not a grain of political savvy in your makeup. That's why I like you, I figure. And why you and I will never reach the top." He pointed his finger. "I'll bet that grease-ball Mark is stealing all the credit, yeah? You'll be the forgotten man in the shadows."

"Something like that. He's not reticent when success is in the air." Haydon paused and frowned. "Pete, you and I said all that needed to be said to each other at Kabbani's party. You told me what you had to do, and why you had to do it. Your friend Buckley. Mughniyeh. I get it. I did what I had to do, stop a huge device from destroying the cradle of democracy."

"My target remains unchanged, Haydon, but don't think my eyes aren't spinning around like radars, maybe I wasn't as smart as I thought. Maybe you were. Now I got the listening boys hoovering up the sky all around the Sheikh, listening to his every fart. Your intel shook me."

"Have you spoken to him?"

"I went to see him in Soba, wanted to look the critter straight in the eye."

"Rashid's involvement? His private secretary A suicide bomber? You need more proof?"

"He seemed surprised that Rashid Al-Duri had become *shaheed*. Told me he'd been recruited to a *takfiri* cell. He'd betrayed his trust, his blood brother, working his own agenda. He was angry, upset. Never seen him like that before."

"You believed him?"

"I believed what he said about Rashid, yes."

He fell silent and waited while the barman brought their refills.

"Told me the usual stuff. He's a farmer, done his fighting, wants to bring up his kids, breed his horses." Monkton took out a cigar and clipped the end. "But he assured me I could rely on his Afghan-Arabs to take action in Khartoum against Mughniyeh."

"He's conning you, Pete. Forces of the Great Satan are despoiling the lands of the Holy Cities, and they're convinced you're never going to leave." Haydon tapped the table. "Now the Shia are rising in Basra, there's going to be a big civil war in Iraq."

"I got a wide-open mind. You helped me out there." He started puffing furiously on his cigar. "I told him straight out. Any of his people take direct action, against us, or against UK, or our allies in Europe, we gonna pound the shit out of him and his houses and his farms and his horses and his Afghan-Arabs and even his goddam beehives, and when we're finished there won't be nothing left to find except a few deep holes in the ground, and the odd empty turban flying through the dusty sky."

"How did he take that?" Haydon scratched his head.

"He smiled graciously and said we Yankees never learned to take yes for an answer, and when was I going to set up the hit on Mughniyeh, he'd give me his best team."

"I've done my bit Pete and now I'm done. Done. I've no responsibility any more, other than to boost Mark's ego for a while. You'll carry on fighting this never-ending war. It'll still be going on when we're dribbling in our wheelchairs. Arabs, Palestinians, Islamists and all the rest. You're welcome to it."

He took a slug of bourbon and realised he was on the verge of getting pickled. *So what?* "I haven't decided what's next for me, I'm in no hurry. After the bomb I'm feeling so good and so positive and happy, and ready to enjoy my life. And don't worry, I won't be getting in your way."

"I wanted to tell you something myself." He reached out and gripped Haydon's arm. "Lena and I are parting ways. We just kinda ran out of steam. Nothing left to say to each other. No one to blame, not even you, goddamit. Just the life we led, or the passage of time, or maybe that we couldn't have kids, or I don't know what else the hell."

"I'm sorry Pete. That must be tough."

"Not really. We spooks can't even be honest with our-selves in the bath, maybe that's why our marriages rarely work. And I prefer fighting wars with guns to arguing with skirts. It's just who I am."

"Is she over here with you?"

"Yeah. We're staying here at Claridges. Maybe you ring her and cheer her up?" He raised his glass. "I'm summoned to Winfield House for dinner. Ambassador's a fellow Yaley. Alpha Sig, my frat. It's an older version of the Agency. More exclusive 'tho. The frat is. Lena won't come, she says she can't stomach more secret society rituals."

He called for the bill and paid it with a black American Express card, dropping a twenty-pound note on the plate as a tip. Standing up, he held out his hand. "I respect you Haydon. You should have stayed in uniform. Maybe we both should have. But it's too late for that now."

"Stay in touch Pete." They shook hands, looking into each other's eyes. "When you're next through London, let me take you to my decrepit club. The food's vile, but the company is rarely banal."

Monkton stubbed his half-smoked cigar out in the ashtray. "See ya round buddy. Call me if I can do anything for you."

He smiled, then strode out of the bar.

That's him, Haydon thought. A man with the self-confidence of a born winner who knows his winning streak will never end. Yet he felt maybe he was the lucky one, that it was his self-doubt that kept him from ever really joining in. No frat. No glory. Just an uncertain future, where he could try to find out who he was.

Passing through the reception area, he paused and stood for a while by the little cubicles housing the house telephones. He saw the receptionist staring at him. Could he be honest now, he wondered, really honest? No more pretence, no more secrecy, no more games? He squeezed in and lifted the handset.

Glossary

Abu Nidal Organisation (ANO): A militant Palestinian splinter group, secular, anti-Zionist, and anti-Western, not associated with any specific ideology, but with its origins within Al-Fatah and the PLO. The ANO carried out worldwide hijackings, assassinations, kidnappings of diplomats, and attacks on synagogues. It was responsible for 90 such attacks between 1974 and 1992.

Afghan-Arabs: Arab and other Muslim Islamist *mujahadeen* who came to Afghanistan during the Soviet–Afghan War to help fellow Muslims fight Soviets and pro-Soviet Afghans. Despite being called 'Afghan' they were not from Afghanistan nor were they citizens of Afghanistan.

Egyptian Islamic Jihad (EIJ): An Egyptian Islamist group active since the late 1970s, which joined with Osama bin Laden in 1988 to form al-Qaeda. The merger was intended to link bin Laden's money and contacts with the military expertise of EIJ and take up jihadist causes elsewhere, after the Soviet withdrawal from Afghanistan.

GID: Jordanian General Intelligence Directorate. The civilian foreign as well as domestic intelligence agency of the Kingdom of Jordan. By repute one of the most important and professional intelligence agencies in the Middle East.

Hamas: a Palestinian Islamic movement, principally Sunni, founded in 1987, with the aim of establishing a Palestinian state incorporating present-day Israel and the West Bank. In 2006, Hamas defeated the more moderate Fatah in the elections for the Palestinian National Authority, campaigning on an anti-corruption ticket. They seized power in Gaza in 2007.

Hezbollah: an extremist Shiite Muslim group with close links with Iran, created after the Iranian revolution of 1979 and active in Lebanon and Syria. In 1983 Hezbollah bombed the US Marine Corps barracks in Beirut, the deadliest single-day death toll for the Marine Corps since the Battle of Iwo Jima in World War II.

Kuffar: is an Arabic and Islamic term referring to any person who does not believe in the Islamic God, who rejects the tenets of Islam, as well as all those who are not Muslims.

Muslim Brothers: a transnational Sunni Islamist organisation founded in Egypt in 1928. The movement's stated aim is the establishment of a state ruled by sharia law under a caliphate. The movement was supported by Saudi Arabia, with which it shared mutual enemies such as communism. Charity is an important aspect of its policy.

Takfiri: Takfiris believe they have the authority to label other Muslims as non-believers, based on their own interpretation of Islamic religious texts. This extreme form of sectarianism often leads to violent actions and has been associated with several radical Islamist movements.

The National Islamic Front (NIF): An Islamist political organisation founded in 1976 and led by Dr. Hassan al-Turabi which influenced the Sudanese government from 1979 until the late 1990s. It was one of only two Islamic revival movements to secure political power in the 20th century (the other being the followers of Ayatollah Khomeini in Iran). The NIF also tried to position itself as the world's predominant Sunni Islamist organisation, leading the only Sunni Islamist state before the Taliban.

Salafist: Salafists strive to emulate the practices and beliefs of early Muslims, promoting an austere and simplistic lifestyle and advocating for social and moral conservatism.

Shaheed: Shaheed is an Arabic term describing Muslims who die while fulfilling a religious commandment, including jihad, and is variously translated as either 'martyr' or 'witness'. In recent conflicts suicide bombers have often been described as Shaheed.

Wahhabism: A strictly orthodox Sunni Muslim sect founded by Muhammad ibn Abd al-Wahhab (1703–92) which advocates a return to the early Islam of the Koran and rejects later innovations. The sect remains the predominant religious force in Saudi Arabia.

The Sheikh

Acknowledgements

My enduring gratitude to my beta-readers, kind enough to read different drafts and provide inspirational feedback – Caroline Cass, Ros Colley, Maryanne Fitzgerald and Robert Graham all provided helpful advice and suggestions. Oliver James, my editor at the Blue Pencil Agency, steered me through several drafts, wielding his blue pencil like a scythe, whilst remaining endlessly encouraging. Sincere thanks to Chris Jackson, Dan Whomes and the team at Northside House for their backing, support and encouragement. And to my wife Bella, for all her encouragement and support.